Phenomenal praise for

Bahamarama

"I was wondering when Bob Morris would finally get around to writing a novel, and it was worth the wait. *Bahamarama* is sly, smart, cheerfully twisted and very funny. Morris is a natural."

—Carl Hiaasen,
New York Times bestselling author of *Skin Tight*

"In *Bahamarama,* Bob Morris is as tough and fast as Elmore Leonard, writes about the Caribbean as knowledgeably as Jimmy Buffett, and also begins to blaze his own, stylish trail as a gifted novelist. *Bahamarama* is a can't-miss hoot."

—Randy Wayne White,
New York Times bestselling author of *Twelve Mile Limit*

"Bob Morris, a terrific writer and pure Florida boy, has created a marvelous tale that perfectly captures the nation's strangest state. Like Florida itself, *Bahamarama* is wild, weird, unpredictable, populated by exotic denizens—and funny as hell."

—Dave Barry,
New York Times bestselling author
and Pulitzer Prize winner

"Bob Morris's *Bahamarama* is as spicy as a bowl of fresh conch salad. Leading good guy Zack Chasteen tells his own story of a Bahama trauma with a voice so fresh that it makes you want to read this book twice."

—Jeffrey Cardenas, author of *Sea Level*

More . . .

"When it comes to books from the lower latitudes, you sometimes can't see the forest for the palm trees. No worries with *Bahamarama*. This book stands out. It's a fun and engrossing read from an author who expertly knows the lay of the land and the sea."

—Michael Connelly,
New York Times bestselling author of *The Narrows*

"[A] hard-boiled, edgy debut novel . . . An array of colorful locals gives the story some much-needed texture, while juicy plotting keeps this impressive page turner simmering. Morris has produced an accomplished first novel with a priceless final scene."

—*Publishers Weekly*

"Cinematic . . . Fast-paced . . . Chasteen makes a fine hero, one who lives by his own rules, disdains firearms and takes care of business with guile, strength and help from a mysterious Caribbean Indian who can smell hurricanes coming and conjure up a sleeping potion when necessary . . . A highly enjoyable way to pass an afternoon."

—*The Miami Herald*

"Morris captures the islands and local people well . . . Morris has ably woven kidnapping plots, subplots, a promiscuous heiress, a Taino medicine man and even a hurricane together to keep the pages turning . . . A great bullets-and-beaches book to pack on your next trip."

—*Caribbean Travel & Life*

"A breezy, energetic debut . . . [S]hould be the start of a long series. Morris's wry sense of humor, coupled with a bit of cynicism, crisp dialogue and seasoned view of Florida and the Bahamas give an extra punch to *Bahamarama*."

—*South Florida Sun-Sentinel*

Bahamarama

Bob Morris

St. Martin's Paperbacks

BAHAMARAMA

Copyright © 2004 by Bob Morris.
Excerpt from *Jamaica Me Crazy* © 2005 by Bob Morris.

Library of Congress Catalog Card Number: 2004046780

ISBN: 0-312-99747-7
EAN: 80312-99747-2

Printed in the United States of America

St. Martin's Press hardcover edition / October 2004
St. Martin's Paperbacks edition / October 2005

St. Martin's Paperbacks are published by St. Martin's Press, 175 Fifth Avenue, New York, NY 10010.

10 9 8 7 6 5 4 3 2 1

For Debbie, Bo, and Dash

ACKnowledgments

No human beings were killed, maimed, or otherwise abused in the writing of this book. A few people, however, did willingly subject themselves to early versions of the manuscript and were gracious enough to offer their wise suggestions for making it better. Among them: Bill Belleville, Lyn and Gary Shader, Josh Shader, Skellie Morris, Eric Estrin, Donald DeVane, Emily Alice Cambron, Bill Sheaffer, Danny and Nancy Morris, and my mother, Georgiana Morris, who will always be the loveliest lady in Leesburg.

Thanks also to Graham and Elizabeth Barr for letting me hunker down on a regular basis at their home in New Smyrna Beach; Tessa Tilden-Smith for advising me on the curious way in which people from England insist upon speaking and writing the American language; Raul Tonzon for his badass Spanish; Valerie Albury, owner of Dilly Dally, for impromptu Bahamian research; and my highly placed confidential source in the U.S. Secret Service Agency who told me way more than I needed to know about counterfeiting. Yeah, Fred, that's you.

I am lucky to have an awesome agent, Joe Veltre, of the

Artists Literary Group. Without his enthusiasm and good counsel this book would still be residing solely in my laptop. Likewise, I am indebted to Marc Resnick, my editor at St. Martin's Press, for his astute skills and gentle tweakings.

While there is indeed a Harbour Island, and the world is a better place because of it, the Harbour Island mentioned herein is pure fabrication, as are all the people on these pages. That much said, LaVaughn Percentie does make the world's best conch salad, and you should never hold back on the hot sauce.

1

The way it works at Baypoint Federal Country Club for Wayward Males, guys sometimes throw a going-away party for their buddies who are checking out, and invite the D.O.'s to join in. Everyone acts all chummy, guzzling Dom, firing up the Cohibas, playing Texas hold 'em for real hard-on money, and letting the good times roll.

It's not like that at most prisons. At most prisons the guards lord it over inmates, treat them like scum, sweeten their lousy state-tit paychecks by muling in merchandise. Skin magazines and dope, those are the major franchises at the low-rent lockups, with cell phones grabbing a chunk of the action—a year contract paid in advance and a flat two hundred and fifty dollars going to the D.O. who sets it up on the outside. Then the D.O. goes home to his double-wide trailer and his Dish Network TV, feeling smug and in control, thinking his tiny little life beats anything the cons can ever hope to have.

But things are different at Federal Prison Camp/Baypoint, where the alumni ranks are swollen with premium-grade white-collar criminals, including, at last count, two former U.S. congressmen, a past president of the Florida Senate, and enough fallen financiers to staff an M.B.A. program in advanced corporate swindling. At Baypoint, the D.O.'s lack leverage. They're just chambermaids with too much testosterone. Because it's not like they can build any equity by catering to inmate cravings. Whole different crowd. Baypointers enjoyed the good life before they got caught and fully intend to start enjoying it again the moment they get out. There's nothing they really need, and even if there were, they wouldn't obligate themselves to the hired help.

So what you have at Baypoint is the D.O.'s being serious suck-ups and gofers and actually thinking that once the Mr. Bigs get back into circulation they will look kindly upon the cheerful detention officer who used to bring fresh towels and fix the leaky toilet. Maybe find a place for him in their organization. Like that ever happens.

No one threw me a bubbly send-off. No slaps on the back, no thirty-dollar cigars. And the D.O. escorting me through all the graduation-day rigamarole—a pork loaf name of Fairbanks—was definitely not playing brownnose. Mainly because he and all the other guards thought they had me figured—just an aging jock, a bottom-feeder among the Baypoint elite, someone who'd pissed away what little he'd had and wound up at Baypoint instead of a lowlier joint where he belonged only because he had charmed someone with a little clout. That she was a beautiful someone ticked them off even more.

I had made all the stops, collected my exit papers, and Fairbanks was ushering me into Building A, the "transition lobby," with its fake leather furniture, and ficus trees dropping leaves in every corner. Two other D.O.'s were manning a counter by the last set of doors between me and the great wide open. They traded talk with Fairbanks as we walked up, making me stand there a minute, then two, playing their D.O. mind games. One of them was this black dude named Williams and the other was this pimply young white guy didn't look like he could have been more than two years out of high school. Probably brandnew on the job, still developing his style, paying close attention to the older guys and mirroring the way they did it.

Williams finally glanced sideways at me and grumbled, "Put your bags on the counter, Chasteen."

"No bags," I said.

Which got me the full turn-around from Williams. He raised up from his swivel chair and looked me over.

"Mean to tell me you're leaving here and you ain't got nothing?"

"Just my good looks."

"Shit, then you really are traveling light, Chasteen. Let's see your papers."

I gave them to him. Williams ran them one by one over a green-light scanner, the pimply kid taking them and sticking them in a see-through plastic pouch that also contained my driver's license, birth certificate, and passport.

"You're supposed to ask me first," I said to the kid.

"Ask you what?"

"Do I want paper or plastic . . ."

The kid was glaring now, only his glaring skills were still pretty lame. I kept looking at him until he looked away.

Williams jerked his head toward the doors.

"Chariot's waiting, Chasteen."

I looked outside. A hundred yards away, beyond a Bahia grass lawn turning brown against the sun and a ten-foot chain-link fence topped with concertina wire, sat a big black SUV. One of those Cadillac Escalades it looked like—the only vehicle in the visitors' parking lot.

"You sure that's here for me?"

"Guy driving it asked for you," said Williams. "Figured he was here to pick you up."

"A guy?"

"Yeah," said Williams. "Two of 'em, as a matter of fact."

Fairbanks said, "They your boyfriends, Chasteen?"

I let it slide. I was trying to figure out who was sitting inside the Escalade. I wasn't expecting two guys to pick me up. I was expecting Barbara. She was the beautiful someone. Just thinking about her gave me . . .

Put it this way: Baypoint might be the Ritz-Carlton of prisons, but the top brass cuts no slack when it comes to conjugal visits. You have to be married. To each other. No license, no nooky. And no amount of bribery could change that. I'd tried.

One year, nine months, and twenty-three days. That's how long it had been. One short stretch for a monk, one giant gulch for my kind.

I grabbed the plastic pouch that held my papers and turned toward the door.

Fairbanks said, "We'll leave the porch light on for ya, Chasteen. So you can find your way back."

"That's sweet, Fairbanks. I'll leave the porch light on for you, too."

"What for?"

"So you'll know where to deliver my pizza."

The doors jolted open, and I left the three of them standing there, Williams saying, "Smart-ass walking . . ."

2

It was one of those August days in Florida that doesn't so much suck the air out of your lungs as it does jam it down your throat. Not even 9 A.M. and already everything felt heavy. Dragonflies buzzed up from the lawn as I walked past, then said to hell with it, folded their wings, and spiraled back down. Mockingbirds perched atop the fence, but not one of them could work up even the faintest song. The sun was on its way to glory.

Halfway to the gate I was lathered in sweat, my white shirt sticking to my back, little rivulets of eau-de-me running down the legs of my jeans. It was too hot to be wearing jeans, but it was all I had. I'd buy some new duds—the Chasteen summer collection—as soon as I got the chance.

As I approached the gate, I kept my eyes on the black Escalade. It definitely wasn't part of the plan. Barbara was supposed to be there, driving her sweet little haul-ass 450 SL convertible, a 1979, with 117,000 miles on it and just getting primed. She called it "Yellow Bird."

"Like the song," she had explained when I asked her why she named it that.

"Dumb song," I told her.

"I happen to like it."

"You ever tried eating breakfast with a bunch of bananaquits hanging around?"

"Bananaquits?"

"Those yellow birds they sing about. You eat breakfast down in the islands and they come out of nowhere. They hop . . ."

"Oh, those, they're adorable."

". . . they hop on the table, pick at your bread, dab at the butter. Swat them away and they just come back stronger, crap on the tablecloth. That's a yellow bird."

"Well," said Barbara, "it's a pretty song."

In three years of knowing each other that was the closest we'd ever come to an argument. Of course, we'd only had a few months together before I got sent up, so maybe if things had been different, maybe if we'd lived together and knew too much about each other, we'd have fought like hell, and split up. But I didn't think so. Neither one of us was quite sure where the whole thing between us was heading, but we were enjoying the ride. Or had been until a run of bad luck—not to mention considerable double-crossing—landed me at Baypoint.

So now Barbara and I were going to spend a few days wending our way down to Key West, just taking our time. That's why I couldn't figure out what the Escalade was doing there.

I stood at the gate, waiting for it to open. Nothing happened. The D.O.'s were making me squirm, milking the last drops of authority. I was hoping they came out curdled.

The Escalade had its motor running. The a.c. belts were whining, straining to cool off whoever was inside. The windows were tinted as dark as the law allows, maybe darker. I couldn't make out who was sitting behind them.

Thirty seconds went by. Then a minute. The gate stayed shut. I was getting prickly around the neck, ready to be moving. Finally, Williams's voice came over a speaker mounted on the fence: "Three steps back, Chasteen."

I moved back; the gate whirred open. I stepped out onto the asphalt parking lot; the gate whirred shut behind me.

No one got out of the Escalade. I looked beyond it, down the two-lane road that led to the main highway. I could see for at least a half mile, until the road curved and disappeared behind pine trees. I was ready to be on that road, ready to see Barbara. The road was empty, no cars headed our way. The heat was rising off it and making the distance look liquid, almost molten, like a painting that was melting, like the whole scene was turning into something else right before my eyes.

I looked back at the Escalade. The driver's window went down. The man at the wheel was thirty-five, maybe. It was hard to tell, but he looked younger than me. He was smoking a cigarette. He took a long draw and flicked ashes out the window, studying me. There was someone sitting up front beside him, but I couldn't make out much more than a shape. It was a pretty big shape. It was slumping so it wouldn't scrape its skull on the headliner.

The driver wore a black T-shirt made out of some shiny synthetic material that was supposed to look more expensive than it really was. He had a thin mustache that wormed across his lip and down to his chin and turned into a skinny goatee. Skinniest goatee I'd ever laid eyes on. He probably had to stand in front of the mirror every morning and pluck it to get it to behave like that. Maybe he took it to goatee obedience school. Maybe he trotted it out at goatee shows. Maybe it had won trophies. His hair was long and black, and pulled back in a ponytail. It was slick and greasy, like he put something on it to make it look that way. Or maybe he hadn't shampooed since the first Bush was in office. I was guessing he put something on it. He seemed like the kind of guy who worked hard on the way he looked. All I knew was, I'd never seen him before.

Goatee flipped his cigarette onto the asphalt. Then he used the same hand to wave me over to the Escalade. He did it like a headwaiter summoning a busboy to clean up a spill that was the headwaiter's fault.

I stayed where I was. I reached behind me and stuck the plastic pouch with my i.d.'s into the waistband of my jeans. That way I had both hands free. Never can tell.

Goatee cocked his head and screwed his mouth around, giving me his hard-ass look. But he didn't have the eyes for it. They were big and round and soft and brown. Pretty girls might swoon over them. I didn't.

He said, "We need to talk, Chasteen."

There was an accent. Spanish, it sounded like.

"So talk," I said.

"It is better you get inside and come with us."

"Better for who?"

Goatee looked at me some more. Then he turned away and said something to the shape sitting next to him, and it opened its door and got out, and I could see its head and shoulders above the roof of the Escalade. It didn't appear to have a neck, just a big square head planted on big square shoulders.

He came around the Escalade and walked toward me. Good thing the sun was already riding high or he would have blocked it. He was wearing one of those nylon workout suits where the top and bottom match and it always looks ridiculous. The workout suit was maroon, with white stripes on the pant legs, and white stripes on the shirt sleeves. The vertical striping didn't have much of a slimming effect. The guy was every bit of three hundred and fifty pounds, maybe bigger. Defensive tackle material, only he didn't move well enough to be a defensive tackle. He'd spent too much time bench-pressing and not enough time running. He was top-heavy and bad on his feet. He rolled from side to side as he walked, meaning his quads were no match for his weight. He was already breathing hard by the time he stopped a couple of yards away from me. He was sweating a lot more than I was. He wore a crewcut. His ears were tiny and pink, in contrast to the rest of him, which was dark, Hispanic, like Goatee. A 'roid muncher for sure. Pumped up and primed, but with a pecker that was probably punier than his ears. That's the downside of steroids. Certain appendages suffer for the sake of a ripped bod. Life is all about trade-offs. Some people just make stupid trades.

I couldn't read anything on the big guy's face. But then, he didn't look like someone who possessed a vast range of emotions. Eat. Sleep. Work out. Bust heads in between. Abstract thinking didn't get in the way.

I had seen all of him I needed to see. I looked at Goatee.

"So. What happens next?"

Goatee rubbed his chin. I suppose it passed for deep thought. He said, "You can make this as difficult as you choose."

"Yeah, you're right, I can," I said. "But let's make it easy."

Goatee shrugged. He didn't say anything.

I said, "Who the hell are you?"

"Just get inside, Chasteen. You are coming with us."

"You're repeating yourself. It's boring."

Goatee looked at the big guy.

"Raul," he said. *"Traemelo."*

The big guy took a step. I spun his way. He reached to grab me.

"Pare, pendejo," I told him.

In a situation like this, if you're a white-bread Anglo like me facing off against a Latino and know just enough Spanish to say "Hold it right there, asshole," then it usually surprises the other guy so much that he actually stops. That's what Raul did. He was a good dog. At least for the time being. At least until his brontosaurus brain told him he was supposed to be taking orders from Goatee, not me.

I looked at Goatee.

"You got anyone else inside there with you?"

"No, it is just the two of us."

"Got any backups on the way?"

"No."

"That's too bad."

"Why is that?"

"Because if Raul here takes one more step, I'm going to clean his plow. Then I'll piss down his throat and set fire to his tiny little balls. Then I'm coming after you. I'm going to break your ribs, and shave you bald, and write haiku on you with a Magic Marker. Then, when I'm done, both of you are going to need someone to drive you to the hospital."

Used to be I wasn't big on trash talk. Never did much of it when I was on the field. At Florida the coaches would bench us for running our mouths during a game. And when I was with the Dolphins, well, Mr. Shula was a class act and he expected the same from his players. But you get older, and you get tired of doing things the way you were taught, and you develop skills that suit your needs. Partly adaptation, partly to break the monotony.

I had knocked heads with more than my share of thick dumb big guys, but that was football. I couldn't remember the last time I'd been in a fight. Junior high, maybe. I really didn't want to get into it with Raul. I could probably hold my own. I knew I could outlast him. But most fights aren't about endurance. They're about who lands the first good punch, or who wraps the other one up, and if Raul wrapped me up it would be all over.

"Just thought it would be fair to warn you before the hurting begins," I told Goatee. "So if you've got backups you might want to call them in now."

Goatee started to say something, but before he could get it out the speaker by the gate crackled and I heard Williams's voice.

"What's the problem out there, Chasteen?"

I looked at Raul. He looked at Goatee. We all looked at each other. Nobody moved. Then Williams was squawking again.

"Chasteen? You hear me? What's going on out there?"

I turned and looked at Goatee.

"You the mastermind of this operation?"

He didn't answer.

"I mean, did you actually plan this thing out or did you make it up when you got here? Because either way you got shit for brains."

I pointed back at Building A.

"Got armed federal guards sitting in there watching everything you do. We get into it and they're going to be out here in about thirty seconds. Which is more than enough time for me to whip both your asses. Then they're going to run your license plate, and run your i.d.'s, and run your fingerprints and anything else you got on you. No offense, but the two of you just don't strike me as the kind of upstanding citizens who get keyed into the system without making any blips. Know what I mean? You might be sitting in there for a long while. They might even drag me back in there. Which is really going to piss me off. And you don't want to piss me off any more than you already have because . . ."

"Chasteen!"

I backed up to the gate. I pushed the talk button and spoke into the speaker.

"Everything's fine," I said. "These guys were just confused about me needing a ride, that's all. I was trying to cheer them up about making such a long drive out here for nothing."

Williams thought about it. Then he said, "So where *is* your ride, Chasteen?"

I didn't have an answer for that. I looked out to the road. Nothing much had changed. I kept looking. The sun glinted off something in the distance, something that took form and became a car. It was coming fast. It was big and white, and getting bigger. A limo. I kept watching it. Goatee turned and watched it, too. Raul kept his eyes on me. He still wanted to play fetch for Goatee.

The limo rolled into the parking lot and made a big loop, and squealed to a stop. It wasn't your everyday limo. Certainly nothing you'd ride in to the cemetery to bury your beloved. It was trimmed out in bright pink piping with pink curlicues and filigree framing the windows. A track of tiny pink lights lined the running board and bumpers. They were blinking on and off. How festive. A real pimpmobile. There were big pieces of cardboard duct-taped to the front doors, covering up whatever was written on the sides of the car.

The driver's door opened and out stepped a guy in a chauffeur's uniform. A young guy, late twenties, a shade bigger than me, but still way shy of Raul. He wore his black chauffeur's cap low on his head. Tweety Bird–yellow hair poked out from under it, proof of a dye job gone bad. His eyes were hidden behind the blue lenses of his reflecto sunglasses, a cheap knockoff of the two-hundred-dollar models that Tour de France bikers wear. A tiny diamond stud sparkled in the lobe of each ear, and the collar of his shirt couldn't completely hide a tattoo, one of those Celtic ring-around-the-neck designs. He looked fairly presentable, in a World Wrestling Federation sort of way.

"You Mr. Chasteen?" he said.

I nodded. The chauffeur opened one of the back doors and gestured me inside. I turned to Goatee.

"Not to hurt your feelings, but this guy is making a much better first impression. Spiffy set of wheels. Dressed up for the occasion. Called me Mr. Chasteen. Nice touches. You could learn something."

I looked at the chauffeur. There was a brass name tag on his uniform. Chip, it said. He was the most un-Chip-looking Chip I had even seen.

"So, Chip," I said. "Who sent you?"

His face was chunky and red and bore a smattering of blemishes that looked more like basal cell carcinoma than acne—a fair-complected kid who had spent too much time outside in disregard of sunblock and his genetic makeup. Florida is full of such folks and dermatologists drive Porsches because of them.

"Ms. Pickering sent me," he said. He spoke with an accent, too. Vaguely British, but with something else tossed in. Couldn't place it. "She hired me to drive you to Fort Lauderdale. Said to give you this."

Chip pulled an envelope from his jacket and handed it to me. I opened it. There was a letter inside, a couple of pages long. I recognized Barbara's handwriting. There were some hundred-dollar bills inside the envelope, too. I didn't count them, but there were a lot of them. I closed the envelope and stuck it in a pocket of my jeans.

"It's been fun, fellas," I told Goatee and Raul. "Maybe next time we'll make formal introductions. Exchange business cards and all that."

It was just beginning to sink in on Raul that he should have grabbed me when he had the chance. Goatee waved him back to the Escalade.

I slid into the limo. Chip shut the door behind me, then went up front and got behind the wheel.

I've been in my share of limos and this one was no less cheesy than any of them—creamy faux-leather upholstery and mahogany veneer cabinets, and a dhurrie rug on the floor. There were all kinds of remote-control gadgetry—three TV monitors, and a VCR, and a Bose wireless system—plus a wet bar with crystal highball glasses that tinkled as I squirmed around on a low-slung divan. The divan wasn't really all that comfortable. It smelled of stale perfume and tutti-frutti deodorizers. Spilled drinks and who knows what else had created a mosaic of grimy stains.

I stashed the plastic pouch with my i.d.'s in a side pocket on the door. Out in the parking lot, Raul was folding his mass back into the Escalade. Goatee was putting it in gear. No doubt they were planning to follow us.

I scooted to the front of the limo and knocked on the Plexiglas divider that separated me from Chip. He slid it open.

"Just wait right here," I told him. "And be ready to roll."

There was a stainless steel corkscrew sitting on the limo's wet bar. A nice hefty one with a big handle. I grabbed it. Then I opened a door and got out and ran behind the Escalade. I jabbed the corkscrew into the left rear tire. I jiggled it around until air started hissing. Then I moved over to the right rear tire.

I was working on it when the passenger door opened and Raul rolled out. He moved faster than I gave him credit for, but instead of coming in low and barreling into me and using all his bulk, he reared back and tried to kick me. Stupid move. It's easier to grab a shoe than it is to wrestle three hundred pounds of goon. I grabbed and twisted and Raul went down. His head smashed against the Escalade's fender. It was more of a thwack than a thud. Didn't knock him out, but it didn't do him any good.

Goatee jumped out. He was holding a crowbar. As he moved toward me I pinned Raul down with a knee between the shoulders. I yanked his head back and stuck the corkscrew under his chin.

Goatee closed in, trying to get behind me, but I slid over, twisting Raul with me, putting the Escalade at my back. Now would have been a good time for Chip to lug his ass out of the limo and lend me a hand. But he hadn't signed on for this. I could hear him revving the limo's engine.

"Put down the crowbar," I told Goatee.

"Fuck you."

"Put it down. Or I'm popping your pal's cork."

Goatee kept coming. Raul grunted and squirmed. I gave the corkscrew a push. Raul stopped squirming. Blood began dribbling down his throat. I'd nicked the skin at the tip of Raul's chin, where the bone is close to the surface and there aren't any major veins or arteries. It looked a whole lot worse than it really was, but it was enough to make Goatee drop the crowbar.

"Now turn off the car and give me the keys," I said.

He didn't move.

"Do it."

I made another nick in Raul's chin and Goatee backed his way to the driver's side. He turned off the ignition, pulled out the keys, and dangled them for me to see.

"Now toss them to me," I said.

He tossed them. There were ten yards between us and they landed halfway. He gave me a smirk.

"That was really stupid," I said.

I slung the corkscrew aside and grabbed Raul by his little pink ears. I slammed his head into the side of the Escalade. Just once was all it took. He went limp. I was pretty sure it hadn't killed him.

Goatee was already diving for the crowbar. And that was the perfect time for a kick. I caught him in the side of the head and sent him spinning. He lay groaning on the asphalt.

"What the hell's going on out there, Chasteen?" Williams hollered over the speaker. The front doors of Building A blew open. Out ran Fairbanks and the pimply kid, hands on their holsters. A couple of other D.O.'s came streaming out behind them.

I picked up the Escalade's keys and tossed them over the prison fence. They landed in the tall Bahia grass. Then I jumped in the limo.

"Haul ass," I told Chip.

He gunned it and we were gone from the parking lot before the D.O.'s made it to the gate. We sped along the two-lane road and around the bend, past pine trees planted in neat green rows and nothing else for miles and miles. After a couple of minutes Chip opened the divider and said: "What was that all about?"

"Beats hell out of me," I said.

I was lying. I didn't want to face the truth. Not yet, anyway. Because the truth meant dealing with a dead man.

Chip put the limo on I–10 and we headed east toward Tallahassee. Every now and then I looked out the back window. No one appeared to be following us.

After we had settled into the flow of traffic, I opened the envelope and unfolded Barbara's letter. The stationery bore the imprint of the Albury Beach Club. It's on Harbour Island, in the Bahamas. It was the very first place Barbara and I had run off to for a weekend together, a dreamy hideout that we had returned to on several subsequent occasions. I guess you could say it was our place. The letter was three pages long, dated Wednesday, August seventh—the day before yesterday—and it was written in Barbara's perfect, British-schoolgirl hand. Brits don't just talk differently than us, they write differently, too. They cross their 7s and their Zs, or zeds as they call them. And their spelling's sometimes a little off, too.

"Dear Zack," the letter began. "I am so sorry I'm not there, but all hell has broken loose. I had to fire the photographer we hired for the Harbour Island shoot. Then I had to drop everything and fly here to salvage the mess and make sure everything gets organised. It's the fashion feature for the January issue, so it is critical that everything go smoothly, and I cannot risk it being anything but perfect. Can you ever forgive me?"

Of course I could. I could forgive Barbara just about anything. She had stuck with me when others had bailed. She had loved me during a time when, through no fault of my own, I really wasn't worth loving. Sure, I would have preferred it if she were sitting in the limo with me and we were toasting my freedom with the bottle of Schramsberg '98 she told me she had bought for the occasion. But I loved her. She loved me. What was there to forgive?

She had tried to call to tell me about her change in plans, but the phones were out on Harbour Island. Typical. If it's not the phones, it's the electricity. Life on a tiny island. Barbara said someone on the island knew a limo driver back in Florida who would make the long haul to the Panhandle to pick me up. I was to join her on Harbour Island. All the commercial flights were booked out of Orlando, so I would be spending the night in Fort Lauderdale. She'd made reservations at Los Altos Inn, a fancy hotel on the Intercoastal.

"I could not arrange a charter until Saturday afternoon. You'll be happy to know you are flying with Charlie Callahan. He said you should be at Fort Lauderdale General Aviation by 3 P.M. He also said he was renaming his charter service 'Con Air' just for you. Zack, you are laughing, aren't you?"

Well, not laughing exactly, but I could only expect such a groaner out of Sorry Charlie Callahan.

"I have us booked at Albury Beach. Same cottage as always, on the hill behind the sea-grape hedge. It is so lonely in this room without you. This bed is much too big, and I am lying under the mozzy net thinking about . . . well, never you mind exactly what I am thinking about, but know that it most definitely involves you. So perhaps this bed is not too big after all. Wings on your feet and all that. Love . . ."

I folded the letter and stuck it back in the envelope. Then I pulled out the hundred-dollar bills. Twenty of them. There was a Post-it note on which Barbara had scrawled: "Paid driver for two days in advance. He will take you to airport on Saturday. This is mad money, spend it foolishly. . . ."

I felt a twinge of guilt, realizing for the first time that if called upon to fill out any official forms or applications, in the space for "Occupation" I would have to write: Kept Man. I stuck the money in the pocket of my jeans and slunk low in the divan, trying to keep the black funk at bay.

Maybe I should have kept my appointments with the Baypoint psychologist, maybe that would have kept me from feeling the way I felt. Part of the "matriculation process" at Baypoint called for a series of one-on-one therapy sessions aimed at preparing inmates for reentry into the outside world. I went to the first one and listened as an earnest young man, probably no more than six months out of grad school, told me the object of our sessions would be to "nurture my sense of self-esteem," "reassess my life goals and core motivations," and "find empowerment by embracing positive values." All of which I translated to mean: Zack, you fucked up and did a bad thing, but you'll feel better about yourself if you promise not to do bad things again and always walk on the sunny side of life. And since I couldn't swallow the first part of the equation—mine was the oldest line in the slammer: I didn't do it, dammit—I thought it would be hypocritical of me to buy into the rest of the program. I listened to the earnest young man's psychobabble for, oh, three minutes, then I shook his hand, thanked him kindly for his time, and walked out.

But at that very moment I could have used a big boost in the self-esteem department. Didn't matter that I wasn't guilty of what had just cost me nearly two years of my life. The system had judged me and so be it. Punch up Zachary Taylor Chasteen on the FBI's master shit list and it would be laid out in black-and-white. There aren't any asterisks in the sentencing books. I was a convicted felon. I had no job, no bank account, no immediate prospects. Hell, I didn't even have any long-range prospects. What I had was diddly-squat.

Then again, screw the pity party. I was riding in a limo with two thousand bucks in my pocket, on my way to the Bahamas and a woman who loved me. Always walk on the sunny side of life. . . .

4

An hour down the road Chip slid open the Plexiglas divider and said we needed to pull off for gas. He stopped at a 7–Eleven. The place was crowded and we had to wait in line. Families in minivans with out-of-state plates, coming to Florida for vacation, beach chairs and bicycles strapped on the racks. Construction workers in pickup trucks, the beds filled with sawhorses and scaffolding. Old people in old Chryslers, washing bugs off windshields and trying to figure out how to work the dagblasted pumps. Finally it was our turn. Chip pumped twenty-four gallons into the limo. Then he went inside to use the bathroom. I got out and stretched.

I was feeling fat and flabby. Probably the worst shape I'd ever been in. Lots of guys in prison, they use the time to work out and sculpt themselves into real brutes. Not me. All I did was lie in bed and read. Stories about sailors and the sea, mostly. I finished the complete Patrick O'Brian series, all twenty books about Jack Aubrey and Stephen Maturin. I reread the *Bounty* trilogy, which I had first devoured when I was twelve or so, and which had more or less ruined me for a land-based lifestyle. Then I finished up with a book about Ernest Shackleton and his torturous expedition to Antarctica. Stories of hardship and peril. They made my own dilemma seem a little less worse than it was.

I kept an eye on vehicles pulling off the interstate and into the 7–Eleven. No thugs behind tinted windows. No one who seemed the least bit interested in dragging me off for a little chat. But sooner or later someone else would be along. No doubt about that. If I was right about who Goatee and Raul worked for—and there was really only one person it could be— I knew the time I'd bought in the Baypoint parking lot wasn't much of a cushion. This person had lots of guys like Goatee and Raul. If he wanted to mess with me, he had all the troops he needed. I just couldn't figure out why he would bother. He was supposed to be dead. That's what had kept him out of prison. And that's what had sent me there. But why would he blow his cover? And why would he blow it now?

I walked around the limo and stopped at the driver's door. The piece of cardboard taped to the side of the limo was coming loose. I pulled it off the rest of the way and stood there looking at a phenomenal piece of airbrush craftsmanship: a pair of women's breasts—humongous, cartoonish breasts—painted in the same bright pink as the limo's chrome piping. Tiny pink lightbulbs marked each of her nipples. The face belonging to the fulsome rack wore big hair and a teasing smile. A curlicue logo read: "Ruby Booby's—Fort Lauderdale's Finest Ladies."

I looked around. People were watching me. Limos tend to draw attention. Big tacky limos with naked women painted on them tend to draw even more.

Chip left the 7–Eleven and walked across the parking lot. He was sipping a Big Gulp. People were watching him, too. He was a sight alright, big guy like that in a too-tight chauffeur's uniform, that crazy blond hair sticking out every which way from under the chauffeur's hat, those wild electric-blue sunglasses—looked like the love child of Hulk Hogan and Captain Kangaroo, something born on another planet.

He walked up beside me. He took a long draw on the Big Gulp, draining it. He looked at the piece of cardboard in my hand. Then he said: "Why'd you take that off?"

"Wanted to see what it said underneath. That where you work?"

He shrugged, didn't say anything.

I said, "What's this? The Ruby Booby's party car?"

"Yeah." He grinned. "They call it the Mercedes-Bangs."

"Cute."

"That sofa back there, where you been sitting, they call it the cockpit."

"Even cuter."

"You wouldn't believe some of the stuff goes on back there."

"Oh, I believe," I said.

I walked around to the passenger side. There was a piece of cardboard on that door. I ripped it off. I stood there looking at another Ruby Booby's logo, a matched set. Then I flipped both pieces of cardboard into a trash can.

"Chip?"

"Yeah."

"Rest of the way, I'll be riding up front with you."

Chip liked to play the radio loud. Real loud. He kept flipping stations. We listened to rock. We listened to country-western. We listened to music—I don't even know what you would call it. I didn't complain. I just looked out the window and watched North Florida go by. Billboards and pastureland, tract homes and trailer parks. Little dried-up towns wishing they were closer to Disney or a beach. Folks call it home.

Just before Live Oak we hit a stretch where Chip couldn't pick up anything on the radio, so he turned it off. We drove for a while. And then Chip said, "So this woman you're hooked up with, she must be loaded, huh?"

"She's done well," I said. "Worked hard."

"She's in the magazine business or something, isn't that it?"

"That's right."

"There a lot of money in that?"

"Can be," I said. "If you're the one who owns the magazines."

"How many she own?"

He was asking a lot of questions, but I didn't mind. Mainly because the topic was Barbara, and I enjoyed bragging about her. Besides, we had to talk about something, I guess, and that was the common ground. I couldn't figure out what friend of Barbara's might know a guy like Chip, but it was getting me where I needed to go, so why think too hard about it?

"Well, there's *Tropics*," I said. "That's the main magazine, the one she started out with. Covers the Caribbean. It's a travel magazine, high-end stuff. Then there're some smaller magazines for different islands—the *Live!* publications. Got *Barbados Live!* and *Jamaica Live!* I forget all of them."

"So how did the two of you get together?" he asked.

"Couple of years back, she booked my boat for an office party, a big Christmas shebang on the river by Minorca Beach."

"That where she lives?"

"No, that's where I live. She lives in Orlando. Winter Park, actually. Little town next to Orlando. Nice place. That's where her offices are. Orb Media."

"How many people she got working for her?"

"Oh, I don't know. Thirty or forty. I don't pay that much attention to her business, tell you the truth."

"So what do you do? You own a boat?" Chip asked.

"Used to. Several of them. Not anymore."

"Giving people boat rides—that was your business?"

"That and a few other things," I said. "I did day trips, sunset sails, deep-sea fishing, charters to the Bahamas. Had a flats boat, too. But . . ."

I'd lost all of it. Every damn bit of it. Gone. But to hell with wallowing in the past. I was itching to be in the Bahamas with Barbara. Only, there was something I needed to do first.

"Which way you going to Fort Lauderdale?" I asked Chip.

"Taking I–10 all the way across to 75, then south until we hit the turnpike. Same way I came."

"I want to get off the highway and cut across to Minorca Beach. I need to stop by my place."

"Too far out of the way," Chip said. "We don't have time."

"What's the hurry? My plane doesn't leave until tomorrow. You got a date or something?"

Chip turned and looked at me. I think he was trying to give

me his whup-ass glare, but it was hard to tell, what with him wearing his fancy shades.

"I got stuff I need to do," he said.

"Well, it'll have to wait. Barbara paid you for two days. We're barely into day one. We're going to Minorca Beach."

We rode along for a minute or so, Chip squeezing the steering wheel, restless in his seat. Then he looked at me and said, "I don't know how to get to there. And there's no map in the car."

"Not a problem," I said. "Just get off 75 at Ocala, take 441 down to Pedro, cut through the forest on 42, hang a right at 452, then catch 44 across to Deland, and follow it until it ends at Minorca Beach. How about that?"

Chip spent a few seconds grinding his jaw, letting me know he was ticked off. Then he flipped on the radio and turned it up to shatter-the-earwax volume, clearly unimpressed that he was chauffeuring Mr. Rand Damn McNally.

We drove, and we didn't talk, except for when I told Chip which way to turn. The news came on a couple of times. A boatload of Cubans had washed up in the Keys. Gas prices were expected to increase as much as fifteen cents a gallon before Labor Day weekend. And a tropical depression seven hundred and fifty miles east of the Turks and Caicos had been upgraded to the third tropical storm of the season. They were calling it Curt.

Just outside of Deland, Chip's cell phone rang. He looked to see who it was, but didn't answer. A couple of minutes later he pulled into another 7–Eleven.

"Need to make a phone call," he said. He got out of the limo and walked to the other side of the parking lot, punching numbers on his cell phone, then talking to someone.

I didn't have anything else better to do, so I started nosing around. Opened the limo's glove compartment. Not much that was interesting or surprising—a couple dozen condoms, along with what appeared to be a hash pipe. Also a first aid kit. Seemed to cover all the bases for a good time on wheels. There were some business cards in the glove compartment, too. They had the Ruby Booby's logo engraved on them. "Chip Willis," the cards read. Under that it said: "Transportation and security." So our boy was a bouncer, too. Seemed more his style. I plucked a card from the stack. Never knew. Maybe I was headed for a midlife crisis. Maybe I might be overcome by the urge to go out on the town, smoke dope, and cavort in the cockpit with bimbos. Then again, maybe someone would have the good sense to shoot me first.

Chip opened the limo door and stuck his head in.

"This might take a while. I need to make a couple more calls."

"Can't you do that in the car?" I said.

He shook his head.

"Reception sucks, need to be outside. You want, you got time to go inside, take a leak, get something to eat."

Sounded like a good idea. I got out of the limo.

"Get you anything?" I said.

"Yeah, I'll take another Big Gulp. Diet Dr Pepper. And how about a bag of Cheetos, something like that?"

He reached in his pocket and pulled out some money, but I waved him off.

"My treat," I said. Figured the two of us might as well kiss and make up. Still had several hours ahead of us.

I went inside the 7–Eleven. Used the facilities, washed my hands and face. Got a bottle of water for myself, and the Big Gulp and Cheetos for Chip. Came to $3.67. Of Barbara's money.

When I stepped outside the limo was gone.

I stood there thinking about all the reasons why Chip would have ditched me. Maybe the little show in the Baypoint parking lot had scared him off. Maybe he really did have a hot date down in Fort Lauderdale. Or maybe he just thought I was a lousy conversationalist. It didn't really bother me until I realized he'd taken off with the plastic envelope containing all my i.d.'s—driver's license, passport, the works. Then it bothered me a lot.

U.S. citizens don't need passports to enter the Bahamas, but they must at least present a driver's license along with a registered birth certificate, the kind with the raised seal on it. I had seen entire families turned away on vacations simply because a by-the-numbers Bahamian bureaucrat wouldn't accept a photocopy of some kid's birth certificate. Lacking even a library card, I had no idea how I was going to pass muster. It was a Friday afternoon and government offices would be closing for the weekend. Even if I could get all the papers filled out and filed, plus have a new photo shot, it would take several days to get a new passport even if I paid the hefty premium for a rush job. I might be able to get a duplicate driver's license, assuming my

felony record didn't gum up the works. But the birth certificate
would be trickier. Requests had to go through the bureau of vital statistics in Jacksonville, and that would take a day or two,
at best.

The short of it—I was screwed unless I could get myself to
Fort Lauderdale, then try to find Chip and the limo. Failing that,
I'd turn to Charlie Callahan for help. He had plenty of Bahamas
experience, a good deal of it on the sly. If anyone could sneak
me into the Bahamas it was Sorry Charlie.

I walked over to the pay phone, stuck in some money, and
called my house. It was a long shot, but maybe Boggy was
there, and maybe he would answer. He could drive over to Deland and pick me up. It was only about twenty miles.

Back when I had my boats and a decent business, Boggy was
my first mate, although that implies a ranking system our relationship doesn't have. Then came the shit storm and my sojourn
at Baypoint. Boggy stuck with me—he always has, even when I
have tried to shake him loose—keeping an eye on things in my
absence.

I let the phone ring ten times, until the automated voice
came on and told me that if I stuck in another seventy five cents
it would forward a message. I hung up.

I looked around the parking lot. Two young guys—seventeen or eighteen, barefoot, shirtless and wearing knee-length
surfer trunks—were checking the straps that fastened their
boards to the top of a rusty Volvo sedan. Orlando kids, heading
for the inlet to catch some waves. I walked over and asked if
they wanted to make an easy hundred bucks. I told them I'd
throw in a Big Gulp and a bag of Cheetos to sweeten the deal. A
couple of minutes later we were on our way.

Minorca Beach hadn't changed all that much in the time that I
had been gone, which is something you can't say about most
Florida beach towns. Two bridges connect it with the mainland.
They're named after a couple of dead politicians, but everyone
calls the old one the Low Bridge, and the new one the High
Bridge. I had hated the new one when it was built several years

ago, but it had grown on me for the view alone, and it was the one we took.

I've driven over that bridge probably a thousand times and never once have I not been completely blown away by all that spreads out before me: To the north, where Coronado Inlet casts its apron unto the ocean, white-capped rip currents slash against granite boulder jetties—a vain attempt to thwart the Atlantic's crusade to reclaim this spit of sand. To the south, mangrove mud flats huddle along the Indian River, eventually leading to the broad inland sea known as Redfish Lagoon. In between, humankind has done its best to blight the landscape, but has come up short compared to its shabby conquests in Daytona, and Cocoa, and too many other places. There is notable excess, of course, because this is, after all, Florida. A slew of too-tall condos snake along the shore. Strip malls sprawl out on turf better served by cabbage palms. And people with too much money and too little sense of grace have erected overdone beachfront homes too close to the dune line. I wouldn't wish a hurricane on anyone, but . . .

We crossed the bridge and followed A–1–A south a few miles, almost to where it ends at the entrance of Coronado National Seashore and where the island is only a few hundred yards wide. Looking left, I could see the ocean. To my right was Redfish Lagoon. And straight ahead, for miles and miles, there was nothing but a skinny sliver of land—beach to the east, dunes in the middle, tidal flats to the west—splitting the two bodies of water.

The Cold War had been good for something. It had sparked the space race, which in turn prompted NASA to claim a giant chunk of Florida's east coast so those pesky Russians couldn't get a peek at what we were up to at Cape Canaveral. Later, after things began loosening up, NASA turned over most of the buffer zone to the National Park Service, the result being that Florida still has twenty-some-odd miles of coastline that remains virtually the way it was centuries ago.

We passed the park's ranger station with its big parking lot for people using the boat ramp. Only a couple of SUVs with trailers were parked there. It was too hot for fishing. We came to a dirt-and-oyster-shell road that hooked off A–1–A and cut past a sign that said: "Leaseholder vehicles only beyond this point."

"Turn in there," I told the kid who was driving.

The road slithered through clumps of saw palmetto and sea grape. It jutted down to the lagoon and hugged it awhile before reaching a clearing where a low wooden pier stuck out fifty yards or so into the river. Just beyond the pier stood the first of several houses that faced the lagoon—big cracker houses with wraparound porches and broad, overhanging eaves, and tin roofs long since gone rusty. None of the houses were particularly grand, but all of them were old, all of them were in various stages of disrepair, and all of them were, quite obviously, empty. Ancient cedar trees, their trunks gnarly and knotty, lined the road as it ran by the houses. There were rotting boat hulls, and the skeletons of vintage pickup trucks, and picket fences falling down.

"This where you live?" one of the kids said. "Looks like a ghost town."

"Welcome to LaDonna," I said. "Population: Two."

That would be me and Boggy. I didn't count Boggy's numerous girlfriends, mainly because I couldn't keep track of them all. And I didn't count Barbara, even though she had been spending more and more time at my place before Baypoint claimed me. I was hoping we might be headed toward something permanent. I think Barbara was hoping the same thing. But it was a subject that hadn't been broached. We had a lot of catching up to do first.

I gave the two surfers their hundred dollars and they immediately began talking about how they would spend it. One of them wanted to "throw a giant kegger." The other planned to put it toward a ticket to Costa Rica so he could check out the surf and the ganja down there. Made me feel all proud and glowing inside, knowing I was helping make the dreams of America's youth come true.

I got out of the rusty Volvo and went the last few hundred yards on foot. I walked past a green historical marker with gold lettering that read: "The Town of LaDonna." Below it, the in-

scription went on to say that while the origins of the name
LaDonna were unknown, it was once the site of a Timucuana
Indian settlement, as evidenced by numerous shell middens and
a network of canals built to connect the ocean with the lagoon.
Later, in the early 1900s, well-to-do citrus growers from inland
built the houses as family retreats.

What the historical marker didn't say was that LaDonna had
been the site of a bitter battle, one fought in the 1960s, by the
descendents of those well-to-do citrus growers, when the federal government confiscated their property as part of its coastal
land-grab spree. Perhaps confiscated is too strong a word, but
that's what it amounted to in the long run. The feds offered each
of the homeowners a pitifully small cash payment, along with a
life-leasehold. Meaning, when the owner of the property died it
would revert directly to the government, and all the heirs be
damned.

My grandfather Chasteen wasn't nearly as well-to-do as his
forebears—it would not be unfair to call him an eccentric—but
he was a hardheaded old coot. All the other LaDonna landown-
ers signed buy-out contracts with the government. Not my
grandfather. Exhausting what little money he possessed, he
hired attorneys and waged war for nearly a decade. He argued
that, unlike the other owners at LaDonna, he used his property
as a place of business, a business that couldn't easily be up-
rooted. So to speak.

Some people go gaga over orchids, others over roses. For
my grandfather, it was palm trees. He roamed the world seeking
them out—Madagascar, the Canary Islands, Thailand, Cuba.
He stashed away seed pods and, in some cases, juvenile trees,
then sneaked them back into the country since he didn't have a
federal research permit. My grandmother was once detained at
Miami International after customs agents found a three-foot-
tall talipot palm from India in her steamer trunk. Just a minor
setback, since my grandfather made it through with a smaller
talipot hidden inside his umbrella. The two of them, they were
the real smugglers in our family, not me.

All in all there were more than two hundred species of palm
on the property, probably thirty thousand trees altogether,

crammed into a little more than seventeen acres. It was an exotic tropical jungle that miraculously sprouted on a scrubby barrier island. And it was a great place to grow up.

"Our own little Eden," my mother used to call it.

I was seven when she and my father died in a horrible accident on Redfish Lagoon. They were out shrimping one summer evening when a thunderstorm blew in out of nowhere. Lightning struck their little boat and the gas tank exploded. They were gone in an instant.

My grandparents raised me. They smothered me with love. And they dug in their heels when the federal government came along and tried to take away their idyllic little domain on the river.

The sad truth about us Chasteens is that we are genetically disinclined toward entrepreneurialism. We work hard, but we just don't make good businesspeople. While my grandfather sold some palm trees from time to time, enough to pay the bills and keep us in groceries, he wasn't all that aggressive about attracting new clients, or tapping into the vast and lucrative landscaping market that grew out of Florida's full-throttle rush to develop every square inch of the state. He much preferred collecting rare specimens and nurturing them to maturity. He traded trees with other collectors and donated them to any botanical garden or public park that asked. He never made much money from his obsession. The palm trees were just something he loved. Still, a federal judge eventually ruled that Chasteen Palm Nursery represented a "unique and indigenous livelihood, one that is intrinsically connected to its physical place." The government lost its bid to buy us out. And our homestead endured as a private oasis surrounded by national park.

I followed the dirt road until it ended at a cul-de-sac where an eight-foot wood fence ran from the river to about a hundred yards inland. Behind the fence, in lush and flagrant contrast to the surroundings, loomed a mass of green—palm tree after palm tree after palm tree.

After my grandfather died, and my grandmother soon after him, the grounds were tough to maintain. The house was in good shape, or at least in as good shape as a hundred-year-old wooden house in Florida can be with salt winds and thunder-storms and all manner of semitropical vermin always nipping away at it. I had all the work I could handle keeping my boats running and bringing in customers on that front. Besides, I wasn't much of a horticulturalist. I enjoyed all the trees, but I really didn't know what to do with them. The palm nursery slipped into neglect, with blight and disease wiping out a few of the more fragile species.

Still, it was home, and aside from my time in college and the few years I'd spent in Miami, it was the only home I'd ever really known. And even though I was expecting it, even though I was the one who had set the wheels in motion, I wasn't fully prepared for seeing the sign in the driveway, the one that said FOR SALE.

6

I didn't want to sell the place, but it wasn't as if I had a choice. I was broke. And without my boats I had no way of generating income. I couldn't even pay the property taxes, much less the regular upkeep.

The FOR SALE sign bore the logo of Jo Hardwick Realty and gave a phone number to call. Jo was an old family friend and, as realtors go, she had some principles. The property was worth a lot of money and her commission would be sizable. Still, she balked when I told her I had decided to put it on the market.

"Zack, all you have to do is contact the park service and you know they'll grab it in a heartbeat," she said. "You don't need me slicing seven percent out of the deal."

"Already called them," I said. "Talked to some muckety-muck up in Washington. Said the park service would have to lobby Congress for a special appropriation. Said a sale could take three or four years. I can't afford to wait that long. I need the money now."

Jo sent me the listing papers and I signed them a week before they sprung me from Baypoint. I'd avoided thinking about it since then, but the FOR SALE sign delivered a sharp slap of wake-up-and-smell-the-dismal-reality. The market for waterfront property in Florida is always vigorous. Jo knew a couple of potential buyers and thought we would have a contract within a month.

There wasn't anything I really needed to do at LaDonna. I just wanted to be there, to take it all in, to reset my compass, get my bearings, say the first of many good-byes, and then head for the Bahamas and Barbara.

We typically kept the driveway gate closed. But as I approached I saw that it was wide open. There were fresh tire tracks in the dirt. It was unlikely that Boggy had made them. He drives only when he has to and then only with a monumental amount of bitching. So who had paid me a visit? Could Goatee and Raul have contacted their associates to tell them I'd given them the slip? Maybe. Would they have left the gate open and advertised what they were up to? Maybe. These weren't subtle guys. I edged to the side of the driveway and took it slow, on the lookout.

I couldn't help noticing that someone had put serious sweat equity into the place. The undergrowth had been whacked away. A pile of PVC pipe was stacked and ready to be set out for irrigation. The trees looked as healthy as I'd ever seen them. There were even some new plantings.

I turned the last bend before the house and saw a flatbed truck parked in the driveway. A man about my age was tying down a big sago palm on the back of the truck. A teenage boy was helping him. The sago had a half dozen or so crowns—a prize specimen—and its root ball was wrapped in burlap. Over the years we'd always kept an eye out for people sneaking onto the property and digging up palms to decorate their yards. But pulling right up in the driveway? That was pretty damn brazen.

The man and the boy stopped what they were doing and watched me walking toward them. The man was lean and lanky. He took off his cap, wiped his forehead with a shirtsleeve, and grinned at me.

"How you doin', Zack?" he said.

Only then did I spot the name on the side of the truck—Burleson Landscape—and recognize Tom Burleson. We had grown up together, but I hadn't seen him in at least a dozen years.

"Tom," I said, shaking his hand. "Been a long time."

"Yeah, it has. Zack, this here's my son, Tom Jr." I shook Tom Jr.'s hand, his father saying: "Tommy, when you were just a kid you used to watch Mr. Chasteen here playing on the TV for the Gators and the Dolphins."

"I remember," said Tom, Jr. "Zack the Sack, number forty-four."

"I'm flattered."

Tom Jr. stared at me, as if he wanted to say something but couldn't make up his mind about it. Then finally, "I thought it sucked what the high school did."

"What's that?" I said.

Tom Jr. looked at his dad. And then both of them looked away, embarrassed. Finally, Burleson said, "Aw, hell, Zack, I thought you'd heard about it. It was all over the newspaper. You know that trophy case they had in the school lobby? The one with the photos of you in it and your jerseys from the Gators and the Dolphins?"

I nodded.

"A bunch of goodie-goodies didn't think it looked right honoring somebody who was in prison. They kept raising hell until the school took it down."

"Well, I guess there's always going to be people like that," I said.

"You oughta make 'em put it back up," said Tom Jr.

"Probably not worth the fight," I said. "But I appreciate you saying it."

We were quiet for a couple of seconds. I didn't quite know how to ask Tom Burleson what he was doing stealing palm trees from my property. And he didn't seem the least bit embarrassed that I'd caught him at it.

"Saw the FOR SALE sign," Burleson said.

I shrugged. I really didn't want to talk about it. But did he think a FOR SALE sign meant he could just come and plunder as he pleased?

"That fella you got running this place been doing a pretty

good job of it while you were gone," Burleson said. "I've probably bought four or five sagos off him and every one of them is doing fine. What's that fella's name anyway?"

"I call him Boggy."

"Bobby?"

"No, Boggy. Like muck. You seen him around?"

"Nah. I was by earlier in the week, and he said he might be gone awhile. Said if he wasn't here, for me just to pull on in here and load up," said Burleson. "What is he, Mexican or something?"

"He's from the Dominican Republic," I said.

"Kinda Indian-looking."

"He's Taino."

"Tie what?"

"Taino. They're Caribbean Indians."

"Never heard of such a thing," Burleson said. "Tell you what, though, Zack, that fella sure likes to dicker. Me and him, we must have gone around for at least an hour or so before we settled on a price for this sago. And he's a stickler about getting paid in cash."

Burleson reached into the cab of his truck, then handed me a bank envelope.

"Should be twenty-five hundred in there," he said.

"That how much Boggy charged you for this sago?"

"Yep. Like I said, he likes to dicker. Started out asking four thousand dollars. But it's a fair enough price. Big sagos like this take fifty years to grow, and they're getting scarce. You got another one up there, by the midden, pretty near twice the size. Me and Boggy have just about settled in at three thousand dollars for it. You get a better offer than that, you let me know."

I told him I'd keep that in mind. I helped them finish tying down the sago, then we said our good-byes, and Burleson backed his truck out of the driveway. I closed the gate behind them.

I felt equal parts fury and betrayal. It was like I'd been kicked in the stomach. Boggy had been selling off palm trees and pocketing the cash. Four or five sagos for two or three thousand apiece. That was a pretty good bundle. And who knew what all else he'd dug up? There were some Canary Island date palms I knew could fetch four or five thousand each. And some of the rare specimen palms, hell, you could just about name any price you wanted for them.

I could only guess that Boggy had seen the future and figured he didn't want any part of it. The palm trees were just sitting there, easy pickings, a fair amount of stake money for hitting the road. I wondered where he had run off to, wondered if I'd ever see him again.

7

I left the driveway and followed a stone path that led me to the house. It stood solid and permanent, as everlasting as anything I'd ever known. Giant live oaks, older even than the house, encircled it and provided cool shade. It was all locked up, the storm shutters latched tight. Boggy had fled the scene, but at least he'd had the decency to shut the doors on his way out. I could get inside the house easy enough, but if I did that I'd be knocking around in there for hours, communing with ghosts and reliving memories. I didn't have time for that.

I moved past the house and down a gentle grassy slope toward the river. The sun was bright here, the back side of the property kept clear to offer a view of the water from the back porch of the house. There was another FOR SALE sign stuck in the backyard, all the better for attracting the attention of boaters passing by. The river was narrow at LaDonna, only forty or fifty yards across, and dotted with little islands that weren't much more than wiregrass and mangrove, and piles of broken, bleached-out shells. The tide was out, and the mud flats sat exposed. Ibis and herons stalked tiny crabs in puddles by the boathouse.

I opened the door of the boathouse and stepped inside. It looked pretty much the way I'd left it—empty and lonesome. My boats were gone. The only thing occupying the three slips were thick clusters of oysters and barnacles that encrusted the wooden pilings. Last I'd heard, the boats were scheduled for auction at the U.S. Coast Guard station in Minorca Beach. I could only assume they'd been sold to the highest bidders while I was still in Baypoint, the proceeds going to the government. I'd been too torn up about it to seek out the details.

I walked past a row of closets and storage lockers, flipping them open and checking them out as I went. Most of my gear was still there—fishing tackle, diving paraphernalia, cleats and lines, anchors, rigging, five-gallon gas tanks, Q-beams, marine batteries, boxes of Coast Guard–certified emergency flares— the endless clutter that comes with owning boats. Or having once owned them.

I walked to the end of the largest boat slip—the one that once held my trawler, *Miz Blitz*—and looked up and down the river. About the only change I noticed was in the seawall that ran on either side of the boathouse. The last time I'd been here, shortly before the trial that sent me away, a tropical depression was pounding the East Coast. It had dropped about a foot of rain and, coupled with some kind of freak alignment of the moon and sun that swelled the tides and flooded the river, had cracked and broken away most of my seawall.

But I saw now that it was fixed. The work was new and Boggy had quite obviously done it himself. I could tell this because the new seawall was a thing of both function and art, although the art part of it might have been obscure to anyone who did not appreciate Boggy's artistic vision. Instead of buying steel rebar to reinforce the concrete and rock in the seawall, Boggy had relied on whatever he could find lying around— chicken wire, old axles and wheel rims, several driveshafts from ancient outboard motors, old scuba tanks, and other castoff gear from over the years. Broken pieces of tile and glass were set in the face of the seawall, creating a wild mosaic of blues and yellows and reds. It might not have been the way I would have repaired the seawall, but it had saved me a bundle of money, and at least I could thank Boggy for something.

I walked out on the seawall and stood there, gazing across the lagoon. The last time I'd seen my parents I was standing at the very same spot, waving good-bye to them as they pushed off in the boat. I could still recall tiny details of that day—the turquoise bracelet my mother wore, the Marlboro hanging from my father's mouth, the eight-track tape deck that was playing the soundtrack from *South Pacific*. They loved listening to music on the water. My father was hamming it up and singing along with "There Is Nothing Like a Dame." My mother was rolling her eyes, but loving it. Then they were gone.

I broke away and returned to the boathouse. My tiny office occupied a corner by the last boat slip. I stepped inside and switched on the light. Everything looked OK. A fax machine/printer and a prehistoric laptop sat on the pinewood picnic table that was my desk. A three-drawer metal filing cabinet, a few plastic chairs, nautical charts thumbtacked to the particleboard walls, a ceiling fan with the blades covered in dust—the executive suite of what used to be LaDonna Charters.

When it came to chartering I was a generalist. Flats fishing, deep-sea trips, scuba diving, leisure outings for the booze-cruise crowd—whatever it took to cover the overhead and give me a little wiggle room, I had boats for every purpose. I could have sat back, hired other captains, and kept the entire fleet in operation on a semi-regular basis. But I liked doing it all myself. I was lucky. I had socked away a little money and could afford to run my business in an inefficient manner. Doing it the other way wouldn't have been any fun. I didn't claim to be the savviest fishing guide, or the best divemaster, or the most knowledgeable tour captain. I spread myself too thin to excel in any one area. Blame it on a chronically short attention span. I will do anything to avoid boredom or sidestep the routine. Besides, I knew too many specialty guides who had grown to hate their occupations. They became sour and bitter at the prospect of taking people out on the water. I didn't want it to ever come to that. I still enjoyed the hell out of what I did. Only problem, I wasn't doing it anymore.

I didn't have a grasp on the current real estate market, but I was hoping the property would fetch enough to allow me to buy a decent boat and start all over again. If I was fortunate enough to find another trawler like *Miz Blitz*—not damn likely, but I could dream—I might even be able to live on board at Minorca Beach Marina.

I was on my way out when the phone rang. I answered it.

"LaDonna Charters," I said.

"Zack, that you?"

I recognized Jo Hardwick's voice.

"In the dazzling flesh," I said. "I was just thinking about you."

"Were your thoughts pure?"

I had to laugh. Jo was closing in on seventy-five. A very well-maintained and attractive seventy-five, but still . . .

"As pure as you deserve," I said.

"My, my. Then they were totally indecent. You should be ashamed of yourself."

Had to admire the old girl. She still had plenty of spark.

"Good news on your listing," Jo said, getting down to business. "I have one offer in hand and I expect at least two more by this evening."

"That was fast."

"Not really, not when you consider the uniqueness of the property," Jo said. "Zack, I want you to know that I have qualified the potential buyers. Not based on whether they have money—they've all got too much money, bucketfuls of it. No, I'm only accepting offers from people who will be good stewards of that land, people who will give it the respect it deserves. I won't let you sell it to someone who is going to come in there and build something big and awful just to show off. I just won't have that."

"That means a lot to me," I said. "It means more than the money."

Then Jo mentioned the amount of the first offer. It was more than I had expected, a lot more. I might be able to buy a couple of boats. Might even be able to put a little aside and pretend like I was flush.

"You think you can get that much?"

"God isn't making property like that anymore, Zack. It's a precious, precious parcel. You'll get top dollar for it. The people who are interested in your place, I wouldn't be surprised if they got into a bidding war. Of course, some of that will be ego. But mostly it's the property. There's nothing else out there like it."

Yes, the place was precious beyond anyone's imagining. And here I was, on the verge of letting it go. But I'd already beaten myself up about that. It was time to move on.

"You want me to drop by this evening with the offers?" Jo asked.

I told her no, it would have to wait. I was only sticking around for a few more minutes. I'd give her a call as soon as I got back from the Bahamas.

After we said our good-byes, I pulled out Chip Willis's business card and dialed the number for Ruby Booby's. All I got was a recording. It told me the joint opened at 7 P.M., there was a ten-dollar cover charge, two-for-one beer until ten, and twenty naked ladies at all times. But it wouldn't let me leave a message.

I walked back up the hill toward the house and stepped inside the open-air tin-roofed shed that doubled as my garage. It was mostly filled with tools for the nursery—hoes and shovels, pruning shears and post-hole diggers. Swing blades for keeping the grass low. Not much in the way of mechanical equipment. My grandfather had left me a low-tech operation and I had done little to improve it.

My Jeep Wagoneer sat under a canvas tarpaulin. I yanked off the tarp and stepped back to let the cockroaches and spiders skitter away. The Wagoneer was twenty-two years old. I'd bought it with my signing bonus from the Dolphins, and it had weathered the years much better than I had. The key was in the ignition. Before they'd hauled me off to Baypoint, I'd asked Boggy to forgo his disdain for automobiles and crank it up every now and then just to keep the battery charged. I slid behind the wheel, juiced the accelerator a couple of times, and turned the key. The engine sputtered and coughed, and then it rolled over.

But there was a problem—two pallets of fertilizer stacked

behind the Wagoneer, blocking its way out. Must have been fifty bags, seventy-five pounds apiece. Looked like a recent delivery. What had Boggy been thinking? The place was for sale and he knew it. I didn't want to dump money I didn't have into something that soon wouldn't belong to me. Let the new owners worry about fertilizing palm trees.

I turned off the Wagoneer and sized up the chore ahead. I figured it would take at least thirty minutes of lifting and hauling and catching my breath. I'd probably throw out my back as part of the bargain. But there was no other way around it. I couldn't hit the road until I'd moved the bags of fertilizer.

Used to be, when I was younger and helping out my grandfather, I could carry a bag of fertilizer in each arm. I gave it a try. Still had it in me, although I'd probably pay hell for it the next day. I began lugging the bags and stacking them along the side of the shed. My shoulders were burning but they were burning good. My shirt was soon drenched with sweat. I cleared the first pallet and was starting in on the second one when I heard a voice behind me.

"Chasteen . . ."

I swung around. There were three of them, silhouetted by sunlight as it streamed in the shed's entry. I didn't have time to make out their faces. All I saw was one of them swinging something. A shovel, it looked like. I heard the sick crackle as it slammed against the side of my head, and everything went dark.

I'd been knocked out once or twice before, but all the other times it had been on a playing field, and when I came to, a trainer or a team physician was hovering over me with water and towels and a comforting word. When I limped toward the bench there was applause. Teammates gave me pats on the butt. It was much better that way. Which is not to say that I was particularly fond of those pats on the butt.

Coming out of it, I heard them. They were talking in Spanish and I couldn't make out any of it. I was lying facedown on concrete and my hands were tied behind my back. It felt like they had used duct tape. My legs were lashed together at the ankles and the knees. There was duct tape over my eyes, too. I was bleeding from a big chunk that I had bitten out of my tongue and my mouth had pebbles in it. I spit out the blood and realized the pebbles were broken teeth. The whole right side of my face was throbbing. I wiggled my jaw. It stung like hell, but, except for the cracked molars, everything seemed to be in place. Gee, if I'd only been wearing my protective gel mouthpiece.

And then one of them was saying, "Hey, Chasteen, can you hear me?"

"Yeah, I can hear you."

"That's good, that's real good. Because we thought we had fucking killed you. And if we killed you, then we would be fucked, too."

They laughed. They talked some more in Spanish. I could hear water lapping against something. I was in the boathouse. They had dragged me back there so passing boaters wouldn't see what was going on.

I tried to roll over, and all it got me was a kick in the back, and then one of them planted a foot on me and held me down. He ground his heel into my neck.

"How's that feel, asshole? Huh? How's that feel? You lucky Raul's not here or he'd rip your head off. He wants a piece of you, man."

He took his foot off my neck.

"What do you want?" I said.

"You supposed to show us where it's at, man."

"Where what's at?"

"What you got that don't belong to you."

"I don't know what you're talking about."

"You want us to tear this fucking place apart, man? We'll do that. We should have already done that. I don't know why we're fucking waiting around."

"Tell me what you're looking for."

They talked some more in Spanish. And then the one who was doing most of the talking said: "You got something that belongs to Victor Ortiz."

The name I'd been waiting to hear.

"I thought Victor Ortiz was dead."

The men laughed.

"Yeah, he's dead alright. And he wants to stay dead. Only he wants what you got that belongs to him. He wants it back. Or else, you gonna be the real kind of dead. *Sabe*, asshole?"

"You guys work for Ortiz?"

"Like you said, man, Victor Ortiz is dead," the one in charge said. "But there's all kinds of ways of being dead. Like if everyone thinks you're dead, then you're dead. So he's dead. But he wants something from you."

"You tell Ortiz that there's something I want from him."

"What's that?"

"The last two years of my life."

"Maybe Mr. Ortiz, he wants the same thing. It is not easy being a dead man. Very much pressure. Very stressful."

"Cry me a goddam river. Where is Ortiz?"

"He is where men go who are dead like he is dead. Only he cannot find peace because of what it is you owe him."

"Listen, you tell Ortiz I don't have anything that belongs to him. You got it? You tell him that he's the one owes me."

The three men talked in Spanish some more. I could pick up a little of it, but my Spanish is pretty lousy. Then they stopped talking. I could hear them opening gear lockers and rummaging around. It didn't sound as if they were being particularly tidy about it. They stopped tearing things apart and then one of them kicked me in the back.

"Don't go nowhere," he said and his buddies laughed some more.

I listened as they walked away. Minutes passed. They didn't come back. Had they left for good? Probably not. I figured they had moved on to the house to rip it apart and look for whatever they were after. They'd be back soon.

I wiggled my wrists in the duct tape, but couldn't pry them apart. I flailed around with my legs, but couldn't get them loose either. My head was near the edge of the concrete now, and I could hear the water lapping against the wood pilings in one of the boat slips. I tried to remember how high the tide was when I had first arrived at the boathouse. I recalled seeing herons on the mud flats. The river had been still, almost no current. Dead low tide. How long had I been unconscious? Five minutes? An hour? At low tide there could be anywhere from five to six feet of water in the slips, depending on the phase of the moon, just barely enough for me to pull in *Miz Blitz* without scraping her bottom. High tide it rose to eight feet or nine feet.

I had a plan in mind. It wasn't a particularly brilliant plan, but I didn't have a lot of options. I could stay where I was and wait for them to come back. They would kick me and knock me around some, maybe worse. Goatee and Raul had obviously been in touch with these guys. They were probably back on the road by now and headed this way to join their pals. They would want to get in a few licks, too. No reason why I should just hang around and be everyone's favorite punching bag.

So it was my plan or nothing. Might work, might not. All depended on the tide. The lower the better. Too high, I'd most likely drown.

I scooted to the edge of the concrete, tried to judge where I was. They had probably dragged me in through the boathouse door and stopped at the first slip. I tried to visualize it. Eight wood pilings along each side, about six feet apart, with a concrete walkway separating it from the second slip. I didn't think they had dragged me out onto the walkway, toward the end of the slip where the water was deeper. Why bother? They just wanted me inside the boathouse, out of sight.

I teetered facedown on the edge of the concrete. I took long deep breaths, filling my lungs with air. Then I rolled off the concrete and hit the water, and the moment I hit it I knew I was in trouble. What I should have done was sling my legs off first and followed them down. That way I might have had a chance of standing up when I hit the bottom. But now I was sinking sideways and the duct tape wouldn't let me bend my knees. I bumped against the bottom shoulder first and then bobbed to the surface. I grabbed a gulp of air, got water instead. Coughed, got more water, then I was sinking again.

I tried to fight back the panic. I thrashed around in the water, struggling to get back to the surface, but I couldn't leverage against the bottom with my feet. I just kept going sideways. Into deeper water. I had maybe another thirty–forty seconds of air left in me. After that, I'd be a goner. Meat for the crabs.

Then I hit a piling. My head struck against it and the oyster shells ripped chunks out of my scalp. But I didn't mind. Those oyster shells were my salvation. They were my plan. I flipped and turned and managed to grab just enough purchase on the bottom to push my back against the piling and work my duct-taped hands up and down on the shells. I was almost out of air. Blood throbbed in my head. My chest tightened and constricted. Muscles in my gut began to cramp. I kept working the duct tape against the piling. Up and down, up and down. Every now and then I'd slip and gash an arm, then press myself harder against the piling. Tough stuff, that duct tape, but finally there was a rip and I pulled and pulled, and my arms were free, and they were swimming me to the surface.

I hugged the piling, taking in gulps of air. I tore off the duct tape around my eyes. It only cost me about half of each eyebrow, but they were getting a little too bushy anyway. I was near the mouth of the boat slip, in the deeper water. I inched back into the boathouse, piling by piling, until the water was about chin high. I reached down and undid the tape around my knees. Then I worked my ankles free. I lost my shoes somewhere in the mud. But I was planning on swimming out of there and I was going to lose them anyway.

I was exhausted from the struggle, but I didn't have time to lose. The three of them could return at any minute. I might be able to give them a good fight, maybe even take them. But I hadn't actually seen them, so I didn't know what I was up against. Besides that, they probably had guns. In which case the fight would be over real fast.

I sucked in air, filling my lungs. From the mouth of the boathouse, it was about fifty yards across the river to a small island rimmed with mangroves and buttonwood. If I was lucky I could make it most of the way across underwater, then lose myself in the mangroves before they could spot me. After that, it was just a matter of swimming from tiny island to tiny island, hopscotching my way across the lagoon. I figured it would take me a couple of hours to reach Oak Hill. I knew people there who could help me out.

I was inching toward the end of the slip, getting ready to swim away, when the boathouse door opened. I heard steps on the concrete and caught a glimpse of someone stepping inside. There was only one of them. I heard him curse when he saw I was gone. And I knew he'd be running to get the others.

I splashed in the water, made it sound as if I were struggling. "Down here," I called out. "I fell. Help me."

He stepped to the edge of the concrete, and as he leaned down to look under the walkway I surged up and grabbed him, pulling him down with me. In the moment before I wrapped myself around him, I saw his face. It was a face I'll never forget, because it was the face of the first man I ever killed.

He was a young guy, no more than thirty, a wisp of a mustache, and close-cropped hair. I locked my arms and legs around him and down we went. We hit the bottom with me on top, my legs scissored around his legs. He wrenched and fought, but I had him. I hooked my arm around his throat, squeezed and pulled back hard, leveraging a knee against his shoulders. My head was out of the water now, and I was holding him down. I kept squeezing his throat and holding him down until he stopped fighting and went still. Then I held him down for another thirty seconds just to make sure.

I let go of him and his body rose to the surface. I kept him face down. I didn't want to see his face again. I pushed his body under the concrete walkway and, as I was doing it, I felt the gun in his pants pocket. I pulled it out and looked at it. I am not a gun guy. I've never owned a gun, and I wouldn't be able to tell one gun from another gun even if I had a cheat sheet and Charlton Heston was whispering in my ear. This gun was black and shiny and bigger than the palm of my considerably big hand. I dropped it in the water and let it sink. Then I wedged the body behind a piling.

I tried hard not to think about what I'd just done. I had killed a man with my bare hands. And it hadn't been a fair fight. Not a fair fight at all. I was bigger and stronger and he didn't have a chance. But if I'd learned anything over the years, it was that you take the matchups the way they come at you. You put on your game face and give it all you've got. Let up just once and you lose your edge, and then you're done for. Because next time the opponent might be every bit as tough as you are. And you can damn sure bet that they'll be looking to lay you flat, and run up the score, and laugh at you when it's over.

I took a deep breath, pushed off from the pilings, and swam for the other side of the river.

9

I made it all the way across without coming up for air, surfaced slowly in the mangroves, and hung there for a moment, looking back at the boathouse. Nothing going on in there. Nothing going on around the rest of the property either. The other two guys were nowhere to be seen. Probably still inside the house.

I waded chest-deep through the mangroves, moving to the back side of the tiny island. Fiddler crabs skittered along the shore and ducked into their holes. I shuffled my feet along the sandy bottom, hoping to scare off any stingrays that might be in my path. Last thing I needed was to get barbed by one of them. That would have me hobbling for sure.

I made it to a pocket-sized break in the tangle of roots and limbs and stared west, charting my course. I picked out the radio tower behind DeQuesnes Fish Camp on the far side of the lagoon. The sun was still a palm width or two above the tree line on the opposite shore, but it was sinking fast. The mosquitoes were already fierce. I ducked underwater to keep them off me, and when I came up they were buzzing there, waiting, ready to suck me dry. With luck I'd make it to Oak Hill by dark, before the little bastards got any worse.

• • •

For the next two hours, it was swim a little, trudge a little, swim a little more, as I moved across the lagoon. I had plenty of time to think about things, which meant thinking mostly about Victor Ortiz. I thought about the day I first laid eyes on him. It was at the Minorca Beach Marina, where I had taken *Miz Blitz* to get her hull scraped and a new coat of bottom paint put on. I was standing around talking with Robby Greig, the marina owner, when a shiny Mercedes pulled up and Ortiz got out and introduced himself. He was elegant in a way that only Latin men can be, with slick-backed hair and an absurdly skinny mustache. Anglo guys can't pull off that kind of look. They wind up being mistaken for aluminum siding salesmen or pederasts.

Ortiz had a couple of guys with him—big, thick guys, who hung back and let him do the talking. He told me he wanted to take some buddies to the Bahamas and go diving. I told him I could arrange that. I also told him that it would cost him more to run out of Minorca Beach than it would farther south—a twenty-hour haul to get to Grand Bahama. He could charter someone based in Fort Lauderdale or Miami and get to Bimini in less than four hours. And the diving would be just as good, if not better. He said he didn't mind the extra time or the extra money. He said he wanted to go to Grand Bahama and that he preferred leaving from Minorca Beach. I told him the price. He didn't argue. And we set the date. There was nothing to sign, just a shake-hand deal. He paid me the fee up front in cash. All the more reason to trust him. I handed part of the money straight over to Robby Greig to pay for the work on the boat. It was all very convenient.

Ortiz showed up at the appointed time and place with four buddies. They brought a lot of gear—several duffels and two of those gray aluminum suitcases made for carrying photo equipment. It didn't strike me as unusual. Most divers are gearheads, and a good number of them also fancy themselves underwater photographers. *Miz Blitz* had plenty of room. Boggy helped me stash everything below and we set off.

It was a long, slow, sloppy haul—high seas and rain, and a lot of chumming the fishes on the part of Ortiz and his friends.

It was still storming like hell when we hit West End, so ugly that when I radioed Bahamas customs to let them know we were heading in, they told me they were locking up and going home and not to worry about the paperwork until the next morning. Ortiz and his buddies rallied a bit after we tied off at our mooring, and when the weather settled I let them take *Miz Blitz*'s skiff ashore for an evening of bar-hopping. They brought along a couple of their duffels and one of the aluminum suitcases. Again, it didn't strike me as unusual.

A couple of hours later, Ortiz and his pals returned in the skiff. They were just short of drunk. They said they had stopped by a dive shop, worked a good deal on some used scuba tanks, and wanted to get them back on the boat before continuing their night on the town. So Boggy and I unloaded the tanks. There were maybe ten of them and they were pieces of crap—old and dinged, with black paint recently brushed on to cover the defects. Then Ortiz and his friends headed back to shore. That was the last I saw of them.

When they weren't back by 10 A.M. the next day, I was forced to clear customs without them. I had forgotten to gather their passports the night before, so I filed an incomplete manifest, showing Boggy and myself as *Miz Blitz*'s only passengers. In retrospect, hell, yes, I should have mentioned something to the customs officials. But I knew it would create all kinds of bureaucratic snags and I just didn't think it was worth the trouble. Stupid, stupid, stupid.

Boggy went ashore at noon to look for Ortiz. He found the skiff tied up at the marina with nothing in it. He made the rounds of bars and casinos. He visited the police station and was told to take a seat until someone could speak with him. While he was sitting there a reporter from the *Freeport Crier* came in and began interviewing the watch commander about a shooting incident from the night before. The details were sketchy but several people had wound up dead. The reporter asked if it was a drug deal. The watch commander said he was not at liberty to discuss the details, but if the reporter wanted to grab his camera, then he could probably get some good shots next door at the morgue. They were getting ready to unload the bodies. Boggy followed the reporter next door. There were seven bodies, some of them uncovered, and Boggy recognized two of them as Ortiz's friends.

We sat on the boat all that night. No one came to ask us any questions. We sat there all the next day and through the next night. Still, no one came to ask us anything. We read the story in the *Freeport Crier.* It didn't contain much more in the way of information than what Boggy had picked up. It said there had been a gunfight during a suspected drug deal. Four of the dead were Cuban-Americans, and the story listed Victor Ortiz as one of them. The other three were from Panama and had been living in Freeport for six weeks prior to the shootings. The story said authorities were asking for anyone who might have information about the incident to please come forward.

We sat on the boat another day and night trying to decide what to do. If I hadn't botched the whole deal with customs, then I probably would have gone to the police and told them what I knew, which was pretty close to nothing. But it would have looked suspicious.

"So why did you not, at least, tell authorities these men were on your boat?" the police would ask.

"Damn good question," I would say. "Why don't you just go ahead and lock me up?"

And they would have. And I could have taken my chances with the Bahamian justice system.

So we pulled anchor and headed back to Minorca Beach. I went through all the belongings that Ortiz and his friends had left behind. The last thing I wanted was to get caught with dope on the boat. But mostly there was just clothes. They had left one of the aluminum suitcases, and when I opened it, all I saw was a bunch of photography stuff—fancy lenses and what looked like darkroom equipment. All I knew was that it looked expensive and I couldn't see just chunking it overboard.

After the crossing, we cut in at Coronado Inlet and Boggy took off in the skiff. His crab traps had gone untended for several days and he wanted to check them. It would give us something good for dinner. I cruised down to LaDonna, taking my time, cleaning up *Miz Blitz* as I went, thinking about how I would make crab enchilau, cracking the crabs and cooking them with tomatoes and garlic, and a little white wine, and soaking up everything with crusty Cuban bread. I pulled *Miz Blitz* into her stall and tied her off, and then all hell broke loose.

I think just about every branch of law enforcement was represented there that day. First came a squadron of black-clad S.W.A.T. team commandos who swarmed the boathouse and flattened me and read me my rights. Then came the F.B.I. and the D.E.A. and the B.A.T.F.—enough acronyms to provide all the makings for a world-class Scrabble game. The Secret Service was there, too, along with enough local cops to put a serious dent in the day's receipts at Dunkin' Donuts. All of them just for me. I think even *they* were a little embarrassed by the overkill.

The headline in the next morning's *Orlando Sentinel* read: "Former Dolphins Star Arrested for Counterfeiting." Which was totally misleading since I had never been a bona-fide star, just a journeyman strong safety, who only once made All-Pro, and who blew out his knee after four seasons and then hung up his jockstrap. There were two counts of counterfeiting—one for the $1,750 in bogus bills that I had paid Minorca Beach Marina for the paint job, the other for possession of what the newspaper called "sophisticated, state-of-the-art counterfeiting devices." That's what had been inside the aluminum suitcase.

The feds arrested Boggy, too. But when it came to the real nut-cutting, they dropped the case against him to concentrate on me. They took my boats. They took everything I had, except my homestead.

Barbara and I were already tight by that time, and she insisted on paying for the attorneys. She paid too much, because the trial lasted only two days, and even I was impressed by the government's case. The defense rested on my claim that the counterfeiting equipment and the bogus money had belonged to Victor Ortiz. Only, Victor Ortiz was dead. And I had no way to prove that he had ever been on my boat.

My attorneys told me I should be grateful that I wound up with only a three-year sentence. Yeah, I was grateful. About as grateful as I was for the head-whopping I'd just received, thanks to a dead man.

10

It was just past dark when I waded out of the lagoon in Oak Hill and walked into the bait shop at DeQuesnes Fish Camp. Freddy DeQuesnes was sitting behind the counter. He was shirtless and nursing a Budweiser and watching the Cubs play the Braves on a tiny TV beside the cash register. There was no one else in the place.

Freddy raised his beer in salute when he saw me, then drained it off and crumpled the can and flattened it on the counter. He owned about ten acres along the lagoon, part of it the fish camp, and part of it a storage lot where people from up north paid Freddy to keep their boats and trucks and travel trailers until they came down to use them each winter. If today was like most of Freddy DeQuesnes's days, he had collected five dollars a boat from fishermen using his boat ramp, sold a few dozen live shrimp, pumped a little gas, and probably already polished off the better part of a twelve-pack.

Freddy stood from his stool, hitched up his khaki shorts, and opened a rusty refrigerator. He pulled out another Bud and offered me one. I turned it down. Then Freddy said: "What the hell happened to you?"

"Long story. Need to use your bathroom."

"Looks like you need a helluva lot more than that, Zack," said Freddy. "Emergency room comes to mind."

"I'll be alright."

Freddy nodded me toward the bathroom.

He said, "Got a first-aid kit under the sink."

I stepped in the bathroom and studied my face in the mirror. Looked even worse than I'd imagined. Over the years, I had suffered plenty of head bangings, but no one had ever hit me with a shovel before. The right side of my face bore a five-inch-wide welt that ran down to my chin. My jawline was discolored and throbbing. There was a knot on the side of my cheekbone the size of a crab apple and, below it, a gash that could probably have used some stitches. I stuck out my tongue. I'd bit off a flap on one side and it was already turning black. The broken teeth were way in back and I couldn't get a good look at them, but I'd be in the market for a couple of crowns.

I pulled paper towels out of the dispenser, soaked them with water, and washed up. I opened the first-aid kit and found a bottle of hydrogen peroxide and poured it over the gash on my face. It fizzed and stung. I wiped it clean and poured on some more hydrogen peroxide and wiped it clean again. I used a pair of scissors to fashion a couple of butterfly bandages out of some Band-Aids and applied them to the gash on my cheekbone. They drew the wound together nicely. There would be a scar, but it wouldn't be lonesome.

I thought about what to do next. The right thing would have been to call the cops. But my outlook on what was right and what was wrong had been skewed by the circumstances that sent me to Baypoint. Ever since then, I had pitched my tent in Camp To-Thine-Own-Self-Be-True. I would abide the law and honor those who tried to uphold it, but damned if I would trust them to sort out the whole truth and nothing but. Particularly as it applied to me.

If I had called the cops, then things would have gotten messy. For one thing, there was the body in the boathouse. That meant I would have to get lawyered up before I called the cops, and I didn't want to go through all of that. Besides, even if I was reporting nothing more serious than a cat stuck in a cherry tree, my record would make for murky waters. Things would get even murkier considering I wasn't even a full day out of prison. I could forget all about flying to Harbour Island. The cops wouldn't let me leave Minorca Beach. Days might pass before I got to see Barbara. I couldn't accept that.

When I stepped out of the bathroom, the Cubs had taken the lead, 2-0, and Freddy DeQuesnes was pulling a pizza out of the microwave and cutting it into slices. He opened another beer.

"You got a car I can borrow, Freddy?"

He cocked his head and looked me up and down.

"Should I ask what happened to you first?"

"No," I said. "Better that you didn't."

Freddy nodded.

"How long you need the car?" he said.

"A week, maybe. Need to drive down to Fort Lauderdale, catch a plane. I'll return it when I get back."

Freddy took a bite out of the pizza. He took a swig of beer.

"I can pay you for it," I said. "Call it a rental."

Freddy liked the sound of that.

"Hundred bucks?"

I took a hundred from the wad in my pocket and handed it to him.

"Sorry about it being wet."

"It'll spend," said Freddy.

He got up from his stool and walked to a square of pegboard stuck on the wall by the refrigerator. There were dozens of keys hanging from it. Freddy searched through them until he found the one he was looking for, and handed it to me.

"1989 Ford F-150. White, with an over-the-cab camper. Belongs to a fellow out of Michigan won't be coming down this winter on account he had a stroke," said Freddy. "Don't fuck it up. But there ain't no real hurry getting it back."

It was a three-hour drive to Fort Lauderdale and I stopped twice—once in Titusville and once in West Palm Beach—to buy small bags of ice. I wrapped them inside a towel, tied it around my head, and let the ice work on my jaw. The throbbing had just about gone away, but my tongue was swollen the size of a sneaker. The crab apple knot had grown into a small cantaloupe and turned an ugly blue. I already had one black eye and the other one was approaching shiner status.

Just outside of Fort Lauderdale, I found a phone booth and called Ruby Booby's again. This time around someone answered, a man.

"Ruby's," he said, shouting over the music in the background.

"Is Chip Willis there?" I asked.

"Hold on," said the guy on the other end.

A couple of minutes went by. The song in the background ended and a new one began. It was that "We Will Rock You" song they play at too many sporting events. I started picturing the Ruby Booby babes performing lap dances to it. I also started picturing the guys they were performing on. So I tried to picture something else. Finally a voice said: "Yeah."

"Chip?" I said.

"Uh-huh."

"Surprise. It's me."

No reply from the other end.

"Look, Chip, I don't care about you hauling ass and leaving me, I just need to get my things out of the car, alright?"

"What the fuck you talking about?"

"You can keep the money Barbara paid you. I don't care. I just want my things."

"What fucking money? Who the fuck is Barbara?"

It was slowly sinking in on me that this voice didn't belong to the Chip Willis I knew. It was more nasal, with a definite up-north accent.

"This Chip Willis?"

"Yeah, I already told you."

"Look, the club has a limo, right?"

"Yeah. We got a limo. Who is this?"

"And you're the driver, right?"

"I drive it sometimes. What's this about?"

"Someone driving the club's limo picked me up today. And then he went off and left me."

"Sure as shit wasn't me."

"I think we've established that," I said. "Do you know who was driving it? Or where the limo is?"

"Hold on, lemme get Ricky."

Several minutes went by. The song changed from "We Will Rock You" to "Sweet Home Alabama." I tried not to picture anything. I was just trying to figure out what was going on. I was doing a thoroughly crappy job of it. Finally, another voice came on the phone.

"This is Ricky. You know something about the limo?"

"Less by the minute," I said.

"What's that?" Ricky shouted. "I can't hear you real good, the fucking music."

"I said I don't know where the limo is, but I'm trying to find it."

"Well, so are we. It's missing."

"Someone stole it?" I asked.

"You know something about it?"

"All I know is that whoever was driving the limo picked me up but didn't take me where I needed to go," I said. "He went off and left me."

"Where did he pick you up at?"

"Oh, just up the road."

"Who'd you talk to when you booked it?"

"I didn't," I said. "Someone else made the arrangements."

"Who'd they talk to?"

"I don't have a clue," I said. "You think someone stole the limo?"

"What the fuck do I know? The key was off the board this afternoon when I opened up and the chauffeur uniform was gone from the closet. Thought maybe Chip or somebody might have booked something last minute, just didn't have a chance to tell me about it. But none of them know nothing about it. The guy picked you up, what's he look like?"

I described the fake Chip Willis.

"I don't know anyone looks like that."

"Not many people do," I said.

"Uh-huh," said Ricky. I could hear him talking to someone,

saying, "You got a pen? Gimme a pen. Anybody got a fucking pen, for Chrissake?"

And then he was back, talking to me: "What did you say your name was? I'm gonna have to file a fucking police report and I know they're gonna want to talk to you."

I hung up the phone.

11

It was almost midnight when I checked into the Los Altos Inn, the place where Barbara had booked me. The bellman seemed put out that I had no luggage he could carry. He also seemed a little sniffy about the way I looked, as if the Los Altos Inn wasn't used to guests whose afternoon leisure activity involved getting their skulls cracked and who showed up muddy and barefoot. After he finished the walk-through and filled the ice bucket, I rifled through my pocket for tip money. I had hundreds and twenties and a lone one dollar bill. I gave him the single. He didn't even say thank you and good night.

My room turned out to be the master suite—two bedrooms, living room, a wraparound balcony looking out on the Intra-coastal Waterway, and a sprawling bathroom with his-and-hers sinks, a phone by the john, an old-fashioned bathtub, a Jacuzzi perched on a platform, and a shower that could fit the entire starting lineup of the Florida Marlins, along with backups in case someone slipped on the Italian marble floor and got hurt. There was original artwork on the walls and the kind of expensive, muted lighting that would make even thrift-store furniture look good.

I checked the back of the door to see if the maximum room tariff was posted. It was—$1,250 per night. But that included a continental breakfast, so I figured all I had to do was eat about a thousand blueberry muffins the next morning and maybe I'd be getting full value.

I knew Barbara meant well, God bless her, but the whole production was wasted on me. I could slip on the silk bathrobe, tune in the plasma TV, drink Moët & Chandon out of the mini-bar, order every blessed thing on the room service menu, and it would still come down to the fact that I was sitting in a $1,250-a-night suite all alone, passing time, waiting for whatever might happen next. It was just a fancified version of Baypoint.

I spent a couple of minutes wandering room to room and taking in the view. There were all kinds of glorious rigs moored in the marina below—some outfitted for fishing, some for cruising, some for just piddling around. Just the sight of those boats made me wistful for my own. I'd start shopping around after I signed a contract to sell the place in LaDonna.

I took a long, hot shower and washed my shirt and my jeans after I got finished washing myself. Then I put on the silk bathrobe and hung my clothes on the balcony to dry. I went to the minibar and was delighted to see it contained several Mount Gay miniatures, so I poured two of them into a glass and stood on the balcony drinking it, listening to my clothes drip-drip onto the tile, and looking at the big boats some more.

When I walked back inside to visit the minibar again, I noticed the message light blinking on the telephone. Had the phone rung while I was in the shower? I picked up the receiver and punched the button that said "message center." Nothing happened. I punched it again and got a busy tone. I hung up the phone, waited a few seconds, and then tried again. There was a beep when I punched the button and then dead air. I have no patience when it comes to these things and telephones in particular infuriate the hell out of me. I pounded the button panel with my fist and then the phone began to ring.

"What?" I barked into the receiver.

Silence from the other end. And then, "Well, that is certainly no way to greet the love of your life, now is it?"

Some men go for legs in a woman, others obsess over breasts and behinds. Me, I'm a voice man. I've been hopelessly infatuated by countless women after nothing more than a few seconds of listening to them talk. And I think I first fell in love with Barbara the morning she called to book her office party on *Miz Blitz*. Yes, the British accent was alluring, but it wasn't just her highbrow Surrey entonements that got my sap rising. Barbara sounded smart, and I like smart women. But she also sounded funny and down-to-earth and comfortable in her own skin. Can someone extract all of that from a mere snippet of conversation? Sure, if you're a connoisseur of women's voices, like I am; if you're a man who willingly submits himself to rapture by a female's dulcet tones. I once actually looked up the word "dulcet" in Webster's to see if that aptly described Barbara's voice. "Sweet . . . pleasing to the ear," it said. Which was accurate enough, but Barbara's voice carried with it a certain indelible sultriness, too. Hell, she just talked every bit as sexy as she looked, and that's why I had fallen in love with her.

"Hey, baby," I said. "Just having a little problem with the phone. Sorry about that."

"Mmmmm," she murmured, and even that sounded fetching. "You sound funny. Is everything OK?"

"Had a little dental work done, that's all. Everything's fine."

I thought I'd spare her the details. She had enough on her mind with the photo shoot. I'd tell her everything when I got to Harbour Island . . . if I got to Harbour Island. I was counting on Charlie Callahan to work some magic to make it happen. And if not magic, then something felonious would have to do.

"I called earlier, hoping I'd catch you. Twin Air had an 8 P.M. flight to North Eleuthera and there was an empty seat, a cancellation. You could have been on your way to join me tonight, but now I'll just have to wait until tomorrow evening to feast my eyes upon you."

"I'm working up a pretty good appetite, too."

Neither one of us said anything. It felt good being connected, even if it was just by phone.

"Speaking of food, Chef Ludo went all out tonight. Grilled triggerfish with a sweet potato souffle. Spiny lobster drizzled with a lemon-vanilla sauce. Jerked pork loin atop a mango puree."

"You ate all that?"

"Just the lobster."

"I'd have gone for the triggerfish. Just to get at the sweet potatoes."

"I know. That's what I told Ludo. Don't worry, he said he'd make them again just for you," said Barbara. "So, you enjoyed the ride down?"

"What a limo."

Thought I'd spare her the details about Chip and the limo, too.

"Were you surprised?"

"You have no idea. How'd you arrange that?"

"Through Lord Downey. I stopped in to see him shortly after I arrived on-island."

"He set it up?"

"Yes, I suppose. Or one of his people did. I mean, I mentioned to him that I was having difficulty finding a driver, and when I returned to the Albury that evening there was a message saying that the arrangements had been made, and that I should leave payment here at the front desk. So I wrote you that note and stuck it in there with the money."

"When was that?"

"It was . . . it was Wednesday. Why? Was there a problem? Did you not get the money?"

"No, I got it. Everything's fine, just fine," I said. "How's Lord Downey, anyway?"

"Not too well, I'm afraid. He's failed miserably since you and I visited him the last time we were here. Indeed, I don't think he even remembered me dropping by to introduce you to him."

"I have a knack for making highly forgettable first impressions."

"I beg to differ on that. But it is a pity how he seems to have aged so very quickly."

"Well, he's getting up there. What would you guess—he's seventy-five or so?"

"At the very least. He once courted my mother. Still, he has always been so . . . so vital. And now . . ."

She let it hang. She took a deep breath. And then she said: "Zack, there is one thing I must tell you."

"Okay, lay it on me."

"Bryce is here."

At first, I didn't know who she was talking about. And then it sank in. Bryce Gannon, the photographer. Barbara's former fiancé. The guy she dumped just before I waltzed into her life.

"What a coincidence," I managed to sputter.

"Not really. I asked him to come here."

"You what?"

"Zack, I had no choice. After I got rid of the original photographer and his crew—they were horrid, absolutely horrid— I needed help and I needed it in a hurry. Bryce dropped everything he was doing and caught the first plane over from London."

"Always at your service."

"Now, Zack, don't get petulant on me. It really doesn't suit you. I assure you that there is absolutely nothing between Bryce and myself."

"Does he know that?"

"Of course he does. This is a shoot, strictly business. He is a professional. I am a professional. And we are both very grown up about this."

"Okay, then I'll be grown up about it, too. It's just kinda weird, that's all."

"Hang around magazines long enough and, I assure you, it will seem absolutely normal. You want weird, you should see the models the other photographer hired."

"Real lookers, huh?"

"If you like slut-chic."

"I'm a big, big fan."

"Well then, you would have been in heaven. Those girls looked like they had been living off cigarettes and methadone for the last six weeks," Barbara said. "Perfect for some urban-industrial shoot. But not for Bahamarama."

"For what?"

"Bahamarama. That's what we are calling the entire photo spread."

"Did Bryce Gannon come up with that?"

"No, actually, I did. Don't you like it?"

"Sounds very festive."

"Well, I happen to think it is perfect. Tropical fashions, fun in the sun. But those other models, they just wouldn't do," Barbara said. "Fortunately, Bryce took a quick spin around the island and found several local girls—fresh and natural, full of life—and I think we have managed to salvage that. Bryce is quite the genius at spotting talent. He is really saving me on this one."

Grown up. I was going to act grown up.

"That's nice," I said. "I look forward to meeting him."

My mouth hurt even more just from saying it. Barbara let out a long yawn.

"Sorry, darling, but I'm exhausted. I know you must be, too."

"I could stand to stretch out for a little while."

"Kisses then."

She made smacky-mouth sounds into the phone. I made some back.

"Can't wait to see you," she said.

"Me, too."

Barbara hung up the phone. I got more rum from the minibar.

12

I don't think I got more than two hours' sleep. The bed was too big, the mattress too comfortable. Every time I started to nod off I kept seeing the shovel right before it hit my head. Then my jaw started throbbing. And then I started worrying about how I was going to get into the Bahamas without my IDs. And then my jaw started throbbing even more.

I spent Saturday morning doing something I do only under circumstances of extreme duress—I shopped for clothes. Not that I had much choice. My shirt and jeans hadn't cleaned up all that well. Wanting to get an early start, I had taken them off the balcony and put them on before they were totally dry. And now they were beginning to sour. My face alone would scare people off—both eyes were full-on black now, the gash a scabby mess. But to wear that funkified outfit on the airplane would be to prompt my fellow passengers to bail out over Bimini.

The marina near the Los Altos Inn had a ship's store, a decent one, and there was an end-of-summer sale going on. Never mind it was the middle of August, which in Florida means there's still another good three months of summer before the two-day interlude that passes for fall. The owner was just being hopeful, I guess. So to help bolster his spirits I bought a canvas duffel bag, three Tarponwear shirts (two white, one blue), a white Patagonia polo, three pairs of khaki cargo shorts, a leather Orvis belt with bonefish imprinted on it, a longbill fishing cap, and a pair of Reef Riders, the best boat sandals ever made.

"Rough night?" asked the clerk when I paid, studying my banged-up face.

"Yeah," I said. "Undertipped the hotel bellman and he lashed me with a garment bag."

I went into a dressing room, changed into shorts and one of the Tarponwear shirts, and dropped the old clothes into a Dumpster on the street. I walked down U.S. 1 to the Beachside Mall, my new canvas duffel bag slung over my shoulder, my new cap keeping my chiseled visage well shaded, and my size-thirteen dogs happy to be out of the Top-Siders and breathing free in new sandals. I went straight to Burdines and bought a blue blazer (gentlemen must wear jackets for dinner at the Albury Beach Club), a white Oxford button-down, a blue Oxford button-down, a blue-and-white pinstriped Oxford button-down, two identical pairs of khaki pants, two pairs of linen pants, and two linen shirts. It wasn't a particularly cutting-edge wardrobe, but I liked to think that the sheer force of my personality, combined with my elevated sense of style and the way in which I wore the clothes, transformed the look into something that defied all couture boundaries and bespoke the manly essence that is Zack Chasteen. Then again, I have always lived in a state of mild delusion. All told, the little shopping spree cost me $946.18. Of Barbara's money.

I stopped in at a bookstore and scoped out the magazine rack. They had the most recent issue of *Tropics,* stuck way in the back behind *Travel & Leisure* and *Condé Nast Traveler* and all the city magazines. It's tough being a small publisher in the magazine business. Barbara has carved out a niche for her titles and certainly holds her own against the competition, but it's not as if Orb Media has endlessly deep pockets. It can't fork over twenty thousand dollars to a bookstore chain just to make sure *Tropics* gets favorable rack placement for a particular issue.

And then there are the distributors to pay off on top of that. So I grabbed the dozen or so copies of *Tropics* from the back and stuck them up front. Then I took a copy for myself, paid for it, and walked back out into the mall.

This issue of *Tropics* had a cover story on private island retreats in the Grenadines—Petit St. Vincent, Palm Island, Saltwhistle Bay—and a feature about the Cockpit Country of Jamaica. But I flipped straight to the Publisher's Letter. Barbara smiled out at me from the page, her head cocked slightly to one side, her thick black hair pulled back and temporarily at bay. The photo had been taken on the beach in Cancún, where Barbara had attended the annual Caribbean Tourism Organization convention. I didn't read the Publisher's Letter. I just looked at Barbara's photo. She looked great, far too beautiful to be a magazine publisher, far too beautiful to hang out with the likes of me.

I drove the man from Michigan's F-150 to the airport and left it in long-term parking. A shuttle bus took me to General Aviation where Charlie Callahan was already on the tarmac, standing by his eight-seat twin-engine Navajo, ready to go.

Charlie was wearing his uniform—red flip-flops, faded madras shorts and a T-shirt that said: "I'm the fucking pilot. You got a problem with that?" Just to make it look even more official, Charlie had pinned army-surplus gold braid epaulets to the shoulders of his T-shirt. The six other passengers—three young couples from Tampa off for a week of diving and fishing—were already inside the plane. From their wide-eyed expressions, I could tell they were entertaining serious doubts about the likelihood of their surviving the flight. Had I not known Charlie for better than twenty years, and been comforted by the knowledge that he had spent the last twelve of them sober, then I might have had some doubts of my own. But he was a steady hand, a good man in a tight spot, and his getup was a clever piece of marketing that branded him as a bona fide Colorful Character. Charlie would get us there safe and sound. The folks from Tampa would return with stories that began "You shoulda seen the guy who was our pilot . . ." And the legend of Sorry Charlie Callahan, along with his lucrative charter business, would continue to flourish.

I told Charlie about my i.d. dilemma.

"No shit," he said.

"Exactly the kind of problem solving I knew I could count on you for," I said.

"How those knees of yours, Zack-o?" Charlie asked.

"Only hurt when I breathe air."

"You know, you oughta sue whoever it was invented Astro-Turf. That shit has fucked up too many careers."

"While I'm at it, maybe I oughta sue whoever it was who invented football. Figure if it didn't exist I'd have found a real career."

"Well, count me in on the class-action. I'd be retired by now if I could stop betting the games."

"What the hell would you do if you retired?"

"Fly airplanes and chase women. Only I wouldn't have to work so hard at it as I do now."

He opened a compartment by the nose of the plane and put my bag in it.

"Look, Charlie, if you think it's going to be a problem, me not having identification and all . . ."

"Won't be any problem. Got it all figured out. That's why I asked about your knees. See, on the approach to North Eleuthera, I'll bring 'er in real low over the salt marsh. You swing out on the struts, then jump. How's that?"

He might have been serious. With Charlie, it was hard to tell.

"Just get your ass in the plane, Zack-o," he said. "We'll think of something."

13

I rode copilot, as the plane lifted off the runway, and Charlie set course due east from the mainland. I stretched my legs, looked out the window, and let my mind wander. There's something about flying off the coast of Florida that does the soul good. Just when you're convinced that greed and stupidity have ruined the entire state, you look down on that deep-blue ocean, and think: Well, things aren't all that bad. Okay, so maybe the dunes have been bulldozed, condos block the afternoon sun, and hatchling sea turtles, disoriented by all the lights, crawl out of their nests, head to U.S. 1, and get flattened. From the air, at least, the Atlantic still looks unblemished, its vastness rendering the concrete-armored coastline puny and impermanent.

Ten minutes out of Fort Lauderdale and we breached the Gulf Stream's air space, the silty backwash of the tidal shelf cleaved by the virulent, dream-blue river, which churns out of the Florida Straits and courses northward on its mission to save higher latitudes from the Arctic's full wrath. Ireland would be a damn sight less cheery and green if it weren't for the Stream. Hell, it would be Norway.

Cross the Stream and you've officially surrendered yourself

to the tropics. It's the demarcation line between "I-need-it-now" and "Mon, soon come," the checkpoint for chucking out the notion that schedules are essential to the everyday needs of humanity.

Oldtime Floridians will tell you the Stream isn't as blue as it used to be. Let them believe what they want to if it preserves some sense of better days. All I know is that gazing upon the Stream at that particular moment, on my way to meet as good a woman as I could ever hope to know, it was a blue full of promise, a blue to make you ache, a blue to help you doze off even though your mind is wired, and you are thinking about thugs who are on your tail for God knows why, and how you left one of them dead in a boathouse.

I slept as we skirted past Bimini and didn't wake up until the plane banked at Spanish Wells to begin its descent to North Eleuthera. I spotted Harbour Island just a couple of miles to the east, picked out the government dock on the lee side and straight across, on the ocean side, a tennis court that looked like it might belong to the Albury Beach Club, which was hidden under a canopy of gumbo-limbos and poinciana. Harbour Island isn't big enough to have its own airport. You have to land on North Eleuthera and then catch a water taxi. But first you have to clear customs. I was anxious to hear Charlie's plan for how I was going to do that.

"It's your lucky day," said Charlie. "We got rain."

He nodded to the southeast, where a dark gray thunderhead was churning and roiling and beginning to consume the horizon.

"We're a little ahead of it," said Charlie. "I'm gonna have to stall for a bit."

He turned to the other passengers, cupped a hand to his mouth, and put on his best Chuck Yeager drawl: "Ladies and gentlemen, this is your pilot speaking. The control tower has asked us to delay our landing for just a few minutes." Charlie coughed and hacked a couple of times, making it sound like static coming over an intercom. The couples from Tampa laughed, eating it up. "So, as an extra-added bonus, you get the fifty-cent aerial tour."

Charlie flipped the plane hard to the left and dipped low. One of the women let out a shriek and grabbed her husband. One of the men said, "Holy shit." Charlie leveled off at three hundred feet, and we zipped along above Dunmore Bight, the two-mile-wide channel that runs between Harbour Island and North Eleuthera.

"Off to your left, those are some of the Loyalist houses," Charlie shouted above the whine of the engines, pointing to a row of pink and yellow and blue cottages lining the Harbour Island waterfront. "Date from the 1770s or so, back when the first settlers came to these islands. Bunch of King George–loving Brits from Virginia and the Carolinas who knew their asses were gonna be in a sling once the Revolution cranked up. Descendants are still thick through some of these islands. Been marrying and inbreeding for going on two hundred and fifty years now."

We followed the curve of Harbour Island, passing over Valentine's dive resort and the Island Marina, until the land tailed off to the south. Then we cut west to Eleuthera. The thunderhead was rolling in faster now. There were flashes of lightning and the wind began to gust.

One of the men in the back leaned forward and asked Charlie, "That isn't the tropical storm coming in, is it?"

"Oh, hell no. That thing's still way out in the Atlantic," said Charlie. "Doesn't even know which way it's going yet."

Eleuthera is a long skinny island—never more than a mile or two across, but running a hundred miles from north to south. Charlie swooped in at Glass Window Bridge, the island's narrowest spot, a limestone backbone just wide enough to drive a car over. On one side, the water was the almost-violet blue of the Atlantic. On the other, it was a balmy Caribbean green.

"Right up there, that's where the caves begin," said Charlie, pointing beyond the bridge to miles of craggy limestone bluffs pocked with holes and arches. "The whole island's like a piece of goddam Swiss cheese, got tunnels and passages running all through it. Used to be, when a bad hurricane was bearing down, that's where the islanders would go and take shelter, in the caves."

"Looks pretty cool," said one of the men from Tampa. "They let people explore them?"

"Sure, I guess," said Charlie. "But you damn sure better go with someone who knows them or else we'll never see you again. And watch out for that limestone. It will flat-out tear you up."

When the first fat raindrops began splattering the Navajo's windshield, Charlie pointed us toward the North Eleuthera airport. We bumped, then skidded on the runway, the rain coming down in sheets as Charlie pulled to a stop, still a good hundred yards from the tiny terminal. The AC was off and the little plane was an oven. One of the young women was fanning herself with a magazine. The others looked flushed and miserable.

"Folks," said Charlie, turning around to them. "We're gonna have to make a break for it."

"Can't we pull any closer to the terminal?" asked one of the women.

"'Fraid not," said Charlie. "Federal regulations."

I knew that was a crock. Charlie had always pulled right up to the terminal before.

"I vote to get the hell out of here," said one of the guys. The others nodded in quick agreement. As they unsnapped seat belts and grabbed bags, Charlie turned to me, speaking low: "Over there by the shed. That's where you wanna go. There's a gap in the fence."

He nodded to a small tin lean-to that I could just barely make out through the rain.

"Good luck," said Charlie. "But if you fuck up . . ."

"It's my ass."

"Bingo," said Charlie, and he was out his door, onto the wing, then hopping down to open the rear hatch.

"OK, folks, let's shit and git," he shouted, helping the six of them down the three-rung ladder and pointing them toward the terminal. When I got to the hatch he stopped me.

"Let us get halfway to the terminal, then you go. They won't be looking for anyone after me."

And then Charlie was gone, running after the others as the rain started coming down even harder. When I lost sight of him through the downpour, I jumped down to the tarmac, grabbed my duffel from the compartment and beelined it to the tin shed. The gap in the fence wasn't quite as big as I might have hoped for, but I squeezed through, managing only to rip my brand-new shorts and put a small gash in my thigh. It didn't bleed much. But my brand-new shorts, jeez . . .

The main road was right there, and I followed it, away from the terminal and toward the water taxi dock. It was about a two-mile walk. A couple of cars passed me, but no one paid me any mind or offered me shelter from the storm or ran me down with sirens screaming and locked me up in jail. After the first mile, the rain stopped, and the sun came back out. It was like a greenhouse by the time I reached the dock. One of the water taxis was getting ready to pull out for Harbour Island and I hopped on board. The captain took my canvas duffel and put it on the transom with luggage belonging to the three or four other passengers.

"Four dollars," said the captain. I gave him a five and he kept it.

14

A horde of young boys—at least a dozen of them, none older than thirteen or fourteen—swarmed around the end of Government Dock as the water taxi pulled up after its ten-minute sprint from North Eleuthera. A couple of the boys grabbed lines tossed by the captain, while three or four others leapt onto the water taxi before it came to a stop. One of them, a skinny kid in a Miami Heat T-shirt that covered his knees, grabbed my duffel.

"Hey, Mr. Big Man," he said to me. "You belong 'dis?"

I told him I did. He gave me a big smile.

"You follow me, sir, come-come. Watch your steppin' off the boat, sir."

I hopped onto the dock and the boy told me to wait right there with my bag while he found me a taxi. Not a difficult task, since there were four minivan taxis parked on the other side of the dock, just ten yards away, with their drivers looking straight at us. The boy walked up to one of them, they spoke, the driver finally nodded grimly—as if the bond between taxi driver and passenger was a solemn sacrament—and then the boy ran back, picked up my duffel, and lugged it to the taxi.

I didn't really need a taxi. The Albury Beach Club was only

a five-minute walk, but I knew the drill at the dock from previous trips. It was like an unofficial entry tax to Harbour Island—benign and fairly cheap, and if you got all huffy and Ugly American about it, then it was bad juju for the rest of your stay. Harbour Island is a small place—less than a thousand people—and in the course of a few days you're likely to run across most of them. A little good will at the get-go stretches a long way. The boy in the Heat T-shirt put my duffel in the backseat of the taxi with all the care and attention one might give a cuddly puppy. I gave him two bucks. He stuck out a clenched fist and I bumped it with mine.

"You be needing anything, Mr. Big Man, you look for me," he said.

The taxi jostled along the buckling timbers of Government Dock, stopping where the dock met Bay Street to let a couple of old women cross in front of us. Actually, it would be more accurate to call them old ladies. They wore long pastel dresses and hats with silk flowers, and they carried umbrellas against the late afternoon sun. They nodded at the driver as they passed by.

"Afternoon, Maurice," they both said.

"Afternoon, aunties," said the driver.

A big sign at the foot of the dock announced: WELCOME TO HARBOUR ISLAND, THE FRIENDLIEST ISLAND IN THE BAHAMAS. It wasn't just tourism board hokum. Brilanders, as the people of Harbour Island call themselves, are gracious and polite to a fault. And, aside from the shakedown by the boys at the dock, it's not a put-on just to pry loose tourist dollars. I guarantee that if you walked from one end of the island to the other, every single person you passed, be they five or ninety-five, would at least say hello. Just a small thing, perhaps, but a small thing that has been discarded elsewhere, a small thing that helps keep a smattering of civilization in everyday life.

The straw market along Bay Street—a half dozen or so plywood stalls selling everything from hats and woven placemats to T-shirts and coconut purses—was open for business that was anything but booming. The vendors were drowsing or talking among themselves. A couple of fishermen cleaned their catch of snapper and grouper on the hull of an overturned skiff. Golf carts, the main mode of Harbour Island transportation, were parked at weird angles along the curb outside the Harbour Lounge. Tourists in snazzy resort wear held down a table on the deck, munching fish sandwiches. Between the street and the bay, a couple of old men sat chatting on rickety wooden stools perched on the lip of a broad pit in the sand.

Something seemed a little off. And then I realized what it was. The old men were sitting at the exact spot where a giant, century-old fig tree had once stood. It had been a landmark, the main gathering spot on the island, its canopy big enough and thick enough to shade a hundred people. Public ceremonies, island council meetings, school concerts, and plays—all were held under the fig tree. If you wanted the lowdown about anything that was happening on Harbour Island, all you had to do was go to the fig tree and you could find out. And now it was gone.

I asked the driver what had happened to it.

"Floyd took 'er down, man."

"Hurricane Floyd?"

"He da one. Helluva blow. Took down the fig tree and carried her clear up Bay Street into the Landing Hotel. Knocked off the hotel's verandah. Had to build it all back new-new again."

"Where's everyone hang out now?"

"Oh, here and there. But some of the old-timers they just keep sitting at that big hole where the fig tree used to be," said the driver. "Fig tree gone, but the gossip still alive."

"So what's the latest gossip?"

The driver let out a big laugh.

"Oh hell, man, you know. Mostly about somebody been stealing somebody else's woman, same as it always is. The gossip don't never change, just the people getting gossiped about. Tongues are always burning on this island."

15

Pembroke Pindle, the Albury Beach Club's ancient bellman/bartender/man-about-the-premises, was resting in the shade of a bougainvillea arbor as the taxi crunched into the shell driveway by the reception area. He wore a long-sleeved white shirt with a navy blue tie, brown pants, and brown shoes. He snapped an Atlanta Braves cap down on his head, eased himself up from the bench, and walked to the taxi. He was a slow walker. Then again, maybe he was somebody who stood still at an extremely fast pace. It was hard to tell. I could have opened the taxi door myself, but that was Mr. Pindle's job, and I knew it would upset him if he didn't get to do it. I paid the driver and tipped him and traded some idle chitchat about fishing and the weather. Finally Mr. Pindle opened the taxi door.

"Welcome back, Mr. Chasteen."

"Thank you, Mr. Pindle. Good to be here."

I let Mr. Pindle take my bag, and I followed him along a gravel path as the taxi pulled away. It was a lot like following a statue. It gave me plenty of time to soak up the surroundings. The Albury Beach Club wasn't fancy by any means, but it evoked a sense of timelessness. Built in the 1930s by a rich British industrialist who wanted a family enclave, it had passed first to his heirs and then to a succession of other owners who opened it to the public. Its ten cottages were simple, almost spartan. No televisions, no radios, and the only telephone was the one that Barbara had called me on from the salon. Maximum occupancy was twenty guests, most of whom had been coming there for years. On our last visit, Barbara and I had met a multigenerational family from North Carolina who had been visiting each April since the 1960s. They said Mr. Pindle had been old even then.

We passed an allamanda hedge in full golden bloom and came to a convergence of several other gravel paths. A signpost pointed the way to different cottages—Orchid, Whelk, Dolphin—and a concrete sidewalk led to the main house with the salon, dining room, and bar.

"You care for something to drink first?" Mr. Pindle asked.

"No, thanks. I'll wait."

"I expect you ready to see Miss Pickering, huh?"

"Yes, I am."

"She down on the beach still."

"Hard at work, huh?"

"Oh yah, man. She up and at 'em early this morning. Didn't even take breakfast, she didn't. That picture man, he up early with her."

Bryce Gannon. Up early with Barbara? I didn't like the sound of that.

"The photographer, you mean?"

"Yah, English fellow. Mr. Gannon."

"Is he staying here, too?"

"Oh, no. He staying at Bahama Sands with all the rest of the magazine people. But he came by to pick up Miss Pickering first thing, before the sun up even."

That sounded a little better. Not that I was concerned about the love of my life running around with her old boyfriend. Oh, no. Because I was an adult. And I was going to act like one. Really I was.

A path led up a low hill toward Hibiscus Cottage. About halfway up, Mr. Pindle stopped at a gazebo perched above the dune line. He pointed north along the beach.

"There Miss Pickering now. See 'em way up there?"

A cluster of people stood near the edge of the ocean about a half mile away. I could just barely make out what looked like two big blue beach cabanas. I had visited Barbara at another photo shoot, on Miami Beach, so I knew that one of the cabanas probably held all the outfits and served as a dressing room, while the other was for makeup. What with sylists, makeup artists, caterers, photo assistants, and various other minions, the crew and models probably totaled about twenty people. The rest of the crowd were likely just tourists and a few Brilanders, hanging around to gawk.

A table and chairs sat under the Albury's gazebo. A pair of binoculars was slung over the back of one of the chairs, left there so guests could indulge in one of the great pleasures of the beach—spying on other people from a distance.

"Try these," said Mr. Pindle, handing me the binoculars. They had suffered from being left out in the salt air, but after wiping clean the lenses and making a few adjustments, I was able to get a better glimpse of the scene. I picked out Barbara, standing near the edge of the water, one hip cocked, a floppy straw hat atop her head, her hair tied back with a long purplish scarf. I'd bought her the scarf from one of the vendors at the straw market on our first visit to Harbour Island. Barbara had liked it not so much because it was purplish, but because it had tiny dolphins on it. She said they were lucky dolphins. She said they reminded her of me.

"That whole football thing's behind me," I'd told her.

"Has nothing to do with a silly football team," she said. "Dolphins just make me happy. Like you."

Barbara was wearing what she referred to as her "has-been ballerina's outfit"—a black leotard top and baggy white pants. She had danced professionally as a young woman and still visited the studio on a regular basis. Just standing around on the beach she had more grace than any woman I had ever known. I got this squishy feeling inside just looking at her.

A man approached Barbara, a tall man with shaggy dark hair. He kept tossing his head back to keep it out of his face. He wore a long-sleeved black T-shirt and baggy black pants. A camera dangled around his neck. Nice meeting you, Bryce Gannon. But who the heck wears black on the beach in the Bahamas, buddy? This isn't London.

Gannon stood close to Barbara. He pointed to a model who was stretched out on a chaise longue and being tended to by a stylist. Barbara and Gannon talked and nodded, and when Gannon walked away, Barbara turned and looked in my direction. She knew when I'd be arriving and was probably keeping an eye out for me. I raised an arm and waved. Barbara shaded her eyes, and for a brief moment I thought she might have seen me. But then one of the crew members approached and handed Barbara a bottle of water. She took a sip from it and turned away.

I kept looking through the binoculars until Mr. Pindle cleared his throat.

"Best head on up to the cottage," he said.

16

After Mr. Pindle deposited my duffel and returned to the shade of the bougainvillea, I spent a few minutes snooping around the cottage. It was small and simple—a single bedroom, a tiny living room with a broad triptych of jalousie windows, and a bathroom that could hold no more than one occupant at a time.

The living room displayed evidence of Barbara at work— manila folders, magazines, a *Tropics* tote bag filled with page proofs of the upcoming issue, an unopened bottle of Beefeater gin, three limes, a bottle of tonic, and, chilling in the ice bucket, a magnum of Schramsberg 1998, which I could only assume was there to celebrate my arrival.

Barbara's laptop was on, with the "Deep Space" screensaver repeating its monotonous cycling. I tapped the space bar. The cosmos dissolved to reveal a spreadsheet. It looked like a tally of costs for the photo shoot. Didn't interest me in the least.

Sweet notes of Barbara hung everywhere in the bedroom—a paisley scarf draped over a chair, a pair of pink flip-flops by the bedside table, a white silk bathrobe on the bathroom doorknob. The bathroom counter was not the temple of bottles and squeeze tubes and aerosol cans often erected by females on the road. There was only moisturizer, baby powder, and a small bottle of Coco Chanel that I had bought for her at a duty-free shop at the airport in Trinidad, when we had gone down to Carnival a couple of weeks before my arrest. It was almost empty. Time to get her a new one. On a hook by the vanity hung a linen blouse, white and gauzy, with a filigree of rosebuds. I rubbed it between my fingers, then drew it to my nose, seeking a scent of Barbara. It was there, all lavender and sweetness, and I summoned a vision of Barbara and the nape of her neck, where I liked to bury my face when we slept. But to hell with fantasies, it was time for the real thing.

I left the cottage and followed the path down through the dunes to the beach. There were maybe thirty minutes of daylight left, and the photo shoot appeared to be breaking up—some people were hauling off boxes and coolers, some were breaking down the blue cabanas, some were just standing around talking. Given the distance, I couldn't make out who was who.

The sun was playing its twilight tricks. Not an hour earlier, the ocean had been a shimmering turquoise, mottled with gray-green reefs and coral heads. Now a deep blue blanket spread out from shore and covered what lay below. The famous pink sand of Harbour Island, which is actually more of a salmon color, was taking on the hue of a slightly bruised peach as the sun went down. It is truly remarkable, the sand here, finer than sugar and of a color I've never seen anywhere else. It's the result of mighty forces and countless elements conscripted over eons—Atlantic currents washing away decaying flecks of coral, hurricanes pounding the limestone shelf on which the archipelago rests, the churn and roil of water battling land against time. I've read stories that describe the sand of Harbour Island as having the texture of talcum powder. It's only a slight exaggeration. I stooped down and gathered a small handful of it, rubbing it and letting it drip between my fingers like silky grout.

I saw a seagull in the water, a white and gray speck bobbing atop the darkening waves. Then I looked closer. It wasn't a seagull, but a man—an old man, white-haired and withered. He was neck-deep in a trough between sandbars about fifty yards offshore, and although he didn't seem to be struggling, he clearly wasn't in control of the situation. The surf wasn't that big, but the brief squall had made it choppier than normal. Each wave that rolled in covered the old man completely. As it passed he would emerge, gulping for air.

I looked around. Other than the photo-shoot crowd a quarter mile away, there was no one else on the beach. The old man kept slipping farther and farther from shore, the intervals when he could catch a breath between waves becoming shorter and shorter.

I pulled off my shirt, kicked off my sandals, and hit the water at what passed for a respectable gallop. I hurtled the first set of waves, dove, and came up in a rescue crawl, keeping sight of the old man as I swam. A couple of dozen strokes and I was almost on him. He hadn't spotted me yet, but I caught a glimpse of his face—eyes wild, mouth wrenched, his expression tortured. And I could see now that he was holding something in one hand—a walking stick, thick and knobby, with a brass handle.

I floated over a wave and closed in on the old man as he bobbed up.

"You OK?" I called out.

At the sound of my voice he swung around and, whether by accident or not, just missed whacking me with his cane. I ducked below the water. I grabbed the old man by the knees and flipped him around, then came up from under him, hooking my right arm beneath his jaw and thrusting my hip into the small of his back for support. There wasn't much to him, just sinew and bone. It was like holding a sack of twigs.

"Just take it easy," I told the old man. "It's gonna be OK."

He didn't fight me. He coughed and sputtered as I stroked the water with my left arm, pulling us in. Catching a wave as it crested and broke, I bumped along the sandy bottom, then got my footing and dragged us ashore. I stretched the old man out on the sand, but he insisted on sitting up.

"Leave off, will you?" he said, indignant. His accent was British. "I'm quite alright."

That was a matter of debate. He was thin to the point of emaciation, and he wore the haunted, hollow look of a sub-Saharan refugee. As he sucked in air with a raspy wheeze, his jaw hung open, making his sunken cheeks seem even more pronounced. Dark circles ringed his gray eyes. His hair needed trimming and was the yellowish ivory of old piano keys. He wore a white linen suit and a white linen shirt. His shoes were still on—camel-and-white wingtips à la Jay Gatsby. Except for the fact that he was drenched, the old man looked as if he had just stepped away from a cocktail party for the cadaver crowd. He was anything but quite alright. And he was certainly not the same fit and engaging gentleman Barbara had introduced me to three years earlier.

"Lord Downey?" I said.

He studied my face, trying to place it, coming up with nothing.

"Zack Chasteen," I said. "I met you a few summers ago. I was here with Barbara Pickering."

"Pickering?"

"Yes, Barbara Pickering. Caroline Pickering's daughter."

"Caroline Pickering. Ah yes, Caroline Pickering," he said, eyes suddenly aglimmer. "I once diddled her, you know."

I couldn't think of a suitable response.

"Mmmm," I said.

"Quite fine, she was," said Lord Downey. "Quite fine."

"Mmmm," I said. Once you find a line that works, then you might as well stick with it. I'd be sure to share Lord Downey's endorsement with Barbara. She'd be delighted to know her dear, departed Mums had made such a lasting impression.

"Where's Burma?" Lord Downey cried out suddenly, panic returning to his face.

"Excuse me?"

"Burma. Where is Burma?"

He tried to stand, but fell. I kneeled by his side. His eyes rolled back in his head. He was out of it, but his breathing seemed steady enough. I grabbed his cane, picked him up, and put him over a shoulder.

I remembered where Lord Downey lived from when Barbara had taken me there. It sat just a short way beyond the Albury Beach Club, in the direction from which I'd come. I headed there.

17

Technically, I suppose, Lord Downey's place qualified as a compound. It sat on several acres, all by itself, open to the ocean and with a high block wall running along the other three sides. There was nothing stately or manorly or British-lordly about it. It was divided into several different pods, each comprised of a gangly stilt house, and each painted a different color—bright blue, bright green, bright pink. The houses were connected by lattice-covered walkways that radiated from a low-slung main pod, which was all angles and glass and painted black, topped off with a spindly turret, as if inspired by the Seattle Space Needle. It was a place of whimsy, something Dr. Seuss might have imagined, and it had been designed by a famous Dutch architect, whose name I forget. Barbara told me the compound had won all kinds of awards for its design, and during our visit I recalled seeing a framed story from *Architectural Digest*, which gushed praise, saying it seemed to "sprout organically from the natural landscape." To me it didn't resemble anything sprouting so much as it looked like a LEGO space ship that had crash-landed on the sand dunes. It was almost dark by the time we got there.

"Hello," I yelled up from the beach. "Anybody home?"

Lord Downey was slipping in and out of consciousness, limp as linguini. The dunes were high, and there weren't any steps that sprouted organically from the natural landscape to help me up them. After much slipping and sliding, I reached a stone landing at the top of the dunes. I was catching my breath when a woman appeared on the path through the hedge. She was a slim, striking, black woman, mid-thirties. She wore a white sleeveless blouse and a flowery skirt that rustled as she knelt beside me, gently cupping Lord Downey's head in her hands. He didn't stir. The woman looked up at me. Her hair was pulled back tight against her head and tied in a bun at the back. Her big almond-shaped eyes looked almost oriental.

She said, "Is he alright?"

"I think so. We just need to get him laid down somewhere."

"Come, come," she said, leading me along the path through the sea-grape hedge and toward the house. She moved briskly. For such an otherwise slender woman, she had full hips and they swung freely. She was a pleasure to follow.

We passed an empty swimming pool with a forlorn ceramic cherub fountain stranded in the middle. We passed a rose garden that wasn't blooming and that had seen far better days. Then we walked through a sculpture garden. Or, at least, I think it was a sculpture garden. I didn't see any Confederate generals sitting atop rearing horses or naked Roman goddesses holding wine jugs. But there were some big pieces of polished rock cut into different shapes—ovals and squares and triangles—sitting on top of tall white pedestals with spotlights shining on them. It was like walking through a 3-D geometry textbook.

We headed for the main pod. The woman pushed a button by a sliding glass door, it purred open, and we entered the same living room where Lord Downey had once entertained Barbara and me. The air inside was stale and stuffy. Either the air conditioner wasn't working right, or it was set to run in the eighties.

I lowered Lord Downey onto a leather L-shaped couch. He still hadn't stirred, but he was breathing regularly and appeared to have fallen into a deep sleep.

"I'll be right back," the woman said. She left the room. I

looked around. The room seemed considerably barer than it had two years ago. There were still floor-to-ceiling bookcases along one wall, complete with a library ladder on wheels. Gone, though, was the Steinway grand piano where Lord Downey and Barbara had, after several martinis, teamed up on show tune after show tune—he played, she sang, I hummed along pretending like I'd heard them before.

Gone, too, were three big paintings that had hung along another wall. The wall still bore the outline of the canvases. They were Jamalis. It's not that I know my art—although I can tell a Van Gogh from a Norman Rockwell—but I do know Jamali. He's a Florida guy, by way of India, and one of Barbara's many artsy acquaintances. She had connected Lord Downey with Jamali, who had sold him a series called "Woman Giving Birth to the World." It looked better than it sounds, and the room was the less for its absence.

A glass-topped sofa table held an assortment of framed photographs. There were black-and-white shots of a young Lord Downey in a British army uniform, posed atop an elephant; shots of him playing croquet with friends; shots of him with various beautiful women. The largest photograph looked fairly recent and appeared to have been taken at the compound with the dunes and the ocean in the background. It showed Lord Downey standing arm-in-arm with a gorgeous, willowy young woman with long brown hair, both of them laughing and holding glasses of champagne.

"Where did you find him?" said the young black woman, as she returned carrying a wet washcloth and a bottle of Evian. She knelt by Lord Downey and wiped the sand from his face. She tried to get him to drink some of the water, but couldn't wake him. She stood, looking up at me with those big eyes of hers.

I told her how I had spotted Lord Downey struggling in the water and pulled him to shore.

"He seemed kinda out of it. Is he on medication?"

"No, not really. Every now and then for his arthritis, but that's about it."

"Are you his nurse?"

"No," she said. "But I do take care of him."

She stuck out a hand.

"I'm Clarissa. Clarissa Percival."

"Zack," I said, shaking her hand. "Zack Chasteen."

She studied me more closely.

"Barbara Pickering's friend?"

I nodded. Clarissa smiled.

"I heard you were coming. Ms. Pickering stopped by here just the other day. Lord Downey was so glad to see her. He seemed so much better after her visit. And then . . ."

She stopped as Lord Downey bolted upright on the couch, his face wrenched in terror.

"Burma!" he shouted. "Where's Burma?"

He cast about, looking at Clarissa, then at me, not seeming to really see either of us. Clarissa sat down beside him. She gently placed her hands on his cheeks, like a mother caressing a child.

"Look at me," she almost whispered. "Look at me."

He looked at her. And immediately he began to calm down. It was those eyes of hers. They would have soothed the beast in me, too.

Clarissa eased Lord Downey back down on the couch. She stroked his face and soon he was asleep again.

"That's the same thing he was yelling when I pulled him out of the water," I said. "What's the deal with Burma?"

"Burma is his daughter." She nodded at the big color photograph on the sofa table. "That's her."

"She lives here?"

"Sometimes. When it suits her."

The way she said it told me it wasn't a subject I needed to pry into. Clarissa stood up from the couch and offered her hand again. I took it. It was a very nice hand.

"Mr. Chasteen, I cannot thank you enough for what you did," she said. "But if you don't mind . . ."

"No problem. I have to go meet Barbara."

"You haven't seen her yet?"

"No, I just got here an hour ago, and she's been busy with the photo shoot."

"Oh, I know all about that. They hired several girls from

the island, and they say it has been such a thrill. Plus, they get to work with that famous photographer. Mr. Gannon, I believe it is?"

"Yes, the one and only."

"The girls say he makes them all feel like movie stars. He must be very charming."

"So I've heard," I said. "I can find my way out."

I stepped to the sliding glass door, but Clarissa stopped me.

"Oh no, go out the front," she said, leading me across the living room and into the foyer. The door was stainless steel. It looked like it could have been the door of a meat locker. "That way you won't break your neck going down the dunes."

"Why didn't that Dutch architect think of building some steps out there?"

"I guess for the same reason he didn't think of building any windows that open to catch the ocean breeze," she said.

"What do you mean?"

"I mean, none of the windows in any of the houses will crank open. They are just glass to look through. We have to run air conditioning all the time. You don't want to know what the electric bills are," she said. "I apologize if it was uncomfortable in there. I like to keep the thermostat up high and I guess I'm just used to it."

"No problem," I said. "It keeps me loose and supple."

Clarissa bit back a smile as I stepped through the door. With the sun down, it was actually cooler outside than inside.

"Good night, Mr. Chasteen," Clarissa said. "Do give Ms. Pickering my regards."

"The moment I see her," I said.

18

It was after seven when I made it back to the cottage. I thought Barbara might be there, but she wasn't. I took off my clothes, tossed them in a hamper, and hopped in the shower. Maybe Barbara would surprise me while I was in the shower. Maybe I would turn and look and she would be standing there smiling at me. Maybe she would be holding the Schramsberg '98. Maybe she would take off all her clothes, toss them in the hamper, and get in the shower with me. Maybe we'd skip dinner.

Barbara still hadn't shown by the time I was toweling off, and as I stepped into my new dress-up-for-dinner duds—tan linen pants, white linen shirt, blue blazer—it occurred to me that perhaps she had been to the room before I returned from Lord Downey's and, not finding me there, had gone looking for me in the main house. She was probably sitting down there waiting on me.

"No, sir," said Mr. Pindle, as I claimed the only empty stool at the bar. "Haven't seen her."

Mr. Pindle was wearing his bartender's outfit—a black tux with a red bowtie and a red cummerbund. He wore red sneakers. His Atlanta Braves cap was stashed under the counter.

There was fifteen-year-old Barbancourt Reserve du Do-
maine on the shelf, and I asked Mr. Pindle to pour me some of
that. He was a much swifter bartender than he was a bellman—
mainly because the bar was tiny and everything was within
arm's reach. Mr. Pindle poured two fingers of the Barbancourt
into a lead crystal tumbler, then he looked at it and poured another finger on top of that.

"Neat, right?" he said.

"Neat," I said.

The Barbancourt wasn't nearly as sweet as Mount Gay. It
was smoky and smooth, hardly any bite at all. Dangerous stuff.
I felt like I could drink about a gallon of it. Pacing was clearly
in order. Too bad I am a lousy pacer.

I nodded to a couple sitting next to me. They introduced
themselves—the Something-or-Others from Somewhere. He
was a doctor. She was a doctor's wife. Lovely place, isn't it?
Yes, it is. We've been coming here for years. Me, too.

"What line of work you in?" asked Dr. Something-or-Other.

"No line," I said.

"Retired?"

"Mmmmm," I said.

"Lucky you."

"Mmmmm," I said again.

The people on the other side of me were four couples from
Charleston, South Carolina. The women all wore Lilly Pulitzer
dresses and were drinking white wine. They were talking about
the last trip they had taken together, to Bermuda. The men were
partners in the same law firm. They were drinking bourbon,
talking about mutual funds, and wore blue blazers just like
mine. Yep, I fit right in.

I asked Mr. Pindle for another Barbancourt, and I took it and
stepped over to one of the salon windows and looked up the hill
to the cottage. The lights were off, no sign of Barbara. When I
returned to the bar, Chrissie and Charlie Hineman were there,
talking to Dr. and Mrs. Something-or-Other and the Charleston
crowd.

The Hinemans had been managing the Albury Beach Club
for nearly ten years, since about the time I first started visiting

Harbour Island. Chrissie was big and loud and bosomy, but in a good way. The bigness (she was almost as tall as me), the loudness (it was operatic), the bosomyness (we're talking grand tetons), all of it worked for her in a manner that was charming, sort of like a chunkier version of Julia Child. Chrissie had taught Renaissance poetry at Duke, but she wasn't a stuffy academic. She was a born conversationalist, someone who seemed to know a little something about everything. I once stayed up half the night at the bar with her discussing the coral reef ecology of the Indian Ocean, while she matched me rum for rum and offered a brief discourse on how the small distilleries of the French West Indies turned out a more traditional and pleasing product than those of Barbados, where they had been swallowed up by big liquor corporations like Hennessy.

Chrissie was the extrovert in the marriage, the Albury Beach Club's p.r. department, the force that kept the clients happy, and kept them coming back. Not only did she remember the names of all the guests, but she knew the names of their kids and their grandkids, where they all came from, and what they all did, and who preferred Miles Davis on the salon stereo, and who preferred Buffett. Charlie Hineman had retired from Delta after thirty years as a pilot and stayed mostly behind the scenes at the Albury. He made sure the plumbing worked and the gardeners kept the hedges trimmed and the food order arrived on the daily boat from Nassau. He was strong-jawed and handsome and played tennis every day, mostly with female guests whose husbands were off fishing. Other, lesser, men in his position might have enjoyed occasional, discreet post-match dalliances— Charlie certainly looked like a ladies' man—but he only had eyes for Chrissie.

"Oh, Zachary, come here to me this instant," trilled Chrissie, giving me a kiss and a bear hug, and not spilling a drop of her champagne.

I shook hands with Charlie Hineman.

"Zack," he said, which was about as much as Charlie Hineman ever said. A pleasant guy, just quiet.

"Where's Barbara?" asked Chrissie.

"Your guess is as good as mine," I said.

Chrissie gave me a funny look, but didn't say anything. She pulled me into the circle of people at the bar. I stood around doing my best to keep up my end of the banter, mostly by smiling and saying "Mmmm" when it seemed appropriate, and being as agreeable as I could manage to be, which wasn't very.

Where the hell *was* Barbara, anyway?

19

After a few minutes of playing party hostess, Chrissie Hineman took me aside.

"You look like the canary who swallowed the cat," she said.

"I'm not sure what that means."

"Neither am I, but you are clearly uncomfortable and your mind is elsewhere, Zachary."

"Guess I'm just anxious to see Barbara, that's all."

"And you would probably prefer seeing her alone, just the two of you, and not standing around this bar making small talk."

"Mmmm," I said.

Chrissie turned her back to the crowd at the bar and lowered her voice.

"Was that you I saw just before sunset, carrying Lord Downey from the beach?"

Yes, I told her, it was. Then I told her how I'd come across him struggling in the water and how I had delivered him into the very capable hands of Clarissa Percival.

"That poor, poor man. That makes at least the sixth or seventh time he has wandered off in the last couple of weeks."

"He's getting old."

"Old, hell. It's the daughter. He's worried sick about her."

"Burma?"

"Yes, do you know her?"

"Only by name."

"Well, surely you've heard about her."

"No. Clarissa Percival mentioned her. But other than that . . ."

"Zack, where have you been?" Chrissie immediately caught herself, and said, "Oh, I'm sorry. I didn't mean it like that."

"No problem. I didn't take it like that."

"What I meant was, Burma Downey is, well, I don't know any other way to put it except to say she is notorious. I can't believe you've never heard of her," said Chrissie. "But then I must admit that I do follow these things a bit more closely than others might."

During her years on-island Chrissie Hineman had become a devoted Anglophile. She read all the London newspapers and immersed herself in the minutiae of British royalty and titled folk, several of whom had homes on Harbour Island.

"Burma is Lord Downey's only child. Came very late in his life. I believe it was with his fourth wife, Lady Paula, just before she died in that plane crash in Kenya. Lord Downey's a dear, but he has always been something of a libertine himself, and I rather doubt he raised Burma with anything that even came close to resembling a firm hand. Which would explain a lot."

"Like what?"

"Like if you've got the rest of the evening, Zachary, then I might be able to tell you about a tenth of it. Burma Downey had a short run as a fashion model. Did the whole thing—sex, drugs, and total excess. She's the original wild child, that one."

"Maybe she has a 'Boy Named Sue' complex."

"Say what?"

"The name. How would you like to be called Burma? Good thing her father isn't Lord Shave."

"Oh, I don't know. Burma—I think it's rather exotic. It was quite the thing amongst all those upper-class British gents who served abroad and did their damnedest to prop up the Empire.

Named their daughters after the places where they did battle, or where they were stationed, or where they once had a rubber plantation or something."

"What did they name their sons after?"

"Themselves for God's sake. All Nigels and Phillips and Johns. But the girls—I know of at least three Indias, a couple of Chinas, and one Rangoon."

"You're kidding."

"Not at all. The Rangoon even goes by 'Goonie.'"

"Ah, may there always be a Britain."

"Burma Downey is the one who had the affair with Celia Ashton a few years back."

"Sorry, I'm blanking on that one, too."

"Well, at the time, Celia Ashton was the chancellor of the exchequer's wife," said Chrissie. "Meantime, the chancellor was cavorting with choirboys in a closet. Or so that rumor goes."

"Burma Downey's a lesbian?"

"She can be." Chrissie let it ride, sipped her champagne. "She's had some very public affairs with men, too. I don't think it really makes much difference to her one way or the other."

"How veddy, veddy British," I said.

"Burma is also the one who, shortly after all the sordid details about her and Celia Ashton were aired out in *The Sunday Telegraph,* posed for *Tatler* on the front stoop at No. 9 Downing Street, draped in the Union Jack and wearing nothing but her birthmarks. I suppose she must have been off-island the last time you and Barbara were here or you would definitely remember her. She always went topless down on the beach. Not a bit of decency."

"Appalling."

"Oh, spare me."

I caught Mr. Pindle's eye and signaled for another drink. Chrissie wiggled her glass for a refill, too.

"Burma used to shuttle quite a lot between here and South Florida. Quite the club girl, always bringing back some of her club friends and putting them up for weeks on end at the house here. A very rough trade they were, too. Not nice people at all. Then came the accident."

"Accident?"

"Yes, in Fort Lauderdale, I believe it was. A collision. Must have been six weeks or so ago. The details are a bit sketchy, but the *Island Voice* ran a front page piece about it. Burma suffered broken bones, horrible lacerations, a crushed larynx. Lost her voice and everything. Whether it's permanent remains to be seen. She's confined to a wheelchair. And heaven knows how many plastic surgeons have struggled to put her back together again. She's at the house here now, recuperating, still covered in bandages."

"And that's what has Lord Downey all torn up."

"That, and the fact—from what I hear, anyway—that Burma won't have anything to do with him. Ignores him completely. Wheels herself out the moment he steps into the room."

One of the dining room servers, a young woman in a starched white uniform with a pale blue collar, came to the door by the bar and tinkled a tiny brass bell. The 8 P.M. call to dinner. The crowd at the bar began filing to their tables.

"Come," said Chrissie, ushering me toward the dining room. "You and Barbara will be sitting with Charlie and me tonight."

"Look, if you don't mind . . ."

Chrissie stopped. She smiled.

"Oh, I'm sorry, Zachary. You'd probably prefer to wait out here for her, have a moment for yourselves before you join us."

I nodded.

"Ah, sweet boy, you are smitten, aren't you? Well, it's good to see, good to see." Chrissie gave me a peck on the cheek. "I can only think that Barbara might have gotten caught up in something down at the Bahama Sands. I understand they were finishing the shoot today and perhaps she might have spotted the crew a drink at the bar. Shall I call down there for you and see?"

I told her no, I'd just sit in the salon and wait, maybe go check the room again if Barbara hadn't shown up in a few minutes. Mr. Pindle arrived with our drinks and Chrissie went off to join Charlie in the dining room. I took a chair in the salon, flipping through magazines, not even paying attention to what magazine I was flipping through, sipping the Barbancourt much faster than I should have been sipping it.

Wonderful aromas wafted from the dining room. The evening's menu was posted outside the dining room door and I got up to look at it. Pan-seared snapper with toasted couscous. Barbecued breast of duck with peanut-whipped potatoes. Grilled double-thick veal chop with vegetable tart. I would have to order one of everything. Couldn't risk insulting Chef Ludo.

Mr. Pindle was no longer tending bar, so I poured a rum for myself. I found my name on the bar sheet and made another mark under the "Brand Name" column. That made four rums—four big rums. And not much in the way of food. I was pacing myself, it was just a fast pace. I was definitely feeling it, all giddy and pretty and gay.

My ass . . .

I was antsy and grouchy and tired of sitting around. I walked outside and up the hill to the cottage. No one there, just as I'd left it. I drained the last of the Barbancourt and headed for the Bahama Sands.

20

I took the back way to the Bahama Sands, cutting behind the Albury's tennis courts and following Barrack Street as it wound north, buffering the other beachfront properties—big homes and small hotels and a few vacant lots that were on the market for more money than I would ever see. Barbara wasn't one to walk alone on the beach at night. And the only other way to get between the Albury and the Bahama Sands was to follow Barrack Street.

I walked past the Coral Inn and the Castaway Beach Club. I walked past a big yellow French Provençal house owned by a famous clothing designer and past a giant Mediterranean-style villa that belonged to a former co-owner of the Tampa Bay Bucs. Barrack Street skirted the edge of Dunmore Town, the only town on Harbour Island. It was hopping on Saturday night, at least as much as it can hop. A small crowd of young men and women stood around a Honda Civic wired for sound with two bass-thumping speakers blaring from its open rear hatch. Little kids zipped around on shiny scooters. The Faith in Jesus Victory Tabernacle Church carried on its gospel sing-in with the windows and doors thrown open and a choir of twenty belting out hymns backed up by electric guitars, piano, trumpets, and tambourines. And the take-away shops did brisk business—the proprietors dipped up fried fish and cracked conch from sizzling cast iron skillets, spooned out mounds of peas 'n' rice, and plopped everything into Styrofoam containers for their customers. I was sorely tempted to chow down, but I was a man on a mission.

I walked past Briland Bakery, which also doubled as the ice cream shop. The kid in the Miami Heat T-shirt, the one who had carried my bag from the water taxi, was sitting outside by himself. He held the nub of an ice cream cone that was melting faster than he could lick it. I nodded at him and he leapt up, polishing off the cone and wiping his hands on his shirt. He fell in step beside me, saying, "Hey, Mr. Big Man, you need a guide?"

"A guide for what?"

"To get where you're going."

"I know where I'm going."

"Where's that?"

"The Bahama Sands."

"I'll guide you there."

I smiled and he smiled back, the scammee acknowledging the scammer.

"What's your name?" I asked.

"Nixon."

"Nixon? Like the president?"

"No," Nixon said. "Like me."

"How old are you, Nixon?"

"Soon be thirteen."

"You get paid more for being a guide than you get for carrying bags?"

"Uh-huh. Being a guide, I tell you all about the history. Now, see, what we are walking through, this is Dunmore Town."

"I know that."

"Yeah, but you know when it was founded?"

"No, I don't."

"That's why you need a guide."

"OK, you're hired." I stuck out my hand and he slapped it. Deal sealed.

Then Nixon said: "It was founded in 1713."

"So who was Dunmore?"

"You mean why they call it Dunmore Town?"

"Uh-huh."

"Well, you see, the slaves that came here, they were freed slaves, they named it that. The first one got off the boat, he looked around and he said: 'They shoulda done more to fix up this scruffy-ass town than they did.'"

Nixon glanced at me to see if it got a laugh. It did.

Then he said, "Dunmore was this Englishman used to be governor of the Bahamas. Back then, Dunmore Town was bigger than Nassau, used to be the capital of all the Bahamas. Nassau wasn't nothing. Except it had a big fort, Fort Montagu, built in 1741, oldest fort in the Bahamas. Then came the Revolutionary War and the Americans, they captured Fort Montagu. So this group of Brilanders, about fifty of them, they got in their ship and they sailed to Nassau and they attacked the fort. There was about two hundred of them Americans and the Brilanders they whipped hell out of them and got the fort back. You American?"

"Uh-huh."

"Well, the Brilanders they whipped hell out of the Americans, did you know that?"

"No, I didn't."

"That's because your history books don't tell that story, do they? But it's true. You can look it up. Whipped hell out of them."

"I believe you."

"I read all the history books. Then I give it my own special sauce."

"You been in the guide business long, Nixon?"

"Just started tonight," he said.

Barrack Street narrowed as it neared the Bahama Sands, the road dark, the undergrowth thick on both sides.

"Look out for the holes," said Nixon. "This road's all broke up."

I followed him, making my way carefully. The four rums didn't help my surefootedness. We aimed for the spotlights on the Bahama Sands' stone arch entry, then walked up the driveway to where a pair of uniformed security guards stood on either side of the double front door. I gave Nixon a five dollar bill. He studied it on both sides and then stuck it in a pocket.

"You want, I can wait here and guide you back."

"Nah, that'll be alright, Nixon."

"I know lots more than what I told you," he said. "I know everything there is to know about this island."

"I bet you do."

"You need guiding, then you come get me."

I shook his hand good-bye and told him I would keep him in mind for all my guiding needs. He smiled and took off running.

21

Bahama Sands was an outpost of hipness, part of a chain of boutique properties in the Caribbean owned by an Italian sportswear mogul turned hotelier. All the pretty people stayed here—fashion models, fashion photographers, rock stars, actors, agents, producers, and plenty of others pretending to be one of the above.

I walked through the reception area. It didn't really look like a hotel reception area. It looked more like a Soho art gallery. Huge canvases hung on the walls, the paintings all variations on a theme of beats-the-hell-out-of-me. The front desk clerk stood behind a polished slab of granite that was free of all clutter except a telephone and a laptop computer no thicker than a manila envelope. He didn't really look like a front desk clerk. He looked like someone auditioning for the part of the idealistic but troubled young doctor on a daytime soap opera. I smiled and gave him a nod as I walked by, auditioning for the part of the tragically maimed love interest of the beautiful leading lady.

I walked into the bar. It didn't really look like a bar. It looked like the sultan's harem quarters. White tile, bleached sandstone walls, gauzy damask sheets hanging ceiling to floor and dividing the long narrow room into a series of intimate sitting areas with couches and overstuffed chairs. I half expected Scheherazade to beckon me to her settee and beguile me with tales.

Waiters, all wearing some kind of Vietnamese black silk pajama outfit, filled drink orders at a grottolike chamber that was cram full with bottles of liquor and wine. There were a few stools in front of it, and people sitting on them, but no one I knew. Oil lamps gave the room a glow of just-past-twilight. The music was cool and jazzy, and playing just low enough that I could hear the sounds of people partying above it. But the layout made it impossible for me to see who was there without parting the gauzy sheets and poking my head into each of the cozy little sitting areas. I made my way through the place, sticking my head through sheets and looking around. I startled a man and a woman making out on a couch. I startled two men making out on a couch. I startled a group of men smoking cigars and drinking brandy.

Finally, I stuck my head through some sheets and saw people I knew. Or, at least, recognized. They worked for Barbara at the magazine. I just couldn't remember their names or what they did. One of them, a guy in black horn-rimmed glasses with spiky black hair, spotted me and waved me in.

"Zack," he said.

"Hi," I said.

"Peter Prentice," he said. "I'm the style editor."

"Right."

"We met on your boat at the office party."

"Sure, I remember."

And before I could ask about Barbara, Prentice had turned to the twenty or so others in the sitting area, and announced: "Hey, everybody. This is Zack, Barbara's friend." There were hi's and hellos and someone said "Hi, Zack, Barbara's friend" and the others laughed. Prentice introduced me around. I met the assistant art director, the makeup person, two lighting technicians, and the caterer. I met the stylist and three of the models. I had to agree with Barbara. Bryce Gannon did have an eye for talent. I met other people whose functions were uncertain, but who were associated with the shoot in one way or another. After a few minutes, I finally found myself back with Peter Prentice, and asked if he had seen Barbara.

"Oh," he said, looking around as if he had suddenly noticed she wasn't there. "I guess she left. Yeah, that's right. She left with Bryce. It was a while ago."

I stepped out, not bothering with good-byes. Back in the reception area, I asked the front desk clerk if he would mind calling the Albury Beach Club.

"Certainly, sir." He handed me the receiver and punched the numbers. The Albury receptionist answered and got Chrissie Hineman on the line. No, Barbara still hadn't been to the dining room. I waited while she checked to see if the lights were on in Hibiscus cottage. No, she said, no sign of her there either. I thanked her.

I handed the clerk the phone and asked him: "Can you tell me what room Bryce Gannon is in?"

"Why no, sir, I can't." He smiled. "But I can ring it if you like."

"I like."

He handed me the receiver again and began punching the numbers on the console. I let the phone ring ten times. No one answered.

"Would you mind dialing it again?"

"Excuse me, sir?"

"Dial it again. Just in case you got it wrong the first time."

The front desk clerk was clearly offended. How dare I question his switchboard capabilities? But he redialed the number anyway. He did it slowly, overexaggerating for my benefit. This time I watched him punch the numbers: 2–1–1–4. I let the phone ring a few times.

"Guess no one's home," I said. I handed the clerk the receiver. He didn't wish me a pleasant good night.

I walked out of the reception area and onto the hotel grounds. The Bahama Sands was a swank place, but it wasn't a big place, maybe twenty or so duplex bungalows sitting close to one another and connected by shell paths. I found a door marked 114. Dim light shone from under the door, but there were no windows on this side of the bungalow so I couldn't tell if anyone was inside.

I knocked on the door.

"Hello," I hollered. "Anyone there?"

I wasn't quite sure what I was going to do if Gannon opened the door, even less sure what I might do if it turned out that Barbara was with him. I pounded on the door again, and when it didn't open, I walked around to the back of the bungalow. I had to cut through a croton hedge, breaking a few branches and making a minor racket.

Each side of the bungalow had a small terrace that opened onto a view of the ocean, and I stepped to the terrace behind 114. The sliding glass door was pulled shut, the blinds drawn.

I rapped on the sliding glass door.

"Gannon," I said. "Are you in there?"

I rapped again.

"Goddammit, open up."

I grabbed the sliding door's handle and rattled it, trying to jiggle the lock loose. That's when a voice said, "May I help you, sir?"

A flashlight cast a beam in my face, and when it lowered, I could see one of the security guards standing on a pathway.

"Is this your room, sir?"

"No, I was looking for a friend."

The guard shone the light in my face again.

"Are you a guest here, sir?"

"No, I'm not," I said.

And I walked away.

I wanted a drink when I got back to the Albury, but I didn't want to stand around making happy talk with the crew at the bar. So I went back to the cottage. I had a choice between the Schramsberg '98 and the Beefeater's. I picked the gin. I poured some in a glass and squeezed lime in with it. Then I sat outside in an Adirondack chair facing the ocean.

The wind was blowing stiff and it felt fresh and good. I looked at the stars. There were lots of them. I picked out the easy ones—Orion and the Big Dipper and Scorpio. Then I started making up constellations of my own—Oreo and the Gravy Ladle and Scallopini. Christ, I was hungry.

I poured another drink. I looked at the stars some more. One of them looked particularly bright. It might have been Venus, not a star, I don't know. I yelled at the star that might have been Venus as loud as I could yell. It felt good to yell, so I yelled again. How long would it take for those yells to reach the stars? Light years, millions of light years. What if my yells didn't hit the stars but just kept right on going and going and going? Would that make me immortal? Sure it would. I yelled again.

Then I went inside to make another drink. Only I fell onto the bed instead.

22

First light seeped through the jalousie windows and nudged my brain toward something that, in lower life forms, might almost pass for consciousness. Catbirds tittered. A lonesome dog yelped. A rooster did its rooster thing, a rival crowed in counterpoint, and then the first rooster started in again. The ocean boomed its backbeat. It was the Bahamas Philharmonic in full crescendo.

I willed open a reluctant eye.

The pillow I embraced was comely as far as pillows go, its foam as responsive as foam can reasonably be. Given time and utter depravity, we might have gotten to know each other on a much more meaningful level. The sheets were twisted and knotted. The blanket was on the floor. My mouth was sour, my skull throbbed, and life at that moment truly sucked.

There is a particular hell that lies between rage and despair. And I was stranded there. By strict definition, cuckoldry requires a state of marriage. While no vows officially joined us, Barbara and I had—or, at least, I'd thought we had—an understanding. So, if indeed she had spurned me for another, I figured I was at least a common-law cuckold. What was that song

all the Carnival road-marchers were singing on our trip to
Trinidad? Something by Shadow, the reigning calypso king.
"Man, why you act so surprised?/You got no money/You got no
house in town/Your woman done horned you/That's what a
woman do." Caribbean lyricism—it always cut to the chase.

Then again . . .

Barbara simply wasn't the kind of person who would let
someone down so hard. Especially someone she professed to
love. She had not a shred of cruelty in her. She was loving and
good, and even if she had suddenly decided the two of us were
not meant to be, she would at least be gentle and forthright
about it. She would not disappear into the night and leave me so
alone. It was shabby behavior, and it was beneath her.

Then again . . .

Bryce Gannon was an impressive guy. He and Barbara did
have a history. There had even been a ring and a wedding date
and all that. Then, enter Chasteen and exit Gannon. Yet, forgiv-
ing all, Gannon rushes across the wide, wide ocean and rescues
his damsel from impending calamity. I knew Gannon must have
some substance, some core of goodness, or else Barbara never
would have taken up with him in the first place. Reunited in
such idyllic circumstances, maybe the old chemistry had gone
to work. And maybe Barbara had responded in a way that might
seem altogether out of character.

Then again . . .

I felt the wave of nausea that comes when one has drunk too
much and eaten too little and must have food immediately or
else sink farther into the mire. When had I eaten last? The closest thing to a meal had been the minibar peanuts at the Los Altos Inn. That was Friday, this was Sunday. No wonder I felt like
hell. It wasn't the rum and the gin, it was hunger. OK, maybe it
was both. But I definitely needed some breakfast.

I looked at the bedside clock. Its face was blank, not even
blinking. I pulled the chain on the bedside lamp. Nothing happened. The power must have gone off. It happens a lot in the
Out Islands.

I went into the bathroom and looked in the mirror. Not much
improvement over the day before. My eyes weren't quite so

puffy, but the cut on my cheekbone was festering. I ran hot water on a washcloth, then held the washcloth against the scab until it softened. Then I worked up some soap lather on the washcloth and rubbed the cut. It stung, so I figured it must be doing some good. I brushed my teeth. I drank three cups of tepid tap water, then forced myself to drink a fourth. I tried not to look at the Beefeater bottle to see how much damage I had done. I slipped on shorts and a T-shirt, and headed down to the main house.

I found Mr. Pindle and some of the kitchen staff sitting on stools at the back door of the kitchen. I asked them if there was any chance a man might get a cup of coffee.

"No chance at all," said Mr. Pindle. "Electric broke up."

"Got any idea when it might come back on?"

There were snorts and laughs, and a big woman wearing a white apron said, "You want, I got some orange juice in the icebox."

"I want."

She fetched me a big glass of it, then another, and then a third.

"Got some hot pipes this morning, don't you?" said Mr. Pindle, and the others laughed.

The orange juice made me feel better, but only just barely. I needed to fight pain with pain. I left the main house and cut across the dunes and onto the beach. I had it all to myself. I eyed the north end of the island, about two miles away, and set my course. I stuck to the narrow hard-packed stretch that lay in between the loose dry sand and the lip of the incoming tide. A hundred yards and I was into a pretty good rhythm. Maybe a nine-minute mile. Not all that impressive, but not all that bad considering how long it had been since I had worked out. I might even make it the whole way without upchucking.

Every now and then a wave would roll in and I'd go splashing through it thinking it might make a good shot for a TV commercial about some new pill to combat impotence or depression or pattern baldness. Happy music would be playing. I'd have a couple of golden retrievers running along beside me. About halfway through the commercial I'd jog up to the front steps of a charmingly restored Cape Cod beach bungalow where my chemically balanced wife would hand me a glass of fresh-squeezed lemonade. We'd laugh about the golden retrievers romping in the yard. I wouldn't be sweating nearly as much as I was sweating now.

I ran past the spot where I had plucked Lord Downey from the ocean the evening before. Should I drop by and check on him today? Nah, probably best just to let it go. If the old guy had recouped his good senses, then the incident would only embarrass him. If he was still out of it, then he wouldn't know the difference. I ran past the Bahama Sands. Should I drop by and check on Bryce Gannon? Nah, probably just best to let that go, too. Whatever was going to happen would soon play itself out.

23

I was pretty winded by the time I reached the end of the island. I stood there watching the current rip through the bight. It was an outgoing tide and it was draining the flats on the back side of the island. Blue heron and white ibises were stalking prey on the emerging slivers of sandbars. The air carried the sour, fetid smell of sea things drying in the sun.

I followed a path off the beach and pretty soon I was walking through Dunmore Town. Church bells were ringing and people were walking along Chapel Street decked out in their Sunday best. For such a small place, Harbour Island has an abundance of churches, at least a dozen within Dunmore Town alone. I stopped on the street outside St. John's Anglican Church and watched as the crucifer led the procession from where they were gathered on the stone steps out front, through the doors, and down the aisle. The congregation joined in on "I Sing a Song of the Saints of God." It was one of my favorite hymns. I considered slipping in the door and finding a spot in a back pew and singing along with them. But I wasn't dressed for it. Plus, sweating out the previous night's overindulgence had created an aura around me that would not be appreciated by my pewmates.

I was walking up the hilly driveway to the Albury Beach Club when I heard the crunch of tires on rocks behind me. A voice chimed out, "Beep-beep!"

I turned to see Steffie Plank at the wheel of a golf cart.

"Hello, stranger," she beamed, pulling the golf cart to a stop. Steffie works with Barbara. Her official title is "assistant to the publisher." She is three years out of Rollins College and on the fast track for whatever the heck she sets her mind on doing. Steffie started at Orb Media as an intern, working for free just to get a little experience in the magazine business, then quickly made herself indispensable, knocking off every task that was thrown at her with grace and good humor and consummate skill. Now Barbara lives in fear that Steffie will jump ship, head to New York, and go to work for a big magazine, one that would pay her two or three times what she gets at Orb Media.

Steffie's long brown hair was streaked with blond, and she had a yellow hibiscus tucked behind one ear. On anyone else it might have look affected, but not on Steffie. She was wearing a long green sarong and a plain white T-shirt that had been gathered tight around the bottom and knotted on one side. I noticed right away that she had nothing on under the T-shirt, so I tried to concentrate on her face, which is easy to concentrate on. It is wide and friendly and flawless, set off by big brown eyes flecked with the tiniest specks of gold. The eyes add to the impression that Steffie actually glows.

"It's so good to see you," Steffie said, giving me a hug. I hugged back. The hug was, perhaps, just a beat or two longer than it needed to be, which was all my doing, but I don't think Steffie minded. I felt more uplifted by the hug than if I had gone to church. Maybe I would start my own church and station Steffie at the door to give people hugs on the way out. St. Zack's Cathedral of the Much-Needed Embrace, we'd call it. It would be a big hit with forty-plus men who are fresh-sprung from prison and beginning to feel a little sorry for themselves because their girlfriends have ditched them.

"Want a lift?" Steffie asked.

I hopped in beside her and we puttered up the driveway. Steffie swerved to miss a coconut in the road. She said: "So where's Barbara? She decide to sleep in?"

I am pretty lousy at masking emotion. Steffie saw it on my face.

"What is it?"

"I haven't seen Barbara."

"You what?"

"I haven't seen her."

"Not since you got here?"

"She didn't come in last night."

We pulled into the driveway under the shade of the bougainvillea arbor. Steffie turned off the golf cart.

"Wow," she said.

"Yeah, wow."

"Where do you think . . . ?" She shook her head, not finishing the sentence. I put a hand on her shoulder.

"Let me just go ahead and ask you straight. Is there a chance that Barbara might have gotten back together with Bryce Gannon or something?"

"No way. Why would you even think that?"

"Because I don't know what else to think."

We sat there, quiet, the day getting hotter by the moment. There was no breeze. The air was sticky and sodden. On the ground, by one of the golf cart tires, a green anole caught a small white butterfly, but was having trouble turning it into breakfast. The butterfly flapped its wings and the lizard let it go, watching calmly as it fluttered off in a wobbly flight pattern. When the butterfly crash-landed a few feet away, the green anole pounced upon it again.

Finally, Steffie said, "There's no way Barbara was with Bryce."

"Why not?"

"Because there's just no way. He's so not Barbara."

"He used to be her fiancé."

Steffie shrugged it off.

"Bryce Gannon is good-looking and all. And he's a great

photographer. But he's such a lech. He was hitting on me from the moment he got here and he was hitting on all the models. And what's he, like forty, or something?"

"A real old-timer."

"You know what I mean. He should just act his age, that's all I'm saying."

"When did you last see Barbara?"

"It was after the shoot broke up. She bought drinks for everyone."

"At Bahama Sands?"

"Uh-huh. It was kind of fun, actually. Everyone was stoked about the shoot. I mean, we got great stuff. The weather was good; the clothes were cute. The models Bryce found were awesome. The whole thing just came together. I think we really nailed it. So we were celebrating."

"Yeah, I caught the tail end of it, but Barbara had already left."

"What time was that?"

"Must have been almost nine o'clock."

"Oh, she was long gone by then. I left after she did and that was barely eight. She had one drink and that was just because she had to. She was ready to leave, I could tell. I mean, on the beach she kept turning to me and whispering: 'Do you think he's here yet?' And then she kept looking for you. 'Do you see him? Do you see him?' I swear, Zack, she was like a little girl. You know how she can be sometimes."

I knew exactly how she could be sometimes. It was one of about a million reasons why I adored her.

"So that's how I know she didn't do anything stupid with Bryce Gannon," said Steffie.

"But the two of them did leave the bar together."

"Yeah, but that meant nothing, believe me. I was standing right there with them. Barbara said she was in a hurry to get back here to see you, and Bryce offered to give her a ride. He asked me to ride with them, but I said no. Mostly because I didn't want to be alone with him on the ride back."

"So it was just Barbara and Gannon?"

"Yes." Steffie stopped, thought about it. "Actually, no. On

the way out, this woman pulled Bryce aside and started talking to him. Maybe talking to him isn't the best way to describe it. She was all over him, rubbing herself up against him. It was kind of disgusting, actually, but Bryce was eating it up. I remember Barbara was just standing there waiting while Bryce and this woman were going on and on. Barbara finally got tired of it and walked off. Bryce followed her and the woman went with him."

"Who was she?"

"No idea. I'd seen her hanging around the night before, flirting with Bryce then. But there were lots of people hanging around and I had no idea who they were, either. A crowd tends to attract a crowd, especially with models and photographers and all that. This woman . . . hey, maybe Bryce got lucky."

"Which still doesn't explain where Barbara is."

"You don't think something could have happened to her, do you?" Steffie asked, in a tiny voice. "Have you contacted the police?"

"Not yet."

"Well, shouldn't you? I mean, they do have police here, don't they?"

"I'm sure there's someone. I haven't checked into that yet." I patted Steffie on the back. "There's no reason for you to get upset."

I got out of the golf cart.

"Do you want me to stick around?" Steffie asked. "Until she shows up? My plane leaves at one o'clock. I was just coming to say good-bye. But I could cancel."

"No," I told her. "It'll be alright."

I almost believed it.

24

The power was on when I returned to the cottage. I lay on the bed underneath the ceiling fan and let it cool me off while I decided what to do next. Ten minutes later I was still lying there. I had decided exactly nothing. I attributed it to the fact that my stomach was grumbling so loudly that my brain, in an act of solidarity, had staged a sympathy strike. I would get lunch. Then I would do something. Only I wasn't sure what.

There was a knock at the door. Before I could open it, I heard Chrissie Hineman saying, "Stop! You have no authority . . ."

And in stepped a tall young man wearing a uniform—somber blue pants with red piping, a starched white shirt with gold and blue epaulets. He wore a white helmet with a silver crest on it and a strap that was pulled tight under his chin.

"Mr. Chasteen?" he said.

"Yes."

"You must come with me."

"I must?"

The policeman sputtered, and I said: "Where must I come with you to?"

"To the inspector's office," he said.

I looked at Chrissie. She offered a sympathetic shrug.

"He wouldn't tell me why, Zack."

"Is this about what happened at the airport yesterday?" I asked the policeman.

"The inspector will explain," he said. "You must come with me. Now."

He grabbed hold of my right arm. He pulled. I didn't go anywhere. He grabbed hold tighter.

"You want me to make a big muscle?" I said. "It impresses small children and excites loose women."

The policeman let go of my arm. I slipped into my sandals and he nodded me outside, following right behind me. Chrissie stood in the doorway watching as the policeman pointed me down the pathway.

"Zack, if there's anything we can do . . ."

"Mind delivering lunch to the inspector's office?" I asked.

For some reason, she thought I was joking.

The inspector's office sat on Gaol Street, just up the street from the Harbour Island All-Ages School. I had walked past it many times on previous visits and never noticed it, not even with the Royal Bahamian Police crest on the wall out front. The policeman drove a white Mitsubishi van. He parked it on the street. When I reached for my door, he said, "I'll get that." He stepped around, opened the door, and escorted me inside the office.

The office smelled musty and was lit by a single fluorescent bulb that was in the middle of the ceiling and appeared to be in its final flickering throes. Along the back wall, several gray metal filing cabinets stood on either side of a closed door. A sign on the door said: OFFICIAL BUSINESS ONLY. Two metal desks sat at opposite ends of the room on the bare concrete floor. One of the desks held a radio dispatch unit. Its speakers blared a steady crackle of static. The other desk had a computer on it. There was a yellow legal pad next to the computer and, on top of it, a sharpened No. 2 pencil.

The young policeman pointed me to a chair by the desk with the computer. He stood right behind me so I couldn't see him. I could only hear him breathe. A couple of minutes went by. I studied the framed photographs on the wall. There was a photograph of the current prime minister and a photograph of the chief commissioner of the Royal Bahamian Police. There were photographs of the seven members of the Eleuthera council. After I had studied all the photographs, I passed the time trying to figure out how I was going to explain my little end run at the airport the day before.

"You see, Inspector, it was pouring down rain and I couldn't tell where I was going. The next thing I knew I was out on the road and . . ."

Of course, that still wouldn't explain why I didn't have proper documentation. But maybe I could talk my way through it.

"All you have to do is call Ruby Booby's. It's this topless joint in Fort Lauderdale and they'll tell you . . ."

I was trying to come up with something better than that when the door on the back wall opened and a broad-shouldered black man in a blue suit and a red tie stepped through it, closing the door behind him. His close-cropped hair was mostly white and so was his mustache, but his face didn't look any older than mine. He was well fed, but he hadn't gone soft. He wore wire-rimmed glasses and clenched his jaw as he walked across the room to the desk where I sat. He did not look at me. He picked up the pencil and spent a minute or two writing something on the yellow legal pad, still standing. Finally, he put down the legal pad, and his eyes met mine.

"Mr. Chasteen . . ."

I stuck out my hand. He shook it with a firm grip, studying my face.

"I'm Lynfield Pederson."

"The inspector?"

He nodded and let go of my hand. He sat on a corner of the desk, looking down at me.

"If you don't mind, Mr. Chasteen, I need to see some identification. Passport will do, along with the yellow form you got when you came through immigration."

"Sorry," I said. "Didn't bring that with me."

"Oh?" said Pederson.

"No, Barney Fife here was in a hurry."

I turned and smiled at the young policeman. He didn't smile back.

Pederson said, "But you do have documentation, don't you?"

"Why wouldn't I?" I said.

Pederson studied my face some more, chewing his lip. And then he said: "Mr. Chasteen, I'll get right to it. We have found a body . . ."

He paused, and in that instant I was just a speck on the ceiling looking down. The room was spinning, the damn fluorescent light was flickering. I was tiny—deep inside myself. Barbara, oh my God . . .

And then I heard him saying, "It is the body of a man."

"A man?"

"A man we believe to be a Mr. Bryce Gannon. Do you know Mr. Gannon?"

"I know of him. What about Barbara?"

Pederson rubbed his mustache. He looked straight at me. I looked straight at him.

"How do you know *of* Bryce Gannon, Mr. Chasteen?"

"He was a friend of . . . a friend."

"That would be . . ." Pederson looked at his legal pad. "That would be Barbara Pickering?"

"Yes, where is she?"

"But you did not personally know Mr. Gannon?"

"No, I did not."

"And Barbara Pickering, would you know where we might find her?"

"No, I just asked you if—"

"Why is that, Mr. Chasteen?"

"Why is what?"

"Why don't you know where she is?"

"Because . . ." I let it hang. And then I said, "Where did you find the body?"

Pederson stood. He walked away from me, hands folded behind his back. When he reached the filing cabinets, he turned around and said, "I'd prefer not to discuss the details at this time. And I'd prefer to ask the questions here."

He said, "What was your relationship with Barbara Pickering?"

"Was?"

"Is. Sorry."

"She's a friend. A very good friend."

"Exclusively?"

"Excuse me?"

"You saw her exclusively? And she you?"

"Yes, I . . . it's not like I . . ."

"I understand you were released from Baypoint Federal Prison Camp, let me see . . ." Pederson studied his legal pad. "The day before yesterday, is that right?"

I nodded.

"And when did you last see Ms. Pickering?"

"It was late yesterday afternoon, just after I arrived on-island. She was down on the beach."

"And did you speak with her at that time?"

"No, I didn't."

"But you saw her?"

"Yes, I was watching her through binoculars."

"Through binoculars?"

"Yes, she was on the beach, working. There was a photo shoot . . ."

"Ms. Pickering is editor of a magazine, is that correct?"

"Not exactly. She owns a magazine, several of them."

"And Bryce Gannon worked for her?"

"He's a photographer. Was a photographer. A freelancer from London. He and Barbara used to . . ." I stopped.

And Pederson said, "They used to what, Mr. Chasteen?"

"They used to be engaged."

Pederson walked back to his desk and scrawled something on the legal pad.

"And you were watching the two of them through binoculars, is that right?"

"I wasn't spying on them, if that's what you are getting at."

"Oh?"

"No. I was just . . . watching them. Just seeing where they were. And then I went down on the beach looking for them."

"You went looking for Ms. Pickering and Bryce Gannon?"

"No, just Barbara. Ms. Pickering. Look . . ."

"Yes, Mr. Chasteen?"

"Are you suggesting that I had something to do with Bryce Gannon's murder?"

"No one has said anything about a murder."

"You said you found his body."

"Yes."

I stood up from the chair. The young policeman stepped beside me.

"Listen, goddamit, I want to know where Barbara is."

Pederson stepped across the room and stood in front of me. I had a couple of inches on him. He didn't seem the least bit intimidated by it. He spoke in a low voice, "I want to know where she is, too."

Pederson picked up his legal pad and tucked it under an arm. He looked at the young policeman.

"Brindley," he said. "I want you to stay here with Mr. Chasteen."

Then he walked to the door.

"Wait a damn minute," I said. Pederson stopped and turned around. "Am I under arrest?"

"No, you are not. But it would please me very much if you would remain right here until I return."

He stepped outside, got in the white van, and drove away.

25

There was a clock on the wall. I watched it. Lynfield Pederson left at 11:20 A.M. About thirty minutes later, the churches let out, and people began passing by on Gaol Street. A couple of young kids stopped and looked inside the window, and when they saw me sitting there, they started giggling and pointing, and more kids came and looked and giggled, and finally Brindley got up and pulled the blinds shut. I sat there some more, listening to the static and occasional chatter coming from the radio and re-studying the photographs on the wall.

At 12:30 P.M., an advisory from BASRA, the Bahamas Air Sea Rescue Association, broke in to say Tropical Storm Curt was located five hundred miles east of the Turks and Caicos Islands and moving almost due west.

At 12:47 P.M. Brindley undid the chin strap on his helmet and took off the helmet and began polishing it with a cloth he took from a desk drawer.

At 1:03 P.M. a woman's voice broke through on the radio.

"Harbour Island, this is Nassau. Harbour Island . . ."

Brindley clicked on the mike.

"Harbour Island. Good day."

"Good day. You got anything to log?"

"No, everything quiet."

The woman on the other end said something I couldn't understand, and Brindley said something back and I couldn't understand that either. They talked for a little bit and I never made out a bit of it. Then Brindley clicked off the mike.

We sat there some more.

At 1:22 P.M. the phone rang. Brindley answered it and I heard him say, "No. I'll have him call you." Then he hung up.

At 1:35 P.M. I told Brindley I needed to use the rest room. He stood, put on his helmet, and opened the door that said OFFICIAL BUSINESS ONLY. He motioned me forward and I stepped through the door and into a room that was dark. Brindley flipped on a light. I saw that the room was really a garage. It was hot and stuffy. I saw a gun case with three rifles in it. I saw a pile of tools—shovels and rakes and hoes. I saw a shiny red Yamaha motor scooter sitting by the garage door. I saw a blue tarpaulin covering something on the floor. I looked some more and saw that the tarpaulin was covering a body. Water pooled around it, seeping into the porous concrete.

Brindley nodded me toward the bathroom. I stepped in and pulled the door closed behind me. Brindley opened the door halfway. He stood outside while I did my official business. Then we walked back into the other room, and I sat down at the desk with the computer on it and watched the clock some more. Brindley took off his helmet and went to work on it with the cloth.

At 2:25 P.M. the white Mitsubishi van pulled back out front and Lynfield Pederson stepped into the office. He was no longer wearing his suit jacket. His red tie was loosened and his white shirtsleeves were rolled up above his elbows. His yellow legal pad was tucked under one arm and he carried a tall paper sack with both hands. He put the paper sack on the desk where I was sitting. He sat down on the other side of the desk and opened the paper sack.

"You hungry, Brindley?" he asked.

Brindley said, "I could eat some."

I thought I had handled myself pretty well so far. For three hours I'd sat there. I had been giggled at by small children. I had seen Bryce Gannon's body in the back room. And I was trying not to go crazy worrying about Barbara.

I slammed a fist on the desk. Pederson looked at me.

"Did you find Barbara?" I said.

Pederson turned to Brindley. He said, "Why don't you run home, Brindley, get yourself some lunch? I'll sit here and talk with Mr. Chasteen awhile."

Brindley strapped on his helmet and stepped to the door.

"And on your way back here, go by the fish house," said Pederson. "Tell Mr. Otis we're going to need his freezer. Tell him it might be for a couple of days. Tell him he'll get twenty-five dollars a day."

"You want me to take the dead man there?"

"You eat first. Then we'll both take him."

Brindley left. Pederson finished tearing open the paper sack. He took out two Styrofoam bowls that were covered with aluminum foil. He took out two plastic spoons. He slid one of the bowls and one of the spoons to my side of the desk.

"You like conch salad?" he said.

I nodded. I sat down.

"This the best you gonna find. Lavaughn, down at the Queen Conch stand, she just made it. I had her put hot pepper sauce on it. That alright? Lavaughn makes that sauce herself."

"That's fine, thanks. How much I owe you for it?"

"Don't owe me nothing. Just figured you were hungry, might need a little something after sitting here all that time."

I took the foil off the bowl. The conch salad was heaped high in the bowl—big chunks of white and pink conch meat and tiny chunks of green pepper and onion. I dipped the spoon into the marinade and took a sip and tasted the sour orange juice and the pepper sauce. It was some good sauce alright. Then I dug in with the spoon and ate for a couple of minutes. I had to chew on the left side of my mouth because the other side was where the shovel had broken my teeth. But it didn't slow me down much. When I was half finished with the conch salad, I took a break.

"So this is how you do it, huh?" I asked Pederson.

"Do what?"

"Play good cop, bad cop. But you only got a two-man department. And Brindley isn't the sharpest knife in the drawer. So you have to play the good cop and the bad cop."

"Brindley is my nephew."

"Sorry, no offense."

"None taken. He don't know shit about police work."

"But he looks good in that uniform."

Pederson laughed.

"That he does, that he does. He sit here polishing his helmet for you?"

"Uh-huh."

"He good at polishing. He can polish hell out of that helmet. He's my sister's boy. He does what I tell him. That counts for a lot."

I ate the rest of the conch salad and waited for Pederson to finish his. When he was done he reached into his suit pocket and pulled out some toothpicks. He offered me one and I took it. We sat there picking our teeth, Pederson watching me, then saying, "I don't have to play bad cop with you anymore."

"Why's that?"

"Because now I know you didn't kill that man."

26

Pederson flicked his toothpick in a wastebasket by the desk.

"So you're telling me that Bryce Gannon was definitely murdered?"

"Oh, most definitely. You want to look at the body?"

"Not particularly."

"Don't blame you. I didn't like looking at it either. Gunshot tore off half his face. Shotgun, probably a 12-gauge. Got shot three times. Once here . . ." Pederson patted the back of his head. "Once in the shoulder. And once in his right leg. Fisherman pulled him out of the water first thing this morning, all the way south near Hawk Cay Cut. Body could have floated from damn near anywhere, tides running the way they are.

"I'm thinking he was already in the water when he got shot. And someone was standing in a boat shooting down at him. Because there wasn't any gravel or sand in any of the wounds. But that's just a guess. There's still a lot I don't know."

Pederson picked up our bowls and dropped them in the trash can. He cleaned off the desktop with a paper napkin.

"One thing I don't know," he said. "I don't know where Ms. Pickering is."

I sat there and took it all in. And then I said, "You checked Gannon's room?"

"Checked it first thing," Pederson said. "Just like you checked it last night."

Pederson watched me. I watched him back. He said, "You want, I can tell you everything you did last night."

"That's up to you."

"Then I think I'll give you a little rundown. Just so you can verify it. And just so you'll know what I was doing for the past three hours while you were sitting here letting Brindley entertain you. It's how I know it wasn't you who killed that man."

So he went through what he knew. He knew it all. He picked it up from when I had watched Barbara through the binoculars and took it through me pulling Lord Downey from the ocean and taking him home. He knew that I sat at the Albury Beach Club bar from seven-thirty until approximately eight-thirty, at which point I walked to the Bahama Sands, arriving in the company of one Nixon Styles.

"That Nixon, he's a piece of work, isn't he?" said Pederson.

"Yes, he is."

"He's my wife's cousin."

"You related to everyone on the island?"

"Nah, only about half," said Pederson. "Wilson Bonner, I'm not related to him."

"Who's he?"

"Security guard at the Bahama Sands, the one came upon you trying to break into Bryce Gannon's room."

"I wasn't trying to break in. I was just seeing if . . . seeing if Barbara and Gannon were there."

"Uh-huh. And when you left there it was about 9:40 P.M. You walked down Barrack Street. You stopped to take a leak in the wax myrtle bushes right before Barrack Street crosses with High Street. And then you walked on the left-hand side of the street straight from there back to the Albury."

"How you know all that?"

"Because Wilson followed you. He was getting off work anyway. Didn't have anything else to do. You oughta be glad he did it. Otherwise, you'd have a little gap in there where I couldn't account for you," he said. "Mr. Pindle said he saw you going up to your cottage. Said about ten-thirty he heard you hollering about something. Said he went up there to check, make sure everything was alright, only when he got there you were asleep on the bed. What was it you were you hollering about?"

"Just hollering."

"Uh-huh," he said. "A man does that sometimes."

And then I remembered something.

"There was a woman, I don't know who she was," I said. "But someone told me she left the Bahama Sands with Barbara and Gannon."

"Yeah, that's right. Woman name of . . ." Pederson flipped pages on his legal pad. "Name of Tiffani St. James. And that is Tiffani with an 'i' on the end. Age nineteen, but plays it much older. I talked to her already. She's a houseguest of Burma Downey's. According to Ms. St. James, Bryce Gannon offered to give her a ride back to the Downey house in his golf cart, and Ms. Pickering rode with them. Ms. St. James said they dropped her off a little after 8 P.M. and that was the last she saw of them."

"You believe her?"

"No reason not to. Ms. Downey and a friend vouched for her whereabouts."

Pederson stepped to the window and opened the blinds. The afternoon sun was blazing in across North Eleuthera Sound. He looked at the water awhile. Then he closed the blinds and turned to face me.

"I know you pulled something funny at the airport yesterday," he said. "No record of you passing through immigration. Ought to lock you up just for lying to me about that."

"I didn't lie to you."

"You said you had the papers. You said you left them in your room."

"No, I said I didn't bring them with me. Which I didn't. Because I don't have any."

"Now you talking shit. I can still lock you up."

So I told Pederson all about the fake Chip Willis and the

limo. And when I got finished, he asked me, "What happened to your face?"

So I told him all about that, too.

And then he said, "Victor Ortiz, huh?"

"You know him?"

"No, just know about him. Good friend of mine's the inspector in Freeport. Know he wasn't ever convinced that Ortiz was one of those dead men they dragged out of that house."

I said, "Me neither. I hauled five of them over, only four bodies were ever accounted for. Math was off somewhere."

"Yeah," said Pederson. "Things have a way of not adding up once Nassau police step in. And they step in everywhere there appears to be a profit. Word has it that Ortiz and his bunch were carrying some serious money on them."

"You saying he paid his way out?"

"I'm not saying shit. I just know that whole thing was a cluster fuck once Nassau got involved, including what happened to you."

"It's over and done," I said.

"Yeah, but it's why I'm gonna play it close with this one."

"What you mean?"

"I mean, I haven't told Nassau about this yet."

"You haven't reported Bryce Gannon getting shot?"

Pederson shook his head. I got up from the chair. I walked toward the window and, halfway there, I turned around and went back to the desk and stood looking down at Pederson.

"Look, Barbara is missing. And I don't like the idea of you dicking around."

He stood up and put both hands on the desk and squared off facing me.

"I don't dick around," he said.

"Then call in the F.B.I.," I said. "Gannon's British. Ought to call in Scotland Yard, too."

"Yeah, ought to. But if I want to call in anyone, then that goes through Nassau. And, Nassau gets involved, they will fuck it up. You ought to know that as good as anyone."

He was right. I had the Nassau police to thank for the fact that Victor Ortiz was still breathing air.

"You got any ideas about finding Barbara?"

"Not a one. I can't even honestly tell you that I believe she's still alive."

There, he'd said it. I'd been thinking it. I sat down in the chair. Pederson sat down, too. He gave me a minute. Finally, I said: "How long you think you can play it close?"

"Not long. A couple-three days on the outside. Everyone I talked to, I told them to keep it tight."

"Yeah, what are the chances of that?"

"Better than you might think. Brilanders are Brilanders. Might talk amongst themselves, damn sure might do that. But if I spread the word that I don't want them letting it out, then they won't be letting it out," Pederson said. "I'm going to take care of this myself."

"I'm going to find Barbara."

Pederson smiled.

"Always good when two men know what they're going to do."

27

Pederson offered me a ride back to the Albury, but I told him I'd
walk. I don't know why I told him that, because I was bone
tired, and there is nothing I remember about the walk except
that one moment I was stepping into the late afternoon sunlight
on Gaol Street, and the next moment I was in the bathroom at
the cottage taking off my clothes. I got in the shower and turned
on the taps full blast. After I'd lathered and rinsed, I sat down
on the tile floor and let the hot water beat on the back of my
neck. I closed my eyes and put my head in my hands and let the
steam roll up and cover me. I tried to get lost in it.

I don't know the last time I cried and it didn't happen then. I
tried, but I just couldn't. I'm not sure what that says about me,
except maybe it means I wasn't feeling hopeless. I was more
optimistic about things than Lynfield Pederson. Still, there was
this gnawing hole, this big emptiness, this looming uncertainty,
and I was glad I hadn't looked at Bryce Gannon's body, because
I didn't want to even begin imagining Barbara meeting that
same end. It hurts—wanting to cry, not being able to. It hurts
worse than crying. The long, hot shower felt good.

I was getting dressed when I heard a knock at the door. Mr.

Pindle spoke from outside, saying there was a call for me in the main house. When I got there and picked up the phone in the parlor, Clarissa Percival said hello and told me she had heard about Bryce Gannon and Barbara, and she was sorry to disturb me. She said she was calling on behalf of Burma Downey.

"Ms. Downey was hoping that you could come down here," said Clarissa, "as soon as it's convenient."

It took me fifteen minutes to walk down Front Street to the Downey compound. Clarissa escorted me across the grounds to one of the stilt houses. It was painted a bright pink. A couple of times, Clarissa dabbed at her eyes with a tissue. She didn't speak, and I didn't attempt to make small talk.

A golf cart sat on a concrete slab under the pink house, next to a massive air-conditioning unit. We walked up a wooden staircase that led to the front door. It opened before we got to it and a young woman—surfer-girl blonde, sparkly green eyes, big and healthy—motioned us inside.

She looked me up and down.

"Whoa, you're a big one, aren't you?"

I've never known what to say when people tell me this, so I just smiled and followed her as she led us down a hallway. She wore a long white cotton shift and I could see her orange bikini under it. She was barefoot and she walked with a bounce. A lot of bounces, actually. I think the bounciness meant that everything she had was real. She had a lot.

Two women were waiting for us in the living room. One of them stood and she was taller even than the blonde who showed us in. Every bit of six feet. She wore a tight wraparound skirt over what looked like a black unitard. It showed off a fine physique, the result of dedicated training. Muscles where she needed them, not a bit of flab. Maybe a few too many muscles, but then I am prejudiced about too many muscles in women, so sue me. She wore her black hair straight and long, and parted severely in the middle. A single gold hoop dangled from each of her ears. The other woman, I could only presume, was Burma Downey. She sat in a wheelchair, facing away from us, looking out a picture window toward the ocean. I could see only the back of her white hooded robe.

"I'm Zoe Applequist," said the woman with the long black hair. She pronounced Zoe so it rhymed with "no way." She gestured to the blonde. "This is Tiffani St. James."

Tiffani waved a hand and plopped down on a leather couch. Pederson was right. She didn't look nineteen. But then none of them do these days.

There was a glass-top coffee table in front of the couch, and Tiffani put her feet on it, but quickly removed them when Zoe Applequist shot her a look. Tiffani crossed her long legs at the knees, and when she did it she looked at me and rolled her eyes. As if we were coconspirators against the tyranny of those who don't like smudge marks on their glass-top coffee tables. I think it meant she liked me. Yes, Chasteen, you've still got it. You're not yet invisible to the sweet young things. Give it time. You'll fade.

There was a whirring sound, the wheelchair spun around, and Burma Downey sat facing us. I tried not to look shocked, but I didn't pull it off. I've never seen so many bandages on a person. Except for the tip of her sharp fine nose and her full lips, her entire face was enshrouded by gauze. She wore big amber sunglasses that covered her eyes. No hair showed from beneath the hooded robe. There were casts on both of her legs, below the knees, and on both of her arms, below the elbows. It hurt just to look at her.

She raised an arm and made a V with two fingers. Zoe Applequist shook a cigarette from a pack on the coffee table, lit it, and nestled it between the two fingers. Burma Downey took a long drag and exhaled slowly. I noticed a small chalkboard sitting on her lap and on it a piece of yellow chalk.

"Please sit," Zoe Applequist told me, and I found a chair. She ignored Clarissa, who hung back on the other side of the room. "Care for a drink, Mr. Chasteen?"

"Rum, if you have it," I said.

Zoe Applequist looked at Tiffani, and Tiffani made a cute little pout and uncrossed her legs and got up from the couch. A long counter separated the living room from a small kitchen and there were bottles sitting on it. Tiffani walked to the counter, bouncing all the way.

"Neat," I called after her.

Tiffani turned and smiled.

"Thanks," she said.

It was Zoe Applequist's turn to roll her eyes.

"He means no ice with the rum, Tiffani," she said. "Just pour it in a glass and bring it to him."

No one said anything while Tiffani poured the rum—it was Myers's, not my favorite, too heavy on the molasses. She walked back across the room and handed me the glass.

"Neat-o," she said. She sat back down on the couch.

Zoe Applequist said, "As you may know, Mr. Chasteen, Burma was injured. She can't speak."

"I understand that." I nodded at Burma Downey. "Sorry about your accident."

She didn't respond. She seemed to have forgotten about her cigarette. The ash was long and, as I watched, it fell on the chalkboard. Zoe picked up the chalkboard and swept the ashes into a wastebasket by the couch.

"Burma, honey, do you really want that cigarette?" Zoe said.

The gauze-wrapped head under the hood moved, almost imperceptibly. I took it for a yes. And if I had to guess, I'd say Burma Downey was doped to the gills. Maybe I'd be doped up, too, if I had wrong with me all that she had wrong with her.

"I will tell you what I know and Burma will help out as she can," said Zoe. "Yesterday evening, after you left here, we discovered that Lord Downey was missing. Again." She looked across the room at Clarissa, who kept her eyes on the floor. "We were alarmed, certainly. We began looking for him immediately, but had to stop when it got late. We went out again this morning. We combed the island, but couldn't find him. When we got back here, it was shortly before noon, and we found this."

Zoe Applequist reached in a pocket of her skirt and pulled out a shiny chrome cell phone. She handed it to me. I looked at it. Just a cell phone, nothing special. I gave it back to her.

"It was sitting on top of a post by the gate. We didn't think anything of it, thought that someone, one of the groundskeepers, maybe, had left it by accident. We brought it inside with us, set it right there on the coffee table, and a little while later it began to ring. I answered it.

"There was a man on the other end. He asked to speak to Burma. I told him that Burma was unable to talk, but that I would gladly take a message. Then the man became very abusive. He said, 'I know she can't talk, but she can fucking listen, can't she?'

"So I hung up the phone. But it rang again. I answered, and it was the same man, and he said, 'The old man is going to fucking die. We'll kill him. Let me speak to his daughter.'

"So I gave the phone to Burma. And the man said what he had to say. I tried to listen and I could hear part of it, but afterwards I had Burma write down everything. This is it, this is what he told her."

Zoe handed me a sheet of paper. The words were written in pen with a shaky hand:

We have your father and Barbara Pickering. We want two million dollars. We will call again.

I stared at the writing on the paper until I heard Zoe say, "When they left the cell phone, they left something else, too."

She reached into her pocket and pulled out a scarf. She handed it to me. It was a long purplish scarf. With tiny dolphins on it. Lucky ones.

28

I sat back in the chair. I let out some air. It was more than just a sigh. It was like something had popped loose inside and I could finally get rid of it. Barbara was alive. Alive. The scarf wasn't much of a connection, but it was all I had. I rubbed it against my cheek. It was damp and smelled of brine, not Barbara. I smoothed it out and folded it and tucked it away in the pocket of my shorts.

Then I finished the rum.

"More?" asked Tiffani.

"Please," I said.

I handed the sheet of paper back to Zoe. She said, "The man called back an hour later. And he insisted on speaking to Burma again. This is what he told her the second time." She handed me another sheet of paper.

It said: "Show us we have a deal. Have two hundred fifty thousand dollars ready by Monday. We'll be in touch."

Tiffani returned with my rum and another smile.

I asked Zoe, "Have you called the police about this?"

Before she could answer, there was a grunt from the wheel-chair, and I saw Burma shaking and the cigarette dropping from her hand. As Zoe picked it up and snubbed it out, Burma reached down for the chalk and wrote something on the chalkboard. Zoe took the chalkboard, read it, and then showed it to me.

"NO POLICE!" it said.

Zoe patted Burma on the shoulder.

"It's alright, honey, it's alright." And then she turned to me. "Burma and I have discussed this. It is her wish to not inform the police. She does not trust them. She does not want to risk the life of her father. And I am sure that you do not wish to endanger your friend's life, either."

"So what do you propose we do?"

Burma Downey scribbled again on the chalkboard. This time it said: "GET THE MONEY."

I stayed there for another hour and we talked about getting the money.

The first two hundred fifty thousand dollars wouldn't be a problem, Zoe Applequist told me. She said they could have it by the next morning. She said she had talked it over with Burma and she felt certain that, given a few days, and depending on how quickly the bankers in London moved, they could put together another seven hundred fifty thousand dollars, totaling their half of what the man on the phone had demanded.

Which meant I had to come up with a million dollars.

I told them I didn't have that kind of money. I didn't get specific, but I made them understand I wasn't long on liquid assets. I say "them," but it was mostly Zoe Applequist. Burma Downey just sat there and smoked cigarettes. Tiffani St. James just sat there. Every now and then she would pout or readjust her legs.

"Surely Ms. Pickering has resources, doesn't she?" asked Zoe.

Yes, I told her, she did. But I told her I knew nothing about Barbara's finances. That was her business.

Burma wrote something on her chalkboard and held it up.

"JEWELRY?" it said.

"Barbara's not big on jewelry," I told her. "She might have something in a safe-deposit box, but I couldn't even tell you where it is."

"Relatives, next of kin?" asked Zoe.

I told her Barbara's mother had died two years earlier and that, as far I knew, she had no other relatives.

"Then you'll have to contact her attorney," said Zoe.

I had no idea who Barbara's attorney was, but I told Zoe I would make some calls and go from there. That didn't leave us much else to talk about. We were playing a waiting game. Waiting on that cell phone to ring again so the man could tell us what to do next. I told them I would stay there until the call came. We were all in this together.

"Thanks so much, but it really isn't necessary," said Zoe Applequist. "I'm afraid we're all quite exhausted. If anything happens, we'll get in touch."

She stood, and I got up to shake her hand, but she gave me a hug instead. I hugged back. It was like hugging a steel girder. The woman was solid. She told me, "We must keep this quiet. Do you understand?"

Actually, I didn't understand. And I wasn't sure I agreed. I was ready to call in the troops. This was bigger and more dangerous than we could handle. But before I could say anything, Tiffani got up and gave me a hug, too. It was considerably softer than the one Zoe had given me.

I told Burma Downey good-bye. She scribbled something on her chalkboard.

"THANK YOU," it said.

29

Funny how you can hold things together when you have to. The whole time I was inside Burma Downey's house, I was Zack the Detached, absorbing the details of the kidnapping and coolly discussing a plan to come up with the ransom. The moment I stepped outside I became Zack the Zombie. I walked away in a daze, not paying attention to where I was going. Instead of heading out through the compound gate and on the road back to town, I wound up by the dunes.

I sat down in the sand and looked at the ocean, trying to focus, trying to get my mind to settle down long enough to figure everything out. But my thoughts, wild and awful thoughts, were shooting in all directions, like someone was poking my brain with a hot wire every time I almost got a handle on things. The whole world was jumpy and spinning, and I sat there clenched up, unable to set it right again.

Once, when I was just fifteen or sixteen, a rich guy from Orlando asked me to crew on his sailboat during the Coronado Cup, this big-deal offshore regatta the Minorca Yacht Club sponsors every year. We were on the last leg of the course, a haul-ass spinnaker run to Coronado Inlet, when a squall line blew in out of nowhere. In half an instant the wind shifted, the boat jibed, the mast snapped, and the spinnaker began filling with water, threatening to suck the boat down after it. That was the first time I ever confronted real, true panic. There was an excruciating moment when everything inside of me was going helter-skelter while I stood there frozen, utterly incapable of action. Then came a calmness as I realized: It could be worse. It's not my boat. And I'm not going to drown. The next thing I knew I was up on the foredeck, cutting the spinnaker sheets. Someone cranked the engine and we made it in just fine.

Slowly, sitting there in the dunes, that same calmness returned. This wasn't going to suck me down. Things could be worse. Less than twenty-four hours ago I thought Barbara had run off with another man. Then he turned up dead and I feared Barbara might be dead, too. But the situation had improved. Hell, things were downright rosy: Barbara was alive. And I was going to get her back. Just a matter of finding a million dollars.

I got up and walked through the compound toward the road. Clarissa Percival was pulling away in a golf cart. She stopped when she saw me and offered a ride back to the Albury. We weren't a hundred yards down Front Street when Clarissa broke down in sobs. She pulled the golf cart onto the side of the road. I let her cry awhile.

Finally, she said, "They blame me. They say it's my fault."

"It's not your fault. Someone came in and kidnapped him."

"But I left him, I left him there. And then they came and took him. And now . . ."

She cried some more. When she was done I asked her to tell me how it had happened. I had heard a little bit of the story before, but Zoe Applequist had done the talking.

"After you left yesterday evening, I let Lord Downey stay sleeping on the couch," she said. "I didn't want to move him. He looked so peaceful and he hasn't been sleeping well at all lately. So I let him stay there.

"I went to the kitchen to make something for dinner. And that's when the power went out. Do you remember?"

I told Clarissa I didn't remember the power going out in the evening. It had been on at the Albury and elsewhere on the island. I just remembered that it wasn't on when I woke up that morning.

"Well, there's no predicting when or where. It goes out some places and not others. It's a mess, the power on this island. All the time broke up," she said. "So I go looking around in the kitchen for the candles we keep there. But I can't find them. And the kerosene lamp, it's gone, too. Sometimes the power, it can be out for hours, and I didn't want to sit here in the dark. I'm a little bit afraid of it, you know?"

She laughed a sad laugh.

"Sometimes, when Lord Downey was feeling better, he'd play tricks on me. Everyone, they know I'm scared of the dark. And he'd go flipping off the main power switch just to scare me some, just to see me throw a fit. They'd all get a laugh out of that. Then he'd flip it back on and laugh some more. Oh, that man . . ."

Just thinking about him made her cry a little bit more and then she calmed down again.

"So last night I got on the phone and I called my mother. She only just lives down the road. She said she had power, but if I came down there, then she'd let me borrow her lamp and some candles.

"So I went down there. And I wasn't gone long. It couldn't have been ten minutes. I came back here and I went straight in the kitchen and lit the lamp and I cooked dinner. I cooked peas and rice and chicken, and made some johnnycakes. And then I took a plate of it out into the living room, just to see if maybe Lord Downey, he'd like to eat a little. Johnnycakes usually perk him right up. But he was gone."

"What time was that?" I asked her.

"I don't know, maybe then it was eight-thirty or nine. I can't say for sure when they might have come in the house and took him away. Could have been while I was gone, or it could have been while I was in the kitchen. I didn't lock the house. No one on the island ever locks their houses. And they just came in and snatched him up. Poor man, he didn't weigh a thing."

She started crying again.

The no-see-ums were coming out. They were getting in my

hair and biting, and I slapped some off my ankles. They didn't seem to be bothering Clarissa. Or else she was just too upset to notice them.

I asked her, "So when you found him gone, did you go and tell Burma?"

"Not right away, no. I went looking for him first, carrying the lamp. I looked around in the yard. And then I went down on the beach, but not too far. I went by a couple of the neighbors' houses because sometimes before he has gone there. And only after I'd checked all those places did I come back and tell Burma about it. By then it must have been ten o'clock or so. Yes, it was a little after ten because, when I got back here, the power was on, and I had to reset all the clocks."

Clarissa found a tissue in her purse and dried around her eyes.

"How long has Lord Downey been like this?" I asked her.

"You mean the wandering off and all?"

"Yeah, is it something that has just been getting gradually worse or what?"

"No, it came on fast. Just since Burma's accident, actually."

"He was OK before that?"

"Well, he is seventy-eight and he has some troubles. But his mind, it was always alright. I've been taking care of him, let's see, almost a year now. And it has only been in the last month or so that he's gone down. After Burma came back here. The sight of her, it was like that set him off, like it was more than he could handle."

I said, "It's a lot to handle, all those bandages and casts, and her not being able to talk. What do the doctors say?"

Clarissa shrugged.

"I don't know. I don't talk to the doctors. I just barely talk to Burma and her crowd. They keep pretty much to themselves." She shook her head. "They say they can get that two hundred fifty thousand dollars, but I don't know where they can get it from."

"Does Burma have money of her own?"

"No, not that I know of. She's all the time been asking her father for some, especially this last month or so, since the accident. That's one of the reasons they weren't getting along."

"What about Zoe Applequist? Do you think she has money?"

"I don't know much about her. Not much at all. Claims to be a physical therapist or something."

I slapped at the no-see-ums. They were getting worse.

"We get moving, they'll stop biting," Clarissa said.

She turned on the golf cart and pulled back on Front Street. We bumped along for a few blocks. It was almost dark. People were out visiting, enjoying the cool of the day. Most everyone we passed waved or said good evening. We smiled and waved back, as if everything were right with the world.

30

Back at the cottage, I noticed that someone had come in and straightened up and filled the ice bucket with the bottle of Schramsberg in it. I went through a stack of Barbara's things until I found an address book. I looked up Steffie Plank's home phone number, then went down to the main house to give her a call.

One of the Charleston women was using the phone in the salon. She saw me and gave a little wave—I'll just be a minute, dear—and kept on talking. The other Charleston women were sipping cocktails in the salon while their husbands played gin rummy. It looked like a serious game. They had a pad for keeping score and everything. The television was on, but the sound was off, and the picture was all gray and speckly with horizontal bands cycling over and over. Dr. and Mrs. Something-or-Other were chatting with another couple in a corner of the salon by the stereo. Sarah Vaughan was singing, all deep and husky, "I Can't Give You Anything But Love." It was like being back in the 1950s—highballs and card games, songs with sweet lyrics, and shitty TV reception.

No one was sitting at the bar. I sat there.

"Barbancourt?" said Mr. Pindle.

"No, think I'll go light tonight. How about a Kalik?"

"Silver or gold?"

"Silver," I said.

"Smart man. That gold will kick your ass."

"Yeah, I know. It's kicked me before."

"That what kick you last night, made you do all that hollering up there?"

"No, that was rum, all rum. And a little Beefeater's."

"Oh, man. Put the clear on the brown, you wake up with a frown."

"Never heard that one before," I said. "What about you put the brown on the clear?"

"You wake up pissing beer. Or you wake up lost an ear. I've heard it both ways."

Dr. Something-or-Other came for a round of drinks. Mr. Pindle poured them. Dr. Something-or-Other stepped away and Mr. Pindle leaned on the bar by me.

"I heard about the picture man. Some bad business. Things like that don't happen here," he said. "They got any ideas about it?"

I shook my head.

"What about Ms. Pickering?" he asked.

I shrugged. It was better than lying about the kidnapping.

The woman from Charleston finished her telephone conversation. I stood and walked to the salon, but one of the other Charleston women beat me to the phone.

"Do you mind?" she smiled.

She started dialing. I went back to the bar. Sarah Vaughan started singing "Perdido." A busboy was setting tables in the dining room. Chrissie Hineman was making sure all the tables had fresh flowers in their vases. She saw me and rushed over and gave me a hug.

She said, "You OK?"

"Fine," I said. "Just trying to take it all in and figure out what to do next."

"Well, you know Charlie and I are here for you, whatever you need."

After Chrissie stepped away, Mr. Pindle said, "I know some-one who saw 'em."

"Saw who?"

"Ms. Pickering and that Gannon fellow. Last night."

"Who's that?"

"Jesteen, works in the kitchen, the one gave you the orange juice this morning. She saw 'em on her way home last night. Ms. Pickering, the picture man, and this blonde woman. In a golf cart. The blonde woman driving, the picture man up front with her, Ms. Pickering in the back."

"The blonde woman was driving?"

"That's what Jesteen said."

That seemed a little off. I thought Bryce Gannon had offered to give Tiffani St. James a ride. That's what Tiffani had told Lynfield Pederson.

"Has Jesteen gone and told Lynfield Pederson about this?"

"I don't know about that. I suspect not. Most people, they wait until the police come to them. Not the other way around."

The young woman in the starched blue uniform came out and rang her little bell. People started making their way toward the dining room. The Charleston woman was still talking on the phone.

I asked Mr. Pindle, "What do you think of him?"

"Who, Pederson? I like him alright. He plays it pretty straight. Not a man you want to cross though." Mr. Pindle took my empty Kalik and brought me another one. "You knew him when you were playing ball, didn't you?"

"Knew who?"

"Lynfield Pederson, man. Who you think?"

"He played football?"

"Yeah."

"Where?"

"Florida Gators, just like you. About the same time, too. At least, that's what he said."

"He said he played football with me?"

"He don't have to say it, I know it. I remember when he went off there. Maybe twenty years ago. Stories about it in the paper here. Some kinda news when a boy from Harbour Island starts playing football for a big college team."

"You sure about that?"

"Yeah, I'm sure. But why don't you just ask him?" said Mr. Pindle. "There he is."

I turned to see Lynfield Pederson striding across the salon toward the bar. He had gotten rid of his suit and tie and was wearing a plain white T-shirt and khaki shorts. He didn't look particularly happy. Matter of fact, he looked mad as hell.

"Speaking of the devil," I said.

"You ain't begun to see the fucking devil yet," said Pederson. "We need to talk."

31

"So when were you planning on letting me know about this shit, huh?"

We had gone back to the cottage to talk. Only I wasn't doing much talking. Mostly I was listening to Lynfield Pederson unload on me for not telling him about the phone calls from the man who wanted two million for Barbara and Lord Downey.

"I just found out about it," I said. "It isn't like I've been sitting on it. I just got back here a little while ago."

"And so you went down there and you were sitting at the bar, drinking, and then you were getting ready to go in and eat dinner. And then maybe sometime when you got around to it, after dessert maybe, or after you drank a glass of cognac, then you were going to let me know?"

"I was waiting to use the phone. They've only got one phone here, you know."

"And you were going to call me?"

"Who else would I call?"

He looked at me, eyes narrowed.

"You got a way of worming around a question. I almost took that for a yes."

He reached into a shirt pocket and pulled out a toothpick. He chewed on it. And then he said, "But I'll give you that one. I still don't believe you. But I'll give it to you."

"Thanks," I said. "So how'd you find out about the phone calls?"

"Got my sources," said Pederson.

"That would be Clarissa Percival?" I said.

"My, my," he said. "You're pretty good."

"Process of elimination. It wasn't me. And it wasn't those three other women. Had to be her. She one of your cousins, too?"

"Not hardly."

He arched his eyebrows, smiled.

"Oh?" I said.

"Me and Clarissa," he said. "We're friendly-friendly."

"I'm envious."

"Oughta be."

"Thought you had a wife."

"I do." He gave it a beat. "She stays in Nassau. Says she likes it better there. I like her better there, too."

"Nice arrangement."

"No, it isn't nice. It's got-damn expensive, that's what it is. It's why I have to rely on graft and corruption to pay my bills." He worked the toothpick around in his mouth. "That's a joke, Chasteen."

"I'm laughing," I said. "So what do you make of it all?"

"Meaning, who do I think the bad guys are?"

"For starters."

"Don't have a clue. All I've got is guesses. And my best guess is that it's someone who wants two million."

"Impressive," I said. "You get an A in deductive reasoning at Gainesville?"

Pederson sat there studying me. His mouth worked into a grin.

"Actually, it was Logic 101 and 102 and, yeah, I aced them both." Then he said, "Wondering when you were going to make that UF connection."

"I'm still making it, still kinda foggy. How come you didn't mention it before?"

"Didn't want to embarrass you," he said.

"Embarrass me how? For not remembering you?"

"No," said Pederson. "Embarrass you when you did remember me and how I knocked you on your ass."

"You knocked me on my ass?"

"Uh-huh. Flat on your ass."

"When was that?"

"Oh, I'd say it was about twenty-two years ago, almost twenty-two years ago exactly."

"Twenty-two years ago, I was . . . I would have been a senior."

"Uh-huh, I know that. I was a freshman."

"You played ball?"

"I did."

"And you knocked me on my ass?"

"I did indeed."

"Sorry," I said. "But you're gonna have to refresh my memory."

"Be glad to. It's alright you don't remember me, I was hardly worth remembering. Just a walk-on freshman, playing on the scrimmage team. It was a Wednesday, before the opening game. Against Southwest Louisiana."

"We beat them forty-eight–zip."

"Uh-huh, and to get warmed up for it they threw the freshmen meat against the first team. Our first offensive series we ran a quarterback draw that ripped up the middle and went all the way. Mainly because you got taken out of the play. And Coach Rowlin . . ."

"Howlin' Rowlin . . ."

"That's him, he chewed your ass out. Chewed it out up and down. Wanted to know how you could have possibly missed tackling that quarterback. And you remember what you told him?"

"No, what?"

"You said, 'That right guard threw a pretty good block.' You didn't make up any excuses. You just told it like it was."

"And you were the right guard."

"I was. And I did throw a pretty good block. One of the best damn blocks I ever threw."

"Mmmm."

"You still don't remember, do you?"

"No, sorry."

"That's alright. Doesn't matter. Got me a little notice with the coaches though, blocking out a preseason second-string All-American. Got me some playing time on the freshman team. And come the end of the season they offered me some scholarship money."

"You move up the next year?"

"Was going to," said Pederson. "Only I screwed up my hip next spring at the Orange and Blue game. Didn't play after that. But they made good on the scholarship. Paid for my full ride. Got a degree in criminology and public administration."

"How'd you wind up here?"

"Oh, I was raised on Harbour Island. Came time for high school though, I went to Miami and lived with my aunt. Played at Coral Gables. Then went on up to Gainesville. Got out, I worked Miami PD for three years. Hated it. Got word the inspector here was retiring and I was first in line for the job. Been at it going on fifteen years now."

Pederson looked around the room.

"You got anything to drink besides gin and champagne?" he said.

"I got ice and I got water," I said.

"I'll take some of that."

I poured him a glass and one for myself.

I asked him, "So you got any other guesses about who we're up against here?"

"Got a couple. They say what the man on the phone sounded like?"

"No, they didn't. I didn't ask," I said. "I should have asked."

"Yeah, you should have. But what you really should have done was call me up while you were sitting there and told me what was going on, and then I would have come over there and asked the questions that needed asking."

I said, "You want, we can go there right now and find out. Let's go."

"Nah, that'll wait until morning. I got plenty else to keep me busy tonight."

"You think it could be somebody here on island?"

"No, I don't. I don't think that at all. Don't know why I don't think it. Just don't. Just know the people. Just don't think there's anyone here would pull something like that," he said. "Now, up on French Jug . . . that's a different story."

"French Jug?"

"A few islands north, other side of Bitter Channel, about a thirty-minute run by boat. Another old Loyalist community. Only it's Loyalist through and through."

"Meaning?"

"Meaning, French Juggers don't exactly embrace the concept of ethnic diversity. You won't find any black folks living there. Hell, you won't find any white folks living there unless they had family on French Jug two hundred and fifty years ago."

"Family tree doesn't have any branches, huh?"

"Oh it's got branches. Exactly four of them. Got the Hailes, got the Crowes, got the Blounts, and got the Snows. And they're all twisted together and growing in on themselves. You aren't one of them, then you aren't living on French Jug."

"They don't let anyone else on the island?"

"Oh, you can go visit. There's a marina and a restaurant and a bar and some shops. Even got a little museum about the history of French Jug and all that. People on French Jug, they aren't going to turn down tourist dollars. Especially now."

"Why now?"

"Let's just say their traditional source of revenue has been drying up."

"Smuggling?"

"The drug part of it, anyway. Back some years ago, in the heydays, there were a lot of millionaire lobster fishermen living on French Jug. Then the drug business got centralized and streamlined, and there wasn't room for freelancers running boats anymore. Some of them, they started hauling Haitians, but there's not nearly as much money in that. So they're scrambling. Some of them are actually forced to go fishing lobster. Some of them are just petty got-dam criminals. I've hauled a few of them in for stealing boats and breaking into houses here on Harbour Island, that sort of thing."

"So you think it could be someone from French Jug?"

"Nothing says it is and nothing says it isn't." Pederson drained the water in his glass and shook loose an ice cube and chewed on it. "You know who I'd put my money on?"

"Victor Ortiz?"

"You got it," Pederson said. "Knowing what little I know and knowing what you told me—not that I can believe all of your shit, but I am looking at those black eyes of yours—then I'd say Ortiz is squeezing you."

"That's what I've been thinking, too. Only I don't know what he's squeezing me for."

"You got something he wants."

"It damn sure isn't money," I said.

"Could be something that you know."

"Yeah, but if it was something I knew and he didn't want me to know it, then all he'd have to do is kill me. And he could have done that already," I said. "Besides, they were looking for something when they tore everything apart at my place."

"You've got no idea what it is they were looking for?"

"No. And believe me, I've been racking my brain trying to think of something."

I looked at the Beefeater's. I was about ready for one. But I didn't think Pederson would join me. And I didn't want to ask him and then wind up drinking alone. Drink clear on Kalik, wake up with a . . . what? A limp dick? Just one gin, that couldn't hurt.

Then Pederson said, "You know where it all falls apart, don't you? The whole thing with Victor Ortiz?"

"If he's squeezing me, then why would he snatch Lord Downey? Why not just take Barbara?"

"Yep. That's the part I can't get around."

"Maybe it's just about the money," I said. "He squeezes me and doubles his money by squeezing Lord Downey."

"Maybe," said Pederson.

"Maybe we don't know shit, do we?"

"Maybe that, too." He stood to go. "Been nice, but I need to go interrogate an informant."

"Clarissa?"

"I'm real good at interrogating," he said. "My informants are always asking me to interrogate them some more."

He opened the door and stepped out and started off down the pathway.

"Did you really knock me on my ass?" I called out after him.

He didn't turn around.

"Flat on it, man. Flat flucking on it . . ."

32

After Pederson was gone, I walked around the room trying to decide if I really wanted some Beefeater's, and then I remembered that I still hadn't phoned Steffi Plank. On the way down to the main house I remembered something else: I hadn't told Pederson about what Mr. Pindle had mentioned to me, about Jesteen from the kitchen seeing Tiffani St. James driving the golf cart. Maybe there was nothing to it, maybe there was. But I didn't want Pederson accusing me of holding out on him again.

Everyone was in the dining room eating and no one was using the phone. Steffie answered on the third ring. We exchanged quick pleasantries and then I asked her if she could put me in touch with Barbara's attorney.

There was a long pause on her end, and then: "What's the matter?"

"Nothing's the matter."

"I don't believe you, Zack. Why do you suddenly need to speak to Barbara's attorney? Something has happened, hasn't it?"

So I told her about it. And when I was done, Steffie shrieked and cried, and then she pulled herself together and said she would call Barbara's attorney that night if she could find her, first thing Monday morning for sure. She said she would get back to me as soon as she knew something.

I walked past the dining room. The menu posted outside said the entrees were rosemary-skewered scallops with a shrimp and white bean salad, honey-glazed squab in a lemon-olive sauce, and porcini-crusted rack of lamb with black pepper spaetzle. It looked like Chrissie and Charlie Hineman had saved a spot for me at their table. I was hungry, but I wasn't feeling all that sociable.

I walked back up the hill to the cottage. The door was open. I didn't remember leaving it like that. I opened it slowly and looked inside. I saw someone sitting on the bed. It was Tiffani St. James.

"Well, if it isn't Mr. Neat," she said.

I stepped inside the cottage.

"Surprised?" asked Tiffani.

"Words can't express," I said.

"Glad to see me?"

"Should I be?"

She scrunched up her nose.

"You're supposed to say yes."

She had changed clothes. She was no longer Little Miss Beach Babe. She wore a slinky black dress and strappy black shoes with heels the shape of daggers. The look was Downtown Saturday Night. Only it was Sunday and we were on Harbour Island. So the effect was more All Dressed Up with No Place to Go.

"What's happening here, Tiffani?"

"I got tired of sitting around. I want to do something." She twisted the end of her hair with a finger and played with it, sticking it in her mouth and sucking on it, and looking up at me with her green eyes. The look was fetching. And it was well practiced, which made it pathetic.

She said, "Wanna go out and do something?"

"No."

"Wanna stay here and do something?"

"I don't think that would be a good idea."

"Oh, I think it would." She slipped off her shoes and eased back on the bed. "Come here. Just relax."

There was a mirror over the dresser by the bed. I went and stood in front of it and checked myself out. Then I turned to her and said, "Do I really look that goddam stupid?"

Tiffani flipped over on the bed and turned her back on me. She sighed a mighty sigh. I sat down in a chair by the ice bucket. Screw it. I took a glass and put some Beefeater's in it and put some ice on top of that. Rum I drink neat. Gin I don't. I took a sip. I took another.

Tiffani sprang up on the bed. She bounced on the side of it, all smiley and ready to play again.

"What are you drinking?"

"Poor man's martini."

"Oh, I love martinis. Make me one, OK?"

"No."

"Why not?"

"Because you aren't old enough."

"How do you know?"

"You're nineteen."

"How do you know that?"

"Lynfield Pederson told me."

"Who?"

"Lynfield Pederson, the police inspector. The man who came and talked to you about Bryce Gannon."

"Oh, him. He's mean. He asked a lot of questions."

"What did you tell him?"

"Not much. Zoe did most of the talking."

"Does Zoe always do most of the talking?"

"Yeah, pretty much. She's smart. She knows how to handle things."

"How do you know each other?"

"What do you mean?"

"I mean, how did you meet, how did you get to know her and Burma Downey?"

"Oh, clubs, you know. Just hanging out. Burma knew I wanted to be a model and she said she could help me. She used to be one you know. A model. Only she's, like, thirty now."

"What about Zoe?"

"What about her?"

"Did you meet her hanging out in clubs, too?"

"Yeah, she's a friend of Cheri's."

"Cheri?"

"Uh-huh. Cheri Swanson. She wants to be a model, too. Me and her, we used to work together, but then Burma started helping Cheri, and she stopped working. Cheri's beautiful. She's tall and thin, and she's hardly got any boobs at all. Me, my boobs are too big, way too big. Don't you think so?"

I rattled the ice in my glass. The gin was gone.

I said, "So tell me about Zoe. What does she do?"

Tiffani shrugged.

"I don't know. Takes care of . . . of Burma mostly." She chewed at a fingernail and spit it out. "Before that I think she was like a personal trainer or something. She works out a lot. Runs, like, ten miles a day. She knows karate and everything. Only it's not called karate. It's like tie one . . . something."

"Tae kwan do."

"That's it. You're smart, you know that? Smart and handsome. I really think me and you should party."

"Cut the crap, Tiffani."

She had a patent on pouting. She gave me one of her best ones.

"You don't have to be so grouchy. I just came by to cheer you up."

"Did you cheer up Bryce Gannon?"

She flinched a little, but only a little.

"I tried to. But he was always too busy. He kept saying me and him were going to hook up, and then he . . ." She stopped. "It's too bad he's dead. He was nice. I liked the way he talked. He sounded like Paul McCartney."

"How did you know Gannon?"

"Oh, I just went down to the Bahama Sands and hung out and, you know, these things just have a way of happening."

I sat there trying to figure out who I would cast in the role of Tiffani St. James if my life became a movie. I think one of those

Arquette sisters, the plump one with the baby-doll voice. All sweetness and innocence and not nearly as dumb as she acts.

"Did you sleep with Gannon?"

"That's personal, you." She tried to act offended. She was a lousy actor. "But no, I didn't. I mean, I only knew him for a couple of nights."

"And he gave you a ride home last night?"

"Yes."

"So why were you driving the golf cart?"

"What's with all the questions? You ask more questions than that policeman did."

"I'm just wondering why, if Gannon offered to give you a ride, you were the one who was driving, that's all."

"Well, so what? I like driving those little golf carts. They're fun. They remind me of those rides at the fair, those bumper car thingies. I asked Bryce if I could drive and he said yes."

"And you drove to your place and you got out. Then they drove off. And that was the last you saw of them."

"That's right."

Tiffani stood up from the bed. She reached behind her back, unzipped her dress, and it fell to the floor. Just like that. She stood there naked, smiling.

"What are you doing, Tiffani?"

"Relaxing. You need to relax, too."

I picked up the dress and handed it to her.

"Put it back on."

"Are you sure? Are you really, really sure?"

"Tiffani, this isn't going anywhere. You should really, really leave."

She slipped back into the black dress. She picked up her shoes and carried them with her as she walked to the door. I opened it for her and she stepped outside. She turned to me and said, "You're no fun."

"I've heard that before."

"And, yes, you really do look that goddam stupid."

I'd heard that before, too.

33

I sat there awhile sipping the Beefeater's and feeling virtuous. What other man, fresh sprung from nearly twenty-two months in jail, would turn down a pretty young woman who was standing buck naked in his bedroom? Just call me St. Zack, the Chaste. But the more I thought about it, the creepier the whole scene seemed, and the less virtuous I felt, and then I remembered I still hadn't eaten dinner.

The dining room was closed when I got down to the main house and no one was sitting in the bar or the salon. The place was empty. It was 10 P.M. Yes, fast times in the tropics. I walked through the dining room and back to the kitchen. It was empty, too. But not as empty as my stomach. Surely Chrissie and Charlie wouldn't mind if I went foraging.

I opened a big, double-door stainless-steel refrigerator. I found a leftover rack of the porcini-crusted lamb. I found some of the black pepper spaetzle. I found a jar of Dijon mustard. I hauled all my goodies to a counter and stood there eating with my hands—dipping lamb chops in the mustard, dipping spaetzle in the mustard, dipping both of them together, licking my fingers, and making contented swinelike sounds. I went back to the refrigerator. I found a shelf with several individual bowls of orange caramel flan. I only ate three of them. I used a spoon. Then I cleaned up after myself and went outside.

I wasn't ready for bed and I didn't feel like going back to the room. There was too much stuff knocking around in my head. The night was nice, the humidity low. And there was a halo around the moon. It was supposed to mean bad weather was on its way. Last I'd heard, Curt was still a tropical storm and still west and south of Grand Turk Island. Typically, that meant it would continue south of Florida and then maybe make a run up the Gulf of Mexico and slam into Pensacola or Mobile or Biloxi, or maybe head on west and hit Honduras or the Yucatán. But there's nothing typical about tropical storms, even less so when they turn into hurricanes.

I took Chapel Street down the hill until it came to the foot of Government Dock. A water taxi was tying off and a few people began unloading. I went south on Bay Street and was walking past The Landing Hotel when I heard a voice call out, "Hey, Mr. Big Man."

I turned to see Nixon Styles running off the dock to catch up with me. He was carrying a big grocery sack under each arm.

"Where you going?" he asked.

"Just out walking," I said. "But I can always use a guide."

Nixon beamed and fell in beside me.

"Been grocery shopping?" I asked him.

"No, I grew this."

I looked down in the bags. I could see spinach and yams and okra in one of them. I couldn't tell what was in the other one.

"You grew all that?"

"Yeah, I did. Grew it on my family land."

"So you're a guide and a farmer?"

He thought about it.

"Yeah, I am," he said. "'Course, mostly I just pull the weeds. My momma and my daddy and my auntie and my uncle, they do the planting, and the farming."

"Where do you farm?"

"Over on the mainland."

"The mainland?"

"Yeah," he said and pointed west, across the sound. "Over on Eleuthera. The mainland. That's what Brilanders call it."

"So your family has a farm over there?"

"Uh-huh," he said. "Remember last night, remember when I was telling you about the fort in Nassau and how the Brilanders whipped hell out of them Americans?"

"Uh-huh."

"Well, King George number three, he was the king of England then, see? And when he heard that the Brilanders had whipped hell out of the Americans and got his fort back he wanted to reward them for what they had done. The land on Harbour Island wasn't any good for farming, so the king, he gave the Brilanders some land over on the mainland. And to this day, when a Brilander wants to farm the land, all they have to do is go over there to the mainland and they farm some of the land King George gave them. Every family got some land over there."

"Sounds like a pretty good deal."

"Yeah, it's real good. I was over there today, helping my auntie, and I brought home all this."

He stopped and put the bags down on the ground.

"You ever eat Eleuthera pineapple?" he asked.

"Nope, I haven't."

"Best pineapple in the world. Sweeter than any other pineapple there is. Makes Hawaii pineapple taste like dog turd." He pulled two pineapples out of the bag and gave them to me. They were small for pineapples, just barely the size of big Idaho potatoes. Their skin was almost garnet.

"Thanks, Nixon. How much I owe you for them?"

"Nothing. Part of my guiding fee. You decided where you going yet?"

"Probably just head on up here to Valentine's, see if there's anything going on."

"Most always something going on there."

We rounded a curve and just ahead of us we saw the lights of Valentine's Resort. Valentine's caters mostly to divers and fishermen and people with boats—a crowd that tends to ramble later into the evening than the genteel folk who favor the Albury. It has a tiki bar that sits between Bay Street and the resort's marina. There was a goodly crowd holding down stools, and music was playing, and it seemed as good a place as any to urge the night onward, possibly into oblivion. Frankly, I was a little weary of the things knocking around in my head.

I told Nixon I thought I'd stop awhile and thanked him for guiding me. I reached in my pocket, found a five-dollar bill, and gave it to him.

"You need guiding tomorrow, I'll be around," he said. "I'll be looking for you."

He took off running down the road. Kid probably had a savings account bigger than mine. Come to think of it, I didn't have a savings account. Or a checking account. Just the dwindling chunk of cash in my pocket.

I could make out the music coming from Valentine's— UB40's version of "Red, Red Wine," reggae lite—and I saw a likely spot where I could squeeze in at the bar. I was heading for it when I cast a glance at the boats at berth in the marina, just a waterman's quickie survey of the inventory at hand. There were maybe forty slips strung out along two short docks. They were all full. And tied off at the end of the first dock, in a space for the overflow and latecomers, sat *Miz Blitz*.

Even in the dark, I had no doubt it was her. And, as I stepped closer, the dock lights made it easier to make out her profile— the haughty bowsprit, the smooth swoop of her gunwales, the forthrightness of her flying bridge. Far be it from me to overanthropomorphize an inanimate object, but she was one fine-looking babe of a boat.

I walked to the end of the dock and checked her out from stem to stern. Whoever owned her now hadn't scrimped on the upkeep. She shone where she was supposed to shine and every bit of her looked as good as I'd ever seen her. That made seeing her hurt all the worse.

I looked at the transom. It still read:

Miz Blitz
LaDonna, Florida

I hoped the new owner would keep the name. I hoped he knew it was bad luck to change it.

A light shone in the cabin. Maybe someone was awake inside. I wouldn't go rapping on the hatch this late at night, but I didn't see why I couldn't at least steal a peek and size up the new owner. Maybe I'd drop by in the morning, introduce myself, congratulate him on his purchase and his upkeep.

The cabin curtains were partly drawn and I crouched on the dock to look inside. A man sat at the little table in the galley, his back to me. He was shirtless, his hair long and black and falling below his shoulders. There was a mortar and pestle on the table, and he was grinding up something, some kind of leaves and roots. I leaned out and grabbed hold of one of *Miz Blitz*'s stanchions to get a better look, and as I did, the boat rocked, ever so slightly. The man whipped around. He looked out the window right at me.

It was Boggy.

34

"So, you're saying *Miz Blitz* still belongs to me?"

"By law, no," said Boggy. "But for all intense porpoises . . ."

"Intents and purposes . . ."

"Yes, for all that, yes, she is yours, Zachary."

It was twenty minutes later. Boggy was nursing a hot cup of what he called "blue spirit," a wretched, sulfurous brew made from roots and leaves and things I'd just as soon not know about. It was some kind of Taino concoction, something Boggy had been brought up drinking in the Dominican Republic. He said it promoted "lucid dreaming." Over the past two and a half days, my wide-awake hours had been all too lucid, so I passed when Boggy offered to share his batch. I was drinking ice water and feeling like a shitheel. A happy shitheel, but a shitheel nonetheless. Boggy, it turned out, hadn't betrayed me. And I had my boat back. Well, I kinda had my boat back.

Six months earlier, the government, true to its word, had put *Miz Blitz* up for auction at the Coast Guard station in Minorca Beach.

"But you have friends, many friends, Zachary," said Boggy. "Is like, I don't know, is like the Mafia, these friends."

Robby Greig, at Minorca Beach Marina, had played the don, making the calls, hatching the plan, spreading the word. No doubt he'd felt bad about pulling the string on the counterfeiting charges against me. It hadn't been his fault. After I had paid Robby in funny money for the work the marina had done on *Miz Blitz*, he had deposited it, the bank had caught it, and the Secret Service was soon hot on the case. Still, Robby had nurtured a deep sense of guilt and wanted to make up for my fall from grace. He contacted marinas up and down the coast, other charter captains, friends around Minorca Beach. He even got in touch with several of my old teammates and coaches from the Dolphins and UF. Most everyone kicked in a little money. And some of them showed up on auction day just to give Robby moral support.

The feds had set a minimum opening bid of seventy-five thousand dollars in what was to be an absolute auction. Top money walked away with everything, no matter what. That included the rods and reels, plus all the scuba diving gear. Robby Greig was the opening bidder.

"My friends anted up seventy-five thousand dollars?" I asked Boggy.

"Not exactly, but we come to that."

The plan was that Robby Greig would be the only bidder on *Miz Blitz*. But not everyone at the auction was in on the plan. Several people had seen the legal ads and driven great distances to put in their bids. A retired businessman from Atlanta had bumped Robby's bid by ten thousand dollars. And then two brothers from Jacksonville had jumped in, taking it to an even hundred thousand dollars.

"But the great defensive end, Mr. Lawrence Meyer . . ."

"Larry-Bud was there?"

"Oh yes, and the great offensive guard, Mr. Mac Steen . . ."

"Steenboat was there, too?"

"Yes, yes. Both of them. They are very . . . they are very considerable men, no?"

"They're fucking monsters. But I mean that in a good way."

"Yes, well, Mr. Meyer and Mr. Steen, they convinced the other bidders that they did not really want your boat."

"How did they do that?"

"They went and stood by them and said things like, 'How you going to enjoy that boat if you gotta breathe through tubes?' Things like that. I think maybe I saw Mr. Steen squeezing one of the brothers where he should not be squeezed. Anyway, after a while, the other people, they stopped bidding, and Robby, he got the boat."

"What was the final bid?" I asked.

"It went for $127,500."

A steal. *Miz Blitz* was worth five or six times that, easy.

"So how much did Robby and the gang pitch in for it?"

"About fifty-three thousand dollars, more or less," said Boggy.

"Who paid for the rest?"

"You did."

And that's when I felt like a shitheel for ever having doubted Boggy. That's when I learned that I had sold him short, way short, and that he had stuck with me all the way. Yes, Boggy had indeed been conducting a booming business in specimen palms—cash on the barrelhead for premium quality trees. But aside from living expenses and upkeep on the property, all the money had gone toward getting *Miz Blitz* back. The palm tree business had been so good that Boggy had even begun repaying those who had chipped in to help out at the auction.

The feds weren't dumb to what had gone down. But there wasn't anything they could do to nullify the results of the auction. Legally, the title to *Miz Blitz* belonged to Robby Greig.

"Robby, he say he can loan the boat to whoever he wants to loan it to. And that is you, Zachary."

"What about Barbara? She knew about all this?"

"Oh yes. She put in twenty thousand dollars. She say she can be the last one for us to pay back."

"And it was her idea for you to make the run over here in *Miz Blitz*?"

"Yes, that is why I was not in LaDonna when you stopped by. Barbara, she call me the day she was leaving. She said she thought it would make a big surprise if I was to bring the boat here. She say we can all ride back on *Miz Blitz* together. Only now . . ."

We sat there awhile, not talking, just thinking about the "only now" part. Only now I didn't know exactly where Barbara was. Only now I didn't know exactly how I was going to get her back. Only now, only now . . .

"I know you want badly to see her, Zachary," Boggy said. "I know your patients, they are running thin."

"Yes, Boggy, my patients are running very thin."

"The blue spirit," he said. "It is good for an anxious mind."

I told him, what the hell, I might as well try a cup of it. He smiled and told me that was a wise idea. He poured it. I drank it all in one big gulp. And I slept that night on *Miz Blitz*.

35

I slept late on Monday morning. It was almost eight o'clock when I woke up to the sound of a hose running on deck. I walked out topside to find Boggy washing down a cleaning board where he had just finished filleting what had been a fairly sizeable black grouper. He'd gone out early in the skiff to free-dive in the bight and had taken along a Hawaiian sling. Like always, he came back with something to eat. There would be grits and grouper for breakfast.

"You oughta sell that blue spirit stuff," I said. "I haven't slept that well in I don't know when."

"What did you dream?"

"Not a thing, thank God. I've got enough on my mind without worrying about dreams."

Boggy considered it, concern etched in his face.

"Tonight, I give you something else. It is always good to know your dreams," he said. "And for today? What do we do?"

So I laid out the plan, which consisted mostly of hooking up with Lynfield Pederson, then checking in with Burma Downey and Zoe Applequist. Maybe they'd received another phone call.

I told Boggy I'd be back in time for breakfast. Then I walked

back to the Albury to slip into clean shorts and one of my new
Tarponwear shirts. When I dropped by the main house there
was a message to call Steffie Plank. She was in her office at Orb
Media when I caught up with her. She had spoken to Barbara's
attorney, and the news was about what I had expected. Barbara's assets were considerable, but not exactly liquid. And
even if they were, it would be difficult for anyone besides Barbara to touch them.

"Did he ask you why you wanted to know all this?"

"It was a she," said Steffie. "And of course she did. At first,
she didn't even want to talk to me about Barbara's affairs. Then,
after I convinced her who I was—turns out we had met at a
fund-raiser for Rollins College a couple of months ago—she
loosened up. But she was suspicious."

"So what did you tell her?"

"I lied my butt off. I told her that Barbara had hired a corporate trainer for Orb Media who was working with various inter-
departmental groups to develop team-building and strategize
for worst-case scenarios. And the scenario our group had to
work on was, What if the owner of the company goes on a foreign business trip only to get kidnapped and held for ransom?"

"So she thought she was discussing a hypothetical situation.
Very clever."

"She got a big laugh out of it, actually. She said Barbara was
such a hard-ass negotiator that she would probably charm the
kidnappers and get them to pay her the money. She said that in
such a situation it might be possible to make loans against assets without the presence of the owner. But it would require, in
her words, 'significant legal standing' in order to get it moving.
Like the intervention of a government agency."

"Like the F.B.I."

"More than that. Since it's in a foreign country and involves
the potential transfer of a large amount of cash, then it has to
move through diplomatic channels. It would have to go through
the State Department. And even then it would take time, lots of
time. She said that's why more big companies are starting to
take out kidnapping insurance."

"There's actually such a thing?"

"Apparently. And I already checked. Barbara wasn't covered by anything like that in the company policy. Then while I was waiting for you to call, I got on the Internet and just looked around some. Kidnapping has become a growth industry—up something like three hundred percent over the last five years. These are political kidnappings, or kidnappings where the kidnappers target executives from big corporations. Lots of *Fortune* Five Hundred companies, when their people have to travel to kidnapping hotspots—like Colombia or Mexico or the Philippines—they take out policies that can run in the neighborhood of ten thousand dollars a month."

"I can understand why Barbara wouldn't buy into something like that. Besides, it's not like the Bahamas is a kidnapping hotspot."

"I did check into another way to get the money, Zack."

"What's that?"

"Cash on hand. Orb Media has to pay several different production vendors each month. Mostly these are pre-press companies that make color separations for the magazines, and then there are the various printing houses. It's the biggest cash account, bigger even than payroll, and we keep it separate. I could talk to the different vendors. We're current and in good standing with all of them. Maybe we could work something out."

"How much would that get us?"

"Not a million. Maybe four or five hundred thousand. I don't know for sure. It would depend on how many of them would buy into it and let us ride for a few months."

"Well, that seems like the best direction for the time being. Why don't you get moving on that end of it?"

"OK, but . . ."

"But what?"

"What's wrong with working all the ends, Zack? Why not just go ahead and contact the F.B.I. and contact the State Department and let everyone know what's going on?"

I could sense her anxiety slipping out. I had to remember that Steffi was just a kid, maybe twenty-four or twenty-five, and

I was asking her to help orchestrate something with which damn few people twice her age have any experience. Plus, I was trying not to let my own anxieties slip out and upset her.

"I told Lynfield Pederson that I would give him a couple of days to see what he could do."

There was a long pause on Steffi's end. Finally, she said, "Zack, I know I'm no authority on this, and I don't want you to think I am trying to tell you what to do here, because I'm not. But this one Web site I checked—and, I know, there's lots of whacko Web sites, but this was one run by a security group that works for companies that issue kidnap insurance—it had these tips for, as they called it, 'dealing with a kidnap and rescue situation.' I know, it sounds crazy that someone even comes up with something like this, but I printed it out and, I've got it right here. Is it OK if I read you what it says?"

"Sure, let's hear it."

"It says: 'If someone you know is kidnapped in a foreign country do not call the local police. In many cases, the police are likely to be working in conjunction with the kidnappers and will only help them jack up the ransom demands. Your first order of business should be to call the U.S. Embassy.'"

"Well, I'm afraid we're way past that point, Steffie."

"You trust this Pederson guy?"

"I've got to," I said.

And after I hung up with Steffie, that was who I called.

36

Lynfield Pederson was just leaving the police station when I got him on the phone. He said he had some business to take care of and that he'd swing by Valentine's and meet me at the boat about ten o'clock. I didn't want to wait around that long, so I told him I'd go on to the Downey compound and he could meet me there.

"No," he said. "I don't want you going back there again without me. Wait for me on the boat."

After sidestepping him the day before, I felt like I owed him something. So I went back to the marina and waited for him. It was equal parts hell and heaven—the agony of waiting to hear from the kidnappers, the joy of being aboard *Miz Blitz* once again. Naw, scratch that. It was mostly hell. I couldn't enjoy anything until I knew Barbara was safe.

Ten o'clock came and went. Then eleven, then noon. It was almost 1 P.M. when Pederson finally got there, and I was pacing the deck. He didn't apologize for being late, nor did he seem to be in any particular hurry. Island time. It takes more than murder and a kidnapping to speed it up.

Pederson spent a few moments admiring *Miz Blitz* and, at

Boggy's insistence, polished off a leftover plateful of grouper and grits. Then he and I loaded up in the white van.

"So where's that buddy of yours come from?" he asked as we rolled along Bay Street, then turned east toward the beachside.

"You mean Boggy?"

"Yeah, he's got an Indian look to him."

"He's Taino."

Pederson cut me a look.

"Taino? Like in the Dominican Republic?"

"Yeah, I'm impressed. Most people have never heard of the Taino."

"Oh, I've heard of them. Just thought they were all long dead. Thought the Spanish conquistadors killed them off."

"Don't tell Boggy that. Nothing riles him up as much as people thinking he's extinct."

So I gave Pederson the short version of how I had met Boggy. It was on a solo cruise through the Caribbean the season after I'd left the Dolphins. I was snorkeling around some rocks on the southeast coast of the Dominican Republic, near Punta Azu, when a tidal surge sucked me into a thicket of black sea urchins, the kind with those wicked poisonous spines. I was rolling around on the beach, hollering like a baby, when I looked up to see a short, stout brown man with a long, black ponytail gazing down on me. He had a face like one of those monolithic deities from Easter Island—at first glance it seemed devoid of expression, but the more I looked at it the more it seemed connected to eternity. He might have been twenty, then again, he might have been sixty. Even now, I have no idea how old Boggy is.

As I lay there howling, the short brown man pulled down his pants, unfurled his not-so-short member, and unleashed a stream of hot pee all over me. Before I could protest, he was kneeling in the sand, rubbing the urine into my wounds.

"Is medicine," he said.

A few minutes later, after I was back on my feet and the pain was miraculously gone, Boggy announced, "I work for you."

As it turned out, *Miz Blitz* needed some work done on her and I could use an extra hand. But after all the repairs were finished, it became evident that Boggy's offer extended past my stay in the D.R. He intended to keep working for me and go wherever I went. I tried my best to convince him otherwise. I told him I wasn't in the market for hired help.

"I do not want money," Boggy said. "This is something I must do."

"Why must you do it?"

"Because it was foretold," he said.

"Foretold? You mean, like somebody predicted it?"

Boggy nodded.

"My grandfather," he said. "He saw my future."

"Yeah, right," I said. "You mean to tell me your grandfather looked into the future and saw you walking along the rocks at Punta Azul and saw me getting stung by a sea urchin and saw you pissing on me and the two of us meeting up because of that?"

Boggy shrugged.

"More or less," he said. "My grandfather spoke in symbols. It was left to me to interpret them."

There was no talking him out of it. He wrapped a few belongings in an old blanket, strung a hammock on the sailboat, and when I set course back to Florida he was on board. I figured they'd waylay him when we went through immigration, but he produced a U.S. passport. Turns out he'd been born in Miami, but returned to the D.R. as a child.

"His real name is Cachique Baugtanaxata," I told Pederson.

"I can understand why you call him Boggy."

"In Taino his name means 'Chief of the Cenote.'"

"Cenote? Those are caves, right?"

"Caverns, really. Giant sinkholes. The Taino call them 'Navels of the Earth.' They're sacred, places of worship. Boggy says he comes from a long line of priests and shamans."

"You believe him?"

"Yeah," I said. "I do."

I had plenty of reasons for believing Boggy was exactly who he said he was, stories galore. And I would have gladly shared them with Pederson, but we were pulling into the Downey compound. The time for reminiscing was over.

37

"You did what?" Lynfield Pederson said.

I would have asked the same thing, only I was speechless.

"We gave them the money," said Zoe Applequist.

We were sitting in the living room at the pink house, just Zoe Applequist, Pederson, and me. Zoe said Burma was in her bedroom, resting. And if Tiffani St. James was around, then she wasn't showing herself. Neither was Clarissa Percival.

"When did you give them the money?" asked Pederson.

Zoe closed her eyes and took a deep breath, letting Pederson know that it required every fiber of her mortal being just to tolerate his presence. There had already been a major scene after I showed up with Pederson in tow. Zoe had called me a traitor and liar. At first, she had refused to let us inside, but I had managed to calm her down.

Now Zoe looked at Pederson, and said, "They called approximately one hour and forty-five minutes ago. I know, because it was only moments after Burma and I returned from the bank. And we gave them the money shortly after that."

Zoe Applequist was wearing a blue unitard and looked like she had just finished a workout. Her long black hair was kept at bay with a Nike headband and she was dripping sweat. The arches of both feet were wrapped in white tape. So were the knuckles of both hands. There was one of those big Everlast punching bags hanging in a corner of the living room. Nothing sexier than a woman boxer. Unless it's a guy who's a synchronized swimmer.

"Why didn't you call me?" I asked Zoe.

"We didn't have time. They called us. We had the money. And we gave it to them."

"What did they do?" said Pederson. "Did they just drive up, ring the doorbell and say, 'Hello, we're here for the money'? And then you handed it to them and they drove away?"

"This is not a joking matter," said Zoe.

"You're got-dam right it's not. That's why you should have gotten in touch with my office from the outset." He turned to me. "That goes for you, too."

Pederson sat down in a chair. He flipped his legal pad to a blank page and took out a pencil from a shirt pocket. He said to Zoe Applequist: "You gave them two hundred fifty thousand dollars, is that right?"

"Yes, that is correct."

"If you don't mind me asking," said Pederson, "exactly how did you get that kind of money so quickly? It's Monday morning. Banks were closed yesterday."

"Actually, I do mind you asking. Miss Downey's financial affairs are none of your business."

"Listen, I don't care how much money she has," Pederson said. "I'm just trying to figure out how she managed to get her hands on so much of it so fast. I understood the money would be coming from London."

"It did," said Zoe. "And for your information, London is five hours ahead of us here. We were up quite early calling Burma's bank in London and making arrangements."

Pederson thought about it. Then he said, "How did you deliver the money to them?"

"We delivered it to them in the manner in which they requested."

I could see Lynfield Pederson flexing his jaw. He said, "And in which manner would that be?"

"Miss Downey has made it clear that she does not want police intervention in this matter."

"Too bad," said Pederson. "You've got it anyway. How did you deliver the money?"

Zoe Applequist unwrapped the tape from one of her hands. She stretched her fingers and rolled her wrist. She took the tape off the other hand and did the same thing. Maybe she was trying to intimidate us. So far, she'd been doing a pretty good job of it. She sat down directly across the coffee table from me and said, "Mr. Chasteen, if you insist upon involving the police in this matter, then we must insist that we go about settling this in our separate fashions."

"What the hell does that mean?" I asked.

"It means that we are prepared to negotiate individually with the kidnappers for Lord Downey and Lord Downey alone. It means that we will follow their instructions to the very letter. It means that we will provide them with our half of the money and then we will await Lord Downey's safe return. This is not some kind of package deal."

"What makes you think they would go for that?" I asked.

"Oh, please, Mr. Chasteen. We've already discussed it with them."

I looked at Pederson. As far as I was concerned, this was his cue for breaking out the handcuffs and hauling Zoe Applequist and her bod of steel to the Harbour Island slammer. Which was probably the same stuffy garage where they had kept Bryce Gannon's body before carting him off to get iced down at the fish house. Better yet, put her in the cooler with Gannon's body. A few hours of that and she might suddenly become a more reasonable human being.

"This cell phone they've been calling you on," I said. "Where is it?"

Zoe went to the kitchen counter and came back holding the chrome cell phone. When I reached for it, she pulled away.

"Let me see it," I said.

She gave me an icy look. Then she put the phone in the palm of her hand and stuck it out to me. I grabbed it and punched the power button. Nothing happened. I punched redial. Then I punched power again. Nothing and more nothing.

"It doesn't work," I said.

"Battery's dead. It died not long after we last spoke with them."

"So how do they plan on getting in touch with you now?"

"In our last conversation, they said we would be receiving a new cell phone each time they wanted to contact us."

"What did the guy on the phone sound like?" asked Pederson.

"What do you mean?"

"I mean, did he speak with an accent? Was he American? Was he Bahamian? What did he sound like?"

"No accent," Zoe said. "At least not one that I noticed."

"So, you talked to him this time?" I said.

"What?" said Zoe.

"The first time he called, he insisted on talking to Burma. This time he spoke to you?"

"Yes. When he called I answered and then I gave the phone to Burma. Just like before. And he gave her the instructions."

"Did she write them down?" I asked.

"Why yes, of course."

"May I see what she wrote down?" I said.

"She wrote on the chalkboard," Zoe said. "We erased it."

"Could you ask her to write it again?"

"Like I told you, Burma is resting and I don't think it is in her best interest to be disturbed at this time. Why can't you just take my word for what the man on the phone told her?"

"Please," I said. "We're all upset here. I'm just trying to understand everything that's going on."

Zoe stood up in a huff.

"Alright, alright," she said. "I'll go back there and ask her to write down exactly what the man told her. And then, if you don't mind, I'll be asking you to leave."

Pederson and I sat in the living room and waited while Zoe went back to Burma Downey's bedroom. We didn't talk. About five minutes later Zoe returned with a piece of notebook paper. She handed it to me. I recognized Burma Downey's shaky handwriting from my previous visit.

I read the note with Pederson looking over my shoulder. It said:

> The man on the phone said put the money in a white pillow case. He said where to leave it. He said someone would be watching. He said no one should be with Zoe or they would kill my father and Ms. Pickering. He said he would call about how to deliver the other $750,000. Zoe put the money in the pillowcase and left it where the man said. They seem very well organized.

I tucked the note in a pocket.

Then Zoe said, "If you don't mind me asking, Mr. Chasteen, when do you think you might have your part of the money ready?"

"I don't mind you asking at all. But I don't really have an answer. All I can tell you is that we're working on it. There are lots of things that have to fall in place."

Zoe nodded.

"I understand," she said. "Good luck."

I stood. So did Pederson.

"Miss Applequist," he said, "I expect you to get in touch with me the moment you have any further contact with the other party. Do you understand?"

Zoe Applequist didn't reply. She walked to the door. "Good day, gentlemen," she said.

This time there were no good-bye hugs.

38

"So what do you think?" asked Pederson.

We were standing by the white van in the driveway at the Downey compound.

"I'll tell you what I think," I said. "I think I shouldn't have been sitting on my dead ass for three hours waiting for you to come pick me up at the boat. I should have been here when they got the phone call, dammit."

Pederson didn't say anything. It was getting hot. He fanned himself with the legal pad.

I said, "What were you doing anyway?"

"What do you mean what was I doing?"

"I mean, what were you doing for those three hours that was so goddam important that we couldn't have come here first thing like I wanted to?"

"Police business," he said.

"That's it? Police business? You can't do better than that? That's all you got?"

"Yeah," he said. "That's all I got."

We had squared off, and I was trying to figure out what to say next, trying to figure out if maybe Zoe and Burma had been right in wanting to leave the police out of this. Then a voice called out, "Lyn . . ."

We both turned to see Clarissa Percival standing at the back door of Lord Downey's house.

"Excuse me," Pederson said.

"Gladly," I said.

He walked off to join Clarissa. And I headed back to *Miz Blitz*.

I was just a couple of hundred yards down Front Street when I began to suspect that I was being followed. The guy was maybe fifty yards behind me. I couldn't tell much about him except that he was definitely overdressed for August in the Bahamas. He was wearing long pants and a navy blue windbreaker zipped up tight. He looked to be medium build, a little on the chunky side. Any more than that I couldn't tell from the distance, but it was a good bet he was sweating something fierce in that getup he was wearing. I didn't have on half as many clothes and the perspiration was pouring off me.

I had picked up some gravel in one of my sandals, and when I stopped to shake it loose, the guy stopped, too. He pretended to admire the blossoms on a royal poinciana tree by the side of the road. I started walking again; he started walking again.

Looking back on it, I had noticed the same guy a couple of other times that morning when I was going back and forth between the marina and the Albury. He was obviously a tourist, and I remembered thinking it was unusual to see a tourist walking around Harbour Island alone. Most people who visit Harbour Island are on honeymoons or romantic getaways and they tend to hang out in couples. This guy just didn't fit in. Yeah, he was definitely tailing me.

I had never been tailed before and I thought I might as well make the most of it. I picked up the pace. I hadn't gotten in my run that morning and, after that exasperating sitdown with Zoe Applequist and the little faceoff afterwards with Pederson, I had some pent-up energy to burn. I hit power-walk stride and plowed down Front Street. I hung a left at Bay Street and shot a quick glance behind. The guy in the windbreaker was almost jogging, trying to keep up. When I reached The Landing Hotel, Toby Tyler, one of the Aussie owners, was standing out front. I stopped just long enough to exchange pleasantries and listen to Toby tell me about the swell that was expected to come in from the tropical storm and how it meant eight-foot surf for parts of Eleuthera.

"I've got an extra board, Zack," said Toby, "should you want to give it a shot."

"Thanks," I said. "But I've had all the humiliation I can handle lately."

As I stepped away, I looked back at the guy in the windbreaker. He had pulled up in the shade of a casuarina tree to catch his breath and was looking across the bay, making like he was enjoying the scenery.

I headed up Chapel Street and beelined it through Dunmore Town, not looking back until I reached the top of the hill by Angela's Starfish Restaurant. The guy had fallen behind, but he was hanging in there. He had his head down now, just concentrating on keeping up, didn't even see me turning around and looking at him.

I kept on walking. I looped back through Dunmore Town on Colebrook Street, looked in the window at the Dilly Dally Shop, then followed Front Street all the way to Uncle Ralph's Aura Corner. Other than its pink-sand beach, the closest thing Harbour Island has to a tourist attraction is Aura Corner. Several years back, a local housepainter by the name of Ralph Sawyer began painting slogans, inspirational verses, and other nuggets of wisdom on pieces of driftwood and hanging them in the trees outside his home. There are hundreds of them now. Mostly it is bumper-sticker philosophy: "Good things come to those who wait . . . and I'm damn tired of waiting," or "Work like you don't need money/Love like you've never been hurt/And dance like no one is watching." Uncle Ralph has strung a couple of hammocks so visitors can rest in the shade. Each morning he gets up and picks fresh hibiscus to stick in the bleached-out conch shells that line his property. And there are a couple of plastic jugs with "Donations" painted on them.

There wasn't anyone at Aura Corner when I got there. I

ducked under the trees, crouched behind a croton hedge and waited. A couple of minutes later, the guy in the windbreaker came walking past. He stopped at the intersection and looked in all directions. He was solid looking, thick shoulders, a bull of a guy. His face was flushed and he was breathing hard. He wiped the sweat off his forehead and started off down Eunice Street toward the bay.

I stepped out from the hedge and followed him. I wasn't sneaky about it. I pulled close, just a few feet behind him, and scuffed my sandals on the pavement to make sure he heard me. He stole a peek over his shoulder and started walking faster. I stayed with him.

"So how's Victor Ortiz?" I said.

He ignored me and kept on walking. I pulled alongside him.

"I know what the hell you're up to," I said.

"Go fuck yourself," said the guy, not looking at me.

I stepped in front of him, shot out an arm, and thumped his chest. He stopped and reached inside his windbreaker, but I caught him by the wrist, spun him around, and yanked his arm backwards, wrenching it at the shoulder. He grunted and went down on his knees. I held him there and stuck a hand inside the windbreaker. I pulled out the gun that was stuck in the waistband of his pants. It was flat-black with a snub-nosed barrel. More than that I can't tell you. It was just another damn gun.

"What kind of cheapshit operation is Ortiz running these days?" I said. "You can't even afford a holster for this thing?"

I eased off him and stuck the gun in the pocket of my shorts. That's when he squirmed loose. He came at me, head tucked down, legs pumping. He moved pretty well. He landed a shoulder square in my chest and knocked me backwards onto the pavement. He got off a flurry of stinging punches before I flipped him over and sent an elbow to the side of his head. It took the fight out of him. He lay there looking up at me.

"Empty your pockets," I told him.

He didn't move. I kicked him in the side.

"Empty your pockets."

He did it. He wasn't carrying much, just his wallet and a room key. The wallet had a Florida driver's license that said his name was Hector Suarez of 1122 San Rafael Drive, Hialeah. He was thirty-three years old and in the event of a fatal accident he wanted his vital organs to go to the state donor program. Thoughtful guy for a thug. The key was for room six at the Heron Inn. It was on St. Ann Street, just a couple of blocks away.

"OK, on your feet, Hector," I said. I gave him back his wallet, but kept the key. "We're going to your place."

He stood up slowly and took his time dusting himself off. He looked me up and down.

He said, "You kill me, he'll just send someone else."

"I'm not going to kill you, Hector."

"So why you kill his nephew?"

"His nephew?"

"Yes, his sister's son, Eduardo. You kill him in the water, leave his body there."

The young guy in the boathouse. So that had been Ortiz's nephew.

"I didn't have a choice," I said.

Hector shrugged.

"Just as Ortiz, he does not have a choice."

"So that's why he kidnapped them? Because I killed his nephew?"

Hector just looked at me, his face blank. He said nothing.

"Start walking," I said.

Five minutes later we were standing in room six at the Heron Inn. It was a threadbare joint that was closer to a boardinghouse than an inn. But it had a room phone and I was using it to call Continental Airlines. I was holding Hector's round-trip ticket from Miami to North Eleuthera. He wasn't scheduled to leave for another four days, but I was changing that.

"There's a flight at 2:20 P.M.," said the agent at the other end of the line. "But it will cost one hundred dollars to change over."

"No problem," I said. "Just put it on Visa."

I read off the number on the card that I had taken from Hector's wallet. Hector, meanwhile, had finished packing his bag and was sitting on the bed. I hadn't been able to get anything out of him since we had returned to his room.

I hung up the phone and handed Hector his ticket.

"You're good to go," I told him.

I found a notepad and pen by the phone and wrote down the phone number at the Albury Beach Club. I folded it and gave it to Hector.

"You give that to Ortiz and you tell him to call me. You got that?"

Hector stuck the note in a pocket. He said, "Yeah, I got it. But it don't make no difference. There's nothing you got to say that he wants to hear."

"Just tell him to call me, Hector."

I opened the door and motioned Hector outside. I followed him out to St. Ann's Street and pointed to Government Dock.

"You go straight there and get on a water taxi and take a cab to the airport," I said. "Don't let me see you back on this island again."

I patted the gun in my pocket.

Hector started walking. He didn't look back. I stood there watching until he got on a water taxi that sped him away to North Eleuthera, then I headed back to Valentine's marina. When I reached the water I took Hector's gun out of my pocket and flung it into the bay.

39

Boggy stood on the dock by *Miz Blitz,* his head tilted back, his eyes closed. He appeared to be sniffing the air. I walked up behind him and watched him. His nostrils flared and he breathed in deeply, and then he did it again. After a moment he opened his eyes and turned to me, and said, "The storm, it comes this way."

"You can smell it?" I asked.

"Smell it, feel it, taste it. It is growing, this storm. Three days, it will be here."

Most of the time I can handle Boggy's mumbo jumbo. But at that particular moment I wasn't in any mood for it.

"If you're so damn good, how come you can't sniff out where Barbara is?"

I hopped on the boat, swung through the hatch, and stepped down to the galley. A coffeepot sat on the stove. It felt warm. I looked in the cupboard and found a mug. Boggy came down and sat on a bench by the big teak table. I picked up the coffeepot. I put my nose to the spout. Smelled like coffee.

"This coffee?" I asked Boggy.

He nodded. I poured a cup and drank some.

Boggy said, "With dogweed in it."

I stopped drinking.

"For the stomach. Drink. It's good. That way the coffee it doesn't give you shits."

"I can hear them now at Starbucks," I said. "'Give me a skinny latte, no foam, with a double shot of shitstopper.'"

I sat down across from Boggy. His hands were folded in front of him on the table. If he was ticked off about the way I had spoken to him on the dock, then his face didn't show it. His face rarely showed anything, actually. I don't know if it was a matter of him having complete control over his emotions or complete control over the way he displayed them, but every now and then I wished he would just give me a little something to work with, some way to read him.

"With people is different," he said.

"What's different? What are you talking about?"

"People. Predicting how they will behave. Is not like a storm. Is not like a fish. Is not like the stars or the moon," he said. "I wish to find Barbara, too."

"I know you do," I said.

"I need to know what you know," he said.

So we sat there, and I drank the coffee with dogweed in it and told him about Hector and how I had caught him tailing me. Then I told him about Burma Downey and Zoe Applequist and how they had turned over the two hundred fifty thousand dollars. I told him how I had asked Burma Downey to write down what the man on the cell phone had told her. I pulled the note from my shorts and let him read it.

When he was done, he said: "The one who wrote this, she is the one who is injured?"

"Yes, she was in a car accident. In Fort Lauderdale."

"She had many years of school?" asked Boggy.

"I have no idea. She grew up in England. I suppose she went to school there."

"Barbara, she went to school in England, too. Is that right?"

"Yes, it is. Why?"

"No reason," he said. "Just to know."

Then I told him about how I had gotten into it with Lynfield Pederson after we had left Burma Downey's house.

Boggy said, "You think there was a reason why he made you sit here waiting?"

"I don't know. I just think it's real strange that he insisted on me staying on the boat for three hours when I could have been there at the house when Zoe and Burma got the phone call and delivered the money."

"He is police."

"Yeah. And your point is?"

"Sometimes, the police, they must insist that other people do things just so the people know that the police are the police."

"Pederson got that point across when he hauled me into his office and made me sit there for half of yesterday. I don't have time for these little control games. I'm tired of sitting around and waiting on people."

"Yes, Zachary, that is good," said Boggy. "It is always better to put things in motion than it is to sit and wait for the motion to begin."

"So how do you propose we put things in motion?"

"You have a boat. You do not wish to know your boat again, to see how she moves?"

A few minutes later, the engine was rumbling, and Boggy was untying the lines while I stood at the wheel. I don't know why I hadn't thought of doing this earlier, but now I was itching to take a ride on *Miz Blitz*, to let her rip awhile. I didn't know where we were heading, but we would blow out the pipes, and I would think about things without even knowing I was thinking about them, and maybe something would fall into place. Even if nothing came of it, it beat heck out of just sitting around.

I glanced toward Bay Street and saw Nixon Styles walking with some of his buddies. When he looked my way I gave him a wave. He split off from his pals and walked out on the dock.

"Hey, Mr. Big Man. That your boat?"

"Yeah, it is. How you like it?"

"Fine-looking boat."

Nixon studied the name on the transom.

"*Miz Blitz*. Why you name it that?"

"Football. I used to play."

"You the quarterback?"

"No, I played safety."

"You any good?"

"I was OK. The safety blitz was something I did best."

"Safety blitz?"

"Yeah, it's when the safety runs in and tries to knock the quarterback on his ass before he can throw the ball."

Nixon thought about it.

"You getting ready to take this ass-knocking boat for a ride?"

"Sure am," I said. "You want to go?"

Nixon was on the boat before the words were out of my mouth. He scurried up the ladder to the bridge and stood beside me at the wheel as I moved *Miz Blitz* away from the dock.

"How long we be gone?" asked Nixon.

"Not long."

"I need to be back in a couple hours. Supposed to go over to the mainland to help my auntie."

"Oh, we'll be back by then. I just want to run my boat in the open water, get the feel for her again," I said. "You going to help your auntie at the farm?"

"Yeah, they working the stew out of me," said Nixon. "You eat those pineapple I gave you?"

No, I told him, they were still sitting down below in the galley. I asked him to run down and get them, and when he came back up, Boggy was with him. Boggy had a knife—he always has a knife—and as we idled out to the main channel, Boggy sliced the two pineapples and served us wedges that were dripping with juice. It was the best-tasting pineapple I'd ever eaten and I told Nixon so.

"You want, I can bring you back some more when I come back from Eluthera tonight," he said.

"I want," I said.

Just before we hit the main channel, I heard the telltale

three-beep signal on the radio, then a voice saying, "This is the National Hurricane Center in Miami."

I flipped up the volume. I have been listening to hurricane updates on the radio ever since I was a kid and I have this theory about the guys who read them. I think they must come from a family dynasty of hurricane update announcers, just like Harry Caray, and Skip Caray, and Chip Caray in sports. Every hurricane update announcer I've ever heard speaks in the same flat, rural, utterly trustworthy Southern voice. They could just as easily be reporting on soybean futures or boll weevil infestations. I guess the whole idea is not to sound excited or alarmed.

The announcer said, "At 1 P.M. Eastern Standard Time today Tropical Storm Curt was located at 37.6 degrees latitude and 84.2 degrees longitude, or approximately two hundred nautical miles east-southeast of Grand Turk Island. Winds at the storm's center were estimated at sixty-five miles per hour, just short of hurricane strength. The storm is expected to intensify as it continues over warm water. Its present course is due west at fifteen miles per hour, which would take it well south of the Bahamas and the U.S. mainland with a possible landfall in Cuba. The next report will be at 5 P.M. Eastern Standard Time."

I turned down the radio and looked at Boggy.

"You want me to radio the National Hurricane Service and tell them they got it all wrong?"

"No, that is not necessary," Boggy said. "Soon enough they will know."

40

We skipped along North Eleuthera Sound, past the tip of Harbour Island. There were some good-sized swells rolling in from the Atlantic as we skirted the lee of Man Cay, and *Miz Blitz* took them without a hitch, slicing through with enthusiasm. It was good to be at her helm again.

Checking depths and shoals on the nautical chart, I came across the green blotch that was French Jug. I eyeballed it on the near horizon—a saucer-shaped island with a bit more elevation than the surrounding cays—and pointed *Miz Blitz* at it, opening the throttle.

After we negotiated a tricky cut at Blind Taylor Shoals, Nixon sidled alongside me on the bridge. He said, "We going to French Jug?"

"Thought we might stop for lunch," I said. "What's it like?"

He shook his head.

"Don't know. Hadn't ever been there."

Only then did I remember what Lynfield Pederson had said about French Jug and its unofficial apartheid policy.

"We don't have to go," I told Nixon.

"I want to," he said. "Besides, none of them French Juggers

gonna mess with me if I got you and that Indian man at my back."

The chart showed a small harbor just past the south tip, at Blountston, the island's only settlement. Boggy grabbed the binoculars, found the channel markers, and stood on the bow, pointing the way in. The channel was narrow, barely wide enough to let two vessels of any size pass at the same time. Once, when I was looking at the chart and not paying close attention, I let the boat stray just a hair, and felt the bump-bump of bottom against the hull before I cut hard on the wheel to avoid running aground.

There wasn't much to Blountston from a distance and even less as we drew near. The harbor was pocket-sized and shallow, and not all that well protected. Like Harbour Island, a big concrete dock sat at the center of everything, but there the similarities ended. No pastel palette of gingerbread cottages and tin-roofed houses lined the waterfront. No aunties promenading under parasols, no fishermen shooting the breeze by their boats. Indeed, no one seemed to be out on the streets. The houses were charmless and built from cinderblock. They were painted white or not at all. I saw the shells of several buildings that had been started and then left unfinished, weeds growing up along windowless walls. There was nothing to catch the eye, no beckoning focal point. The landscape was hardscrabble—stunted trees trying to gain a foothold against ironshore and craggy limestone—and in two hundred and fifty years of living here, the residents had not improved upon it. The scene was not so much one of poverty as it was lethargy and neglect.

I pulled up to a long wooden dock where several other boats were moored, including a couple of sloops bearing the logo of a bareboat outfitter from the Abacos. A white block building sat at the foot of the dock. A sign on it said SNOW LANDING. FOOD. ICE. GAS. We put down the rubber bumpers and I maneuvered *Miz Blitz* into a narrow slot at the end, between two fancy offshore fishing boats with sturdy rods and big shiny Penn reels all ready to haul in trophy billfish.

We walked past the gas pumps and onto the glassed-in porch of the white block building. The air inside was cold and thick with cigarette smoke, and it was so dark it took a few moments for our eyes to adjust. A half-dozen tables sat by the windows, looking out on the water. They were occupied by two parties of fishermen and several handsome young couples, who looked like they belonged to the sloops. They all wore the dismal countenances of people who had arrived at a place expecting a jolly good time and then suffered a grievous letdown.

Several men sat on stools at the bar. They had the look of locals and there was a similarity about all of them—the blotchy complexions, the slope of their shoulders, the general thickness of their bodies. The men were watching a television that hung from the ceiling behind the bar. *Hogan's Heroes* was on and the volume was full blast, consuming the place. Hogan and his pals were teaching Schultz how to play poker. A fat, sixtyish woman stood behind the bar, and she was watching the television, too.

I left Boggy and Nixon by the door and stepped to the bar. A couple of the men glanced my way, then turned their attention back to the television. After a minute or so, a commercial came on and the fat woman looked at me. She was a poster child for the ravages of gravity. Wrinkles started in her forehead and drooped below her eyes, the corners of her skinny lips drooped down to her slack jaw and, beneath a worn T-shirt, her boobs drooped almost to her waist. She still had three or four of her original teeth, which dangled, brown and yellow, like a whittler's work in progress.

"Huh?" she said.

I pointed out to *Miz Blitz* and asked if it would be alright to dock there. She squinted outside.

"How big's that boat a yours?" she said.

"It's a fifty-two-footer."

"Be fifty-two dollars," she said.

"We're only going to be here an hour or so."

"Doesn't matter," she said. "We take the fifty-two dollars now, and if you eat lunch, then we'll take it out of that. You want gas we'll take it out of that, too. Be at least fifty-two dollars no matter what. Be another dollar a foot should you decide to spend the night."

"Ah, the life of a pirate," I said.

I gave her three twenties and she handed me change, looking at Boggy and Nixon.

"Them two with you?" she said.

"Yeah. Thought we'd walk around town, then come back and get something to eat."

She thought about it.

"We got take-away," she said.

Then she turned her attention to *Hogan's Heroes*. Schultz was now wearing a bucket on his head.

41

Our grand tour of Blountston didn't last more than thirty minutes. We walked the length of the waterfront and didn't see anything that compelled us to stop. We passed a grocery store, Blount's, just down the street from Snow Landing. Two brand-new shiny pickup trucks were parked outside, the motors running, small children sitting inside of both of them with the windows rolled up and the AC on, while their mothers—thirty-year-old versions of the fat woman in the bar—stood between the trucks talking. I said hello and they looked our way, and then they went back to talking.

We were the only people walking on the street. Every now and then a big shiny pickup truck would roll by filled with people who looked a lot like all the other people we had seen. Far be it from me to jump to conclusions, but I'd guess the gene pool on French Jug wasn't too much more than ankle deep. No one sat on the front porches of the houses because the houses didn't have any porches. They were closed up tight with the shades drawn and the prevailing sound was the hum of air conditioner compressors. The dogs were mean and bounded out to the ends of driveways to bark at us. They all looked alike, too—

black, short-haired hounds, a subbreed of Bahamian mongrels known as potlicks. There were lots of satellite dishes in backyards and lots of rusting junk. Blountston wasn't so much a town in the tropics as it was a displaced chunk of Appalachia.

At the end of the street we came to a plaque erected by The Bahamas National Trust. Nixon read it out loud for us: "Settled in the 1750s by colonists from the Carolinas who remained loyal to the British Crown, this island was originally called St. Mary. Beset by falling fortunes, the islanders were known to erect false beacons that tricked passing ships into sailing through the nearby perilous shoals, whereupon they crashed and became easy targets for plunder. Transports from France were the favored prey since they typically carried large shipments of wine and brandy that could be sold at a premium—the French jugs from which the island assumed its popular name."

After he finished reading it, we turned around and walked back to Snow Landing. The fishermen and the sailboat party had moved on to bluer waters, but the same crew was still watching television. Only now it was *I Dream of Jeannie*.

We took a table by the window. During a commercial the fat woman brought us menus and stood there waiting while we looked them over. Everything was priced about double what was reasonable, but I told Nixon to order anything he wanted since we had already paid for it.

"You gonna sit inside here and eat it?" the fat woman asked. It was pretty obvious she preferred that we didn't.

"Yeah," I said. "Thought we'd soak up the atmosphere."

The food was better than I expected. Boggy and I both had cracked conch, which was fried with lots of pepper and came with a pile of rice 'n' peas. Nixon had fried chicken and french fries.

While we were eating, I looked outside and saw a man pushing a cart from the grocery store down to the dock. It was filled with five-gallon jugs of water, cans of food, and loaves of bread. He stopped by a lobster boat, a twenty-four-footer. It had plenty of wear on the hull, but sported brand new twin Evinrude 150s. The name was on the transom—*Cat Sass*. The man loaded the supplies into the boat. He was big and well built. He wore short black trunks that were tight where his thighs bulged out. His upper body was so ripped that it made his big arms hang at angles and look shorter than they really were.

He hopped off the boat, flipped on the gas pump, and stuck a hose in the boat's tank. He let the pump run while he stepped to the restaurant and popped his head in the door. He wore a tiny diamond stud in each ear. And one of those Celtic tattoos ringed his neck.

"Hey," he grunted. The fat woman turned away from the TV. "Put me down for seventy-five dollars' worth out here."

The fat woman nodded, the guy walked back to the boat, and only then did I realize he was Chip Willis. Or, at least, the guy who pretended to be Chip Willis when he picked me up at Baypoint. Gone was the blond Tweety-Bird cut. His hair was dark and cropped short, but I had no doubt it was him. The swagger, the voice, the earrings, the tattoo.

"Be right back," I told Boggy and Nixon.

As I started out the door, the fat woman hollered: "Hey, mister, you owe me eight dollars."

I stepped back to the bar.

"Your meal came to sixty dollars even," she said.

I gave her back the eight dollars she had given me in change earlier. I looked out the window. The guy who wasn't Chip Willis had cranked the Evinrudes and was untying his dock lines.

"You know that guy?"

"Uh-huh," the woman said.

"He got a name?"

One of the men at the bar turned his attention from the TV to me. He said, "Why you asking?"

"I like that boat of his. Thought I might make him an offer for it."

The man looked at the fat woman, then back at me.

"That's Dwayne Crowe," he said. "But that boat ain't his. Belongs to his uncle."

"Does Dwayne live here on French Jug?"

But the two of them just looked at me. That was all I was getting out of them.

I waved Boggy and Nixon to follow me, and told them what was going on as we headed to the dock. The lobster boat was already pulling away as we jumped aboard *Miz Blitz*. By the time we made it to the channel we were a hundred yards behind, with about a half mile to go before we hit open water. I watched the *Cat Sass* through the binoculars, saw its bow lift as it picked up speed, then settle down as it began to plane. I gave *Miz Blitz* some throttle and we kept pace.

With three markers to go before the end of the channel, the *Cat Sass* veered left over the shallows, taking a shortcut to the deeper water. When I got to the spot where it had left the channel I could make out the traces of its wake and turned to follow it.

Miz Blitz pulls six feet of draft and we weren't twenty yards out of the channel when we ran hard aground. Nixon slammed against a bulkhead. Boggy yanked loose one of the stanchions trying to hold on. I braced against the wheel as I heard pots and plates and pans crashing around in the galley. The engine died. And the *Cat Sass* disappeared, running to the south.

Dwayne Crowe. So that was his real name, was it? Just what the hell was he doing here?

Lucky for us it was an incoming tide. We only had to wait a couple of hours for it to float *Miz Blitz* and give us enough leeway to trudge to the channel. On the run back, we swung into North Eleuthera and dropped off Nixon so he could go help his aunt. Then we shot across the sound to Harbour Island.

We were pulling into the marina at Valentine's when the radio emitted its trio of beeps and I turned up the volume to hear the announcer from the National Hurricane Center give the 5 P.M. coordinates for what was now Hurricane Curt. He said the storm had moved to less than a hundred miles east of Grand Turk Island with a projected landfall in the southern Bahamas.

I looked at Boggy. He offered no smug I-told-you-so's. He just nodded. Then he went down to the foredeck to fend us off as we pulled into the marina.

Five minutes later I heard someone calling my name and looked out to see Charlie Hineman standing on the dock.

"Phone's been ringing off the hook for you."

He handed me a notepad. It showed three calls from Steffie Plank and two from Zoe Applequist. At the bottom someone had written "????? Call back 7."

"The last one, the man wouldn't give his name or a number where he could be reached," said Charlie. "He said he would try again at 7 P.M. He seemed rather insistent that you be there."

Victor Ortiz? Hector hadn't waited to get back to Miami to call him. And I couldn't wait to talk to him myself.

42

Rather than return Zoe Applequist's call I went straight to the Downey compound. I had to knock twice before Tiffani St. James opened the door at the pink house. She was glassy-eyed. It took her a moment to focus and then she smiled and said, "Oh, hi. Come on in."

No sooner had I stepped inside than I heard Zoe Applequist yelling from the living room, "Dammit, Tiffani, I told you to wait just a minute."

"OK, OK!" Tiffani yelled back. She looked at me and shrugged. "Sorry. We better wait here."

We stood in the foyer, me leaning against one wall, and Tiffani leaning against the other. She was wearing a long white T-shirt and not much else.

"So," she said. "Whatchya been doing?"

"Running around. Mostly in circles," I said. "Have there been any more calls?"

"No, we never get any calls. It's so boring." Then she thought about it and said, "Oh, you mean those other calls. You better talk to Zoe about that."

Zoe appeared and led us into the living room.

"Go put on some clothes," she told Tiffani. After she was gone, Zoe said, "My apologies, but Burma wasn't . . . she isn't presentable."

The empty wheelchair sat by the kitchen counter, the terry-cloth robe draped over the back. Zoe motioned to the sofa and I sat down. She took a chair. She had changed out of her workout duds and was wearing pleated khaki shorts with a green polo shirt tucked in at the waist, no belt.

"I got your messages," I said.

"That was hours ago," she said, a peevish edge to her voice. "I called you the moment we found the second cell phone. And I rang you again right after they called. I am trying not to exclude you from this, Mr. Chasteen."

"I told you before that I'd stay here until the next call came."

She ignored it, taking a cell phone, a red Nokia, out of a pocket in her shorts. She told me how Tiffani had found it sitting on the seat of one of the golf carts at about 2 P.M. She brought it to Zoe. The man called about two-thirty.

"He said they had received the money and took it as a sign of our commitment to continue in good faith. He kept asking if we had said anything to the police."

"What did you tell him?"

"I told him no, *we* hadn't."

Zoe gave me a look that was meant to be withering. When I didn't wither, she said, "I am offering you the chance to proceed in this without any further involvement from the police."

I didn't say anything.

Zoe said, "I have no doubt that they are watching our house. If Lynfield Pederson comes here again, then they will see him, and I don't want to risk that, Mr. Chasteen. We have established a level of trust with them and we can't lose it. That is why we let Clarissa go."

"Let her go? You mean, you fired her?"

"Yes, shortly after she had finished another little rendezvous with Pederson. We know now, Mr. Chasteen, that it was Clarissa who first told him about the kidnaping, and not you. That is why we are still willing to work with you to make sure everything goes smoothly. Have you had any success in obtaining your part of the money?"

I told her I was still waiting to hear about a transfer of funds. That was stretching the truth just a tad, but I was certain that Steffie Plank would come through with something.

Then Zoe said, "Will you be able to come up with the entire million dollars?"

"That I'm not sure about. Will you?"

"We already have."

"You what?"

"We have the remaining seven hundred fifty thousand dollars in hand. We are prepared to give it to them according to their instructions. How much more time do you think you will need?"

Before I could answer, Tiffani walked into the living room. She had changed into a short yellow sundress and pulled her hair into a ponytail.

"I'm going out," she announced, wobbling toward the front door.

Zoe shot up from her chair.

"Like hell you are."

"You can't stop me," said Tiffani.

Zoe grabbed Tiffani's arm, slung her into a wall, and stood blocking the door.

It would have been fun to sit there and watch it all play out, but my lunch was suddenly speaking to me. That fat woman at Snow's Landing must have fed me some bad conch.

"If you don't mind, I'm going to . . ."

I headed down the hall to the bathroom and took care of what needed taking care of. I could hear muffled arguing between Tiffani and Zoe. And then someone stomped down the hallway and slammed a bedroom door, no doubt Tiffani going to her room to sulk and pout.

Washing up, I noticed prescription containers sitting on the counter. Lots of them. I checked out the labels. Yes, ye shall know them by the meds they take. There were painkillers, mostly—fentanyl and Vicodin and Lortab. I wasn't a pharma-

cological expert, by any means, but three knee surgeries had offered me a crash course in barbiturates, so to speak. These were
some strong doses, enough to lay you out in la-la land.

The prescriptions came from various drugstores in Fort
Lauderdale. Some had Zoe Applequist's name on them, some
had the name of a C. L. Swanson. Hadn't Tiffani mentioned
something about a friend, somebody Swanson?

When I returned to the living room, Zoe Applequist was
standing by the big glass window, looking out at the ocean.

"Where will you be if they call again?" she asked, not bothering to look at me.

"Thought I'd sit here and wait with you."

"No, I'd prefer you didn't."

"Then you can find me either at the Albury or at Valentine's,
on my boat."

She nodded.

I showed myself to the door.

43

At 6:55 P.M. I was sitting by the phone in the Albury's salon. The stereo was playing Diana Krall's version of "Peel Me a Grape." It was a dandy version. I would have peeled Diana Krall just about anything she asked for—an onion, a cucumber, the skin off my nose.

Some of the guests were already clearing out, and for those who were left the talk at the bar was about the hurricane. Mr. Pindle was holding court with stories about all the blows he'd weathered on the island. Once, he said, during Hurricane Helene, must have been 1962 or '63, he'd gone to sleep in his little cottage at the Albury only to wake up to discover he couldn't get out the front door. Sand drifts had covered the cottage almost to the roof.

"Had to hoist up my skinny little sweetheart and get her to crawl out the bathroom window and then go find somebody to shovel open the door," he said.

The call came promptly at seven o'clock.

"Hello," I said.

I'd been trying to think of something better than that, but nothing good had come to me.

"You wished for me to call?" a man said.

"Ortiz?"

A pause. And then he said, "Eduardo, he was my sister's youngest son. Only thirty. We had his funeral today. A very private funeral. Because of the circumstances. My sister, she does not understand why I do not just kill you. I tell her it is not so easy as that."

There was so much I wanted to say, so much that had been building up, and it all came out in a rush.

"Listen, I don't know what it is I've got that you want, but whatever it is, I'll do whatever it takes to get it to you, OK? You got that? You don't have to send anyone else to follow me around or whack me in the head with a shovel, OK? But first you have to release Barbara and Lord Downey. I don't have a million dollars, I can't get a million dollars. You've already got some of the money from Burma. So let's work out something else, just you and me."

He didn't say anything. And I thought for a moment that he had hung up.

"Ortiz?"

"I am here," he said. "But I understand nothing of which you speak. What is this million dollars? Who are these people that you want me to release, but that I do not have? And what money has been given to me by this person I do not know?"

"Where are you?"

"Please, this you do not need to know."

The connection was clear and crisp. I could hear music in the background, the chatter of people. It sounded as if he might be in a restaurant.

"You swear to me you aren't behind the kidnapping?"

"You mean that you would take me at my word?"

"Just tell me, you son of a bitch, and let's go from there."

"I am not in the business of kidnapping, if that is what you wish to know. And the million dollars of which you speak . . ."

"Yeah, what about it?"

"You have something worth far more than that, Chasteen."

I heard a click. The line went dead.

44

I stopped at a take-away shop in Dunmore Town and picked up dinner—fried snapper, cole slaw, macaroni and cheese, and two big slices of banana cream pie. Boggy and I polished it off while sitting on the aft deck of *Miz Blitz*. Afterwards, I poured a glass of rum and stretched out on one of the cushioned lazarettes to plot exactly what the hell I should do. Next thing I knew it was morning. The rum sat untouched and Boggy was hosing down the deck.

I sucked down a cup of coffee and headed for the Piggly Wiggly, where I bought a ten-dollar BaTelCo phone card. Steffie Plank picked up on the first ring.

"Zack? Where the hell have you been? Why haven't you called?"

"Sorry, but . . ."

"What about Barbara?"

"Everything's OK, at least as OK as it can be," I said, and caught her up with everything.

When I was finished, Steffie said, "I got the money."

"You did?"

"Well, some of it. Like three hundred fifty thousand dollars.

All the vendors except one went for it. Of course, they wanted details, like were we having problems, and could they expect the same thing again next month? And I said no. I said this was just a temporary thing. But now I don't know what to do, Zack. I don't know where to wire the money, or how to do that exactly. And I don't know what to tell the bank here. And I don't know the name of the bank there. And I don't . . ."

"Take a deep breath, Steffie."

She did.

Then she said, "So what do I do?"

"I don't know."

"You're kidding me."

"It's not like I've done this before," I said. "I've never wired money from a bank to another bank overseas."

"What's the name of the bank there, Zack?"

"I don't know. I mean, I've walked by it a hundred times, but—"

An automated voice broke in: "You have ten seconds remaining for this call."

"Shit," I said.

"Zack . . ."

"Steffie, you've done good, you've done great. I'll call back later today."

"Zack . . ."

The automated voice broke in again: "Thank you for using BaTelCo. Good-bye."

I stood there trying to figure out what I should do next. Seems like I had been spending a lot of time doing that. Hadn't gotten me anywhere. I was just muddling along, knocking heads with Victor Ortiz's hired hands, killing his nephew, and just generally screwing up things. Steffie had done more to help Barbara than I had. She had found a way to get some of the money and she was ready to send it to me. Now all I had to do was go into the bank and make the arrangements.

There were two banks in Dunmore Town—Bank of the Commonwealth, and Bank of the Bahamas. I didn't think it would make much difference which one I chose. But it was early, not even eight o'clock. They wouldn't open until nine. It gave me a chance to head back to the Albury, wash up, and put on some fresh clothes. Wanted to make a good impression on the bankers.

I did all that and when I was done it was only eight-thirty. The day was just dragging along. So I headed back to *Miz Blitz* to let Boggy know what I was up to. I was almost there when I heard feet pounding the pavement and turned around to see Nixon Styles running toward me from Government Dock.

"I know where it is," he said, out of breath.

"Where what is?"

"The boat, the one you were chasing yesterday. That lobster boat from French Jug. I know where it is."

45

We sat around the big teak table in the galley listening to Nixon tell his story. After we had dropped him off at North Eleuthera, he had taken the package to his aunt and then gone out fishing with his uncle. They ran along the windwardside of the island and were drift-fishing the water just north of Glass Bridge when Nixon spotted a lobster boat tucked into a small cove beneath the limestone cliffs.

"Where all the caves are," said Nixon. "And there's all kinds of rocks in the water, too, some of them sticking out and some of them just under the water waiting to poke holes right through a boat. My uncle, he wouldn't pull up all the way in that cove, didn't want to risk it. But he got close enough so I could see the name—*Cat Sass,* just like the boat yesterday."

"Did you see the man?" I asked him.

"No, didn't see him. Figured he might be up there in one of those caves. No other place for him to be around there. No roads going in or out. About the only way you can get to those caves is by boat. Climbing up the back side of those cliffs will tear you up."

I pulled out the chartbook and asked Nixon to show me

where he found the boat. It only took him a few seconds to zero in on the general location, about two miles north of the Glass Bridge.

"This map even shows those pointy rocks that stick up out of the water," Nixon said. "There's five or six of them. My uncle, he says they call them the Steeples because they look like steeples on a church."

Nixon had taken the first water taxi leaving from North Eleuthera that morning and had come straight to the marina so he could tell us about finding the *Cat Sass*. He said he needed to get home or his mother would be worrying about him. I thanked him and fished around in my pocket and found a five dollar bill. He wouldn't take it.

"This one's on the house," he said.

Boggy made us more coffee. We sat on the boat drinking it. Outside, you'd have never guessed a hurricane was barreling down on the Bahamas. The way it is with hurricanes, the big ones, they suck all the moisture out of the path that lies in front of them, feeding on that, just paving the way. The sky was clear and blue. The wind barely stirred.

Finally, I said, "What do you think?"

Boggy said, "I think this man, Dwayne Crowe, he is in too many places."

"Yeah, I'm thinking that, too. And those supplies on his boat. Why would he be taking all that stuff to those caves? It doesn't sound like a place where you set up housekeeping. Unless you're trying to keep it a secret."

"You think he is working maybe with Victor Ortiz?"

"I don't know," I said. "Ortiz told me he didn't know anything about the kidnapping, but I don't have any reason to believe him. And I don't think Dwayne Crowe has the smarts to put something like this together and pull it off."

"No, he would need someone to help him, someone here on Harbour Island," said Boggy. "A man like him, he could not come and go from here—bring the cell phones, pick up the money—without attracting attention. It is very much organized. It takes many people."

I got up and poured another cup of coffee. I looked out the cabin window. A couple of boats had already left the marina and others were getting ready to. Making the haul back to Florida, hoping to tuck in before the big winds hit.

Boggy said, "You are thinking about the police inspector?"

"Yeah, I'm thinking about him. I'm thinking about him a lot. Big gray area there. I'd sure like to know what he's been doing the last twenty-four hours. I thought he would have checked in with me by now. Whatever he's up to, he's playing a close hand."

So the two of us came up with a plan. Actually, it wasn't so much a plan as it was a matter of wandering off blindly in two different directions and seeing what happened. But at least it would keep things in motion.

We decided Boggy would take *Miz Blitz*'s skiff and go snooping around near the caves. If Dwayne Crowe happened to see Boggy then, at least, he wouldn't recognize him.

As for me, I had a lot of items on my to-do list. But having a chat with Lynfield Pederson was number one.

46

Brindley was sitting at his desk when I walked into the inspector's office. He was listening to the police radio, his helmet on the desk, the polishing cloth beside it. I picked up the helmet and looked at it.

"Sorry, Brindley, but I still can't see my reflection in this thing."

Brindley took the helmet and frowned at me.

I said, "Where's Pederson?"

"Wait here," Brindley said.

He opened the door that said OFFICIAL BUSINESS ONLY and stepped into the garage out back where I had seen Bryce Gannon's body two days earlier. He closed the door behind him. A few seconds later the door opened and Brindley said, "Inspector will see you now."

I stepped into the garage. The big garage door was open and light streamed in. A golf cart sat on blocks inside the garage and Lynfield Pederson was squatting down behind it, fiddling around with something. He stood up and dusted himself off. He was wearing blue suit pants, a long-sleeve white shirt, and the same red tie he'd worn before. It must have been ninety-five degrees in that garage, but he was barely sweating. Bahamas heat is different from Florida heat. Florida heat sits on your skin awhile. Bahamas heat goes straight to the bone. They say you get used to it. I hadn't. I was drenched.

Pederson said, "I was just getting ready to come see you."

"Oh, really?" I said. "You mean, after you got finished doing some repairs on the golf cart, then ate lunch, and visited your girlfriend?"

He looked at me, his tongue working over his teeth. He said, "You still got a bug up your ass, Chasteen?"

"Yeah, matter of fact I do."

"Must be a big bug and it's buzzing all around driving you crazy."

"Let's cut the shit, Pederson."

"Yeah, let's do," he said. "Where you want to start cutting at?"

"How about you tell me what you were doing for those three hours yesterday, when I sat and waited for you and the people we are trying to catch collected a quarter-million dollars?"

"Want me to account for my time, that it?"

"Yeah, that's it exactly."

Pederson reached for his back pocket and pulled out his wallet. He opened it up and plucked out a folded piece of paper, and handed it to me.

"What you see there?"

"It's a pay stub."

"Uh-huh," he said. "It's my pay stub. Now you look close at it and tell me how much I get paid."

"It says $941.52."

"That's right. Every two weeks. Ain't shit, is it?"

"I didn't come here to listen to you bitch about your salary."

"No, you get the bitching as a bonus, on top of listening to everything else I'm going to tell you." He leaned back against the golf cart, folded his big arms across his chest. "Mailboat comes from Nassau every Monday morning. Gets here about 9:30 A.M., all depending. And every other Monday it brings my paycheck. So I was down there at the dock yesterday morning waiting on the mailboat. You know why I was waiting on the mailboat?"

"No, why?"

"Because I had next to nothing in my bank account, that's why. Had $17.13 to be exact. And I had to get my hands on one hundred and fifty dollars right away or some dead English fellow's body was gonna be sitting on the dock at Mr. Otis's fish house, swelling up and stinking in the sun."

"Bryce Gannon."

"Oh yeah, Mr. Gannon. He's OK now, don't you worry. We got him on ice. But Mr. Otis was raising hell the other day. Said he wanted fifty dollars a day, not twenty-five dollars. Said none of the fishermen would buy ice from him as long as he's storing that body. Said he wanted three days' money in advance. And it's not like I can just write out a requisition to Nassau and ask for that one hundred and fifty dollars, because Nassau doesn't know anything about that dead body. So I had to wait on the mailboat, then go to the bank and cash my check, and take my own money to Mr. Otis. And so now I'm minus that one hundred fifty dollars until I don't know when because it can take months getting reimbursements out of Nassau. And that's once I can file the paperwork. Which I can't, because I'm still working on this rat's ass of a mess and trying to keep Nassau out of it."

"You could have told me that yesterday," I said.

"Didn't figure my personal finances were anything you needed to know about. It's why I told you it was police business."

"I still don't see why it took you almost three hours."

"Believe me," Pederson said. "I've been kicking my own ass for not telling Mr. Otis to go to hell so I could hook up with you earlier than I did. It was a mistake. Don't blame you for being pissed off. I'm sorry."

He stuck out his hand. I shook it.

"So now that we've kissed and made up," I said, "I still don't see why it took you almost three hours."

Pederson shook his head. This time there was a sliver of a smile.

"Got-dam, I knew I never should've told you about knocking you on your ass. You ain't about to let me have that," he said. "You know Jesteen Clements?"

"No, don't believe so . . ."

"Sure you do. Works in the kitchen at the Albury? Big old gal."

"Oh, that Jesteen."

"Yeah, that Jesteen, the one who saw somebody driving Bryce Gannon and Ms. Pickering in a golf cart the night Gannon was murdered. The same Jesteen you didn't tell me about."

"Forgot," I said. "I meant to, but . . ."

Pederson waved me off.

"That's alright. Would have been good to know a little earlier than I found out about it, but Jesteen, she caught me right when I was leaving the fish house after paying Mr. Otis. Said Mr. Pindle told her she better come talk to me. And then she told me how she'd seen that girl . . ."

"Tiffani St. James."

"Uh-huh. Jesteen told me she saw her driving all three of them in the golf cart. And that got me thinking: What happened to that golf cart of Bryce Gannon's anyway? There's a half dozen places on the island that rent golf carts, so I came back here to the office and I had to call four of them before I found the one that rented to Bryce Gannon. And they told me it hadn't been returned, which didn't really surprise me. I didn't have time to go out looking for it then because I was already late meeting up with you. But I finally tracked it down yesterday afternoon."

He turned around and looked at the golf cart he'd been leaning up against.

"That's it?" I asked.

"Oh, yeah. Want to know where I found it?"

I nodded.

"In the parking lot at Bahama Sands."

Pederson watched my reaction, saying, "Yeah, that's the same kinda look I had on my face when I found it there. Like, what the hell is it doing there? Which means, either the three of them didn't take it in the first place, and they rode in someone else's golf cart, or they did take it, and then somebody drove it all the way back there and left it. Me, I don't think that second choice is too damn likely."

Pederson walked around to the back of the golf cart. I followed him. A black battery sat on a rack above the rear bumper.

A heavy duty black cord was plugged into the battery. Pederson unplugged it.

"That's how I found it," he said. "Battery was unplugged. Cart wouldn't run."

"Meaning, they rode in someone else's. Tiffani's. One of Lord Downey's carts."

"Could be."

"So Tiffani lied to me about that. She told me Bryce Gannon offered her a ride home in his golf cart and then let her do the driving. She said Gannon and Barbara dropped her off and then drove away."

"You talked to Tiffani St. James?" Pederson said. "That something else you forgot to tell me about?"

So I told Pederson how Tiffani had visited my cottage Sunday night. I told him how she had slipped off her black dress and pitched a hissy fit when I asked her to leave.

"You a strong man," he said. "Figure you and me ought to go have a talk with Miss Tiffani?"

"Yeah, I do. Only I don't think Zoe Applequist will let you inside the house again."

"You're probably right."

"Then again, you are the police inspector. I don't know how the Bahamian legal system works, but . . ."

"It works in strange and fucked-up ways," said Pederson. "You wanting to know why I don't tell Zoe Applequist to go screw herself and just go in there and talk to Tiffani St. James myself?"

"Kinda wondering about that."

"Lord Downey's a Belonger. Know what that is?"

"Isn't it someone who's not a native Bahamian, but who has been here a long time and been granted citizenship? Like the next best thing to being a native?"

"Even better sometimes than being a native. Sort of like unofficial royalty. Got to tread lightly with Belongers and their families. Else a police inspector will find himself out of a job."

Pederson plucked a toothpick from a pocket and chewed on it. Then he said, "Of course, if you were to ask me to give you a lift to the general vicinity of the Downey compound, and you were to go in and talk to Tiffani St. James, and then come out and tell me about it, then I can't see how that would upset anyone."

I told him I'd meet him back at the station in an hour. I had a couple of other things to check off my list.

I left the police station and walked into Dunmore Town. The Commonwealth Bank sat on the same block as Maurice's Hardware and Anthony's Bakery.

I waited fifteen minutes to speak with the manager, a grave young man in his thirties, who told me what I needed to do to transfer three hundred fifty thousand dollars from a bank in the United States. He said there would be some paperwork, and a few minor fees, but there was no reason the transaction couldn't be taken care of within forty-eight hours.

"Is there any way to get it faster than that?" I asked him.

"If you had an account with us, then we might be able to expedite the transaction in twenty-four hours," he said. "Otherwise, a sum of that magnitude, it generally takes two days."

I told him I'd get back in touch.

The office of the *Island Voice* sat across the street. I went inside. The only person in the office was a man with curly gray hair and a Mark Twain mustache. He was in his sixties, and he wore a long-sleeve white shirt with the sleeves rolled up and baggy seersucker pants that were held up by red suspenders. He was working at a computer, and a brass nameplate on top of it said RONALD DIXON, EDITOR-IN-CHIEF. He looked up when I walked in.

"What can I do you for?" he said, smiling. The accent was American, I'd guess the Midwest.

"I'm looking for a story that ran in your paper several weeks ago. It was about a woman named Burma Downey, something about a car accident. Do you remember that?"

"You betcha," said Ronald Dixon.

He got up from the computer and started rifling through a stack of newspapers by his desk.

"Here's what you're looking for, right there on the front page," said Ronald Dixon, handing me a paper. It was dated July sixth, about six weeks ago. "Back copies are two dollars."

The phone rang as I was paying him and he answered it. I stood at the counter looking at the paper. The story was played prominently, stripped across the top under a headline that said: "Burma Downey Suffers Critical Injuries in Florida Accident."

There wasn't all that much more to the story than there was in the headline. It read:

One of Harbour Island's most prominent residents was critically injured last week in an automobile accident that happened while she was in Florida. Miss Burma Lindsay Downey, 32, sustained multiple injuries as a result of the accident, which took place in Fort Lauderdale. A spokeswoman for Miss Downey said she was undergoing extensive treatment at a Fort Lauderdale hospital and would be in recovery for several months.

"Burma is hoping to return soon to Harbour Island to continue her convalescence there," said spokeswoman Zoe Applequist. "She thanks her friends and neighbors for their prayers."

Miss Downey is a former fashion model who splits her time between Harbour Island and her international travels. She is the daughter of Lord Frederickson Downey, O.B.E., who has maintained an estate on Harbour Island for many years and is well known throughout the Bahamas for his numerous civic deeds.

When Ronald Dixon finished talking on the phone, I asked him, "Who wrote the story about Burma Downey?"

"That would be me. Got a staff of two. I handle news and advertising. My wife lays it out, gets it to the printer in Nassau, and takes care of the books."

"Mind if I ask how you found out about the accident?"

"Not at all," he said. "Got a phone call. It was from her friend, that woman mentioned in the story, as I remember. Funny name . . ."

"Zoe Applequist?"

"That's the one. She called and told me what had happened and said she thought people might be interested in it. As you can tell, there's not much that goes on here. It was worth the front page."

"Was Ms. Downey driving the car when the accident happened?"

Dixon thought about it. Then he said, "Couldn't tell you that. Don't know."

"Was there anyone else hurt? What about the other car?"

"Beats me. I just wrote what the woman told me. I didn't ask a lot of questions," he said. "I don't claim to be a great investigative reporter, mister. I used to sell insurance in Iowa before we moved here and decided the island could use a newspaper. Hell, I'm supposed to be retired."

I thanked Ronald Dixon for his time and left the newspaper office.

48

It was raining by the time I got to the Albury Beach Club. It wasn't the hard, needle rain of a summer thunderstorm, one that would all-too quickly fade and be gone, but something that started slowly and resolutely and gave notice that it intended to stick around. The sky had gone gray and the ocean had gone gray with it.

There was no one in the Albury's salon, no one at the bar, no one in the dining room. I knocked on the door of the office. Charlie Hineman opened it and I stepped in. Chrissie was sitting at her desk, tapping away at a computer, a phone cradled between shoulder and ear.

"Why, certainly, Mrs. Moss, we understand completely, and we would be delighted to have you in September," Chrissie spoke into the phone.

Chrissie hung up the phone, and said, "Well, looks like you've got the run of the place, Zack."

"Everyone else has checked out?" I said.

Chrissie nodded.

"And the ones who were scheduled to come in have already cancelled on account of the storm. Mrs. Moss was the last of them. Ah, the life of an innkeeper," she said. "Just so you'll know, we'll be shutting down the kitchen for the next couple of days. Until everything blows over."

"Well, hell, if there's no food, then I'm getting the hell out of Dodge, too," I said. "Really, though, it doesn't make any sense for me to stay here when I can just as easily bunk down on the boat."

They tried to talk me out of it, but that was just their hospitable nature. I went back to the cottage and packed up the rest of my stuff. I tried not to look at Barbara's things, just left them where they were. I filled the ice bucket, stuck the Schramsberg '98 in it, and carried it with me.

I met Chrissie and Charlie near the parking lot as I was leaving.

"Has there been any more news, Zack?" Chrissie asked.

Like most everyone else on the island, they still thought Barbara's disappearance was being treated as a missing persons case. I told them about the ransom demand and asked that they not spread it around.

"What can we do?" said Charlie.

"You mean, short of loaning me a million dollars?"

Charlie and Chrissie exchanged a look.

Chrissie said, "Would a hundred thousand help? We could cash in some CDs that are just sitting there. We don't have much, Zack. I mean, we're just resident managers here, but we have saved a little and . . ."

"Thanks, no. But I appreciate it."

"How's Burma holding up in all this?" Chrissie asked.

I told them Zoe Applequist was handling everything.

Chrissie said: "I don't mean to be catty, but . . ."

I waited. Charlie waited.

"Very well, if you insist," said Chrissie. "Who's sleeping with who at Burma's house these days?"

"I'm not exactly privy to that information. But I'm open to speculation."

"Well, if it's anything like it has been in the past, then they are all in the sack together."

"I don't think so. At least not Tiffani and Zoe. No love there."

I told them about the little altercation I had witnessed the day before.

"Quite the alpha bitch, that Zoe," said Chrissie. "Remember the scene she caused here that night, Charlie?"

"Hard to forget. I was the one had to break them up."

"It was several weeks ago, not long before Burma's accident," Chrissie said. "Burma and her entourage showed up here for dinner. There were a few new faces, one of them was that Tiffani girl you mentioned. She and her boyfriend. Both of them rather coarse, if you ask me. But the other gal was a knockout—tall, quite nearly as tall as Burma, looked like she had stepped straight off the runway at Milan. She and Burma walked in together—arm-in-arm, as a matter of fact—and it was like watching a couple of Thoroughbreds pace through the paddock.

"After dinner the two of them were kissing in the salon, practically stretched out on one of the rattan sofas. It was scandalous, even by Burma's standards. I was preparing to ask them to kindly take it home when Zoe came charging out of the dining room and started flailing away at them. I daresay it was a fit of jealousy, but I don't know exactly whom she was jealous of. She was giving both of them the beating of their lives. And then, of course, Charlie stepped in."

Charlie said, "Happens again, I'll just spray cold water on them. Don't ever break up a cat fight."

"Do you happen to remember the name of that woman, the one on the sofa with Burma?"

"I was never introduced," said Chrissie. "I learned later she was a friend of that Tiffani creature. But I never got a name."

Chrissie gave me a peck on the cheek. I shook hands with Charlie. On the way back to the police station I thought about Tiffani describing that beautiful friend of hers who wanted to be a model. I thought about the prescription bottles I'd seen in the bathroom at Burma Downey's house. Sounded to me like the gal on the sofa making out with Burma could have been Cheri Swanson.

But so what if it was? Wasting time trying to figure out who Burma Downey might have slept with wasn't getting me any closer to finding Barbara. Just focus on the prize, Chasteen.

49

Pederson drove us to the Downey compound. On the way I told him about my trip to French Jug the day before, about seeing Dwayne Crowe, and how Nixon had spotted the *Cat Sass* anchored near the Steeples. He seemed a little bent out of shape when I told him Boggy had gone over in the skiff to check it out, said I should have talked that over with him first.

"Sorry," I said. "But I wasn't exactly thinking kind thoughts about you when I got up this morning. Didn't want to share much of anything with you."

"All I'm saying is, Dwayne Crowe is two tons of trouble in a one-ton bag."

"Had some run-ins with him?"

"Yeah, over the years. There was a string of break-ins here on-island a while back that I liked him for, him and his younger brother, Donnie, and a couple of their cousins. All of them big as a house and mean as snakes. But I couldn't make anything stick. One of his cousins got shot over in Nassau not long after that, trying to stick up a grocery store, dumb piece of shit. They got his ass in jail. Been wondering where Dwayne run off to.

Heard he was working over in Florida. Can't say I'm real glad to know he's back."

Pederson pulled his van over in the shade of some casuarina trees just down the road from the Downey compound. I could see thunderheads building up to the south.

"Storm's coming," I said.

"Sure hope so," said Pederson. "I could use some fresh breeze. Hot as Baptist hell right now."

An ice cooler sat on the floor. He opened it and pulled out a jug of water and took a long swig. He passed it to me and I drank some, too.

"How's Clarissa doing? I heard how they let her go."

"Oh, she's fine. I mean, she's torn up about it, but she's fine. She loves that old man, worried sick about him. She's staying down the road at her mother's house. Said to tell you hello."

A ground dove flew off its branch in a casuarina tree and disappeared into the spartina grass along the road.

Pederson said, "Tell you one more thing I did yesterday, and then you will have the full accounting for my time and know you are getting your money's worth. You see that house across the road there?"

He pointed to a two-story gingerbread cottage almost hidden behind palmetto thickets and wax myrtle.

"Miss Melodie Michaels lives there, spinster lady, used to teach at the school, used to teach me, matter of fact. Miss Melodie, she let me sit upstairs in her bedroom yesterday afternoon. Figure I'm the first man to spend time in her bedroom in probably just about forever. But you know why I was sitting up there?"

"Keeping an eye on the Downey compound?"

Pederson nodded.

"Sat up there from two o'clock until must have been five-thirty or six, until whenever it was you showed up and went inside."

"That was closer to six."

"Yeah, guess it was," said Pederson. "What time they tell you they found that second cell phone?"

"Said Tiffani found it in one of the golf carts about two and then they got the call at 2:30 P.M."

"Well, all I know is that whoever left it must have been wearing the fucking cloak of invisibility. Because I didn't see anyone coming or going from that property except for Clarissa after they told her to pack her bags and leave. Matter of fact, I didn't even see Tiffani St. James go out to the golf carts at two o'clock, or whenever it was they said. Didn't anyone leave that house all afternoon. Miss Melodie, she kept bringing me cups of tea. Drank four of them. Kept me up pissing all night."

We sat there listening to the dove coo-cooing in the grass. Then Pederson said, "Listen, I appreciate you giving me some time to handle this. I can understand it if you want to pull the plug, call in the big guns. Finish here we can head back to the station, give Nassau a call, get in touch with the F.B.I. Do whatever you want."

"I was ready to do that last night," I said. "But . . ."

"But what?"

"Figure it's fourth down and long. But I damn sure don't feel like punting."

Zoe Applequist opened the door, and before I even had a chance to speak, she said, "Now is not a good time."

"Look, I'm just checking in with you, wanting to see where things stand."

"I have nothing new to share with you. We have had no further contact with the other party."

She stood firmly in the doorway, not about to let me inside.

"Actually, that's not the only reason I came here."

I told her about Tiffani St. James and her conflicting stories regarding the golf carts.

Zoe said, "I'm sure there's a reasonable explanation."

"I'd like to talk to Tiffani about it, hear what she has to say."

"I'm afraid that's impossible. Tiffani is indisposed."

"Indisposed? What's that supposed to mean? Is she here or not?"

"Oh, she's here. But if you must know—she's incoherent.

Totally out of it. Or at least she was. Now she's sleeping it off. I can only guess that she must have gotten into some of Burma's medication."

"Yeah, I couldn't help but notice all those pills back there. Who's Cheri Swanson, anyway?"

Zoe looked away, but recovered quickly and fixed me with a steely stare.

"Are you in the habit of going through other people's belongings?"

"There wasn't much in the way of reading material in your bathroom. Had to take what I could find."

Neither of us spoke for a long moment. Then Zoe said, "Have you made any progress getting the money?"

I nodded.

"I've spoken to the manager at Bank of the Commonwealth. He told me what I need to do to get the money wired here."

"That's good, Mr. Chasteen. I'd like to have positive news to report when they call again. And now, if you'll excuse me."

She closed the door.

50

I spent the next few hours in the company of Lynfield Pederson as he made the rounds of his tiny domain making sure everyone was strapping down for the blow that was headed our way. Twice I called Zoe Applequist to see if she had heard from the kidnappers, and twice she told me there had been no word. I didn't call Steffie Plank about wiring the money. She was probably beside herself with worry, but there was something holding me back. I just couldn't go through with it.

About midafternoon Pederson drove me back to *Miz Blitz* and said, no, he wouldn't turn down a glass of rum. Boggy had yet to return from his reconnaissance mission to find the *Cat Sass*. I was starting to get a little concerned.

I went to the galley and got out the Mount Gay. I poured a glass for Pederson and a glass for me, and we sat down at the teak table. The first sip burned. The second one burned good.

I flicked on the radio and we listened to the latest hurricane report. It said the storm was skirting west of Mayaguana Island and would likely pass over Acklins Island shortly after midnight. It said top winds at the center had reached one hundred and twenty miles per hour and, if it maintained its present course, it would make landfall on South Andros Island in about twenty-four hours, with near-hurricane-force winds extending as far east as Harbour Island. The hurricane center predicted a landfall in Florida near Daytona Beach.

I heard a thump on the foredeck and opened the cabin door, thinking it might be Boggy. But it was just a plastic bucket, blown onto *Miz Blitz* from the dock. I went out and got it, and stashed it away. The rain had gotten harder and was starting to come down sideways. There weren't that many boats left in the marina—another trawler and a couple of sailboats, their lanyards clanging up a racket.

When I got back inside, Pederson said, "Boggy might be good, but he's going to have to be better than good if he crosses paths over there with Dwayne Crowe."

"I'm not worried."

"The hell you aren't," said Pederson. "Be stupid not to be worried. Be twice as stupid if Dwayne Crowe is mixed up with Victor Ortiz."

I went to the galley and poured us some more rum. We drank quietly awhile, listening to the rain, the boat rocking more and more.

I said, "You ever used to get butterflies before a game?"

"Hell, yes. Every game I ever played. Even the ones we knew we were going to win. The tough ones I used to throw up."

"Me, too."

"Meant you wanted it. Meant you wanted it so bad you'd lose everything to get it."

I finished my rum and went for another one. Pederson said he was fine.

I said, "I'm beginning to get that fluttering feeling inside."

Pederson said, "Uh-huh. Not full-on butterflies yet, but just the beginnings. Yeah, I'm getting that, too."

"Hadn't had that feeling in a while."

"Long while," said Pederson.

"Doesn't feel bad, doesn't feel good."

"Kinda tickles."

I looked at him.

"Tickles?"

He said, "You get your butterflies, I get mine, OK?"

Pederson stood up from the table. He said, "Clarissa wants you to come eat dinner with us this evening, you and Boggy."

"I've never turned down a meal. Thanks."

"Her momma likes to eat real early, around five, but they won't mind holding it awhile."

"We're not there by six, start without us."

Pederson said, "You can damn sure count on that."

He stepped outside and was gone. I sipped rum and listened to rain and kept hearing things smack against the boat, and none of them were Boggy coming back.

When he did come back, the sun was low and I didn't even hear him. The cabin door flew open and he stepped inside.

"I found them," he said. "I saw Barbara."

51

Boggy retold his story after we arrived at Clarissa's mother's house. We sat around the dining room table—me, Pederson, and Boggy—while Clarissa and her mother brought out the plates: stuffed crab backs, peas 'n' dumplings, green bananas stewed in lime juice and sprinkled with cinnamon sugar. For dessert there was pineapple tart and banana bread.

Boggy looked a mess. He had slipped into dry clothes, but there were nicks and cuts on his face and arms, all kinds of debris in his long black hair. He had found the Steeples easily enough, seen the *Cat Sass* right where Nixon had said it would be, and then he had anchored the skiff in a cove about a half mile away. Still, he needed some reason for being there, just in case he ran into Dwayne Crowe. Lucky for Boggy he's part chameleon. Dress him up in Armani and he can pass for an avant-garde artist or a film director or a two-bit gangster. Put him in rags and he's a refugee who just washed ashore from some third-world hell.

"There were many birds in the cliffs there. Terns and gulls and skimmers," said Boggy. "Many, many nests."

So Boggy had taken a bucket from the boat and slowly

worked his way along the cliffs, plucking an occasional egg from the nests, making it look like that's why he was there. A large cave yawned open above where *Cat Sass* was anchored, and he had gotten to within a hundred yards of it when they spotted him.

"A man walked from the cave and came near to me. He was not the man we saw before on the boat, but another man, just as big as the other one," said Boggy.

"Sounds like it could be Donnie Crowe, Dwayne's brother," Pederson said.

Boggy said, "This man, he called out and asked what I was I doing there, and I put up my hands and smiled, and said, '*No habla inglés, señor*.' Then I reached in the bucket and took out one of the bird eggs and showed it to him and smiled some more. The man, he thought I was just an egg poacher. He said, 'Go do that somewhere else.' So I moved away and he went back to the cave."

Boggy said, "These sea caves, they are just like the caves where I come from in Hispaniola. They are all connected down below and there is more than one way in and out."

Boggy meandered his way to the top of the cliffs, where the limestone terrain leveled out into a desolate and pockmarked landscape.

"Is like the face of the moon there," said Boggy. "Everywhere you step there is a hole in the rock."

After following a number of false passages, he finally found a promising point of entry—a long narrow chute that dropped straight down from the surface, then made a sharp turn before transecting the face of the cliff. Again, he encountered several dead ends before eventually finding a tunnel that led to the same cave from which the man had come.

"It is very narrow, this tunnel. I must lay on my back as I go, feeling the way with my feet. The rocks are sharp, very sharp. There is a little water sometimes coming in with the tides. It is damp and it is dark. But then, I make a turn, and the tunnel widens, and I can stand, and then I see a speck of light. I move closer, and I can hear a voice, a woman's voice. And it is Barbara. I cannot hear exactly what it is she says, but it is her.

"I crawl closer, behind a big rock, and I can make out a figure now. It is dark, very dark, and it is hard to see. But yes, it is Barbara and she is sitting up, leaning against the wall of the cave, and the man, Lord Downey, he is lying down beside her. They are talking. Beyond them, it is still some distance to where the cave opens in the cliff, and I can just barely make out the figures of the men—there are three of them, sitting there against the light from outside. I wanted to go nearer, to whisper to Barbara, to tell her that all will be OK, but alone I could not risk it."

Boggy had stuck a spool of fifty-pound-test fishing line in the bucket, and he used it to mark his trail on the way out. When he emerged from the long narrow tunnel, it was still daylight. So he waited until it was dark and then made his way back down the cliffs to the skiff.

"The way it is," Boggy said. "They keep Barbara and Lord Downey far, far in the back of the cave. And they stay just inside the mouth of it, watching. They may not even know there is another way into the cave. I think maybe we can get in there and get out with Barbara and Lord Downey. And the men, if we are lucky, they will not even know."

When we were done eating, Clarissa's mother—Momma Percival, they called her—worried over Boggy's nicks and cuts. Except for her eyes, which were big and clear, and could stare a hole right through you, Momma Percival looked nothing like her daughter. Short and heavyset, she wore her long white hair tied up on the top of her head in a bun. She spoke little, and when she did, it was in the rapid-fire local Bahamian dialect of which I could understand almost nothing at all. She wore a man's flannel shirt, a long calico skirt, and high-top tennis shoes with white socks pulled up high above her knees. She scrubbed Boggy's wounds with a washcloth and then led him to a back room just off the kitchen.

"Momma's mixing up that hoodoo medicine," Pederson laughed. "No telling what she's anointing him with back there."

"Laugh all you want," Clarissa said. "All I know is that when you get a bellyache you're always coming by here asking Momma to make you some bush tea."

I said, "Your mother knows bush medicine?"

"She's a root woman, what they call it here," Clarissa said. "Knows everything that grows and what's good for curing what."

"And if you're burning hot for some sweet young woman," Pederson said, "she can cook up something that'll make sure you get her."

Clarissa said, "She can cook up something that'll make sure you don't, too."

The two of them cut looks at each other, playing it back and forth.

"She and Boggy will hit it off just fine then," I said. "The two of them can compare notes."

Pederson was eyeing the last of the stuffed crab backs left on the platter. He finally gave in. While he was eating, I said, "Clarissa, you happen to know a friend of Burma Downey's by the name of Cheri? Cheri Swanson?"

Clarissa rolled her eyes. She said, "Oh yes, I know her plenty. That one, she's something else."

"She's visited Burma here on-island?"

"Uh-huh, she was here just before Burma left and had her accident," said Clarissa. "Her and Zoe Applequist and Burma and Tiffani—sleeping the days, partying the nights. Must have been two weeks of it. Don't know how they kept the pace."

"Chrissie Hineman told me Tiffani had a boyfriend."

"Yes, but he only came around once or twice. I hardly got a glance of him. Big man. Had a tattoo around his neck."

I looked at Pederson.

"Sounds like our boy Dwayne."

Pederson nodded.

"They were all here right before Burma's accident?"

"Right up to it," Clarissa said. "One night they all went out to eat dinner at the Albury, and when they came back, they were going at it until late, until long after I'd gone to bed, raising a ruckus, drinking and yelling. Next morning, they were gone. Just like that, they run off. Burma didn't even say good-bye to her father. Just gone. Accident must have been two-three days after that."

"How'd Burma meet Tiffani and Cheri Swanson anyway?"

"Tiffani told me it was at some club where she and Cheri Swanson used to work. Had a funny name."

"Ruby Booby's?"

"That sounds like it."

"You get along with Tiffani?"

"Better than with Zoe. At least Tiffani, she's friendly. She used to come over and help me out in the kitchen, do this and that. She wasn't much at cooking, but I taught her how to make lemonade. Lord Downey, he loves his lemonade, drinks it morning, noon, and night. Sometimes with a little gin in the afternoons. So Tiffani, she'd take Lord Downey his lemonade and sit and talk with him awhile." Clarissa smiled, thinking about it. "Lord Downey didn't mind that at all. Pretty young girl waiting on him, and walking around half-dressed the way she did. At first, she put the life back in him, but then he started fading."

"She ever ask him for money?"

"Not that I know of. Besides, he didn't have it to give. Poor man was selling off pictures on the wall just trying to keep up with all the money Burma was spending. He has the house and the things that are in it, and that's about it. I mean, the house and the property are worth a great deal of money and he owns that free and clear. He has a little bit coming in, but only enough to cover the basics and maintain a certain degree of respect."

We cleared off the table. Clarissa stepped into the backroom to check on Momma Percival and Boggy. We heard her say, "Come here, you two, and look at this."

Clarissa stood by the screen door that opened onto the backyard. Outside in the rain, Boggy held an umbrella over Momma Percival while she shined a flashlight on a tangle of plants and vines and bushes that consumed most of the yard.

"Momma's showing him her doctorin' garden," Clarissa said. "The rain just pouring down on them and they don't care."

Pederson said, "Maybe the two of them can cook up something that will scare off this hurricane."

Clarissa wouldn't let Pederson and me help her wash the dishes, said she had her own way of doing them and for us just to go and relax. We sat down in the living room. Outside, there was a flash of lightning and then came the thunder, and the wood-frame house creaked and moaned in the wind.

We sat there listening to the storm awhile. And then I said, "It's going to take at least four of us to get them out of that cave. We'll use *Miz Blitz* to haul us over there. We'll have to do it tomorrow night."

Pederson nodded.

"Great minds," he said, "think alike."

52

By the next morning, the rain had let up some, but the winds were howling, with gusts to fifty miles per hour. The 2 P.M. report out of Miami showed the center of Curt just southwest of Great Exuma. It was crossing the shallow waters of the Great Bahama Bank and nearing the Tongue of the Ocean, where the sea floor suddenly plunges more than a mile below the surface. All that deep, open water meant the storm was likely to strengthen, reaching one hundred and forty miles per hour, or more. A category-four, doozy of a blow.

The forecast called for Curt to follow a path that would take it between Andros and New Providence Island, just missing Nassau. After that, it was anyone's guess. I was hoping that once it reached the Gulf Stream it might drift north and avoid a direct hit on Minorca Beach. No matter what, Florida's east coast, along with Georgia and the Carolinas, would soon have hell to pay.

I bought another phone card and called Steffie Plank at home. She unloaded on me for not getting in touch with her earlier.

"All I could think was that something had gone wrong. I'm about to lose it, Zack."

"Well, just take it easy. Things are going as well as they possibly can."

"Did you find out the name of the bank where I can wire the money?"

"I want to hold off on the money."

"Zack—"

"Wait, just hear me out," I said. I told her about Dwayne Crowe and how Boggy had spotted Barbara and Lord Downey in the caves on North Eleuthera.

"I'm not going to siphon off everything Barbara has worked for and turn it over to these bastards until I know I absolutely have to."

"And when might that be?"

"I don't know. I'm working on it."

"You'll call me the moment you know something?"

"Yes."

"You swear, Zack?"

"All the goddam time."

When I returned to *Miz Blitz* Pederson and Boggy stood in the galley. An open footlocker sat by the big teak table and I watched Pederson pull two rifles from it and put them on the table.

"Enfield L-85s," he said. "Fully automatic pieces of shit. Bahamas police bought them off the British in the late 1980s after the Brits figured out they didn't work worth a damn in that Falklands War of theirs. Got this, too."

He pulled a shotgun out of the trunk and put it on the table.

"Twelve-gauge, semi-auto pump. About as simple as they come. But get close enough, it'll bring down a Crowe," said Pederson. "You two got any preferences?"

Boggy said he had weapons of his own that he planned to take. Pederson looked skeptical, but didn't press him on it.

"Guess I'll take the shotgun," I said. Pederson handed it to me, along with a box of shells.

"I guess Brindley can use one of the Enfields."

"What are you going to use?" I asked.

"Oh, I got something special. It's at my house. I asked Brindley to run by and get it and bring it with him."

I didn't say anything. Pederson studied me.

"Look," he said. "I know you aren't real excited about including Brindley in this. But the boy can run a boat. He ought to be doing that instead of dressing up in a uniform and pretending he's a policeman. You can trust him with *Miz Blitz* while we're up there on those cliffs."

I handed him the 12-gauge.

"You want to show me how this thing works?"

"You never fired a shotgun?" Pederson asked.

"Maybe once or twice when I was a kid, one that belonged to a friend. My family wasn't real big on guns," I said. "Don't know much about them."

So Pederson got a box of shells from the locker and showed me where to pop them into the breech. I loaded three shells—*ker-chak, ker-chak, ker-chak*—then Pederson showed me how to click the safety off and on.

"Now step out there on the dock with it," he said.

"Do what?"

"Get out there and fire the damn thing. Just shoot into the water, you aren't going to hurt anything. Shoot once close and then once far off, and then once in between. You need to see how the shot spreads so you got an idea of what the hell you can hit. I'm not having you go into that cave never having even fired the gun you're carrying."

So I went out onto the end of the dock. I aimed the gun at the water and pulled the trigger. Nothing happened.

"Turn off the damn safety," Pederson said. I did. Then I shot three times into the water, watching the splatter of the shot, pumping the stock, and ejecting the empty shells. It was louder than I thought it would be, even with the wind blowing. I didn't know that I could hit anything with it, but at least I knew a little bit about what to expect after I pulled the trigger.

I was walking back to the boat when I saw a golf cart stop at the end of the dock. Zoe Applequist stepped out and walked toward me. She looked at the shotgun. Then she looked at the boat where Pederson and Boggy stood watching us.

"What's this all about?" she said.

"Pederson wants to sell me one of his shotguns. Good for duck hunting. I was just seeing how it works."

She didn't buy it, but she didn't argue.

"They called again," she said. "Burma wrote you this note."

Zoe handed me a piece of paper. It said:

Zoe told the men you might have trouble getting all the money. They said they would take $750,000. When can you have it? We need to finalize this as soon as possible.

I folded the note and stuck it in my pocket.

"I'll bring it to them tomorrow," I said. "After the storm passes."

Zoe turned and walked away.

Brindley arrived about 3 P.M. He had ditched his police uniform and looked the better for it. He was wearing gray sweatpants and a T-shirt and lugging a long metal case. Pederson took the case from him and placed it on the teak table.

"Thanks for tossing in with us," I told Brindley.

He nodded.

"Nice boat," he said. "Stirling diesels?"

"Yeah," I said. "Never had a lick of trouble with them, knock on goddam wood. Feel free to look around."

Brindley headed for the stern and I watched Pederson open the metal case. The rifle inside looked like something out of the George Lucas prop room: sleek, wicked, and shiny. Pederson pulled it out lovingly and held it up for me to see.

"I know the beauty of this weapon is lost on you, Chasteen, but you are looking at an AUG A2. Uses 9mm ammo, and I modified the original clip so that it holds forty-two rounds." He pointed at the case. "Got a titanium bipod and a sniper conversion barrel. If you can't shoot it with this, then it can't be shot."

"Mmmmm," I said.

Pederson smiled, shook his head.

"I might as well be talking Chinese to you, huh?"

"Nice gun," I said. "Now how about we sit down and come up with an actual plan for this thing?"

By 5 P.M. we had talked it all through more times than we could count. The only thing we knew for sure was that we wouldn't know anything for sure until we got there. It could go in all kinds of directions. We were counting on the storm to create our diversion. And we were counting on *Miz Blitz* to stand up to the storm.

No one felt like eating. Pederson said it might be a good idea if we tried to squeeze in a nap before setting out at 9 P.M. So everyone found a bunk and stretched out.

I closed my eyes and tried to sleep, knowing it wouldn't happen. I felt the first flutter of butterflies in my stomach. Pederson was wrong. They damn sure didn't tickle.

53

By 10 P.M. we had bounced our way across Dunmore Bight and were hanging offshore of the Steeples. We could just barely make out the cliffs beyond them, and Boggy showed us the general vicinity of the cave. It was too dark to see *Cat Sass* in the waters below it. Even though the cove was well protected, the storm surge had it churning. Dwayne Crowe and his crew would need stout lines on the lobster boat to keep it from slipping its mooring.

I had let Brindley take the helm of *Miz Blitz* when we were about halfway across the sound, and now he pointed us south, head-on into the swells. We planned to put in about a mile below the cave. The seas were running twelve to fourteen feet, but my sweet trawler was slicing through it. It was a wild sleigh ride and we were taking a pretty good pounding, but Brindley didn't seem the least bit fazed by it. I looked at him, his eyes focused, his mouth scrunched up. Hell, he was whistling. A cool hand under pressure. Maybe *Miz Blitz* would survive to make it back to Minorca Beach. Maybe I would, too.

I slapped Brindley on the back.

"All yours from here on," I said.

"Got her under control," he said.

"You get my boat back in one piece and maybe I'll let you polish it."

Brindley grinned. He said, "And maybe you can kiss my ass."

"Aye, Captain," I said.

We were running with all the lights off, nothing on, even in the cabin, and with *Miz Blitz* pitching and rolling in the storm it was a bitch making my way around below. I banged a shoulder against a bulkhead, cracked a shin on a galley drawer. The rate I was going I'd be on the disabled list before we ever put ashore. I finally found foul-weather gear and put it on, falling down only once in the process. The foul-weather gear was navy blue. Too bad I couldn't see myself in the mirror. Not quite the dashing commando look, but surely a stealthy hunk of manhood, nonetheless.

I worked my way onto the deck. Boggy straddled the bowsprit, holding onto a line, looking ahead into the darkness, trying to find the place he'd scouted out earlier for us to try to come in.

I found Pederson hanging over a lee rail, perfecting his version of the Technicolor yawn. He straightened up as I came and stood beside him, wiping his mouth on the sleeve of his sweatshirt.

"Just got rid of those butterflies," he said.

I doubt I could have handled *Miz Blitz* any better than Brindley did when he put us ashore. Boggy had picked a spot where the cliff wall was recessed just enough to give a little protection from the surge. Brindley went in stern first with the boat, the three of us standing ready on the transom, holding on to each other, holding on to the gunwales, holding on to anything we could. Pederson carried the AUG A2 in a waterproof sling, but there was nothing to keep my shotgun dry. So I'd stuck it in a Hefty garbage bag and wrapped it with duct tape. Call me the hobo commando.

Miz Blitz rose on the crest of a wave and, in the gully that followed it, Brindley gunned the diesels in reverse, bringing us to the jagged lip of a ledge that cut across the cliff wall, then threw it into forward just before the stern crashed into the rock. We had about a two-second window of opportunity.

"Now!" shouted Boggy and we jumped, landing on the ledge, sliding across the slick rock, trying to get as far ashore as we could, trying to find something to hold on to so we wouldn't get sucked away by the outwash. I heard *Miz Blitz*'s engine's roar above the surf and the wind as Brindley gunned it forward and climbed the face of the incoming wave.

Boggy yelled, "Up, up!" And we followed him, scrambling on the cliff wall, finding a higher ledge, and dodging the torrent of the next wave as it came crashing in, spraying us from below. We kept climbing for a few minutes, finding plenty of footholds in the rock and wide berth on the ledges. We stopped about halfway up, resting on an outcropping no bigger than a twin bed.

Pederson pulled his rifle from its sling and slapped on its clip. He pointed at my shotgun.

"That thing isn't going to do you any good unloaded," he said.

I pulled the shotgun out of the Hefty bag, opened the breach, and put in the shells. We couldn't see *Miz Blitz* through the storm. Pederson flipped on his walkie-talkie and connected with Brindley.

"Got her under control?"

"Roger that," said Brindley.

"Keep her tight then," said Pederson. "I'm clicking off here. You'll hear from us when it's done."

"Affirmative," said Brindley. "Ten-four and over."

Pederson flipped off the walkie-talkie and grinned.

"Boy loves talking that radio shit," he said.

Pederson split off to make his way south, trying to get as close to the mouth of the cave as he could. He was to wait there for three hours. If he heard any sort of commotion coming from inside the cave—namely, gunshots—he was to assume Boggy and I had either been caught or cornered or killed. He was to use his best judgment—give us backup or abort the whole thing. If, after three hours, nothing had happened, he could assume we had succeeded in our mission and were spiriting Barbara and Lord Downey out of the cave's rear entrance. He was to return to the same ledge where we had leapt off the boat and we would meet him there.

A simple plan, and only about two zillion ways for it go wrong.

54

Thirty minutes after we split up with Pederson, Boggy and I reached the top of the cliffs and set out across the moonscape of limestone. With nothing to break the rage of the wind, we had to walk crouched over or risk getting blown sideways. I kept my eyes on Boggy's feet, trying to step where he stepped, avoiding the potholes that could twist an ankle or wrench a knee.

Another fifteen minutes and we were standing over a hole in the limestone about the size of a garbage can lid. Boggy opened the duffel strapped to his back and pulled out a ten-foot length of rope. He tied an end around one of his ankles and the other end around one of mine. Then he started down through the hole. I followed him, cradling the shotgun against my chest.

Never have I been in a darker place. Never have I felt more out of my element. Six feet below the surface and we might as well have been in Middle Freaking Earth. I kept waiting for my eyes to adjust, but everywhere I looked I saw only blackness. Boggy kept pulling on the rope, urging me onward.

It was slow going. Brittle rock crumbled and handholds disappeared. Once or twice I thought I was going to tumble and take Boggy down with me.

Finally we reached the bottom. I stood beside Boggy as he rummaged through his duffel. I heard a scratch, then saw the flare of a kitchen match. We stood in a chamber about twenty feet wide. Three other tunnels branched out from it.

"We take that one," said Boggy, moving to the largest of the tunnels just as a downdraft blew out the match. We crawled on our hands and knees. After a few minutes, Boggy lit another match. Ahead, the tunnel was honeycombed with smaller side passages and a multitude of holes. I sniffed the air. I had never smelled anything quite like it—a mix of salt and rot, and something distinctly animal. Boggy kept lighting matches as we moved deeper in the tunnel, and the odor kept getting stronger.

"There," said Boggy, pointing to where he had marked the way from his earlier trip. A few feet ahead of us, a gull feather hung from a piece of fishing line that dangled from the ceiling of the tunnel. To the right of it, a smaller tunnel sloped downward through the limestone.

We moved in front of the smaller tunnel. Wind rushed out of it, a cool updraft that carried with it the thick, dank odor that filled the air. I caught whiffs of what smelled almost like ammonia.

"What stinks?"

"The smell, that is what led me to this tunnel, what led me to the cave."

"But what is it?"

Boggy didn't answer. He was already worming his way into the tunnel, feet first, on his stomach. I went in after him. The tunnel was slick with mud and goo, and I began to slip. I held on to the shotgun with one hand and tried to grab something with the other, but there was nothing to grab on to. I kept slipping until I slammed into Boggy, and then both of us were sliding down the tunnel, out of control, wrapped up in the rope that held us together. I was losing my grip on the shotgun. I grabbed it tighter and caught the trigger, and the gun discharged a roaring blast, disintegrating the Hefty bag, hitting the limestone ceiling, spraying us with stinging chunks of rock. We hit the bottom of the tunnel and tumbled into what I could only sense was a broad chamber. It was still pitch dark but the sound of the gunshot echoed all around us.

Then there was silence. I could feel another updraft coming from across the chamber. And that smell—so foul and pervasive. Suddenly, Boggy pushed me down and said: "Lay flat, cover your head!"

The sound was faint at first, and then it grew louder and louder. When I was a kid, we used to stick playing cards in the spokes of our bicycle wheels and pretend we were driving hot rods. That's what it sounded like—*click-click-click-click-click,* a wild and manic fluttering. And then they were upon us.

Bats. Hundreds, thousands of bats.

I lay facedown on the slick, damp rock, arms covering the back of my head as they flew over us, racing across the chamber. I suppose they were just as upset to find us there as we were them. It sounded as if they were shrieking and all in a panic. Or maybe that's just typical bat behavior. Beats me. All I know is that the chamber was thick with their furry, mousy little bodies, and there seemed to be no end to them. They bounced off my back, careened into my hands, some of them taking little nips of flesh as they went. And then, as suddenly as they had come, they were gone.

Boggy said, "I didn't tell you about the bats."

"Forgot to tell me? Or didn't tell me?" I said. "Which one?"

"Didn't tell you," he said. "One less thing you had to worry about."

"So that smell . . ."

"Bat shit," Boggy said. "Guano. The cave is filled with it."

"That wasn't mud we were just crawling through."

"No, it was not mud."

"And those cuts on your face . . ."

"Bat bites. From yesterday. They surprised me. That is why, today, we go down on our stomachs and cover up, so there is less to bite."

"Listen, Boggy, I'm no doctor, OK? But bats are mammals. And I'm pretty damn sure they can carry rabies."

"Yes, they can," Boggy said. "Here, take this."

I fumbled in the dark and found his hand. It held a fistful of something that felt wet and spongy.

"What is it?"

"Is milkmoss. Clarissa's mother, she gave it to me when she saw that the cuts on my face had been made by bats. That is why we were out in her backyard. To pick the milkmoss. Take it, chew it, and swallow all the juice it makes. When it has stopped making juice, spit it out. If the bats had rabies, which is doubtful, then the milkmoss will stop it."

I chewed the milkmoss. It tasted sweet, sort of like peaches. And it worked a lot like chewing tobacco. The more you chewed, the more juice it made. So I chewed and I swallowed the juice and tried not to think about all the bats.

And I tried not to think about how I had screwed up with the shotgun.

"You think they heard it?" I asked Boggy.

"Is hard to say. Maybe not. The cave, it is still some distance away."

It took another ten minutes of crawling through a series of tight tunnels until we reached it. We positioned ourselves behind a boulder and looked out across the low-ceilinged chamber. The mouth of the cave lay maybe fifty yards in front of us, a gaping hole that opened onto the night. The roar of the storm was almost deafening. I couldn't imagine that anyone could have heard the shotgun go off over it.

I scanned the chamber, studying the shadows. I could make out the shapes of rocks and outcroppings on the cave wall. But I saw no one. Nothing moved. Were they sleeping? Surely Dwayne and his cronies would take turn standing watches. Besides, who could sleep in the middle of a hurricane?

Boggy untied the rope that joined us. He reached into his duffel and pulled out a leather sheath that held his machete—its steel blade curved like a scimitar and honed to a deadly edge. I racheted open the shotgun's breech and fed in another shell. The fury of the storm swallowed any sound we made.

We crept forward, Boggy on one side of the cave, and me on the other. We took it a couple of yards at a time, moving slowly, finding cover, waiting a moment or two, then moving slowly again. I studied the shadows and the shapes that lay ahead. I kept the shotgun against my hip, low and ready. More than once I thought I spotted someone, but each time it turned out to be only piles of rocks, or tricks of the dim light.

The cave grew wider. I could no longer make out Boggy as he made his way on the other side. I stopped, I listened. I heard nothing but the storm. I saw nothing but rocks and more rocks.

Then the cave floor grew sandy. I could make out a pile of something—plastic jugs, empty cans, cardboard boxes. I moved toward it. Just garbage, nothing more. I stepped to the mouth of the cave. Boggy slipped out of the shadows and joined me. The sea pounded the cliffs below us. No sign of the *Cat Sass*. No sign of anything but the torrent of Hurricane Curt. There was nowhere else to look.

They were gone.

Five minutes later, Pederson had joined us in the cave. We were all drenched and dejected. The wind and the rain had calmed down some. Boggy lit a fire from the cardboard boxes and rubbish. We dried out around the flames.

I was sitting in the exact spot where Boggy had seen Barbara and Lord Downey just the day before. A blanket lay on the ground, maybe the same blanket Barbara had slept upon. I rubbed my hand across the blanket. It didn't offer much in the way of solace.

Five nights she had spent here in this dark and miserable place. Five nights. And I hadn't been able to do a damn thing about it. Now who knew where she was?

I tried to think about what might have spooked the kidnappers. Could have been any number of things. Maybe it was something simple. Maybe they just didn't want to sit out the hurricane in the cave. Or maybe Dwayne had noticed us when we tried to follow the *Cat Sass* out of French Jug. Maybe he had caught a glimpse of Boggy and then seen him snooping around later on the cliffs, and that had caused them to bolt. Or maybe they were in cahoots with Ortiz after all, and he had ordered them to move somewhere else.

Maybe, maybe, maybe. I was sick and tired of maybes. I was ready to find Barbara and get her back, no goddam maybes about it.

"I didn't see their boat in the cove when I was climbing up," said Pederson. "They could have moved out hours ago."

"Yeah," I said. "Could have."

"These cliffs are filled with caves," said Pederson. "Could be they just moved to another one. Sun comes up, we might be able to see something."

"No, I don't think they would have taken the boat just to dip into another cove along the cliffs. Too risky," I said. "It was bad enough out there in *Miz Blitz*. I can't imagine what it would have been like on a boat half that size."

Pederson had been trying to raise Brindley on the walkie-talkie, but with no luck. He stood up from the fire, stepped to the mouth of the cave, and tried again. This time he connected, but I couldn't make out anything that was being said.

Pederson put away the walkie-talkie and rejoined us by the fire.

"Told Brindley what was going on," he said. "Says he might have seen them pulling out of the cove not long after he last heard from us. Caught a glimpse of something that might have been that boat of theirs. Hard to say."

"Could he tell which way they were going?"

"Nah, I asked him that. Said if it was a boat he saw, then it didn't have any running lights on and he couldn't tell shit— weather beating all to hell like it was."

I stood up.

"Let's go," I said. "We aren't getting anything done here."

Pederson and I stepped to the mouth of the cave and got ready for our descent back to the boat. I unloaded the shotgun. Pederson put the AUG 42 back in its sling.

I looked back in the cave. Boggy was still sitting there, sifting through the rubbish scattered around the firepit.

"Come on," I said. "I've seen enough of this place."

But Boggy kept at it.

"Goddamit, Boggy, it's just junk," I said. "Let's go."

When he finally stood up he was holding something. He walked out of the cave and handed it to me—a cell phone.

I punched the power button and the face lit up. I hit the redial button and listened. It rang twice, the tone breaking on and off, the battery almost dead. Then a woman's voice came on the other end.

"Dwayne? Dwayne?"

I grunted into the phone. Seemed like what Dwayne Crowe would do.

"I thought you were coming here," said the woman. "We're sitting here waiting on you."

I punched the off button and turned to the others.

"That was Tiffani St. James," I said. "She's expecting visitors."

55

It was just after sunrise when we arrived at the Downey compound. Despite all its fury the night before, the hurricane was a tight, compact bundle of torment, and it had moved on. The sky was still overcast, but the sun was threatening to break through. It would be another scorcher come afternoon.

Pederson and I had done some arguing, but finally agreed that I would walk up to Burma Downey's house alone. That way they'd know we weren't looking for a fight. At first, Pederson insisted that he should be the one to do it, but I talked him out of it, told him that if things turned bad it was better to lose someone who couldn't handle a gun than someone who could.

I walked slowly, arms hanging loose at my sides. If Dwayne Crowe and his pals were watching—and surely they were—they could see I wasn't carrying a weapon. Just call me Mr. Eager-to-Please: If someone wants to shoot me, I'll make it as easy for them as possible.

But they weren't going to shoot. At least, that's what I kept telling myself as I approached the house, crunching my way along the shell driveway. I was the money hookup. If something happened to me they'd be SOL. It didn't exactly give me bulletproof status, but it tilted the odds enough that I could accept them. As long as I ignored the fact that I didn't have the money and had no intention of getting it. Get right down to it, I had no idea what I intended to do. It was play-it-as-it-lays time.

Behind me, Pederson knelt under the casuarina trees, his fancy-ass rifle trained on the house. Brindley was on the opposite side of the driveway, taking cover in the wax myrtles and palmettos. I couldn't see Boggy, but I suspected he was somewhere in the sand dunes, between the house and the ocean.

I reached the steps and stopped. A golf cart was parked on the concrete slab underneath the stilt house. Next to it sat the air-conditioning unit with its fan whirring, the compressor emitting its steady drone. The intake vents were caked with dead bugs—moths and dragonflies, mostly.

I yelled up at the house, "Come on out, Dwayne. Let's talk."

I gave it a minute.

"Dwayne! I know you're in there."

I put a foot on the first step. On the landing above, the door swung open and Dwayne Crowe crouched on the threshold, rifle leveled. He swung away from me, and as I rolled behind the stairway and under the house, I heard a burst of fire and saw puffs of dust ripping down the driveway.

So this was what it was like getting shot at. Can't say I felt particularly enriched by the experience. Still, it beat hell out of getting shot at and hit.

The shooting stopped. Whatever kind of rifle Dwayne was firing, it was mean and automatic, and seemed every bit a match for the AUG A2.

I couldn't see the others in their hiding spots, but I figured they were OK. The shots hadn't come close to them. If Dwayne was just trying to get our attention, he'd succeeded. But if he was after blood, then I was easy pickings. Even shooting blind, all he had to do was unleash a volley under the house and chances were better than excellent he'd hit me.

I looked for cover. The only thing that presented itself was the big, boxy air-conditioning unit. I crawled behind it.

A couple of minutes went by. I scanned the sand dunes, hoping maybe I'd spot Boggy, but he was nowhere to be seen.

Then, from inside the house, Dwayne Crowe yelled, "Pederson! I know you're out there."

Somewhere in the bushes, Pederson yelled back, "Don't want any trouble, Dwayne. Just want to talk."

"Then throw down and step out where I can see you," Dwayne said.

"You throwing down, too?" said Pederson.

"Doesn't work like that," said Dwayne. "Not going to shoot you. Just want to see you."

A few seconds later, Pederson emerged empty-handed from the bushes and onto the driveway.

"Tell whoever you got with you out there to move back to the road," Dwayne said.

Pederson turned and said something to Brindley, then I watched as Brindley made his way through the wax myrtles toward the road.

I heard voices from inside the house and heavy steps on the landing. Then Dwayne said, "OK, Chasteen. Your turn. Get out front where I can see you."

I stepped from under the house and saw Dwayne Crowe in the doorway, straddling the threshold, one arm crooked around Zoe Applequist's neck, the other one pointing the rifle down at me. It had a dull camo finish and one of those banana-shaped clips that looked like it held about a hundred rounds. Which, at that distance, was about ninety-nine more than it would take to send me trotting off to God's own locker room.

"I could've shot you if I'd wanted. You know that?" Dwayne waved his rifle as he spoke, then spat out the side of his mouth. "Should've done it from the very beginning when I had you in the limo. All you've done is get in the damn way."

I didn't say anything.

Dwayne was shirtless, wearing a pair of cutoff jeans. He seemed jittery, eyes darting in all directions. Zoe squirmed under his hammerlock. She mumbled something I couldn't hear and Dwayne eased his grip.

The hallway behind Dwayne was dark. I glimpsed shadowy figures, but couldn't tell who was who.

"Hey, Pederson. Get on up here with your boyfriend,"

Dwayne yelled. As Pederson walked toward the house, Dwayne looked down at me. "Where's the money, Chasteen?"

"Where's Barbara?"

"For God's sake," said Zoe. "Just give it to him. Or they'll kill us."

"Money's on its way," I said. "The bank will notify me as soon as it arrives."

I hate to lie, really I do. But if I'm on the path to hell, then I prefer it be well paved.

"Now, where's Barbara?" I said.

"Inside," said Dwayne. "With the rest of them."

"Let me see her."

Dwayne ignored me, speaking to Pederson as he came up and stood beside me. "Who have you told about this?"

"Nobody, Dwayne," said Pederson. "Keeping everything just between us."

"Good, that's real good."

Pederson said, "Who else you got in there with you, Dwayne?"

"None of your damn business."

"Listen, Dwayne, I'm ready to bargain with you, make it easier on both of us. But I need to know how it all stacks up." Pederson cocked his head, peering past Dwayne into the hallway. "That you in there, Donnie?"

Dwayne moved to block the doorway.

"Yeah, it's Donnie," said Dwayne. "Him and our cousin Curtis."

"OK, that's good, Dwayne. Appreciate you telling me that." Pederson spoke low and easy. "Let's just lay it all out and keep it cool, like we are now. Then everyone gets what they want."

"I'll tell you what I want," said Dwayne. "Want you to guarantee us a way out of here. Or else everything is off."

"No problem," Pederson said.

"Want a boat, a big one. Don't want you or anyone else following us."

"Sounds fine, Dwayne," said Pederson. "We'll get whatever you want."

I put a foot on the bottom step.

I said, "Now let me tell you what I want, Dwayne."

Pederson reached out to pull me back, but I shook him off.

"I want to see Barbara."

I moved up to the second step. Dwayne slung Zoe inside the house and pointed the rifle at me.

I took another step.

"Stop right there or I'll shoot your ass, I swear to God."

"I want to see Barbara. Now."

Dwayne worked his tongue over his teeth, thinking about it. Eyes locked on me, he said, "Donnie?"

A voice from the hallway said, "Right here, Dwayne."

Donnie moved out from the shadows. He was every bit as big as his brother, with a bad eye that was milky and goggled wide open. His brown teeth clenched a cigarette and both hands gripped a shotgun. He was filthy. Mud and crud covered his clothes. Debris hung from his lank brown hair. To see him was to smell him, and to smell him was pretty bad.

"Tell Curtis to bring her up to the window," Dwayne said.

Donnie stepped away. I heard doors opening and closing inside. Zoe picked herself up from the floor and stood behind Dwayne, just inside the doorway.

I said, "What about Lord Downey?"

"He's OK," Zoe said.

Then the blinds went up on one of the bedroom windows and I saw Barbara standing there. The guy who was with her, Curtis, couldn't have been more than seventeen or eighteen, scrawnier than his cousins, but with a streak of mean that showed on his face. He had one arm wrapped tight around Barbara's shoulders, a pistol held to her head. He looked like he was enjoying himself.

Barbara's eyes found mine and held them. Her hair was tangled, her eyes puffy and tired. But she has never looked anything but beautiful in her life and she looked more beautiful than ever then. She smiled a sad smile. She raised a hand and put it on the window glass. Her lips formed the words: I love you.

It was too much, too much for me to hold back. I bounded up the steps and hit the landing. Dwayne lurched out of the doorway, swiveling with the rifle, slamming the butt against the side of my head. I fell back against the railing. Dwayne swung again and I blocked the blow with both arms, the rifle cracking against bone and stinging like hell. He swung again and I caught it with a shoulder, going down, and then feeling the rifle muzzle jabbing hard against my gut.

Dwayne saying, "You want to die, Chasteen? You want to die?"

Then Zoe was pulling him back, screaming: "Dwayne, stop it, goddamit . . ."

He reared back to swing at her, then stopped himself. Zoe never even flinched. She stood there, defiant, fists clenched. Dwayne turned back to me.

"Get out of here," he said.

I pulled myself up on the railing, my hands and arms tingling from the rifle blows. I looked at the bedroom window. Barbara was gone, the blinds down.

Pederson met me halfway down the steps and helped me the rest of the way. When we reached the bottom, Dwayne said, "Get the money, Chasteen."

He backed inside the house and closed the door.

56

We decided to pull shifts watching the house. Brindley drew the first one. Pederson and I headed back to *Miz Blitz*. Boggy still hadn't shown up. I had no idea where he was.

I sat and listened to Pederson chew me out for getting into it with Dwayne. I tried to act contrite. Then I made some coffee and we sat there drinking it. After he was finished being pissed off at me, Pederson said he figured it had all played out to our advantage.

"Dwayne's sitting in there now, thinking he's in charge of the show. Buys us time," said Pederson.

"How much time you think?"

"Maybe twenty-four hours. Then they're going to start getting fidgety, wondering why you haven't brought them the money yet, wanting some proof that we're doing what we told them we were going to do."

"Meanwhile, we execute our secret plan, capture the bad guys, and save the girl."

"Exactly."

"And that plan would be . . . ?"

"Don't have a clue," said Pederson. "But let me ask you something: Can you get that money?"

"Some of it, not all of it. Not nearly as much as they want."

"But you don't want to get them any of it, do you?"

"No, I don't."

"What if I said I think you might have to get the money even if you don't want to do it?"

I drained my coffee and stood up from the table.

"You hungry?"

"That an answer, Zack?"

"It'll have to do."

I made us each a fried egg sandwich, with mustard and Bermuda onion to go with it. And after we were done eating them, I made us each another one.

Pederson said, "Only way in's through that front door. No way we're going to storm the place."

"What about from underneath the house?"

"I thought about that," Pederson said. "Think there's a garbage chute, one of those dumbwaiters, that dumps down from the kitchen. But we'd be going up one by one. Not good odds in that."

"There's the air-conditioning duct, but that's even smaller than the garbage chute. Don't think you or I could fit in that."

I poured us more coffee. Outside, it had started to rain again, just a sprinkle. The wind had laid a little, but every now and then it would still stir up a gust.

Pederson said, "So what you figure? Dwayne and Tiffani were planning to kidnap Lord Downey all along? Then Barbara showed up and they decided to get more bucks for the bang?"

"Something like that."

"So Dwayne rounded up the muscle and snatched the two of them . . ."

"And killed Bryce Gannon."

"Then Tiffani kept an eye on everything from the inside."

"Yeah, that could be," I said.

"Only something still isn't fitting, is it?"

"No, it's not."

I needed to change clothes and get into something dry. I

went through my pockets, took out everything, and found the note that Zoe had given me the day before, the one from Burma Downey. I was still looking at it when I heard footsteps on the bow and Boggy came in through the hatchway, his machete in a sheath strapped across his back. He shook off water like a dog coming in from a storm. Then he strode past us and into the galley. He opened a drawer and pulled out two big knives, testing their blades with a finger. He grabbed a box of Hefty bags from under the sink.

He handed us each a knife and said, "Come, we must hurry."

"What's going on?" I said.

"The house," he said. "There is a way in."

57

Three hours later, we were back on Front Street, outside the Downey compound. The rain had stopped.

Across the road, in the vacant lot next to Miss Melodie Michaels's house, rubbish and underbrush had been piled into a heap, and a fire was smoldering under it, sending a thick plume of smoke out across the Downey compound. It smelled awful—a mixture of burning tires and garbage and palmetto stumps. Pederson had recruited Nixon Styles to help us out, and he sat off to one side of the lot, keeping an eye on the fire, making sure it didn't get out of control.

This time, Pederson and I walked up the driveway to Burma Downey's house together. I couldn't see Boggy and Brindley, but the plan—such as it was—called for them to be hiding behind the bougainvillea hedge that sat between the house and the dunes.

"Dwayne," Pederson called out. "Need to talk."

The door opened and Dwayne stepped out with Zoe Applequist. He kept her in front of him, his rifle ready.

Pederson said, "Just wanted to let you know that everything is moving forward."

Dwayne sniffed the air, made a face.

"What's that stink?" he said.

Pederson said, "Oh, it's coming from Miss Melodie's, across the road. She decided to burn off her garbage, along with some of the tree limbs got knocked down in the storm. She's got a boy over there watching it. Wind's blowing it right this way."

Dwayne looked beyond us, to where the fire was burning in the vacant lot. Then he looked at me and said, "You got the money?"

"Tomorrow morning," I said. "I can't get it before then."

"How much you getting?"

"I thought we'd agreed on seven hundred fifty thousand dollars."

Zoe Applequist said something that I couldn't hear. And then Dwayne said: "OK, seven hundred fifty thousand dollars. You get that here tomorrow morning."

I said, "There's something else, Dwayne. I want to see everybody."

"What do you mean, everybody?"

"I want to see Barbara and Lord Downey and Burma."

"I'm not dragging them out here," he said.

"Then have your guys bring them to the windows," I said. "I just want to lay eyes on them, make sure they're OK."

"I don't have time for this shit," Dwayne said.

Zoe said, "Everyone's fine, Mr. Chasteen, trust me."

"Look, Dwayne," said Pederson. "We give you a little something. You give us a little something. All we're asking is to get a look at everyone."

Dwayne stuck his head inside the door and said something.

We stood there, the smoke from across the road beginning to sting our eyes. Finally, the blinds went up on one of the bedroom windows. Barbara had an arm around Lord Downey, helping him stand. He looked wobbly and half-asleep. Barbara smiled. She gave me a halfhearted thumbs-up sign. I gave her one back.

"Where's Burma?" I said.

"She's resting," said Zoe. "I thought it best that we let her be. I assure you, she's alright."

"I want to see her."

"Did you hear what the woman told you?" Dwayne said. "She's OK. So drop it already."

"Bring her to the window. Let me see for myself."

Zoe shook her head, exasperated. She turned to Dwayne and said, "I'll go take care of it."

Dwayne let her go and she stepped inside the house.

We stood there, none of us talking. Dwayne kept his rifle pointed at Pederson and me. Five minutes passed. Finally, the blinds parted on the window in Burma Downey's bedroom. Burma Downey sat in her wheelchair, her gauze-wrapped head the only part of her visible above the windowsill. Zoe stood behind the wheelchair, Tiffani St. James beside her.

"There. You satisfied now?" Dwayne said.

I looked at the other bedroom window. Barbara was still standing there with Lord Downey. I could make out Curtis and Donnie behind them. Everyone in the house had their eyes on us.

I looked at Dwayne.

"Yeah, I'm satisfied."

That's when Pederson said, "How about it, Dwayne, you folks need something to eat?"

It was the cue, and as Pederson said it, I caught a glimpse of Boggy and Brindley running out from the bougainvillea hedge behind the house, each dragging two big garbage bags behind them. No one inside the house saw them. They made it to the concrete slab under the house and knelt between the golf cart and the air conditioner. The fan on the AC unit was still whirring. It hadn't let up the whole time. They had the thermostat cranked down low inside. We were counting on that. And we were praying there wouldn't be a power failure.

"Yeah, we could use something to eat," Dwayne said. "We don't have anything in here but saltines and Gatorade."

"How about we go down to the Piggly Wiggly and bring you back some meat and cheese and bread, something to make sandwiches? How about that?"

"Yeah, that'd be good. And cigarettes, too. We could use some cigarettes."

"No problem, Dwayne," said Pederson. "You just sit tight

and wait for us. Might take a while. I have to find Mr. Hanson and get him to open up the Piggly Wiggly for us. But we'll be back, just sit down and take it easy."

Dwayne studied us, wary. For this thing to work, he had to go back inside and stay there. A long moment passed. And then Dwayne said, "What about the rest of it?"

"The rest of what, Dwayne?" I said.

"About getting us out of here. What about the boat?"

I looked at Pederson. We had forgotten to discuss this part. I was going to have to make up something.

I said, "We've got you a boat—a fifty-two-footer, steel hull, cruising range of nine hundred miles. We'll have it stocked and ready to go."

"That your boat?"

I nodded.

Dwayne said, "That the one you came looking for us in?"

I nodded again. I was forcing myself not to glance under the stilt house where Boggy and Brindley were opening the garbage bags and dumping the contents onto the concrete slab.

Dwayne said, "But we tricked you, didn't we? Me and Donnie and Curtis, we cleared out before you could get the drop on us."

Dwayne grinned.

"Better kiss that boat good-bye, Chasteen. We leave here, you won't see us or it again." He pulled back inside the doorway. "Now go on and get us that food."

We didn't go anywhere. We dropped back by the main road and sat in the dark under the casuarina trees. We had no idea how long it would take. An hour, maybe two.

Nixon Styles took a break from tending the fire in the vacant lot and joined us. He kept pestering us with questions and finally we told him how we saw it all going down. Most everything hinged on the Not-Dead Bush.

"The Not-Dead Bush?" Nixon said. "What's that?"

"Oh, it's something grows here, but anymore you really have to go looking for it. Squat little shiny-leaf plant with tiny red berries," said Pederson. "When I was a boy and used to get the croup, my mother would close all the windows in my bedroom and burn some of the leaves in a pan, and it would help me get to sleep. Breathe the smoke off those leaves and it will make you sleep like you're dead. Only you're not."

"Boggy called it something else, some Taino name," I said. "But Momma Percival knew just what he was talking about. She took us all over the island, showing us where to cut it and helping us fill up those garbage bags with leaves."

Nixon said, "And that's what they're burning under the house?"

"Got a wet fire going, so there's lots of smoke and not much flame. Got the garbage bags tented over the AC unit so they catch most of the smoke and it gets sucked in by the fan and up through the main duct."

"And that fire I got burning by Miss Melodie's," said Nixon. "That's so they don't think something's funny when they smell the smoke?"

Pederson and I both nodded our heads yes. Nixon thought about it.

"Might work," he said.

He didn't sound any more convinced than we were. But it wasn't like we had a backup plan.

58

Two hours passed. No one opened the door of Burma Downey's house to see what was happening outside. The lights stayed on behind all the windows. Except for the whir of the AC compressor, everything was quiet. When the fire in the vacant lot burned down, Nixon Styles came to join us again, but Pederson told him he'd done a fine job and insisted it was time for him to go home.

And then, without us even hearing him, Boggy crept out from behind the casuarinas and was beside us in the driveway. His eyes were red and watery.

"The leaves, they are all gone," he said. "We must go in now."

Pederson said, "Where's Brindley?"

"He took in much smoke. He fell down. Now he is asleep," said Boggy. "I carried him into the bushes."

Pederson looked at me.

"Well, at least we know that smoke might have laid them out inside," he said. "But now there's only three of us. You alright with that?"

"Seems like a fair fight," I said.

Pederson opened the door of the van. He took the AUG A2 out of its case and held it out for Boggy.

"I'd feel better if you took this," he said.

"But I wouldn't," said Boggy.

Then he turned and was gone again, back into the night.

Pederson returned the rifle to its case and snapped it shut.

"Doesn't make a bit of goddam sense. When you've got firepower like that, you don't just let it sit around doing nothing," he said.

"Boggy knows what he's doing."

"I hope to hell you're right," Pederson said.

There were two cardboard boxes in the van, each one filled with food and cans of soft drink. It was stuff we had picked up earlier in the afternoon, on the way there. I took one box. Pederson took the other. The food was just window dressing. Wedged in the side of each box was a Smith & Wesson .38, safety off and ready to go. Nothing I had to do but point and shoot. Just like a camera. I wasn't any good with one of those, either.

We walked down the driveway to the house. A few twigs still smoldered around the intake on the AC, and ash from the burnt leaves of the Not-Dead Bush skittered about in the breezy back currents above the concrete slab. When I reached the bottom of the steps, I yelled, "Dwayne! We've got your food out here."

No sound came from inside the house, no shadows moved across the windows.

I yelled again, "Dwayne! Open the door."

We gave it a long moment. And then we started up the stairs. Pederson reached into a pocket and pulled out a house key Clarissa had given him. He stuck it in the lock and turned it. The door opened. Nothing but silence from inside. We stood there. We couldn't hear anything.

And then came the gust of wind. It whooshed in from behind us, blowing open the door and slamming it against the wall with a crack that shook the house. Pederson grabbed his .38, tossed aside the cardboard box, and dove inside onto the hallway floor. I moved beside him, pistol ready. I heard Boggy racing up the steps, and then he was in the hallway with us, his machete in hand.

There was only the sound of the wind as it rushed through the door and into the house. We moved down the hall, toward the living room. I could see a pair of legs, someone sprawled on the floor—Donnie Crowe. We moved into the living room, spreading out along the wall. Donnie was beginning to stir, revived by the burst of fresh air. Beside him lay Tiffani St. James, head rolling from side to side, a thread of drool dangling from her mouth. Curtis was trying to sit up on the sofa. Poker chips and playing cards and dollar bills were scattered across the coffee table. A shotgun lay under the table. Pederson grabbed it and moved with me toward the bedrooms. Boggy stayed in the living room, keeping an eye on Tiffani, Donnie, and Curtis.

Then came a sound, a metallic sound, the sound of a banana-shaped clip ratcheting into action. And in the instant before he started firing, I saw Dwayne Crowe rise up above the kitchen counter. I pulled Pederson down with me as shots ripped into the wall above us, splattering plaster and debris, blowing out big chunks of drywall, shattering lamps and ceiling fans, glass flying all over the place. Dozens and dozens of shots.

The firing stopped. Pederson raised up with the shotgun, blowing open the refrigerator door, blasting twice into the kitchen counter, tearing it apart. And then Dwayne rolled out from the kitchen, taking cover behind the couch. The rifle was gone. He had a pistol and he was firing again and again and again. . . .

"Goddam!"

Pederson grabbed his side. Blood seeped between his fingers.

Dwayne moved out from behind the couch, pistol leveled, closing in on us. Before I could get off a shot, Boggy reared back and flung his machete across the living room. The steel blade glanced off Dwayne's bare shoulder, but dug out a chunk of flesh along the way. Dwayne howled. He whipped around and fired wildly at Boggy, who dashed back into the hallway.

I fired once, twice, three times, missing with all of them. Then Dwayne was charging across the living room, running to the back of the house. I dropped my pistol and caught him from behind, a shoulder in the small of his back, hacking against his hands and stripping him of his pistol as we tumbled against a bedroom door, breaking it open, and rolled onto the floor, pieces of wood flying every which way. One sharp scrap, bigger than a broom handle, jabbed deep into my forearm, blood spurting as I yanked it out. I caught a glimpse of Barbara, sitting up in a corner, Lord Downey's head in her lap. Her eyes fluttered as she began to wake up.

And then Dwayne was on me, hands at my throat. I broke his grip and he head-butted me in the nose, the pain so intense that I kicked and jerked wildly, somehow bucking him off me, onto the floor. I straddled him, pounding his face. Dwayne tossed and flipped, and then I was on my back again, warding off his blows. Dwayne knew how to punch—short strokes, well placed—and no sooner had I covered up one soft spot than he was pounding another.

Gunshots from the living room . . .

And a voice—it was Pederson's—called out, "Zack, we got one of them. Other one's got a shotgun in the kitchen."

Dwayne pinned me and yelled, "Donnie? You OK?"

Then it was Tiffani, crying, "They shot him, Dwayne. They fucking shot him!"

Screams from the living room, the sound of furniture crashing. . . .

And then Dwayne was hammering the bony heel of his hand into the base of my nose again and again. I tasted the blood and fought the darkness and felt it as his weight lifted off my body. He lurched across the room toward Barbara, reaching for her, knowing she was his only way out. Barbara moved along the wall, kicking at Dwayne, fending him off. Lord Downey's eyes were open, and he lay curled up, arms clasped around his knees.

My hand fell on the thick piece of wood that moments before had lanced my arm. I raised up, bracing the butt of it against my shoulder.

I yelled, "Dwayne!"

And in the instant that he turned, Barbara planted both feet in his back and kicked out hard. Dwayne fell toward me, trying to twist away, trying to dodge the sharp and jagged stake, but it caught him under the rib cage and went deep as he came down. I rolled onto him and drove it deeper, thrusting against him, awash in his blood. He kicked and screamed and flailed about. I held him down, my eyes on his eyes, watching as his life seeped away. And then he stopped moving.

I fell back and Barbara was in my arms.

"Omigod, Zack, omigod."

"It's alright, it's alright."

"Zack . . ."

We held each other. I kissed her face, her neck, her eyes. She kissed me. We held each other some more.

"You OK, baby?"

"Uh-huh. Just keep holding me."

She was shaking. And then she was crying. And then when the crying was over we just lay there, squeezing and hugging, drinking in each other and not a thing needed to be said.

Boggy stepped into the room and knelt beside us, holding his blood-splattered machete.

"The two men out there, they are dead," he said. "The girl she is wounded, but not badly."

"What about Pederson?"

"I'll live."

Pederson stood in the doorway, holding a bloody dish towel against his side.

"Went in and went out. Just a big hole."

A moan came from the corner of the room and we turned to see Lord Downey pulling himself up on the windowsill, trying to get to his feet. Barbara went to him.

I said, "Is he OK?"

She nodded.

"He's weak, dehydrated. We both are. But yes, he'll be OK."

"Stay in here with them," I told Pederson.

Boggy and I went into the living room. Tiffani leaned up against a wall, clutching a bloody shoulder and sobbing. Boggy found a towel to tie off her wound. I walked into the kitchen. Behind what was left of the counter, I saw Donnie and Curtis on the floor. Donnie was dead from a single gunshot wound in his head. Curtis was a messier sight, the work of a machete.

Tiffani winced as Boggy finished applying the makeshift bandage to her shoulder. I bent down and looked at her.

"Dwayne's dead," I said.

"I figured that," she said. "So what happens now?"

"You OK to walk?"

She nodded.

I took her good arm and helped her up. We walked down the hall and stopped at the door to Burma Downey's bedroom. It was locked. I knocked on it.

"Zoe?" I said.

The reply was slow in coming.

"Yes," she said.

"Open the door."

59

Zoe Applequist let us in, then quickly retreated behind the wheelchair on the other side of the room. The shrouded figure who sat in it was sobbing, her gauze-covered face buried in her hands. Zoe patted her back.

"There, there, honey," she said. "It's going to be alright."

I led Tiffani to the bed and let her stretch out, then called for Pederson to join us. Boggy had already headed outside to check on Brindley.

"Keep an eye on the three of them," I told Pederson.

I went and got Barbara. We stepped into the bathroom and I turned on the faucet and rinsed out the gash in my arm. I found some hydrogen peroxide in the medicine cabinet and poured that over it. Then I hugged Barbara.

"You need anything?" I asked her.

"Yes, I need lots of things. A hot bath, for starters. And several bottles of wine. And you. I need you, Zack."

"You got me."

We kissed, but she pulled away.

"And a toothbrush," she said. "I don't know how you can

stand to kiss me. I absolutely cannot let you do it anymore."

And then I kissed her again.

When we returned to Burma Downey's bedroom, I led Barbara to a chair by the window. I stood on one side of her, Pederson on the other, as I spoke to the three women who watched us in silence.

"I'm just gonna start talking, explain how I see things. Feel free to jump right in and help me out," I told them. "Now, I figure you all must have met at Ruby Booby's, that right?"

"Uh-huh," said Tiffani. "Cheri and I were both working there then. So was Dwayne. Burma used to come in all the time. She had the hots for Cheri. But Cheri was with Zoe."

"Tiffani . . ." Zoe stepped toward the bed. "Just let me do the talking. It was all Dwayne's doing, you know that."

Tiffani pulled back, fear in her eyes.

"No, it wasn't," she said. "It was you. You, you, you!"

I stepped between them and grabbed Zoe by the shoulders. She wrenched away and resumed her post behind the wheelchair. She gripped the back of it with both hands, shaking with rage as I continued telling them how I saw everything going down. I went through it piece by piece, starting with how they'd arranged for Dwayne to pick me up at Baypoint after Tiffani had eavesdropped on Barbara's visit with Lord Downey.

"By then you'd figured out that Lord Downey didn't have much more than the roof over his head. Then here came Barbara waltzing into your scheme. Too good to pass up. So you sent Dwayne to see exactly what kind of threat I might pose to your plans. I was a cog in the works, but I was also the only one who could pry loose Barbara's money.

"Dwayne was in a big hurry to get back to Fort Lauderdale. That's why he ran off and left me in Minorca Beach. He wanted to grab a seat on the last Twin Air flight here that night so he could pull off the kidnapping before I had a chance to connect with Barbara. It might never have worked had Lord Downey not wandered off and almost drowned while I was on my way to meet Barbara at the photo shoot."

I looked at Tiffani. I said, "That was your doing. You were slipping stuff into his drinks, keeping him all doped up."

Tiffani bit her lip.

"I tried not to hurt him," she said. "Really I did."

"You also unplugged the battery in Bryce Gannon's golf cart that night at the Bahama Sands. Then, when it wouldn't start, you offered to give Gannon and Barbara a ride. Only you brought them here instead of dropping Barbara off at the Albury."

Barbara said, "She told Bryce she wanted to run inside and fetch a little gift for him. The electricity appeared to be off . . ."

I looked at Zoe.

"That was you," I said. "You threw the switch in the fuse box to distract Clarissa and make it easier to snatch Lord Downey."

Zoe didn't even blink. She said nothing.

"No sooner was Tiffani inside the house than Dwayne and the two others were on us," said Barbara. "They tied us up and took us to their boat. Lord Downey was already in it when we arrived. We were in the middle of the sound when Bryce managed to work his arms and legs free from the bindings. He probably knew he would not be able to overcome all three of them. So he jumped off the boat."

Barbara closed her eyes. I put a hand on her shoulder and she held it.

She said, "Bryce was always a strong swimmer. I'm quite sure he could have eventually swum to shore and found help. I suppose he was hoping that they wouldn't be able to find him out there in the darkness. But Dwayne swung the boat around and they were on him in seconds. Then Dwayne had his brother take the wheel while he stood on the bow with the shotgun. They toyed with Bryce, taunting him, laughing. Dwayne fired the gun several times, purposely missing Bryce, turning him this way and that until he was gasping and choking and . . ."

Barbara stopped. She dabbed at her eyes, took a deep breath.

"Dwayne asked Bryce if he wanted back on the boat. Bryce said yes. At that point he could barely stay afloat. Dwayne let him reach up and hold on to the side of the boat. That's when he shot him."

Barbara cried. I held her until she stopped. I looked at Pederson.

"You heard everything you need to hear?"

"Pretty much," he said. "Of course, there's still a few details I'm not clear on."

"Me, too. But I think I know someone who can fill in the gaps."

I stepped across the room and stood in front of the wheelchair.

"Don't you harm her," said Zoe.

"Wouldn't think of it," I said.

The figure in the wheelchair sat erect, eyes fixed on the other side of the room. I reached down and tugged loose a piece of the gauze that was wrapped around her head. She didn't try to stop me. Neither did Zoe. I unwound the gauze, revealing close-cropped brown hair, then a forehead, big brown eyes, high cheeks, a nose, a mouth, a chin . . . and not a scar on her. She was gorgeous.

"Why, if it isn't Cheri Swanson," I said. "Got anything you'd like to add?"

60

It took a while. At first, all Barbara wanted was sleep and for me to hold her. And then more sleep. No objections on my part. I was worn out, too. We were staying at the Albury, back in Hibiscus Cottage, the only guests at the place. Barbara didn't talk much. At least, not about what had happened. Just general, all-purpose comments. "It's lovely out," she'd say. Or, "Oh, look, there's a jay in the allamandas." Or, "That Mr. Pindle, he's such a dear."

But slowly she came around. The long silences became less frequent. She began to laugh again, even at my lousy jokes. On the second night, we popped the Schramsberg '98 and slow-danced to songs from an oldie-goldies station out of Miami. Then we made love. It was as sweet as I could possibly imagine. Afterwards, we nestled together in bed, close as close could be, the jalousie windows open, and the ocean breeze blowing fresh and true.

I told her that Lynfield Pederson had released Bryce Gannon's body to the British consulate.

"It's being flown back to London for burial," I said.

We were quiet awhile.

Finally, she said, "The cave was absolutely wretched. The horrid smell, all those bats. They flew in and out, twice a day, like clockwork. And their squealing, my god, I fear I shall never be able to get it out of my mind."

She shuddered, then rolled over and tucked her head under my chin.

I said, "I really didn't expect Lord Downey to survive it."

"Nor did I, not at first. But it was all those drugs, that's what was dragging him down. Being in the cave was like detox for him. He actually seemed to get stronger by the day, more and more lucid. Once, at the very end, the same night the storm hit, he looked at me and said, 'I've lost her, haven't I?' He knew Burma was dead."

I said, "They found her body this morning."

"Where?"

"In a cave, not far from the one where Dwayne took you," I said. "Pederson had to call in help from Nassau, but not before he sat down with Cheri Swanson and convinced her that it was in her best interest to tell him everything she knew."

"So Zoe killed Burma?"

"It was a fit of rage, jealousy. Zoe was in love with Cheri. They'd been living together in Fort Lauderdale while Cheri danced at different clubs. Burma Downey began frequenting Ruby Booby's and it wasn't long before she fell for Cheri, too. The three of them started hanging out, Burma footing the bill for them to visit her here on Harbour Island, Cheri and Zoe envisioning a never-ending meal ticket. They kept pressing Burma to milk more and more money out of her father, money he didn't have."

Barbara said, "But they didn't know that."

"No, because Burma was too proud, too vain to tell them the truth. And so they began to argue. One night, after they had been out partying and drinking at the Albury, Zoe fell asleep on the couch, and when she went back to the bedroom, there was Burma, in the sack with Cheri, the two of them going at it. Zoe lost it, completely lost it. According to Pederson, the cause of death was strangulation, but there were bruises all over her body. Zoe just beat hell out of her."

"And that's when they hatched the story about Burma being in the automobile accident?"

"Uh-huh. They got Dwayne Crowe to hide Burma's body in the cave, with the promise that they would cut him in on whatever they managed to worm out of Lord Downey."

There was just enough Schramsberg left for us each to have half a glass. I got up and poured it. Then I lay back down beside Barbara.

She said, "So, tell me. What led you to suspect that Burma wasn't really Burma?"

"The handwriting," I said.

"You mean, you compared Cheri Swanson's handwriting with that of Burma Downey's?"

"No," I said. "With yours."

She sat up and looked at me.

"With mine? Whatever for?"

"It's a British thing." I opened a drawer on the bedside table. I pulled out the note Barbara had written, the one Dwayne had delivered when he picked me up at Baypoint. And I pulled out the two notes Burma Downey had supposedly written to describe her alleged cell phone conversations with the kidnappers. I showed them both to Barbara. "You Brits cross your Z's when you write."

"They're zeds, not Z's," said Barbara.

"Whatever. You draw that little line across the middle of them. And you also cross your sevens."

"That is so they will not be mistaken for ones. It's only common sense."

"Hey, you can cross the whole damn alphabet and all the numbers up to a zillion as far as I'm concerned," I said. "Plus, you Brits spell 'organized' with an 's.'"

"The way it is supposed to be spelled."

"Only, in the note that was allegedly from Burma Downey, it was spelled the American way, with a 'z,'" I said. "But Burma Downey was British. She was well educated . . ."

"We attended the same secondary schools—years apart, of course."

"Yes, Chrissie Hineman mentioned that. Which is eventually

what got me thinking," I said. "The story about Burma having a crushed larynx could account for Cheri not speaking, meaning she didn't have to fake a British accent. Even if she were very good at it, she probably couldn't have fooled Lord Downey. But something was off with the notes that she wrote. It just took a while for it to sink in."

Barbara drained her champagne and put the glass on the bedside table. She sat on the side of the bed.

"What now?" she said.

"Your call. I've got no plans," I said. "Just glad to be with you, baby."

She got up and walked across the room and turned up the radio. Van Morrison was singing "Have I Told You Lately That I Love You?" She held out her arms.

"Let's dance."

61

Every day was a better day for Barbara. I knew for sure she'd be alright the afternoon she borrowed Chrissie Hineman's computer to check her e-mails and send memos to the staff back at Orb Media.

The next morning, a FedEx package arrived, sent by Steffie Plank. Barbara opened it to find page proofs of the photo shoot on Harbour Island. The headline said "Bahamarama" and the opening spread showed three of the models holding hands and leaping over the waves in front of the Bahama Sands. The shot could have been a tired cliché—I'd seen the same setup countless times before—but Bryce Gannon had pulled it off with style and flourish. The water was gorgeous, the sand pinker than pink, the models full of joy and life. All the other shots were just as good.

When Barbara finished looking at them, she said, "I'd like to have a little party. Just to celebrate. That alright with you?"

"Fine by me. What are we celebrating?"

She held up the page proofs.

"This," she said. "Bryce would have been proud of it."

"He did a great job."

Barbara nodded.

"You did, too," she said. "That's the other thing I want to celebrate—you, Zack. And me."

"You and me?"

"I love the sound of that," she said.

She gave me a hug.

"I want to celebrate everything," she said.

We gathered on *Miz Blitz*. Lord Downey couldn't make it, having flown to London to attend a memorial service for Burma. But Lynfield Pederson was there, with Clarissa and Momma Percival. Brindley brought a girlfriend—one of the models, as it turned out. Chrissie and Charlie Hineman showed up with Mr. Pindle in tow. Nixon Styles was there with his family, and he helped Boggy and me with the cooking. We grilled lobsters and passed them around and everyone ate them with their hands. There was a big bowl of conch salad and a plateful of sliced Eleuthera pineapple. There was lots of rum and lots of beer. We toasted everything and everyone. And then we danced.

It was after eleven when Barbara and I got back to the Albury. She was in bed and I was brushing my teeth when I heard the knock at the door. Barbara hopped out of bed and opened it. I heard Mr. Pindle tell her I had a telephone call.

Barbara said, "Please, just take a message."

"Already tried that," said Mr. Pindle. "This man says he has to speak with Mr. Chasteen right this moment. Says Mr. Chasteen's been waiting for him to call."

"Zack?" said Barbara. "Do you have any idea who it could be?"

I did. And it turned out to be just who I thought it was.

"Your business there, it is finished?" asked Victor Ortiz, after I picked up the phone.

"Almost."

"It worked out in your favor?"

"Uh-huh, I was lucky."

"Yes, indeed, you are a lucky man. And soon, if we can come to some agreement, you may also be a rich man."

"How rich?"

"Oh, perhaps a half-million dollars."

"That's not so rich."

"It is a half-million dollars more than you have now, is it not?"

"Might be. But it's not even a down payment for settling up on what you put me through," I said. "You still think I've got something of yours, Ortiz?"

"Yes. Or, at the very least, you know where that something might be. Either way I will make it worth your while. I always intended to pay you for your services."

"You'll never have enough money for that," I said. "Why don't you tell me what this thing is that I am supposed to have, and maybe we can save us both a lot of time and trouble?"

"No, no. It is not that easy. If you knew, then you would have it and I would not, and then maybe I would not get it back, don't you see?" Ortiz said. "But you return to your home soon, no?"

"Pretty soon."

"Three days maybe?"

"That sounds about right."

"Good," said Victor Ortiz. "You will hear from me then."

"I don't want to hear from you, Ortiz. I want to see you. I want to look you in the eye."

"I am afraid that cannot happen."

"Then I'm afraid we don't have a deal."

"I can make it very difficult for you."

"You've already made it difficult. If you think you can make it any worse, then bring it on."

There was a long pause.

Ortiz said, "OK, then. Three days from now. At your home. In the evening. You will be there?"

"Bet your ass," I said.

62

Two days later, as the sun was going down, Boggy and I chugged through Coronado Inlet on *Miz Blitz* and pointed her south on the Intracoastal toward LaDonna. Barbara had flown home the morning after the party and was busy getting the next issue of *Tropics* ready for press. I was missing her something fierce.

The crossing from the Bahamas had been smooth and un-eventful. Except for the fishing. We kept four lines rigged with ballyhoo and trolled all the way from Pinders Point, on Grand Bahama, to the mouth of the inlet, a sixteen-hour run. We had twelve dolphin, six kings, and a wahoo to show for it. We'd stuffed ourselves on fresh-from-the-water ceviche, and more fine meals were in our immediate future. What we couldn't eat or fit into the smoker to eat later, I'd sell to Bob at Ocean's Seafood. Might help pay for some of my gas. I'd gone through all the money Barbara had given me and most of the two thou-sand five hundred dollars that Tom Burleson had paid me for the sago palm. I was planning on paying Barbara back. I just hadn't worked out the logistics of how and when.

It was hard to miss the wrath that Hurricane Curt had

wrought. The worst of it was on the back side of Minorca
Beach. The storm had raked past during a high tide. Few docks
or seawalls had escaped damage and roofs were off a couple of
houses. Boggy took the helm as we pulled close to LaDonna
and I stood on the bow. Some trees were down, mostly oaks and
pine along the edge of the property. The FOR SALE signs were
still standing. The house looked fine. And, except for a swath
of missing shingles on its roof, so did the boathouse. But the
seawall . . .

I walked back to the helm.

"You're going to love this," I told Boggy. "All that work you
did patching up after the last storm? *Por nada*, bubba. We're going to have to do it all over again."

"Why? The new owners, let them take care of it."

"There aren't going to be any new owners," I said. "This is
where I live. It's not for sale."

Boggy turned and looked at me. He put a hand on my shoulder and smiled. He didn't say anything. He didn't have to.

We put *Miz Blitz* in her slip and walked along the seawall. At
least half of it—a thirty-yard stretch or more—had crumbled in
the storm surge, exposing all the castoff junk, the flotsam and
jetsam that Boggy had used to reinforce the concrete. I saw
rusty wheel rims and pieces of corrugated tin and the blades of
old lawnmowers.

Boggy said, "I try to save some money, doing it that way."

"Yeah, well, this time I think we'll pop to hire someone to
come out here and wire it in right for us, use some reinforced
steel, put in baffles and pilings."

I was already calculating how many palm trees I'd have to
sell to pay for a new seawall. I was probably looking at twenty
thousand dollars' worth of repairs, easy. Then I had to start paying back Barbara for the lawyers' bills and everything else
she'd bankrolled. Time to get cranking.

We were walking away when I spotted the scuba tanks.
There were thirty or forty of them, various tanks that I had ac-
cumulated over the years and then retired and stashed away
when newer, sleeker models had come on the market. Boggy
had set the tanks smack dab in the middle of the seawall, about

a foot apart, and then poured concrete around them. It wasn't a bad idea. It just hadn't taken into account the fury of a monster hurricane. Some of the tanks were silver, some were green, and some were red. But it was the ten black tanks that caught my attention.

"Those the tanks that Victor Ortiz bought after we put in at West End that night, the ones he and his pals hauled back to the boat?"

Boggy nodded. He said, "They were still on the boat after the auction. Old tanks, no good, very heavy. I put them in the seawall with the others."

I kneeled down to give one of the tanks a closer look. The cracking concrete had banged it up and scraped off some of the black paint. I got out my pocketknife and scraped off more paint.

What lay beneath glittered. And I was pretty sure that it was gold.

63

We worked all that night and into the early morning, hammering away at concrete and prying out the ten black tanks. We pulled out the other tanks, too. There were thirty-four of them altogether. The black tanks were heavier than any of them, a good eighty pounds apiece. I found a couple of gallons of black paint in the boathouse. It didn't take long for us to paint all of the tanks the same color. When we were finished it was hard to tell which ones had belonged to Victor Ortiz.

Once we were done with that and had stood the tanks up to dry, I started making phone calls. It took a while to get in touch with everyone I needed to speak to, but by midafternoon I'd checked off all the names on my list and told each of them exactly how I wanted them to proceed. There was some bitching, some hemming and hawing, but in the end everyone came around to my way of thinking. Mainly because time was short and they were hard-pressed to come up with a better plan. It was now or never.

Chances were that Victor Ortiz had at least one of his men watching us from the moment we had returned to LaDonna. But I was counting on Ortiz to have given strict orders that no one

was to make a move until he got there. So we made a stack of
tanks in the backyard, piled them like cordwood in the middle
of the grassy slope that ran behind the house to the river. It was
wide open there, easy to see, and easy to be seen. We pulled up
a couple old Adirondack chairs and a cooler with bottles of water in it. And then we sat down and waited.

It was just a couple of days before the full moon. The
shrimp were running, making their exodus from the brackish
backwaters to the ocean. Long before dusk, there were already
dozens of boats out on the lagoon with lights hanging over their
sides to attract the shrimp, and long-handled nets for scooping
them in. So, when three more boats glided in at sunset and anchored at fifty-yard intervals along the far bank, they didn't
look out of place. Just local boys enjoying an evening of dip-
pin' and drinkin,' maybe bringing home a few pounds of
shrimp to help fatten up the family. I wasn't sure who was in
which boat. I'd just told them to make sure the boats weren't
government issue and didn't look alike. They'd done that. One
was a Boston Whaler, one was a Carolina Skiff, and the third
was a Mako 17. It looked like there were three guys in each of
them, no telling how many others sitting back, waiting to get
the call.

Boggy dug out a pit near the tanks and piled kindling wood
on the bottom and blackjack oak on top. The mosquitoes were
getting bad. If we lit the fire it would bring a bit of relief from
the bugs, but we were waiting until later to do that.

Just before ten, we heard the sound of tires on gravel, then
car doors slamming. Boggy struck a match and set the kindling
ablaze. We watched the fire spread, listening to the crackle and
sizzle, just sitting by the pit and letting them walk up behind us,
playing it easy as could be.

"Chasteen . . ."

Boggy and I stood and saw them approaching us from behind the house. There were six of them. They weren't showing
weapons, but I knew they were carrying. That's just the kind of
guys they were—big and dark and mean. I recognized two of
them—Goatee and Raul. Goatee seemed to be in charge. Raul
seemed even bigger than the first time I saw him. He rolled his

shoulders and cracked his fingers, flexing, ready to get even with me for what had happened in the Baypoint parking lot.

"Where's Ortiz?" I said.

"In a moment," said Goatee. He signaled four of the men to split up and spread out. He and Raul stood there with us, silent, watching as two of the men went through the boathouse, boarded *Miz Blitz,* checked out every nook and cranny. The other two cased the old house, one of them crawling underneath it and shining a flashlight. When they were done, the men re-grouped and all of them walked to the river and looked around down there. We walked with them. They spoke in Spanish, and then Goatee turned to me and said, "There are many boats on the water. Why?"

"Shrimp are running," I said. "This is a slow night. You ought to see it on the weekends."

Goatee looked out at the river, studying all the boats. Then we all walked back up to the fire. Raul stayed at my back. I could hear him breathing.

The men looked at the stack of scuba tanks. By this point, I wasn't even sure which tanks were which. Goatee pulled out a cell phone, punched numbers, said something in Spanish, and put the cell phone away.

"Sit," Goatee said. "It will be a minute."

It was more like twenty minutes. And then there were more tires on gravel, the slamming of a door. Victor Ortiz appeared at the corner of the house, walking toward us, alone. He came and stood by the fire. He wore a tan linen suit with a black silk shirt, black shoes, no socks. His hair was slicked back and perfect.

He glanced at the stack of scuba tanks, then at me.

"So, I see we do not have to sit and talk and play the game," he said. "You knew all along what it was that you had."

I saw no reason to tell him the truth. So I didn't say anything. Ortiz said, "It is gold, you know."

"I know," I said.

"Seventy-eight pounds of it, more or less, in each of them."

"Pretty clever," I said. "How did you do it?"

"It was the Panamanians' idea, actually. Why risk cash? They made the molds and poured it and then painted over that.

Not even the customs dogs, the ones they use for their noses, are trained to sniff out gold. And there are many, many people who go back and forth between Florida and the Bahamas with scuba tanks on their boats."

"How much was the whole deal for?"

"Ten million dollars," said Ortiz. "A good price for us, a good price for the Panamanians. Their country, it uses the U.S. dollar, only they call it the balboa there. And they do not watch so closely for the counterfeiters. Even if they did, the materials we sold them, what we took to Grand Bahama on your boat, it was very, very good. State of the art."

"Yeah, that's what the U.S. attorney said. And that's why I couldn't cop any kind of a deal."

"I am sorry about that."

"My ass."

"I was hoping that what I offered you would make up for what went wrong."

"I already told you—nothing would make up for that. But as long as we're on the subject, what did go wrong?"

"The police," he said.

"I thought you paid them off."

"I did, weeks before we got there. But then they wanted more. And when I would not give it to them . . ." He turned up his hands. "These things happen. I lost four good men that night. They only let me slip away so that I could live to pay them on another day. Believe me, these last two years have not been so easy for me, either."

I was tired of talking. I had heard all I needed to hear and I was hoping everyone else had, too.

I said, "So, I get half a million. Is that the deal?"

Ortiz smiled. He looked at his men and said something in Spanish. I saw them reaching in pockets and pulling out pistols. Raul clamped a hand on the back of my neck. Goatee held a pistol on Boggy.

Ortiz said, "It was the deal, yes. But that was when I thought it would be more difficult than this. That was when I was still not certain that you did indeed have the tanks. Perhaps the authorities found them when they seized your boat and did not give them back. I could not be sure."

I said, "How can you be sure now?"

Ortiz said, "What do you mean?"

"There are a lot of tanks in that pile, Ortiz. How do you know the ones you're looking for are in there?"

Ortiz shook his head, smiled.

"You think we were not watching you, Chasteen? You think we did not see you pull the black tanks from the wall and then paint the other tanks black as well? It was much work on your part, much work for nothing. But the tanks with the gold, they are in there."

"How do you know, Ortiz? How do you know I didn't hold a couple back for myself? How do you know we didn't slip some into the river hoping you wouldn't find them? How do you know the black tanks we pulled out of the seawall are the same tanks you picked up in Freeport?" I said. "You gonna trust me on this one, Ortiz? You gonna trust me like I was trusting you?"

Ortiz chewed his lip, his eyes narrowed.

"Jorge," he said to one of the men. "You and Valdes, go through the tanks. Find the ones with the gold."

The two men stepped to the pile. They started at the top. They removed a tank, scraped off paint with their knives. Nothing. They moved on to the next one. They were removing the fourth tank when the spring-load snapped and the pile exploded with smoke and flames. All Boggy and I had to work with were U.S. Coast Guard–certified emergency flares, but we had two dozen of them. We had wired them together, counterbalancing the flares between two layers of tanks. I was expecting the explosion and it still scared the hell out of me. The pile of tanks burst apart, sparks shooting out in all directions and blanketing the backyard in smoke. The two men rolled on the ground screaming, partly in pain, partly in terror.

I spun loose from Raul's grip and sent an elbow to the side of his head. It staggered him, but he came at me. As he reached out to grab me I hammered the heel of my hand under his chin, cracking his jaw, and he went down. Boggy wrenched the pistol from Goatee, flipped him onto the ground, and held him there.

Ortiz and the rest of his men looked around, ready to run. And then the whole backyard lit up with stun lights. I heard a voice boom out: "Freeze! Everybody freeze!"

And then it was all of them—F.B.I., B.A.T.F., the D.E.A., and the Secret Service, plus local cops bringing up the rear. The first wave charging out of the three boats as they zoomed ashore, the others swarming in from the far reaches of the nursery, where they'd hidden in the palms. It was the same happy crew, more or less, that had showed up for my party two years before. Ten of them for every one of Ortiz's men, all of them yelling and charging and, sure, being considerably more gung ho and physical than they really needed to be. But not a shot was fired.

Three of them grabbed Ortiz and slung him on the ground.

One of the cops said, "You have the right to remain silent . . ."

And that's exactly what Ortiz did.

64

A week later, Barbara and I were driving south on the Overseas Highway, passing through Marathon, heading for Key West. She was at the wheel of Yellow Bird, the top was down, and all was right with the world. Well, almost.

"I still think it's a stupid, insipid name for your car," I said. "As a calypso song, it's hackneyed and worn out . . ."

"My, a retired professional athlete and a full-time boat bum who can use 'insipid' and 'hackneyed' in the same sentence. I'm impressed."

"You forgot the part about being a farmer. I'm also one of those now. I farm palm trees."

"Does that make you a palmist?"

"No, a palmist is someone who reads palms."

"And you only grow them."

"Well, Boggy does most of the growing," I said. "But I like to think of myself as a gentleman palm farmer."

"A rare breed, indeed."

"And please don't forget it," I said. "But back to Yellow Bird. As a song, no self-respecting calypso singer would ever sing it. And as for the birds themselves . . ."

"They are adorable little birds. I just love watching them down in the islands. Hopping all about. What did you tell me their real name is?"

"Bananaquits. They're called bananaquits. They fly down on your table while you are eating lunch, they eat the bread, they crap on the tablecloth . . ."

"Well, darling, I can't very well change the name from Yellow Bird to Bananaquit, can I? I mean, really, Zack. She's a Yellow Bird. That's what she is. She's pretty. And she flies."

That she did. We flew across the Seven Mile Bridge and Sunshine Key and then Barbara pulled Yellow Bird into the park at Bahia Honda. We found a picnic table with shade near the water. And while Barbara strolled off to use the ladies' room, I spread the tablecloth and set out lunch. There was curried wahoo salad and sliced mangos and a crusty loaf of Cuban bread. There was chardonnay, Rancho Sisquoc, for Barbara, and a Heineken for me. There were no bananaquits. The adorable little bastards don't live as far north as the Keys.

Barbara returned a few minutes later.

"Do you have any quarters?" she said.

I fished out five from a pocket and Barbara added them to the several she had in her hand.

"Why do you need them?"

"You'll see."

When she returned the next time she was carrying a copy of the Sunday *Miami Herald.* Barbara held the paper up so I could see it.

"Front-page story," she said.

There was a shot of me from some ancient media kit, number 44, wearing the old teal and orange. The headline read: "Zack Attack! Former Dolphins Safety Tackles a Crime Lord, Saves the Dame."

"Dame? They called you a dame?"

"I thought it quite clever, actually. You know, saves the game, saves the dame. A forgivable play on words."

"Crime lord?" I said. "I thought Ortiz was just a crook."

"Crime lord has more oomph to it. Plus, it fills up the space rather nicely," said Barbara. "It's a fine story, simply brilliant. Better than all the others. Shall I read it to you?"

"Please."

And so I sat back in the shade and sipped my Heineken and listened to Barbara read the story. I would have listened to her read anything—the small print on sacks of kitty litter, the ingredients on aerosol cans. Being able to look at her while I listened only doubled the pleasure. And my desire. Could I ever get tired of her? Not bloody likely.

"'U.S. attorney William Sheaffer, who prosecuted Chasteen, said he will personally file a motion before the Ninth District Court to reverse Chasteen's two felony convictions.'

"And, this is a quote, Zack, listen: 'Zack Chasteen deserves not only a complete exoneration, but the applause of citizens everywhere,' Sheaffer said."

I sipped the Heineken. I ate a forkful of the wahoo salad. It needed more curry, but it would do. Not a cloud in the sky, plenty of breeze blowing in off the Florida Straits. We'd be spending three nights at the Marquesa Hotel. Ordinarily, it was a little too rich for my blood. But . . .

Barbara kept reading.

"'According to federal agents, Ortiz and his Panamanian associates devised a plan for disguising gold bullion in the shape of compressed air tanks like those used by scuba divers. The tanks, each weighing almost eighty pounds, went undetected when Chasteen was apprehended after returning from the Bahamas to his ancestral home in LaDonna, Florida.'"

"Ancestral? There's not an ancestral home in the entire state of Florida. Doesn't it take five hundred years or something to make a home ancestral? Doesn't it have to have, like, eighteen bedrooms, and twenty-seven bathrooms, and a graveyard out back, and butlers, and—"

"Zack, do be quiet."

Barbara took a sip of wine. She continued reading.

"'After the raid, which was orchestrated through the cooperation of numerous federal agencies, as well as local law enforcement agencies . . .'"

"What a crock! I orchestrated it. With Boggy. We just told those bozos when they needed to show up."

"Zack, please, isn't the applause of citizens everywhere quite enough?"

I shut up.

Barbara read: "'After the raid,' blah-blah-blah-blah. . . . Here we are: 'federal authorities said they confiscated nine such tanks, worth at least nine million dollars. Ortiz was charged with . . .'"

Barbara stopped reading. She put down the paper and looked at me.

"Zack, correct me if I'm wrong, but didn't you tell me there were ten of those gold scuba tanks?"

I finished the Heineken and got out another one. I'd reserved the penthouse suite at the Marquesa Hotel—three thousand dollars a night. We were going to have a big time in old Cayo Waste-o.

"Zack, answer me," said Barbara. "Weren't there ten of those gold scuba tanks?"

I tore off a chunk of Cuban bread. I took a sip of Heineken. What a gorgeous day.

Turn the page for an excerpt from
Bob Morris's next mystery

Jamaica Me Crazy

Available in hardcover from

St. Martin's Minotaur

It was the first game of the season at Florida Field, and in typical fashion the Gators had scheduled something less than a fearsome opponent. This year it was the University of Tulsa. Midway through the second quarter the score was already twenty-seven us, zip for the Golden Hurricanes.

Reality would come home to roost in two weeks when we faced off against Tennessee, but for now the future appeared glorious, and the only thing in life that even mildly concerned me was why a football team from Oklahoma would call itself the Golden Hurricanes.

I turned to Barbara Pickering and said, "Don't you think they ought to call themselves something more geographically appropriate? Like the Golden Cow Patties?"

It got laughs from the people sitting around us.

"Or the Golden Tumbleweeds," said a woman to my left.

Barbara looked up from her book.

"I'm sorry," she said. "Did you say something?"

It was Barbara's first time at Florida Field. In fact, it was her first time at a football game. I was trying hard not to be offended by the fact she had not only brought along a book—*A*

House for Mr. Biswas by V. S. Naipaul—she was actually reading it. I had never seen anyone reading a book at a football game.

A man sitting in front of us turned to Barbara.

"Honey," he said. "Please tell me that's a book about football."

"You'll have to forgive her," I told him. "Barbara's British."

Barbara gave the guy a smile so stunning that this ears turned red. I could relate. I do the same thing whenever she smiles at me.

I reached under my seat and found the pint flask of Mount Gay that I had smuggled into the stadium. I poured a healthy dollop into my cup. Then I pulled a wedge of lime from the plastic Baggie in my pants pocket and squeezed it into the rum.

The man in front of us turned around again. Mainly because I had succeeded in squirting the back of his neck with lime juice.

"You'll have to forgive him," Barbara told the man. "Zack has scurvy."

Moments later, the Gators scored again. I stood to cheer with the rest of the crowd. Barbara took the opportunity to stand and stretch and yawn and work out the kinks. She glanced at the scoreboard.

"Oh my, only two minutes left," she said. "Perhaps we should go now and beat the crowd."

"That's just until halftime."

"Meaning . . ."

"Meaning, with TV timeouts and the Gators' passing game, I'd say we can look forward to at least another two hours of this. Good thing the relative humidity is 187 percent. That way it will seem like a whole lot longer."

She faked a smile. Even her fake smiles are pretty damn stunning.

Just then I heard someone yell: "Yo, Zack!"

Monk DeVane was standing in the aisle, waving for us to join him.

"Come on, there's someone I want you to meet," I told Barbara.

"An old college friend?"

"Yeah, we go way back."

Barbara put her book on her seat and we began edging our way toward the aisle.

Monk DeVane had been my roommate when we played for the Gators. Like me, he had knocked around in the pros for a few years before getting hurt and calling it quits. He opened a car dealership, but it went belly up. So he tried selling real estate and tried selling boats and tried selling himself on the idea that he could stay married. Last I heard there had been three wives, but I had lost track on exactly what he was doing to make a living.

Monk's real name was Donald, but one Saturday night on a bye weekend during my freshman year, when I had gone home for a visit, Coach Rowlin decided to conduct a curfew check at Yon Hall. He caught Monk in bed with not one but two comely representatives of Alpha Delta Pi.

While Coach Rowlin booted players off the team for missing practice or talking back to a coach, and did it in a heartbeat, bonking sorority girls at 2 A.M. was not high on his list of misdeeds. At the following Monday's team meeting, when Coach Rowlin handed out punishments for a variety of weekend infractions, he gave Donald twenty extra windsprints.

"You boys need to be saving your strength during the season," Coach Rowlin told us. "Not engaging in wild monkey sex."

Donald had been Monk ever since.

Despite all Monk's ups and downs over the years, he seemed none the worse for wear. Still fit and handsome, his sun-streaked brown hair was considerably longer than I remembered, and he had grown a beard. It was spackled with just enough gray to lend a note of dignity.

Monk stuck out a hand. I took it without thinking, and a moment later I was grimacing under his grip. Monk had a Super Bowl ring. I didn't. He liked to remind me of that by catching my hand in just the right way for his big gold ring to bear down on my knuckles.

I wrenched away and introduced him to Barbara. Monk pulled her close and wrapped an arm around her.

"How about you dump this joker you're with and come up to the skybox and have a drink with me? We're throwing a little party."

"This skybox of yours, is it air conditioned?" asked Barbara.

"Cool as a TK, with an open bar and food that'll make your eyes bug out."

"Since when do you have a skybox?" I said.

Monk grinned.

"Since never. It's the president's skybox."

"As in president of the university?"

"As in," Monk said.

"Traveling in some pretty swank circles these days, aren't you?"

"Well, it helps that I work for Darcy Whitehall."

Monk saw the look on my face. On Barbara's, too.

"Yeah, *that* Darcy Whitehall," he said. "I'd like for you to meet him, Zack. Plus, there's something I need to talk to you about."

I had seen Darcy Whitehall that very morning at Publix when I went to pick up a few things for our pre-game tailgate lunch. He was staring at me from the cover of *People*, along with a host of other celebrities the magazine had proclaimed "Still Sexy in Their Sixties."

Barbara spoke before I had a chance to.

"We'd love to join you," she told Monk.

After that, things went straight to hell.

· · ·

We cut under the stands and headed for the elevators that would take us to the skybox level. The concrete breezeways echoed with the boisterous buzz of game day, and we wove through a happy crowd all decked out in variations on a theme of orange and blue.

I had been coming to Gator games since I was in diapers, and the seats I now held season tickets to originally belonged to my grandfather. I felt right at home at Florida Field, but it seemed an odd place for the likes of Darcy Whitehall.

Darcy Whitehall was Jamaican, a white Jamaican, part of a family that could trace its roots on the island back to colonial days. He had made his name as a young man in the music industry. Catching reggae's early wave of popularity, Whitehall had started a music label and signed a number of musicians who hit it big.

Since then, he had branched out and was now best known as founder and figurehead of Libido Resorts, a collection of anything-goes, all-inclusive retreats scattered throughout the Caribbean. The first one, in Jamaica, just up the coast from Montego Bay, immediately gained notice as the ultimate swinger haven. Naked volleyball. Group sex in hot tubs. "Formal" dinners for three hundred where the women were clad only in pearl necklaces and high heels, and the men wore black bowties, but not around their necks.

In recent years, Libido had tried to present a more refined image, no doubt to justify the many thousands of dollars it cost to stay there for a week. Gourmet dining. Serene spa treatments. Yoga pavilions under the palms.

Turn on the television and there was Darcy Whitehall, an icon of rakishness, strolling along a dazzling stretch of beach, an umbrella drink in one hand, a gorgeous young woman on his arm, telling would-be guests: "Yield to Libido."

The pitch was upscale, but the subtext was the same as it always had been: Book a week at Libido and you'll definitely get laid.

As we approached the elevators, Monk gave us laminated badges that said "Skybox Access." We clipped them on, and I stood up straight and tried to look presentable. We would soon be mingling with all sorts of movers and shakers. The conversation would be dignified, the company refined. And I wouldn't have to pour my rum out of a plastic flask hidden underneath my seat.

I was wearing my sit-in-the-sun-and-swelter outfit—flip-flops, khaki shorts and a T-shirt from Heller Brothers produce that I had chosen because it had a plump, juicy navel orange on the chest that was my nod to sporting Gator colors. The T-shirt also bore a variety of stains—Zatarain's creole mustard,

Louisiana Bull hot sauce, Big Tom Bloody Mary Mix—which spoke to the success of our tailgate lunch and the zealousness with which I enjoyed it.

The skybox elite might sniff that I was underdressed, but I wasn't concerned. Barbara was at my side and, like always, she looked dazzling. Her outfit was simple—something beige and linen—but she wore it with a grace that few women can claim. She had recently cut her long dark hair and was wearing it in a swept-back style that fell just above her shoulders. I was still getting used to the look, but it was tugging at me in all sorts of pleasing ways.

Barbara caught me staring at her and smiled and gave my hand a squeeze. I knew she was thrilled by the chance to meet Darcy Whitehall. It had nothing to do with his sexiness or his celebrity. Well, maybe it had a little to do with that. But for Barbara it was mostly a matter of business. I saw the look in her eyes. Her mind had undoubtedly slipped into overdrive as she tried to figure out a way to leverage this lucky encounter into an opportunity for *Tropics*.

Tropics is Barbara's baby, her pride and joy, a classy travel magazine that covers Florida and the Caribbean. She launched it on a shoestring and, against long odds, carved out a niche in the market, thanks both to the quality of the magazine and her very considerable will. The success of *Tropics* has allowed her company, Orb Communications, to start tourist magazines on several islands—*Barbados Live!* and *St. Martin Live!* among others—along with occasional custom publications for cruise ships and resorts.

She's done well, very well. Still, in the publishing world she's small fry, and she's on the road often, roping in new advertisers, stroking old ones, and promoting her magazines with dauntless zeal.

I knew she had long tried to land the Libido account, but had made little headway. Now to have this opportunity fall in her lap, well, I was pretty sure she'd forgive me for making her sit through a game of college football.

We got on the elevator and as the doors closed behind us I

thought about Monk DeVane working for Libido Resorts. It was like the fox getting hired to run the henhouse.

"So what do you do for Darcy Whitehall?" I asked Monk. "You the Vice President for Rubbing Suntan Lotion on Female Guests?"

Monk laughed.

"No, I'm in the security business these days, Zack."

"Ah, you make sure the female guests don't get hit by falling coconuts."

"It's slightly more complicated than that," he said. "We'll talk about it."

The elevator dinged as we reached the skybox level. The doors slid open and a crush of people began pushing their way on before we could get off. Not the sort of behavior you'd expect from this exclusive crowd.

It helped that Monk used to be an offensive guard. He bulldozed a path out of the elevator. We followed him into the narrow hallway that led to the skyboxes. It was packed with people, all heading for the elevators.

But something was off, way off. This was not a jolly football gathering. No, these people looked scared, on the edge of panic.

I saw the lieutenant governor using his wife as a battering ram to get to the elevators. I saw a fairly famous golfer elbowing his way through the fray. I saw the junior U.S. Senator from Florida desperately yanking open a fire door. As people split off to follow him down the stairs, the alarm shrieked a sound track to the mayhem.

A short round woman collided with Monk. He caught her as she tumbled and helped her to her feet.

"You alright?" Monk said.

The woman gasped, words hanging in her throat. She shot an anxious look back toward the skyboxes.

"There's a bomb," she said.